Erica Stankewitz shoved the open folder towards me. "When Ms. Fishbeck asked all the children to draw a picture of their home, this is what your daughter came up with!"

Salla had chosen the Fall of Nauzu's Blood in the mountains of Zemauri near my home village. I felt a prickle of nostalgia as I looked at it. She'd even drawn in a cluster of chattering, three-legged krelyk winding around the trees.

"Ms. Konneva, that place looks like nothing on Earth. Your child is in serious trouble!" Her pen jabbed at the paper before her with short, angry downward strokes. "Code EB-4," she announced. "Emotionally disturbed as a result of dysfunctional home! That's all," she announced, standing up.

"Oh, no, it isn't," I said. "We haven't settled anything. I'm not satisfied that you understand Salla at all."

A smirk distorted Erica Stankewitz's pasty face. "On the contrary, Ms. Konneva, I'm afraid it's you who don't understand. We don't need your consent in a serious case like this."

"You don't consider yourself answerable to the parents at all, do you?" I said. "You people will do whatever you please to my child and I'm not supposed to have anything to say about it?"

"We consider ourselves advocates for the child's best interests. This file will convince anyone that Sally should be referred for mandatory counseling, antidelinquent programming and an EBD classroom."

"Fine," I said, taking it from her, "I'll take it home and read it and see if it convinces me."

"Wait a minute!" Stankewitz's voice rose to a pained squeak. "You can't have that—it's school property!" She made an ineffectual grab for the folder. Somehow her nose accidentally came into contact with my elbow. She edged around the desk and tried to block the door. I accidentally stepped on her fat little foot and she tripped and fell into the desk. I left her squealing about assault and battery and theft of school property. . . .

MARGARET BALL

MATHEMAGICS

This is a work of fiction. All the characters and events portrayed in this book are fictional, and any resemblance to real people or incidents is purely coincidental.

A Baen Books Original

Baen Publishing Enterprises
P.O. Box 1403
Riverdale, NY 10471

ISBN: 0-671-87755-0

Cover art by Larry Elmore

First printing, December 1996

Distributed by Simon & Schuster
1230 Avenue of the Americas
New York, NY 10020

Typeset by Windhaven Press, Auburn, NH
Printed in the United States of America

Prologue

Over the years he had formed a habit of checking Vera's underwear drawer for unsuitable objects. No matter how often he explained to her that a habit of nibbling on sweets would only exacerbate her weight problem, she regularly concealed boxes of chocolates in the underwear drawer and he as regularly threw them into the trash. Here, too, he found the worldly magazines like *Redbook* and *Good Housekeeping* that she sneaked home from the supermarket and the sleazy dangling earrings that he had explicitly told her to throw away—so unsuitable for the wife of a man of God. Hiding these things under her panties was Vera's little act of childish rebellion, and he didn't begrudge it her; women had to be allowed their trivial outlets. And at least she had better sense than to complain when her inappropriate possessions disappeared.

But this! Boatright drew the book slowly out of its hiding place. Raised gold foil letters shrieked out a title against a scarlet background: *Love's Tender Promise*. Beneath the letters were two half-naked figures entwined in a shameless embrace, the woman with her eyes closed and leaning back in the arms of a blond brute whose intentions were all too clear. . . .

This time Vera had gone too far. Here he was, as head of the American Values Research Center, fighting the good fight to keep smut off the bookstands and out of the schools, and she was betraying him by smuggling the stuff into their own home! He couldn't just pitch this thing into the garbage can; this time, sterner measures were called for. He would commit this book to the flames. And he would leave the little pile of ashes in the middle of the patio, to let Vera know exactly what he thought of her latest transgression.

Box of matches in one hand, book in the other, Bob Boatright marched with almost military precision towards the flagstone patio where he barbecued steaks on weekends. The September sun glared down on his head, almost hot enough to burn the book without help; already the long Texas summer had turned the grass around the patio to clusters of dry, shriveled stalks. He dropped the book on top of the barbecue grill and held a match to its lurid cover.

The match flickered and went out.

No doubt that glossy stuff they put on the covers made the books harder to burn. No matter; the pages inside would go quickly enough. He had only to lay the book face open on the grill . . .

It fell shut again as soon as he let go of it.

Bob Boatright's lips narrowed to a thin, determined line as he wrestled with the book. Eventually he was able to wedge the back cover and pages 301–346 under one of the greasy wires of the barbecue grill, the front cover and pages 1–30 under another wire, cracking the spine and leaving pages 31–299 fluttering wantonly in the warm September sun.

"Now," he said, and again applied match to paper.

Page 218 burst into flames most satisfactorily, blackening and curling as it burnt until nothing could be read but a few words right at the spine of the book. Pages 216 and 219 also caught fire, but burned only halfway into the book before slowing down to a grudging smolder. The pages between them slowly blackened. A breath of wind fanned the grill and small blue flames burst up for a moment, then died down again.

The pages must be jammed together so tightly that there was no oxygen for the flames to consume. Boatright found a branch in the grass and poked at the book, first gingerly, then more firmly. Each prod was rewarded by a brief spurt of blue flame and the sight of a few more pages blackening.

Sweat rolled down his forehead and spattered his glasses. He looked at his watch. He had been standing in the September sun for nearly half an hour, in front of a blazing fire—well, no, not exactly blazing, that was the problem. It was taking forever to get rid of this one miserable paperback. How had Hitler managed those famous book-burnings of the thirties? Wrong, of course, a different thing entirely, everybody knew the Nazis had been evil; still, Boatright thought wistfully, they knew how to get things done. Mussolini made the trains run on time, and Hitler burned thousands of books. Well, hundreds anyway.

What was their secret? No half measures, that was it! "Ye shall destroy their altars, and break down their images, and cut down their groves, and burn their graven images with fire. Deuteronomy 7:5," Boatright intoned. He grabbed the can of fire-starter fluid and sloshed its contents liberally over the book, the grill,

the ground, and his shoes. Then he backed away and
threw a lighted match into the middle of the barbecue
grill. Flames shot up.

And around.

And all over . . .

The untended stretch of weeds between the patio
and the neighbor's fence, golden-dry from a long Texas
summer, blazed up more gaily even than page 219.
Boatright watched in horror as the fire reached the
neighbor's new wooden fence. The sun-dried boards
crackled and blackened in the heat; a gust of wind
swept a shower of sparks over the fence to catch the
dry grass next door. There was a clanging sound in
Boatright's ears, a howling that seemed to come from
all directions at once, as if Satan Himself and a
hundred devils were mocking him.

Actually, there were only three fire engines. But
Boatright never noticed when the devilish howling
of the sirens ceased; he was being pushed out of the
way by large, crude men in protective gear, who
shouted orders at one another and dragged heavy
equipment across Vera's autumn garden and soaked
his shoes when he didn't move out of the way fast
enough.

And when the brush fire had been reduced to a
soggy black mess covering most of the Boatright
backyard and the two neighboring yards, the men
who'd put it out spoke very crudely to Boatright
himself.

"What kind of a damn fool burns trash outdoors
after a four-month drought? Haven't you ever heard
of the fire ordinance? Oughta write up a citation, but
I don't have time for the (obscenity) (obscenity)
paperwork. Anyway I figure it's gonna cost you

enough getting that fence rebuilt for Miz Riggs. And you are gonna pay for it, right, you (obscenity) (expletive) jackass?"

Bob Boatright nodded and croaked agreement.

When the men had gone away again, he waded through soot and mud to satisfy himself that he had at least cleansed the world of one filthy thing that day. The charred, vaguely rectangular lump on top of the barbecue grill could no longer be considered a book . . . could it?

When he picked the thing up, greasy ashes covered his hands, fell away in clumps and stained his pants.

The pages of the book were a blackened clump of ashes, but the lurid cover leered up at him, charred but still indecent: wisps of pink and scarlet, lush female flesh and floating veils. Boatright crumpled it in his hand and marched toward the back door just as his wife opened it.

"For mercy's sake, dear," she exclaimed, "whatever is going on? Was there a fire?"

Vera's powers of reasoning were apparently undiminished. She could recognize a charred backyard and a burnt fence when she saw them.

"Are you hurt? What happened?" She looked down at the blackened object in his hand. "And what have you done with my book? Darn it, Bob, I hadn't finished yet! Now I'll never find out if Maura married Kenneth and reformed from smuggling!"

"You'll be better off not corrupting your mind with such filth," Boatright said. "What if our little Becky had found it? Did you ever consider that?"

"But what have you been doing? It looks like the whole backyard is gone."

When tried beyond endurance, even a decent
Christian man can yell at his wife. "It wouldn't burn!"
Boatright shouted, and stalked past his wife into the
house. His feet left sooty prints on the beige carpeting.

Chapter e^0

I was just shoving a cart around the supermarket, trying to figure out where the new manager had hidden the star anise and Szechwan peppercorns, when he reared up in front of me: a big blond hulk with thews to die for, piercing blue eyes, gleaming chest and shoulders bared to the blast of the Frozen Foods section.

"Vordo!"

I dropped the package of Bagel Bites I'd been considering as an after school snack for Salla. My right hand went to my hip, automatically. But there wasn't anything there except my blue jeans. Wallet in front pocket, Swiss Army knife in hip pocket. Even granted that the last time I'd seen him he had been running the other way, I wasn't about to go up against Vordo with nothing but a pocketknife.

Except, of course, it wasn't Vordo. In the flesh, that is. It was only a life-sized cardboard picture of him, propped up in front of the magazine stand at the end of the isle. He was brandishing a short sword in one hand and holding up a girl with more hair than clothes in the other hand—I mean, that was the pictured pose.

And I felt like a damned fool. If I'd been armed, I might have been startled into attacking a picture. As it was, I'd already acted silly enough to get more attention than I wanted.

"Riva, what's the matter with you? You've gone absolutely white—well, as white as you can get," tittered Vera Boatright. I knew her slightly from school; her daughter Becky played with Salla whenever she could get sprung from the family regime of homework, housework and Bible study.

"She's found her ideal man," suggested someone else whom I vaguely remembered seeing at PTA meetings; a perfect Junior League size four with one of those hundred-dollar sculpted haircuts, a "jogging" suit that probably cost more than my monthly grocery bill, and bright maroon lips pursed into an expression of permanent discontent. The pouting look was what jogged my memory. She had to be that little pill Orrin's mom. Louise, that was her name.

"I know him," I blurted out. "What's he doing here?"

Vera tittered. "He's not here, silly, that's only a picture."

"Of course you know him," Louise said, "he's on half the covers in the romance section."

"He's the hottest male model for romance covers since Fabio," Vera put in. "Just having him on the cover doubles the sales of a book, they say."

"You must have seen his face every time you walked past the paperback books," Louise added.

"I never look at the romance novels," I said.

"Oh—well—neither do I, of course," Vera said immediately. Her face turned pink. "My husband—I mean, our church doesn't approve of all that filth." She leaned towards me and whispered confidentially,

"You wouldn't believe the sort of dirty stuff they print in those books. Why, in the very first pages of *Love's Tender Promise*—"

"I mean," I interrupted Vera without waiting to hear about the erotic promises of *Love's Tender Promise*, "I know him. From . . . a long time ago." Two years. And that wasn't nearly long enough. What was Vordo doing on this planet?

"Oh, suure," Louise drawled, "and I suppose you used to date Vordo."

"That's his name." I nodded. "Vordo. Though if I were him, I'd have changed it, after the way he behaved."

Louise sighed and rolled her eyes upwards. "Give me a break, Riva. Of course you know his name, I just told you. That doesn't prove anything. You've never seen him except on book covers, just like the rest of us. You've got to learn to distinguish fantasy from reality."

"It's not as easy as you might think," I muttered as she wheeled her cart away. I put the Bagel Bites back. September in Austin was too hot to risk putting frozen foods in the trunk of the car when I had another stop to make on the way home. It shouldn't take long to straighten out this mistake at Salla's school, but even ten minutes would be enough to turn the Bagel Bites into Melted Cheese Slurps.

I had a bad feeling about this meeting at the school as soon as the principal's secretary requested me not to go to Salla's home room. "We prefer to conduct confidential meetings in here," she said, showing me into a cubicle slightly bigger than one of Duke Zolkir's prison cells.

"There's nothing delicate about it," I said, waving

the letter I'd received yesterday at her. "Somebody
made a mistake, that's all, and I'm here to help you
straighten it out. Probably a computer error," I added,
remembering the magic words Dennis used whenever
he called the bank.

"Ms. Stankewitz will be with you shortly," the
secretary said. "We've found that the services of a
professionally trained counselor are invaluable at
stressful times like this."

She closed the door before I could tell her that the
only stressful thing about this interview was having
to wait in this little box of a room while my groceries
cooked by solar heat in the car trunk. It was a flimsy
door, too; in my home reality of Dazau I'd simply have
put my foot through it, then stood on the woman's
throat until she fixed what was probably her mistake
in the first place. But Dennis really liked me to
conform to his people's behavior standards, and after
the third time he'd had to bail me out I'd promised
to act like a Paper-Pusher woman unless Salla or he
were in actual physical danger.

Getting a stupid letter from the superintendent of
schools and having to wait around to straighten it out
probably didn't qualify.

With a sigh I smoothed the creases out of the letter
and read it again. I'd thought I was making progress
in reading English, but I couldn't make any sense at
all out of this—probably because it had been supposed
to go to somebody else, somebody whose kid was in
trouble.

"Dear Parent:
"This school district is required to inform
parents if their child has been determined to meet

one or more criteria for being at risk of dropping out of school. Some of these criteria are: failing the TAAS, not being able to speak English fluently, emotional or psychological problems, engaging in delinquent and/or rebellious behavior, and lack of family support."

None of that applied to Salla. I'd have been told if she'd flunked the TAAS; her English was better than mine, or at least more fluent—I still tend to slip into ki-Dazau to enhance the limited range of expressions available in English. As for family support, well! Here I'd been commuting back and forth between my job on Dazau and a rent house on the Planet of the Piss-Pot Paper-Pushers just so Salla could go to a good school in a good neighborhood. It was only during the last couple of years, thanks to Dennis's inspired negotiating after Baron Rodograunnizo tried to have me offed by wizardly tricks, that I'd been able to afford to stay here and study math while Salla went to school. And the money he'd got from Rodograunnizo was running out. . . .

I yanked my mind away from my personal problems and went back to reading and rereading the letter. The second paragraph was as bad as the first.

"All Austin administrators and teachers are dedicated to providing the support your child may need to stay in school and be successful. Transfer to the Alternative Learning Center, in-school tutorial or counseling sessions, or placement in an EBD classroom may be required. You are encouraged to call the school counselor to learn what is

available to help your child and what you can do
to help.

> Sincerely,
> [illegible scrawl]
> Superintendent of Schools"

The door opened; a short, dark-haired woman in a
blue suit waddled in. "Ms. Konneva? I'm Erica
Stankewitz. I'm so glad you could find the time to
visit us today."

"I can only see one of you," I pointed out. "Are
your colleagues invisible?" It was the sort of dirty trick
Vordo would have pulled, getting a wizard to disguise
his buddies under a cloak of invisibility so that he could
claim to've beaten up an entire troop of brigands
singlehanded. But I didn't think the Paper-Pushers
knew how to do that. Besides, as Dennis had explained
and explained, they didn't use physical force in most
of their combats.

A pity, that. I could have taken this woman with
both hands tied behind my back. I thought about that
while she smiled and explained that she was speaking
for the School when she said "us." "We haven't seen
much of you here, Ms. Konneva," she said. "You didn't
come to the Back-to-School Parents' Party, did you?
Or drive on any of the field trips this year?"

"I study during school hours," I told her.

"Oh," she said. "How nice for you. Still, most really
concerned parents make some effort to appear for
important school functions."

The field trip to the Nature Center. The field trip
to the antique shops of New Braunfels. The field trip
to watch the Dallas Cowboys practice . . . It was only

the end of September, and already Salla's class had been on six field trips. I contemplated suggesting a minor change in school policy; how about we switched roles, so they taught my kid Earth history and literature, and I took her to the zoo? Wasn't that the way it was supposed to work?

But it wasn't what I was there about.

"Look," I said, "we can discuss the proper role of parents in the schools some other time, okay? What I really came about was this."

Ms. Stankewitz nodded and jotted something down on her notepad as I handed the letter over. At last, I thought, we can get this cleared up.

"It's the standard form letter sent to all parents of at-risk students, Ms. Konneva," she said after a brief glance. "I'm very glad that you've finally found some time to think about Sally's problems. Now, if you'll just sign these simple forms, we can get started on applying the test instruments."

Applying the test instruments? Sounded like something Duke Zolkir's chief interrogator would have said while his flunkies were greasing the test instruments and heating them up.

And the "simple" forms were a stack at least three inches thick.

"She doesn't have any problems in school," I said. "This letter was sent by mistake. You've got her mixed up with some other kid. She's in your Gifted and Talented program, for Nauzu's sake!"

"A placement error," said the pasty-faced Stankewitz, "which can be rectified as soon as you sign—"

"It. Is. Not. An. Error," I said. "This is the error." I jabbed my thumb at the letter on top of her stack of forms. "There is absolutely no reason why Salla should be considered at risk of dropping out. Now just check your files and find out who should have received this letter, and we'll be done here."

"Oh, she meets plenty of the district criteria," Ms. Stankewitz said, flipping through a manila folder full of papers. "We're talking about Sally Konneva, right? Sixth grade? Margaret Fishbeck's class?"

"That's another thing I meant to bring up, as long as I'm here," I said. "What on earth is Ms. Fishbeck doing in charge of the G&T class? We were told Cathy Harper would be teaching the sixth grade G&T class this year." Cathy was a friend of Dennis's, as close as this world got to a wizard-scholar. She'd written a dissertation on Central Texas folklore and European mythology that was published as a popular book and earned, she said, far more than she'd ever made teaching. Salla had been looking forward all summer to taking Cathy's special unit on myths and legends in world literature. She complained that Ms. Fishbeck had watered the material down and narrowed the focus and—well, I didn't understand everything she said, not being any expert on this world's mythology, but Salla had not been happy.

"Here we are!" said Erica Stankewitz triumphantly, delving into the depths of her manila folder and coming up with a single typed sheet. "Sally qualifies for the Alternative Education Program under District Codes GT–103A, SD–22, F–1, and F–33b. It's really very fortunate that we caught her problems in time, Ms. Konneva."

"Would you mind telling me," I said as sweetly as I could, "exactly what those codes stand for?"

Erica Stankewitz looked down at her paper. "GT–103A stands for Gifted and Talented, type 103, category A."

"So you admit she's a smart kid."

"Yes, indeed. That's one of the problems that alerted us," she said earnestly. "A child who is so far ahead of her class often becomes bored with school. She can be a disruptive influence in the classroom; in fact, that problem has already been reported. SD–22: Rebellious attitude toward authority figures."

"You're going to flunk her for being smart and having the wrong attitudes?"

"We don't 'flunk' children in this school, Ms. Konneva. We do feel it desirabe to adjust Sally's attitude."

I was feeling a powerful urge to adjust Ms. Stankewitz's attitude. Kneeling in front of me while I prepared to behead her would have been a good attitude. True, I'd left my sword at home, but I was prepared to make some modifications to my usual procedure.

"According to Ms. Fishbeck, Sally has been marking up her homework assignments with red ink—'correcting' her teacher's grammar and spelling."

I couldn't quite see the problem in this. "So, were there mistakes in Ms. Fishbeck's writing or not? And if there were, isn't she glad to have a student alert enough to catch them?"

"Moving on to the remaining at-risk codes," Erica Stankewitz said briskly, "F–1 is the code for a dysfunctional family situation."

"I'm functioning just fine, thank you," I assured her.

She raised her eyebrows. "According to Sally's file, you are unmarried, Ms. Konneva?"

"So?"

"And you were never married to Sally's father?"

"I should think not," I said. "Bad enough I let that sleazeball—well, never mind."

Erica Stankewitz sighed. "And he does not provide child support or communicate with his daughter in any way?"

"Just let him try!"

"You seem to be missing the point." She ticked off what she considered the relevant points on pudgy white fingers. "Single-parent household, history of early promiscuity, no father figure."

She had a few of those facts wrong, but I didn't see any point in correcting her; it probably wouldn't help Salla's situation to point out that in fact I was sharing a house with the eighth-grade math teacher at this very school, and that Dennis was as much of a parent to Salla as I was.

"And," said Erica Stankewitz, swooping on her last point with a gleam of triumph in her beady little eyes, "parent herself a dropout—there's no record here that you finished high school or even middle school, Ms. Konneva."

They didn't have high school where I came from. But that probably wasn't relevant either. I decided to go for the big picture.

"This," I said as clearly as I could, "is a load of crap, Ms. Stankewitz. How dare you presume to judge my daughter on the basis of what you think you know about our home life and what an incompetent teacher says about her? Doesn't her academic record have any place at all in this discussion?"

"F–41A," Stankewitz said, jotting the code down on Salla's file, "parents not educationally supportive of their child's teacher or administrators."

"You're dyvopto right I'm not supportive," I snarled.

"On the basis of Sally's emotional disturbance alone," Stankewitz said, "I can recommend right now that she be referred to an EBD class."

Those initials had been used in the letter. "Translation, please?"

"Emotionally and Behaviorally Disturbed."

"She is not emotionally disturbed."

"Just look at this picture!" Erica Stankewitz flipped the folder open and shoved it towards me. "When Ms. Fishbeck asked all the children to draw a picture of their home as the first six-weeks report on the mythology unit, this is what your daughter came up with!"

I vaguely remembered Salla grousing, that weekend, about how she wanted to write papers and do research, not play with crayons like a little kid. Now, that seemed weird to me—as if school wasn't enough trouble without complaining when once in a while it was easy. Once I learned enough mathemagics to apprentice to a wizard on Dazau, there was no way I was going to open another math book, much less work problems or write papers.

Salla had chosen one of her favorite places to illustrate—the Fall of Nauzu's Blood, in the mountains of Zemauri near my home village. She'd captured the splashing of the red-tinged water and the rounded smiles of the great slow-boulders so well that I felt a prickle of nostalgia as I looked at it. She'd even drawn in a cluster of chattering, three-legged krelyk winding around the trees that overhung the waterfall.

"It looks fine to me," I said. "Okay, the colors are a little off and the perspective could have been better, but what can you expect of a sixth-grader?"

"Colors!" Ms. Stankewitz snorted. "Perspective! I'm talking about the subject matter, Ms. Konneva. That place looks like nothing on Earth. A river of blood hurtling over a cliff, three-legged snakes, rocks with faces? Your child is in serious trouble, and it's about time you admitted the fact!" Her pen jabbed at the paper before her with short, angry downward strokes. "Code EB-4," she announced. "Emotionally disturbed as a result of dysfunctional home situation!"

A bell clanged in the wall over my head. "That's all," Erica Stankewitz announced, standing up and collecting her papers.

"Oh, no, it isn't," I said. "We haven't settled anything. I'm not satisfied that you understand Salla at all."

A smirk distorted Erica Stankewitz's pasty face. "On the contrary, Ms. Konneva. I'm afraid it's you who don't understand. We don't need your consent in a serious case like this, you know. If you'd spent more time at the school earlier, volunteering like the other mothers, perhaps your daughter wouldn't be predelinquent now. Wild assertions to the contrary won't help your case."

"In fact," I said, "you don't consider yourself answerable to the parents at all, do you? You people will do whatever you dyvopto please to my child and I'm not supposed to have anything to say about it?"

"We consider ourselves advocates for the child's best interests. This file will convince anyone that Sally should be referred for mandatory counseling, anti-delinquent programming and an EBD classroom."

"Fine," I said, taking it from her, "I'll take it home and read it and see if it convinces me."

"Wait a minute!" Stankewitz's voice rose to a pained squeak. "You can't have that—it's school property!" She made an ineffectual grab for the folder. Somehow her nose accidentally came into contact with my elbow.

"Abd the codtedts are codfidedtial!" she squeaked while fishing out a handkerchief to stop the blood.

"I promise not to send it to the local newspaper,"

I said. Stankewitz edged around the desk and tried to block the door. This was a mistake. I accidentally stepped on her fat little black foot and she tripped and fell into the desk. I left her squealing about assault and battery and theft of school property and went to see about my groceries, which were pretty thoroughly cooked by this time.

Chapter $(\sqrt{2})^2$

I fumed at the idiot school and the idiot counselors all the time I was putting away the groceries. It was beginning to look like my whole plan of commuting to the Paper-Pushers' planet so Salla could get a good education had been one big mistake. I'd been lulled by the last two years, when things had seemed to be going so easily. Now everything was going wrong at once. Where had I gone wrong?

I didn't know, but I did know that standing in the kitchen counting Dennis's Szechwan cooking supplies wasn't going to help me figure it out.

Our bedroom had been about the size of one of Zolkir's prison cells before Dennis moved in his collection of classic science-fiction paperbacks. Now, with floor-to-ceiling shelves lining three walls, it was more like a walk-in closet. Sasulau, my sword, hung in her sheath from one bedpost, and the rest of my old fighting gear was stashed under the bed in a cardboard box from the Container Store. I shucked my Paper-Pushers costume, hung the jeans and shirt on a handy bookcase, knelt on the floor and fished around under the bed for the box.

"That's a beautiful sight to greet a man after a hard

day of eighth-grade math," said an appreciative voice
behind me.

"Mumph murph phttt," I said. One of us really ought
to do something about the dust bunny collection under
the bed. I backed out, dragging the box of armor by
one hand, and saw Dennis leaning against the door.
"I'm going to work out," I explained to him.

"I can think of better workouts than fooling around
with that sword and shield," he said, reaching for me.

I could, too, but not while I was so mad at the
school. "Hold that thought," I suggested. "I need to—
We need to talk, too, but—Nauzu klevulkedimmu! I'm
too angry to do anything but work out right now." I
kissed him. It was meant to be a brief kiss, but Dennis
managed to involve his hands and my bare rump and
a lot of small muscle control around the mouth, and
by the time we broke off I was breathing even harder
than I had been when I left Stankewitz's office.

An entrancing image of the counselor's head on a pike
swam before my eyes. It would be a waste of good lust
to jump into bed with Dennis right now; he was a man
who kept his mind on what he was doing, and I wanted
to reciprocate, not get side-tracked into fantasies about
Stankewitz's blood. "Really," I said. "I need to work out.
Besides, Salla should be home any minute."

"I'll cook Szechwan for dinner," Dennis said. "Did
you get the star anise?"

Fiend. He knew exactly what star anise, Szechwan
peppercorns and chili oil did to me. Dennis's Chinese
cooking is a sensual experience equaled only by—well,
as I said, Salla would be home any minute. And I was
still too steamed up over Stankewitz to enjoy life's
normal pleasures.

"I don't want to feel happy and relaxed," I muttered.

"I want to slash, hew, maim and destroy. The star anise is in the brown paper bag with the paper towels, and Norah gave us some habañero peppers from her garden."

"Wonderful! I'll improvise." Dennis went off to the kitchen, humming under his breath, and I put on some of my fighting gear. It was too hot for full armor, and anyway I didn't need the protection when I was just running through exercises on my own. On the other hand, it was important to keep in training to fight with the full weight of armor. I compromised by putting on the basics—your standard chain-mail bra with welded D cups, crotch guard and shield—and adding jogging weights at ankles and wrists.

I started with some basic stretches, then went through a full cycle of boklu against an imaginary mirror-fighter. Dennis says this looks like something he used to study called Ty Chee or something like that, but it seems unlikely to me that there's any real connection. Boklu prepares your heart and mind to cleave through any obstacles in your path bare-handed if necessary, always assuming you aren't already in that frame of mind just from waking up alive another day on Dazau. From what I've observed of this universe of the Paper-Pushers, they aren't much on cleaving either opponents or obstacles. They just wrap them up in red tape.

Which was exactly how I felt now—encircled in a wizard's web of words. One might as well fight clouds as try to get sense out of people like Stankewitz. Nothing she said meant anything real—until the end, when she'd as good as told me they could do whatever they wanted with Salla and they didn't need to answer to me for it.

My Dazau life had been simpler, if harder. I earned

a day's pay for a day's fighting and then gave back most of it to Furo Fykrou to pay for the costs of transporting me to Paper-Pushers each afternoon by the time Salla came back from school. What was left barely covered rent and groceries in the Paper-Pushers' neighborhood where I'd established residence as Riva Konneva so that Salla could get the schooling I'd never had.

Just two years ago that way of life had begun to feel like a trap closing in on me. We were just scraping by, but the future did not look bright. As a swords-woman gets older, her earning power diminishes; just when Salla would be needing even more money to pay for higher education on Paper-Pushers, my take-home zolkys would be dwindling to nearly nothing. That was if Duke Zolkir kept me on at all. If he didn't, I'd be just another middle-aged freelance swords-woman, always on the road, and Salla would have to leave her schooling to come with me; I'd never be able to afford Furo Fykrou's transport fees on the odd jobs I would pick up as caravan guard or merchanters' security. The only way out of that trap was to find another way of earning a living, and I didn't have time to learn a new profession while working as Duke Zolkir's top swordswoman.

Then I met Dennis.

We got stuck together chaperoning a fourth-grade field trip to my workplace. It seemed like a bad idea at the time, but I'd learned it was no use arguing with the earnest, dull young women who organized these things. It seemed like an even worse idea when we arrived in my home reality—after paying exorbitant fees to Furo Fykrou for transporting the entire class—and discovered that I was scheduled for a revenge duel with Vordokaunneviko, the acknowledged champion fighter of all Dazau. And it seemed like an absolutely terrible idea when the duel started and Vordo announced his intention of turning me into something suitable for Chinese stir-fry.

It was one of Salla's classmates who saved my butt that day. The kid was called "hyperactive" and "difficult" on Paper-Pushers'; what that meant was that he noticed absolutely everything that was going on around him and insisted on discussing it. At the top of his voice. When he noticed that Vordo was flickering with the activation of a magic shield every time I tried to land a blow, he discussed that in a loud clear voice. Once I realized that the magic shielding was being provided by Baron Rodograunnizo's new house wizard, a sleazeball if ever I saw one, it was a simple matter to work Vordo around so that the wizard couldn't get a clear view of him. And when the wizard—Mikhalleviko, his name was—started throwing differential mathemagics directly at me, Dennis integrated every one of his incantations right back at him.

When the dust cleared, Vordo and Mikh had both run for it, and Dennis talked Baron Rodo into paying me very substantial compensation for having lured me into an unfair fight. (My patron, Duke Zolkir, and about half of the Bronze Bra Guild helped persuade Rodograunnizo to pay up.)

The zolkys I got from that fiasco had been enough to support Salla and me here on Paper-Pushers' for nearly two years. And now that I had some free time, Dennis offered to teach me enough math so that I could go back to Dazau and apprentice to a wizard. (An honorable wizard, needless to say, not a scumbag like Mikhalleviko—even supposing he ever dared show his face in the trade again.)

It had all seemed to be working out perfectly. After a few months of late-night tutoring sessions, Dennis moved in with Salla and me so that he could tutor me all the time when he wasn't at school. In practice that meant he went over the math texts with me first thing in the morning, I sweated out the problems he had fiendishly devised while Salla was in school and he was teaching, he corrected my work in the afternoon, and our nights were free for more interesting pursuits. Did I say "working out perfectly"? Make that better than perfect. Dennis is a very creative man, and he concentrates his full attention on whatever he is doing. Also, he cooks great Szechwan food, which is the only cuisine on Paper-Pushers' that I consider truly superior to Dazau cooking.

It's a dynamite combination of talents, let me tell you.

When Dennis picked up the Chinese cleaver and began chopping the ingredients for dinner, I took up Sasulau and matched his rhythm with my own fybilka practice—short, fast strokes to mince the air around my imaginary opponent while coming closer and closer to her skin. Fybilka was one of the classic arts of swordcraft at home, something every Guild member studied but that few of us mastered. A swordswoman trained in the art could literally flay her opponent by inches. Even those of us who'd passed the final exercises seldom got a chance to put the art into practice, though; hiring a fybilka killing is expensive, and most of our patrons prefer the cheaper and quicker methods. And even back home, there aren't that many people who really deserve to die that way.

I could think of one now, though.

"There—and there—and there!" I shouted at my

imaginary opponent as my sword took precise shavings
of skin from her pasty cheeks, one pudgy thigh, the
tip of a fat white finger. I could feel Sasulau humming
with pleasure as her blade whizzed through the
motions of a fybilka execution. "That's how you'll
answer to me, Stankewitz!"

Fybilka was too slow; I plunged forward to drive
Sasulau through the spot where her heart would be
if she were facing me. Always assuming she had one.

The screen door slammed and Salla came down the
steps, munching an apple. "Why are you yelling at
Stinky Wits?" she inquired through mouthfuls of
Golden Delicious. "You didn't really run her through
the heart, did you? That would be too cool for words."

"You know Ms. Stankewitz?"

Salla shrugged. "Yeah, I hadda go to her office one
afternoon last week. She's always asking these dumb
questions, like, you know, she goes, how do you feel
about puberty, and aren't you confused about boys,
and really gross stuff about like private things, you
know? And I go, like, I'm just a little kid, ma'am, I
don't know what you're talking about."

"She called you in for counseling without asking my
permission? Oh, I forgot. They don't have to ask
permission."

"Mom," Salla said indistinctly through a bite of apple,
"don't snarl, okay? Like, it's no big deal. She's like,
we do this with all the kids, it's just like a routine
checkup, like seeing your doctor."

"And does she call in all the kids?"

Salla shrugged again. "Enough of them that I knew
what to expect. Why do you think we call her Stinky
Wits? She's best friends with Fishbreath," she added.
"About all they use the computers for is to e-mail back

and forth about what rotten kids we are. I think Fishbreath hates our whole class."

"Ms. Fishbeck to you," I said automatically, "and how do you know what teachers say in their private e-mail?"

Salla smirked. "Never mind," I said hastily, "on second thoughts, I don't want to know. I want you to take your sketch pad into the front yard and draw a picture of our house. This house," I emphasized. "This plain, ordinary, Paper-Pushers'—I mean, Earth-style house. Four windows. One door. White siding, green trim, tree in front yard."

"Why?" Salla demanded.

"Because you were idiot enough to draw a picture of Dazau as your homework assignment for the first six-weeks report, and Stinky Wits—I mean, Ms. Stankewitz—got ahold of it and claims you're emotionally disturbed and she wants to have you moved to a special classroom for problem kids. "Mind you," I added, "I'm impressed by how well you remember the Falls of Nauzu's Blood. It must be, what, five years since I took you there for a picnic?"

Salla had that totally blank expression she puts on when you cut too close to her feelings. Well, I was sorry if she was hurt by finding out that she was on the verge of being bounced out of the Gifted and Talented program, but she'd be a lot more hurt if it actually happened. "So you're going to draw a nice normal boring picture of this house and I'm going to substitute it in your folder and say Ms. Stankewitz must be emotionally disturbed herself to imagine such wild fantasies."

Salla looked at me with more respect than I'd seen since I gave up sword work to study mathemagics.

"Like really sneaky, Mom. I didn't know you had it in you. But don't worry about Stinky Wits. For the next assignment I'm doing this like wizard report on the Female Quest. See, I'm gonna like rip Joseph Campbell and his sexist theories to shreds. Even Fishbreath has gotta give me an A+ on this one."

Well, I told you Salla was the one with brains in this family; I didn't have the faintest idea what she was talking about. "Just draw the picture, okay?"

"Okay, Mom. I never argue back to a lady with a sword in her hand." Salla flipped her apple core into the bushes and sauntered back inside.

After dinner Dennis had papers to grade. Salla holed up in her room to practice her new computer skills (like reading other people's e-mail?). And I went into our bedroom to activate Call Trans-Forwarding through the universes to Furo Fykrou.

"It'll cost extra," Furo Fykrou said, predictably, when I explained what I needed. "You can't just transimage the papers to me; I'll have to have them in their physical form. And you want it done tonight? Did you know the Wizards' Guild has approved a minimum Express Magic fee for overnight work?"

"I still have credit with you from the compensation Rodograunnizo paid me," I reminded him.

"Not that much. You've been having a lot of it translated into Paper-Pushers' green stuff. Now, let me see, at forty zolkys for the round-trip cross-universe transform of the physical papers, plus the fee for mathemagical alterations indistinguishable to the mundane or nonwizardly eye . . . You wouldn't want to buy the Anti-Wizard-Detection Warranty for just an extra ten zolkys, would you?"

"I would not," I said. "There aren't any wizards here. If you can fake up the transcripts to pass mundane inspection, that's all I need. But I need them back before 7:00 A.M. on Paper-Pushers'."

After a little discussion of the Express Magic fee, Furo Fykrou announced that the zolkys I'd left with him would, surprise surprise, just cover the cost of magically altering Salla's transcripts and returning the improved file to me by tomorrow morning.

"There might even be a little over," he said. "A few kauven, at least."

Furo Fykrou made a point of never fleecing his victims—clients, I mean—of their last copper kauve. He said it created ill-feeling. All the same, the thought that my assets now amounted to about $1.56 in Paper-Pushers' money did not fill me with a tide of warm feelings towards Fykrou. I cut off the Trans-Forwarding call before he could think about charging me for that, too, and flopped down on the bed.

"I wish you'd take your armor off before collapsing," Dennis said when he came in. "It's hell on the sheets. What was all that about?"

I lifted one hand to unhook my chain mail corselet and decided it was too much trouble. Besides, I could probably get Dennis to do it for me. "I'm broke," I said. "But by tomorrow, Salla's transcripts will show that she is an emotionally stable, responsible, respectful gifted child."

"She is," Dennis said.

"Not according to her files. Do you know a counselor named Erica Stankewitz?" I filled him in on the afternoon's events.

"Bitch," Dennis said when I finished. "I quit referring any of my problem kids to counseling a few years ago when I noticed that they were coming back more mixed up than they went in. Now I know why."

"So," I said, "tomorrow I'll return the files to Stankewitz and go look for a job."

"Why?"

"I'm broke. I told you. Furo Fykrou is skinning me of my last zolkys to do the transcripts up properly."

"So? I make enough for us both to live on. In fact, now that you mention it, why don't we make this arrangement legal? Solves everything." Dennis beamed at me while reaching one hand around to find the clasp of my bronze corselet.

"I can't let you support me!"

"I don't see why not. You're finishing your studies. Lots of women work to put their husbands through school and nobody thinks anything's wrong with that."

"Yeah, well, most of those women are counting on their husbands to get high-paying jobs after school and support them for a while . . . not that it always works out that way," I said, remembering Norah Tibbs and her ex. Dennis had the top half of the corselet unfastened now, but instead of doing anything about it, he was trailing his fingers along the chain mail fringe. The man made it very difficult to concentrate.

"I thought you were going to get one of those high-paying jobs when you'd learned enough math," he said while investigating the lower edges of the fringe. I shivered and felt my stomach muscles tightening.

"Umm . . . there are some complications I didn't mention when we started this project," I said slowly. "Because they weren't complications then, but now they are. I think. See, I don't just need the math; I need the magic, too. Normally I could learn that by apprenticing to a wizard. But that means living full-time on Dazau. An apprentice has to serve the wizard day and night, whatever hour she's called on. Some of those spells have to be checked every three hours for weeks and weeks. I couldn't do that and come back here at night. I'd have to live there."

"For how long?" Dennis asked.

I shrugged. "For however long the wizard decides it takes, I guess."

"Sort of like grad school," he commented, "only worse. No, I take that back; one year I roomed with a guy who was doing his Ph.D. dissertation on oats. He had to get up and measure how much the baby oat seedlings had grown every three hours. How come you didn't mention this little fact when I started tutoring you?"

"I didn't think . . . it would be that important."

"Or when I moved in?" Dennis's voice had an unfamiliar tone, one I wasn't sure I liked; and he'd quit exploring the boundaries of my corselet. "When I was hauling all those boxes of books into your house? You don't think that might have been a good time to mention this little matter?"

"Hey, I carried as many boxes as you did, and they were your books," I pointed out. "Anyway, I guess . . . I guess I was trying not to think about it. I didn't want to . . . I don't want to . . ."

"Go on," Dennis said. "Say it." He sounded as though he was bracing himself for a double-handed sword blow.

"I like living with you," I said miserably. "I don't want anything to change. I . . . oh, all right. I love you. I think. Sort of."

Dennis propped himself up on one elbow and studied me intently. "I want to remember this moment," he said fondly. "Riva the Invincible, Riva the Amazon Warrior of Dazau, waffling and side-stepping an issue. What's the matter? Were you afraid I wouldn't be willing to come to Dazau with you?"

I gasped. "You'd do that?"

"I've always wanted to travel," Dennis said blandly.

"Well, I haven't. I've done more than enough traveling," I told him. "And I'm not even sure I want to go back to Dazau."

"Fine. We can do it either way. We go back to Dazau and you support me in idle luxury, or we stay here and get married and I support you in—well, okay, a teacher's salary isn't exactly luxury, but we can live on it. Plus, once you're married they won't be able to tag Salla with 'dysfunctional family' and 'single-parent household,' and all that other garbage. Solves everything."

"It does not! I told you, I can't just let you support me."

"Why not?" Dennis lay back down and pulled me towards him. I discovered that he had, in fact, been doing something practical all the time I'd thought he was just fiddling with the fringe on my corselet: he'd opened every one of the leather-bound fasteners. The armor stayed on the bed. I sprawled over Dennis. "See?" he murmured in my ear while caressing the areas that had just been freed from the armor. "I'm supporting you right now, and it doesn't hurt a bit, does it?"

I couldn't answer that for a few minutes. Finally I pushed his hand away. "Did I ever tell you how I happened to join the Bronze Bra Guild?"

"Later," Dennis murmured, reaching for me again.

"It's relevant."

"So is this."

"Mmmm, yes . . . but wait a minute, would you? I want to tell you about this. I . . . when Salla was born, I . . ."

"Your ears are turning pink," Dennis said. "I didn't think anything could make you blush. I'll have to try harder."

"I thought I was apprenticing to a wizard," I said. "I was fresh out of the mountains, dumber than a box of rocks, didn't know you have to pass Elementary Mathemagics and Linear Transformations before you can even seal a binding apprenticeship contract. This sleazeball says, 'Apprentice to me, do exactly what I say, you'll learn magic and make a good living.'"

"Is this going to be a story about sex for grades?"

"It's a story about a dumb mountain girl who thought everything the slimy sleazeball did was making magic. And who believed he was using contraceptive spells. Then when I found out I was pregnant, he said that needn't interfere with the apprentice training . . . until Salla was born. Then he smirked and said he'd be perfectly willing to support me, that I didn't know enough to learn wizardry and had no talent anyway but that he'd let me stick around to keep house for him and cook his meals. On Dazau," I explained carefully, "the rules are basically the same as here, only they're a little more explicit. If you take support from somebody without providing services for it, you're his property."

"And housekeeping and cooking and child care don't count as services worth paying for?"

"Do they count for that here? If you're married to the person providing the services?"

Dennis sighed. "I see your point. But I'm not like that. You should know that by now."

"So. I was a dumb mountain girl, but I was big and strong. The Bronze Bra Guild was willing to give me an apprentice loan while I learned fighting, and they're one of the few guilds that provides decent child care. So I became a swordswoman. And," I added after a few moments of silent reflection, "rather a good one, if I do say so myself."

"That's not the only thing you're good at," Dennis said. "How does this leather panty thing come off?"

"You know perfectly well," I said. "I have to wriggle out of it. Like this."

"Uh-huh," Dennis agreed. "And I like to watch you wriggle."

For quite some time after that we didn't argue about anything, partly because our mouths were otherwise occupied. My armor got shoved over the side of the bed, and I felt guilty about that—no way to treat a perfectly good set of armor—but not guilty enough to stop what we were doing and put it away properly.

We were drifting companionably off to sleep when I remembered the other thing I'd forgotten to tell Dennis. "Guess what," I said. "Vordo's here!"

"What? Where?"

"Not here. Here," I explained. "Somewhere in this reality. Probably somewhere in this country." I told him about the display I'd seen in the supermarket. "And Louise Pilkinton knew his name and everything. It was definitely him. Where do they make covers for romance novels?"

"New York? That's where the publishing industry is."

"Then that's where Vordo is," I said with some relief. New York was nice and far away.

"You sound worried."

"Not about Vordo," I said. That was absolutely true, if not quite complete. "He was running for his life last time I saw him; he wouldn't give us any trouble here even if he did know where we were."

"But that wizard who was working with him nearly got you killed first. Maybe it would be a good idea to find out exactly how Vordo got to this universe."

"Yeah, well," I said, trying to sound bored, "mathemagics doesn't work in this world." At least not as far as I knew. "So even if the wizard came here too, he can't be any trouble. But you're right, we might as well check it out. Let's ask Norah Tibbs to dinner and she can give us the scoop on the romance publishing industry." Because it had just dawned on me: even if Vordo was way off in New York, that didn't necessarily mean the wizard who'd helped him was there.

And I would very much like to know whether Mikhalleviko had transported himself as well as Vordo to this reality, and why, and what he was doing here.

That sleazeball.

Chapter [π]

The secretary was a statuesque Hispanic girl with good legs, which she advertised in lace tights and a very short skirt. The long, firm thighs with their sleek lines of muscle reminded Mikh of Riva. Unfortunately, the top half of the secretary didn't match the promise of the bottom half: she had greasy hair and protruding teeth. In his two years on this world, Mikh had yet to get used to people like that. Why didn't they go to a wizard and get themselves fixed up so they weren't so painful to look at? He knew there were equivalents of cosmetic wizards on this world. They were called plastic surgeons. He had learned a great deal from reading; at least that part of the transform spell had worked right, bringing him to this world dressed like a superior businessman and able to read and speak the local language.

Some of the other improvements he'd made to the spell hadn't worked quite as he expected. Mikh looked down ruefully at the palm-size Leibniz Personal Assistant in his right hand. This little black box and the accompanying manual were a poor exchange for his wizard's staff and book of spells. Of course all the magic power

37

that had been stored in his staff still had to be in the Leibniz. Somewhere. The trouble was, in two years he still hadn't figured out how to release most of the magic functions. And an ability to read English was less help than one might have expected in deciphering the manual.

Now, if only he could figure out how to operate the Veil of Illusion function, he would at least be able to cast an appearance of glamour over this woman so that she was a little easier on the eyes. He might even be able to give her the outer semblance of Riva; the basics were there, the long black hair and coffee-colored skin. . . .

Mikh surreptitiously consulted his manual. Most of his magical spells had been translated as Special Functions, briefly described in an appendix. "To activate the Veil of Illusion," he murmured under his breath, "touch function key F6 twice, then direct the infrared beam of the Leibniz at the item to be veiled and call the appropriate virtual functions." What in Nauzu's name were "virtual" functions? Oh, well, it was worth a try.

He punched F6 twice, then pointed the Leibniz at the secretary and ran the tip of his finger over the touchpad at the top of the Leibniz while remembering the luscious shapes of Riva's contours.

The secretary's face popped out in large, lusciously contoured red boils. Hastily Mikh touched the Undo key and saw the boils disappear.

"You don't have to keep staring at me," the woman snapped. "I told you, Reverend Boatright will see you when he has time."

"My appointment was for nine o'clock," Mikh pointed out. It was 9:45 now.

"Reverend Boatright is a very busy man." She swiveled her chair away from Mikh and touched the intercom. "Reverend, I've sorted all those signed petitions you brought in and entered the names into the database. Would you care to go over them now?"

Mikh felt his wizard's temper rising. This woman was no more than a bondserf to the man he'd come to see; how dare she treat him so lightly?

At least he could use the only magical function he'd regained to teach this impudent female a lesson. While she was still facing away from him, he pointed the Leibniz at the stack of petitions she'd been sorting with such care and pressed function key F2, button A, and the little green knob at the bottom of the Leibniz.

The stack of typed papers vanished. The handwritten signatures didn't of course, but with no paper to support them they merely fell onto the bare desk in a little pile of dried ink crumbs.

There was an incomprehensible crackle from the intercom and the secretary sighed irritably. "Very well, I'll send him in now. You c'n g'wan in," she mumbled without looking at Mikh.

The walls of Reverend Boatright's office were covered with a melange of framed diplomas, letters, and posters in primary colors. The poster behind Boatright's desk read, "The Bible isn't a *good* idea— it's *God's* idea." A single bookcase held a collection of books with titles like *A Call to Righteousness* and *Secular Humanism—Satan of the New Age*. Boatright's desk was bare except for a computer, a speakerphone and a couple of battered textbooks. Mikh read the titles upside down: *Make Friends With Mr. Euclid* and

Families of Our World. If the Reverend Boatright was as busy as the secretary implied, he must be very good at keeping his paperwork organized and out of sight.

Boatright was talking into the telephone as Mikh entered. He gestured for Mikh to sit down and went on with what sounded like a prepared speech, something about the importance of supporting family values and fighting creeping humanism in schools and public life. He was in the middle of a sentence when the person at the other end hung up on him. Mikh could hear the buzz of the dial tone, but Boatright didn't stop talking. People in this reality had relatively inefficient hearing; probably Boatright didn't realize Mikh knew he was talking to empty air.

While he waited for the Reverend Boatright to run out of steam, Mikh glanced around the narrow room. The one window overlooked a parking lot and a convenience store, somewhat detracting from the dignity of the framed diplomas and testimonials that covered the walls. He saw that Boatright had a Ph.D. in Physical Education from the College of Holy Works, a doctorate of theology from the same institution, several letters praising his untiring work in support of American values, and a large brass plaque thanking him for the contribution of the Boatright Wing to the chapel of the College of Holy Works. The signatures on all the letters seemed remarkably similar, but Mikh didn't have a chance to examine them in detail; Boatright hung up the telephone and turned to Mikh with a beam of satisfaction on his face.

"So gratifying to bring another sheep into the fold," he said. "Mrs. Rylander didn't actually commit anything to our cause, but I could tell that she was deeply touched by my words."

He pressed the intercom button. "Sandy, send one of our brochures and a petition to Mrs. Rylander. She's very interested in the cause."

"Hey, Rev, about them petitions, I gotta tell you something—" Sandy's voice crackled through the intercom.

"Later, my dear, later." Boatright switched off the intercom and leaned across the desk, fixing his eyes on Mikh. "Now, Mr. Levy, what can I do for you?"

Mikh launched into his prepared speech about being impressed by the great work done by the American Values Research Center and his desire to offer his skills to the cause. He proffered the sheaf of references he'd brought, praising him for his contributions as a political analyst in various California campaigns. The references were no more bogus than the framed letters on the walls of Boatright's office, and considerably better done.

"Ah—yes, I see, I see, but we aren't really looking for a political analyst at this time," Boatright said. "I advertised for a programmer analyst." He waved at the computer. "I could do it myself, of course, but the Lord said to me, He said, 'Bob, you need to spend your time on My work, not on fiddling around with computers.' So I'm looking for someone who could sort and classify the data Sandy has been collecting and direct our next efforts. Now, if you could program computers—"

Mikh sighed. "Can't everybody? But it would be a waste of my talents. I can do considerably more for you than mere data analysis, Mr. Boatright. Why, a simple extrapolation from the figures in your last mailing tells me that your expected return on mailings can be increased exponentially with a probability of $p_i(s|r,n), s=0-n$."

Boatright blinked and looked impressed. Mikh suppressed a smirk of satisfaction. At least mathemagics worked to this extent on the Planet of the Paper-Pushers: you recited an incantatory formula and people backed off and looked impressed.

It was really unfortunate that anything more solid than impressing Paper-Pushers required the power stored in what used to be his magic staff. Mikh felt sure all the magical functions were there; he'd sweated toads and salamanders on converting the transport spell so that everything he brought with him would be transformed intact and in a form appropriate to this world. But he hadn't counted on his book of spells being transformed into something that no human brain could decipher. He'd spent months experimenting with the arcane Paper-Pushers' formulae of "point and click," and "drag and drop," and he still hadn't managed to get more than a handful of the most elementary mathemagical functions to work for him.

Quickly, before Boatright could stop goggling, he added, "A simple finite-horizon dynamic programming model can determine the precise modality which will establish the American Values Research Center as a serious political presence in contact with the mainstream of grass-roots American activism." He wasn't sure that actually meant anything, but these Paper-Pushers didn't seem to notice as long as one took their favorite words and rearranged them in a pleasing syntactical order. "In other words," he went on, "by using my skills as a political analyst to redirect and focus your efforts appropriately, you can have . . ." He slipped into the sort of terms he would have used in ki-Dazau. "Power. Glory. All the wealth and lordship of the world."

Boatright nodded. "Good man. That's from Proverbs, right? I like a man who knows his Scriptures. What made you decide to relocate to Austin, Mr. Levy? According to these references, you were doing quite well in California." He glanced down at the resume in front of him. Mikh considered this one of his finest works of fiction. He had typed it only the night before on a computer at the public library, targeting his "background" specifically to this idiot's tastes. It wasn't the ideal job, but he had to have some source of income while he stayed in Austin, and this pretentious little preacher had seemed like the kind of idiot who would skip details like checking references. "The governor's race, personal advisor to Senator Waxman, fundraising for the League for Human Decency . . . "

Mikh leaned forward and fixed Boatright with an earnest look. "Reverend Boatright, the state of California is a sink of iniquity, a Godless Sodom whose citizens care only for filthy lucre." And very lucrative he'd found it, too, but it was only a stopping place until he located what he'd really come to this world for. And what a dreary task that had been! Every time he tried to invoke the Searching Eye function of the Leibniz he got back "NO DATA FOUND," instead of the clear images the globe topping his magic staff had once given him. He'd been forced to resort to purely mundane means. Reading telephone directories. Tapping into computer data bases. Fortunately, Riva hadn't disguised herself very well: once he worked his way down to this nowhere town in the Bible Belt, it had been easy to recognize "Konneva, Riva" as the Rivakonneva of Dazau.

His Riva.

None of which was any of Boatright's business. "As for settling in Austin," Mikh lied easily, "this is only one of several possibilities that I'm considering. Some of the larger politically oriented Christian foundations have offered me very significant remuneration."

"Mal and Norma Gainer!" Boatright's fist clenched. "They're always one step ahead of me!"

"It would be unprofessional of me to reveal the names of the other groups bidding for my services," Mikh said smoothly. "Suffice it to say that I have chosen you, Robert Boatright, because I desire to work with a man of proven insight and great leadership potential. Working together, we can make the American Values Research Center a force to be reckoned with in national politics, and you can assume your rightful place as founder of the center. I'm afraid you might be required to take on a rather more public role than you would choose. I know you prefer to work behind the scenes, Reverend Boatright, doing your good works in secret and taking no credit for them—"

Boatright looked downright crestfallen. Yes, he was definitely on the right track now. "But," Mikh went on with a flourish of his Leibniz, "I'm afraid you will now be called to stand forth as the leader of your group and all the good American values they stand for. You may even have to make the deep personal sacrifice of immersing yourself in party politics. Your party needs new leadership, responsible leadership, moral leadership." He couldn't quite remember the names of the political parties in this part of the world, but it didn't matter; the statement was doubtless true of both sides. All three sides. However many there were.

And Boatright was puffing himself up like a feathered dilkydeec in heat. "If God wants me to go out in public," he said, "if God says to me, 'Bob, I want you to become a public figure,' then my answer to God is, 'Okay, Lord!' Do you think I should run for mayor?"

"My dear Reverend Boatright! Your talents would be wasted on such a minor role. Congressman Boatright has a better sound, does it not?"

"Senator Boatright . . ."

"High Duke . . . er, I mean, President Boatright," Mikh put in.

Boatright shook his head vigorously as if to clear it of these wisps of glory. "You really interpret the—uh—dynamic programming that way?"

"It's a simple recursion on the optimal strategy. Nothing could be clearer," Mikh assured him. "There are special analysis functions built into my Leibniz, you know; I had it custom-made for my particular specialty." True enough. The fact that he couldn't access those functions was hardly relevant at the moment; neither was the fact that they had nothing to do with political science. The special functions were about mathemagics, and mathemagics was power, and that was what he and Boatright were both talking about.

"Really? Let me have a look." Boatright reached for Mikh's Leibniz.

"The numbers are, uh . . . not in a user-friendly format," Mikh said, but not quickly enough; he'd made the mistake of setting the Leibniz down on the desk in front of him while he used both hands to sketch out the kingdoms of the world in the air before them. Now Boatright had his hands on the disguised magical staff.

"It's okay," Boatright assured him, "I know all about these things. Read an article in the *Journal* just the other day. It said the infrared data transfer function works without any wires or disks or anything. You just point the Leibniz at your other computer, push the right function key, and off . . . we . . ."

"Not F2!" Mikh cried out.

Boatright's broad thumb came down on the F2 key and the A simultaneously.

"Nauzu klevulkedimmu! Whatever you do now," Mikh said, "don't touch the . . ."

"It's not transferring data," Boatright said. "Oh, I see. You need to press this little green knob at the bottom to activate it, don't you?"

The battered textbooks stacked beside the computer disappeared. Boatright's eyes swelled outwards. "What the Sam Hill—?"

The Leibniz dropped from his nerveless fingers and Mikh scooped it up before Boatright could do any more damage. "I did tell you," he said, "that this model had been specially equipped with functions to my personal specifications."

"What else can you do?" Boatright leaned across the desk as if he wanted to grab the Leibniz back; Mikh held it firmly out of his reach. "Can you make things appear?"

Mikh shook his head. All his efforts to invoke the Monster Movement Transform Function had resulted in the obscure message "PARITY ERROR."

"Can you make anything you want to disappear? This desk? No, don't, it cost a bundle. Um, ah—the paper clips?"

Again Mikh shook his head. "Only printed matter," he said with regret. "I apologize for the loss of your books; I'll personally replace them as soon as possible."

Boatright chuckled and rubbed his hands together.

"All in good time, my dear boy, all in good time. You're hired, of course, and I shall want you to show me exactly how to repeat that little trick—or no, it wouldn't do for me to be seen using mechanical aids. Some people might think it a Satanic contraption. You know, the secular humanist liberal commies call us book-burners," he confided in Mikh, "just because we want to keep smut out of our homes and Satanism out of the schoolbooks. But it's actually quite hard to burn a book." A shadow crossed his brow. "Incredibly hard. But with this—it's a miracle. And the state textbook hearings happening right in town this week, too! Oh, this'll show the Gainers a thing or two about who really does the Lord's work and has the Lord's ear. A genuine, public, certified miracle in front of witnesses. I can hardly wait!"

Chapter 4$(\lim_{x \to 2^+} \frac{x-[x]}{x-2})$

I wanted to fix Norah something really special for dinner, like leegryz in caumopi sauce. Of course I couldn't afford to have the ingredients transported from Dazau, especially now that Furo Fykrou had stripped me of my last zolkys to get Salla's transcripts fixed, but I've worked out a pretty good equivalent with duckling in place of the leegryz and a mix of chili oil, Szechwan peppercorns, Tabasco, vinegar, sage honey, and fresh roasted habañero peppers for the caumopi sauce.

Dennis likes it, but he was doubtful about Norah; he says his Chinese cooking is too spicy for a lot of his people and Duke Zolkir's Leegryz might just be going over the top. "Especially for the kids," he pointed out.

We compromised; pizza for Salla and Jason, which they could eat in Salla's room while playing with the computer, and Duke Zolkir's Duck in Pepper Sauce for the adults. Dennis called it Incendiary Gumbo.

"This is delicious," Norah said after the first bite. Dennis was eating his over white rice, and plenty of it, and there was sweat on his forehead. Norah and I competed amiably to see who could finish off the rest of the gumbo undiluted. I won, mostly because she kept pausing between bites to tell me how she hadn't had anything with this much character to it since her grandmother from New Orleans and her mother in Santa Fe used to get together for their annual Thanksgiving cook-off.

"Where'd you get the recipe, anyway?" she demanded.

"Oh, it's a favorite dish around where I used to live," I hedged. "Everybody knew how to make it."

"And where was that? I'd love to sample the rest of your native country's cuisine."

"Of course, Riva had to improvise a bit on ingredients," Dennis interrupted. He took a long draft of his Shiner Bock; I could practically see the steam rising from his tongue. "You can't get everything she wants locally. I used to have the same problem finding stuff for Szechwan cooking before all these Oriental food stores opened up. Don't you think it's strange the way they keep burning down? Do you suppose it's a tong war?"

"In Austin? Nope, I bet they're doing it for the insurance," Norah said, and they argued that point while I scraped the pot.

"I'd fight you for that last bowl," Norah said wistfully, "but I've eaten too much as it is. As usual." She patted her round tummy. "I don't know how you can eat like that and keep your shape, Riva; it's not fair. You and my Jason both. Of course Jason's growing like a weed, he's that age, but what's your secret?"

"I, um, exercise a lot," I mumbled between mouthfuls of duckling and roasted pepper slices. "Every afternoon, lately." Since the day I'd seen Vordo's picture at the supermarket, I hadn't missed a session. My fighting skills had grown rusty in the peaceful years on Paper-Pushers, and I had a feeling I might need to be up to speed again before long.

"Really? I wish I had your willpower," Norah said. "But I probably couldn't handle your kind of workout routine anyway."

"We'd have to start you off slow," I acknowledged. A sparring partner would be useful, but I wouldn't have picked short, fluffy Norah for the role. Still, if she was interested, we might be able to do something. "Begin with a little singlestick work, then practice shield handling before I let you loose on anything resembling a sword—"

"Norah, you ready for another beer?" Dennis interrupted.

"Oh, thanks, Dennis. I'll get it myself."

While Norah wriggled between the chairs and the wall to get to our dinky little kitchen, Dennis leaned over and whispered, "You dork, nobody does sword-fighting here. She thinks you lift weights or something."

"I don't see why I have to keep Dazau such a deep dark secret," I whispered back. "Especially from Norah. I like Norah. And her kid saved my life on Dazau, remember?"

"Her kid," Dennis said between clenched teeth, "is doubtless convinced it was a dream by now. And if you try to tell Norah all about Dazau, you'll be lucky if she thinks you're dreaming. Most likely you'll get a reputation for having psychotic delusions."

"But you accepted—" I began to protest.

"I was there," Dennis said. "I saw. And I read a lot of science fiction, remember? I'm more open-minded than most people to the idea of parallel universes and alternate realities."

"Then Norah should be, too. Remember, she doesn't

just do historical romances. She writes science fiction under her real name."

"I don't care. It's too risky. Look, you've kept Dazau a secret all these years; what's the problem now?"

I shut up. Dennis was right; it was too risky to expect anybody else on Paper-Pushers' to accept the alternate realities of my life. Still, I wished I could tell Norah. There were some heavy decisions coming up soon, and I could use a good friend to talk things over with. Maybe I could find the money to pay Furo Fykrou for one last transform to Dazau. If I couldn't ask Norah's advice, maybe Sikarouvvana, my first friend in the Guild, would have some ideas. But I wanted to see her face to face—none of this crackly, unreliable Call Trans-Forwarding business.

When Norah got back, Dennis started talking about the textbook hearings being held at the Capitol before she could revert to the subject of my workouts. "The Gainers and their buddies are coming up with the usual list of objections. This time they're even trying to censor the math books, can you believe it?"

"I'd believe anything of that crowd," Norah said. "But do tell me, how do you sneaky secular humanists incorporate Satanism into the mathematics textbooks?"

Dennis snorted. "This time they've come up with a new one. They say the elementary geometry textbook 'encourages creative and original thinking.'"

"What's wrong with that?"

"I guess you're only supposed to think the thoughts the Lord puts into your head. Via one of the fundamentalist preachers, of course. Unfortunately," Dennis said, "they vastly overrate the textbooks. Riva! You read *Make Friends With Mr. Euclid*. Anything in there encourage your creative and original thinking?"

I groaned, remembering my struggles with the first math textbook Dennis had handed me. "I'd rather be a living sacrifice to Nauzu than go through that book again."

"Who's—" Norah began, but Dennis interrupted her.

"What's more," he said, "the book is riddled with errors. I'd never have recommended it to Riva as an elementary geometry text if I'd taught out of it before. They start by leaving out a couple of axioms, without which there's no way you can prove the basic geometrical statements they ask the students to do, and whoever went into non-Euclidean geometries completely misunderstood the point of the parallel postulate."

Norah looked slightly dazed.

"I've a good mind to take a personal leave day and go down to testify at the hearings myself," Dennis declared, "only I'm not sure whether to fight the Gainers or protest the textbook on account of its lousy mathematics."

"Fight the Gainers," Norah said immediately. "In fact, I'll come with you. These people are dangerous. They don't stop at textbooks, you know. Last year they pressured Bookstop and B. Daltons and Waldenbooks to stop selling romance novels because they're pornographic."

"Aren't they? The covers—"

"Listen," Norah said, "we have to wrap the fuck scenes up in so many euphemisms that there's no way anybody could tell what's going on if they didn't already know. Mind you," she added, "I'd be happier if the editors didn't pressure us to have those scenes in the first place. I think everybody skips them; they don't have anything to do with the plot, and they're all the same. Mine in particular," she added with a grin. "After the first three books I started recycling the sex scenes. WordPerfect makes it real easy to do a global change on the characters' names and hair colors; then I use the on-line thesaurus to replace a few adjectives and pop the old scene into the next book."

"Doesn't your editor notice?"

"Honey, editors of midlist romance novels come and go so fast, I've yet to have one stick around for three books to notice the cycle."

"Readers?"

"I told you, everybody skips those parts! But can you imagine," Norah said, returning to her original grievance, "what it would do to my income if they took Kathleen Fraser off the shelves of all three major book chains?"

"Who's Kathleen Fraser?"

"My pen name," Norah said. "I save 'Norah Tibbs' for my real books—the science fiction. Those are fun to write, but they don't pay nearly as well as romance; there's no way I could support Jason and me on the SF. Besides, they'll probably go after science fiction next," she added darkly. "Vera Boatright already complained to the school about letting a third-grade teacher read the Narnia books aloud to her class. Not that she's read the Narnia books, you understand. Not that she's aware C. S. Lewis was a noted Christian theologian when he wasn't writing children's stories. No, they have talking animals in the Narnia books, and that's Satanism. Can you imagine what they'd do if they got hold of one of my SF books? Writers are an endangered species anyway," she finished up gloomily. "I'll probably wind up in Hollywood, writing scripts for *Star Trek: The 43rd Generation*."

"I thought Kathleen Fraser was doing pretty well,"

I said. "And that reminds me. I wanted to ask you something about the cover art on your last book." I hadn't really looked at the book when Norah gave me one of her author copies, but after seeing that poster of Vordo I'd studied the cover again.

"Don't ask me, honey, they never invite mere writers to comment on the cover art." Norah wrinkled her round little nose. "That cover in particular. *Love's Tender Promise* is set in Scotland, for pity's sake, where it's been known to snow in June. My heroine would have frozen all her erogenous zones off if she'd trailed around in nothing but that wisp of pink silk she's not wearing on the cover. Shouldn't complain, though," she said cheerfully. "I got a Vordo cover and foil lettering on the title. Yep, I guess Kathleen Fraser is coming up in the world. They might even pay me real money for the next book; this one ought to sell like hot cakes. Anything with Vordo on the cover generally does."

"That's what I wanted to ask you about," I said. "This Vordo. Who is he, and when did he start showing up on book covers, and where did he come from?"

Norah grinned. "Don't tell me you've got a crush on Vordo, Riva? You'll have to get in line behind forty million American housewives."

"He looks like . . . someone I used to know a long time ago," I said, hoping that was vague enough to satisfy Dennis.

"Unlikely," Norah said. "The PR on him is that he was a political prisoner in Russia before the fall of the Evil Empire. When the walls came down, he supposedly walked out of his prison camp and across Russia to the free world. He got as far as Berlin and was discovered by an American fashion photographer doing a location shoot of lingerie models posing on the remains of the Berlin Wall. The truth is probably less romantic," she admitted. "I've met Vordo, and he doesn't have enough brains to get in trouble over politics."

"That sounds like the guy I used to know," I said.

"But he's definitely got an accent you could cut with a knife. I don't know where he's originally from, Riva, but it's not the USA."

Of course, you could say the same of me, but Dennis would explode if I mentioned that again. And why should Vordo have an accent? Cut-rate wizardry, probably. A standard transform ought to include the host country's language; mine had, and Furo Fykrou never gave you anything that wasn't in the basic mathemagical spell.

Then again, perhaps he'd had the full standard transform—only into Russia, not here. That would give him the right background for the rest of his lies. Too bad he hadn't stayed there. I spared a selfish moment to wish that the Iron Curtain had remained intact.

"Tell you what," Norah said, "if you want to check out Vordo in person, buy a ticket to SalamanderCon next weekend—no, don't bother; I'll get you and Dennis guest passes."

"What's a romance model doing at a science-fiction convention?" Dennis asked.

Norah sighed. "Ariel Romances just bought Vordo's exclusive services for their new line of futuristic romances. Zodiac, it's called. They have this idea that they're going to do a crossover marketing strategy targeting both romance and science-fiction readers. It's been tried before, but Vordo might be just what they need to put it across; books with a Vordo cover have better sell-through and order-back than anything else on the list."

Then again, I thought, Furo Fykrou's language transform had evidently not been as thorough as it might have been. Crossover marketing? Sell-through? Order-back? Norah might as well have been speaking ki-Dazau. Except, of course, I understood ki-Dazau.

"Romance novels at SalamanderCon?" Dennis prompted Norah.

"Big promo. They've rented half of the front lobby at the Crimson Griffin Hotel for a booth and display. They're raffling off 'Feast with Vordo,' tickets. The contract requires him to take his shirt off at least three times a day." Norah sighed again. "They're really pulling out all the stops except one. They could have got some competent romance writers who know something about science fiction to write for the new line. But nooo, instead they had to have the top romance writers do their conception of 'futuristic romance.' And nice ladies though they are, I don't think any of them have looked at anything in SF since the days of BEMs. *Locus* sent me a bunch of the galleys to review for their short comments section, but I don't dare say anything about them; all the books are hopeless as science fiction, and all the writers are friends of mine."

"Would you want to write for Zodiac?"

"Well, no," Norah admitted. "I like to keep Kathleen Fraser and Norah Tibbs separate. Kathleen earns the money and Norah writes what she wants to. All the same—"

"There's the problem," Dennis said. "It's like teaching. Good teachers spend half their time working around the bureaucracy instead of teaching. And even then, sometimes they get booted out."

"I don't quite see the connection," Norah said.

"Well, there isn't one," Dennis said, "but I found out what happened to Cathy Harper, who should have been teaching Salla's class this fall, and I wanted to tell Riva about it."

"They told me she quit," I said.

"She got fed up," Dennis said. "I phoned her this afternoon. She said all last year the American Values Research Center gave her trouble about the folklore and mythology unit. She was teaching Satanism, she was corrupting good Christian kids, the usual line. Bob and Vera Boatright got a bunch of their friends to write letters saying they were offended by the course materials and requested alternate study materials for their children, so half the class was reading stories from the Bible while the other half was reading Joseph Campbell. Then, right at the end of the year, they found out she'd never completed her emergency teaching certificate course work and started raising a stink about that. She said she could've gone to summer school and taken Sociocultural Influences on Minority Leadership Issues for her certificate credit, but she figured next year would just be more of the same thing and she'd had enough. She's working as a tech writer for MCC and making twice what AISD paid her."

"Aha!" Norah exclaimed. "Cathy didn't get her brains burnt out by majoring in education. No wonder she was so sharp—oh, sorry, Dennis."

"No need to apologize," Dennis said. "I snuck in through the same back door Cathy used. She was an English major, I was a math major, and we both got Emergency Teaching Certificates on the basis of a vague promise to take some education courses some time in the distant future."

"So are you going to be in trouble, too?" Norah demanded.

Dennis grinned. "I don't think so. Nobody would have noticed Cathy's lack of credentials if the AVRC hadn't targeted her. And I teach math; there's no reason they should go after me. Nothing controversial about algebra and geometry."

"Unless the textbook encourages evaluative and creative thinking," Norah said dryly.

"There is that. I think I will take a personal day to attend the hearings. Want to come with me, Riva?"

I shook my head. "Have fun. Me, I'm going to slip Salla's file back into place at the school when nobody's looking, and if Erica Stankewitz says anything about me taking it in the first place, I'll say she's having hallucinations. I volunteered to cut out orange construction paper pumpkins for the Halloween festival so I'd have an excuse to hang out around the office tomorrow."

"Watch out," Norah said, "Bob Boatright will probably decide Halloween is Satanist."

I thought about suggesting to Dennis that we pay Furo Fykrou to transfax him forged images of the required teaching certificates, but I couldn't bring that up in front of Norah. Besides, it would be awfully expensive, and he didn't seem worried about the problem.

Chapter $f(-1)|f(x) = x^2 - 3x + 1$

Mikhalevviko the Mage (aka Michael Levy) surveyed the proceedings of the Texas Textbook Hearing Commission with a supercilious smile playing about his narrow mouth. No occasion could have better served to demonstrate the inferiority of this world to his own. In the reality from which Mikhalleviko and Rivakonneva and Vordokaunneviko had come, Dazau was the center of the universe. He had already learned that Paper-Pushers considered their own world a small, insignificant part of a marginal section of their universe.

Judging from this shabby display of justice, they were quite right. The man called Boatright had emphatically described the importance of these hearings. Because Texas adopted textbooks statewide, rather than district by district, and because the state was so large, publishers tailored their textbooks to pass any objections raised in the hearing process. Much money was involved, Boatright claimed—the equivalent of a tower filled to the brim with Dazau zolkys, or so Mikhalleviko mentally translated the currency involved. He would have expected such a major justicing to be carried out in the high style of Baron Rodograunnizo's court in Dazau: a cavernous hall draped with gold-and-purple hangings, petitioners dwarfed by the size of the hall and the height of the baron's throne, and the baron's own house wizard drawing mathemagical illusions of light and smoke to heighten the awe of the commoners.

Instead, he and Boatright had pushed their way into a common rectangular room lit by miserable, flickering, pale blue lights. There were too many people in the room for the chairs available, and the chairs themselves were folding stools that clanged and clattered when anybody moved. The high judges, or whatever Boatright had called the dispensers of this justice, were seated behind a table no higher than the rest of the room, and they were dressed in the same dull manner as all the other Paper-Pushers. There were no insignia of rank or quality to be seen, no guards or drums to lend awe to the justicing, no executioner or torturer with his instruments of truth-finding: just the rabble crowding into the room, and the slightly more dignified rabble sitting behind the table. How could anybody take such a justicing seriously?

The smile died away from Mikhalleviko's face as he contemplated the fact that this was now his world, as well as theirs, and that he would henceforth have to content himself with the Paper-Pushers' poverty of spirit and their unimaginative insistence on the forms of "equality."

Unless, of course, he reshaped this world to suit his ends . . . Boatright had insisted that he cared nothing for the money involved in the textbook business; his only interest was the opportunity the textbook hearings gave them to influence the hearts and minds of the nation's young people. The man was lying, of course. Mikhalleviko had not needed to activate his Truth Function (Alt-F10-S-[f(x)], the manual said, but it failed to say what x was supposed to be) in order to perceive Boatright's true aims. He was really interested in personal aggrandizement. He thought that by persuading Mikhalleviko to activate the one function he had mastered, while pretending that the disappearance of the textbooks was his own work, he would receive the awe and adulation of this rabble. Well, maybe so; maybe so. Such tricks might well impress a backward society like this one. But Boatright's single-minded focus showed how short-sighted the man was. Why stop at impressing the handful of people in this room, when—according to him—the minds of a nation were to be moulded through the textbooks the justicers were discussing?

For this session of the hearings, Mikhalleviko regret-fully conceded, he would simply follow Boatright's instructions. He did not yet understand this society well enough to insert his own changes into the books. But he would learn. These things called books seemed to be repositories of whatever magic the Paper-Pushers possessed. He would learn how to use that magic, and then he would require his own changes in the textbooks; changes that would teach a nation of Paper-Pushers to appreciate glory, to bow down before power, to live almost as if they were in the universe of Dazau.

Not quite like Dazau, though. There would be some minor changes. Mikhalleviko had always thought that wizards, not warriors, ought to be the high dukes and justice-givers of the world.

Now, with patience, he had a chance to shape a world according to his dreams.

It did seem to be true that a great deal of patience would be required.

"Passage objected to," one of the women behind the table read in a monotone. "Mrs. Grieg has a full-time job. Mr. Grieg works part-time. After work, Mr. Grieg picks up their daughter Erin at the day-care center, shops for groceries and prepares supper." She looked over her half-spectacles at the young man before her. "And your objection to this passage, Mr. Molinares?"

"Call me Mo," the boy said. "Thass my street name, see? Just old Mo. Yeah, lady, see, I don't like this kinda crud cause it like encourages women to get uppity. Like when my dad cut out my mom went to work at Target, see, she coulda stayed home onna welfare but now just because she got a job she thinks she can tell me what to do! I wouldn't whup a woman, see, but I got my bidness to tend to on the street, see, I got to watch these little old kids they dealin' for me and—"

"That's enough, Mo," interrupted a pallid paper-colored man sitting behind the boy.

The woman raised her hand. "Please. Mr. Molinares still has five of his six minutes, and we find his . . . er . . . reasons for objecting to the passage most revealing."

Beside Mikh, Boatright chortled under his breath. "That SOB Gainer outfoxed himself this time!"

"Pray explain," Mikh said. Even Boatright's puerile political maneuverings were more interesting than the rambling of the teenager now testifying.

"See, you're only supposed to get six minutes to testify," Boatright whispered. "Of course you can submit as long a list of objections as you want, but you only get six minutes to talk about them. It's hard to make much of an impression in six minutes."

Especially, Mikh reflected, if it took you as long to get to the point as it did Boatright.

"Usually the Gainers get around that rule by busing in a bunch of their church members to testify," Boatright went on. "But this year old Malcolm Gainer's trying a new system. These kids sure aren't church members. They look like he got them right off East Seventh Street. Maybe he thought the testimony of these 'innocent children' would impress the board more than hearing the usual batch of Gainer followers."

"It seems to have attracted a certain amount of attention," Mikh pointed out, indicating the cluster of men carrying black boxes in one corner of the room. He had learned that these boxes were somehow equivalent to Dazau's transfer globes, allowing images and sounds to be sent instantaneously from one place to another—even, so he was told, from one place to many. Such devices were potent instruments of control; after he mastered the textbooks, Mikh decided, he would have to take over the "television" industry.

"Wrong kind of publicity." Boatright sniggered. "He didn't rehearse these kids enough." His smile faded. "Any kind of publicity is good publicity, though. And they could use up the whole day with this nonsense."

Under a rain of whispered instructions from Mal Gainer, "Massa Mo" had finally ceded the floor to his friend Ronald, who was speaking against a passage on the nuclear family.

"Mister Gainer, he says this is too weak, and I agree with him," Ronald said firmly. "Says here the New Clear Family is just one possible structure."

"And well suited to children," a man behind the table interpolated.

"Thass not enough," Ronald insisted. "See, the way I see it, this New Clear Family is—it ain't just one way, it's the right way to go, man, and they oughta say so straight up."

"Er—Mr. Vranesh, I mean, Varnish, I mean . . ."

"Vranesik," the boy said. "Call me Ronald."

"Ronald, would you mind explaining to this board exactly what you mean when you say the nuclear family is the wave of the future? Some of us," the man said with a superior smirk, "think it's already been around for a long time."

"Some of us think it's a tool of the patriarchy!" the woman in half-glasses snapped.

"Now, now, Emmagail," the man soothed her, "this is Mr. Va—er, this is Ronald's time. Let's let him speak."

"No!" Mal Gainer mouthed frantically at the boy, but without effect.

"See," Ronald said comfortably, "this New Clear Family means you gotta be Clear about who's in your Family, dig? Now, what's your Family? The folks who look out for you and give you backup when you need it. My old man never give me nothing but a hard time, hell, he's a goddamn criminal, I oughta knock his head off. He ain't my family. My New Clear Family is Massa Mo, here, and Thunderhead over there, and the rest of the Scars."

"Scars?" queried the man behind the table.

Ronald rolled up his sleeve to show a roughly slashed double X on his forearm. The wound had been allowed to heal without treatment, leaving four angry red lines that puffed out above the flesh. "Yeah. All of us here, we're the Scars, and we stick together, dig? We're integrated, too," he pointed out, nodding at Molinares with his coffee-colored skin. "Anglos and Messkins working together to keep the niggers in their place. That's my New Clear Family."

Boatright was doubled up with silent laughter. "A street gang!" he burbled to Mikh. "The idiot hired a street gang to testify for Christian values!"

Mikh didn't see what was so funny about this. The men with the black boxes were making interesting whirring and clicking noises with their machinery, so presumably Mal Gainer was getting some of this "publicity" that everybody seemed to want so much. And Ronald was the sanest-sounding person he'd yet encountered in the Paper-Pushers' universe. His New Clear Family sounded like the nucleus of a House. On Dazau, Ronald would be headed for the status of a Baron with his own House, if he could stay alive long enough to conquer enough of other rulers' territory.

Mikh leaned back in his chair and let his eyes wander neutrally over the room while a third boy expounded on the dangers of a passage implying that other cultures' ways of life were as good as our own. "Never mind the niggers," he said, "you gotta watch out for the slants. They're taking over the fucking world, man, and we gotta teach decent white Americans that our way of life is the right way and any gook gets in the way is gonna get his Chink store torched!"

Perhaps, Mikh thought, he should leave Boatright and offer his services to the Scars. They seemed to have the right ideas; all they lacked was a wizard. Of course, they might not value the one wizardly function he'd managed to implement as much as Boatright did. . . .

A flash of pure panic shot through his body, breaking off his complacent musings. Something was wrong—something was terrifying, and he didn't even know what! Suddenly he was reliving the heart-stopping moments in Dazau when that horrible Paper-Pushers brat caught him giving wizardly support to Vordo in the middle of a duel. That had been the end of his life on Dazau, the end of his career as a wizard. And now, for some reason, he was reliving that sick moment of loss and failure. What had made him think of that now, just when he was finally starting to rebuild his life?

He hadn't really been paying attention to the pasty-faced rabble while his eyes wandered over them; now Mikh looked back around the room, more slowly, trying to identify what had given him this sense of threat. Ah. Of course. Easy enough to recognize the fellow when you remembered the last time you'd seen him. That tall one with the black-rimmed glasses, sitting at the back of the room and tapping one finger on his thigh. Mikh had last seen him making that same impatient gesture while he bargained with Baron Rodograunnizo to pay Riva an exorbitant sum in compensation for having inveigled her into an unfair duel—a sum that Rodograunnizo would doubtless have tried to take out of Mikh's hide, had he not prudently removed himself first from House Rodograunnizo and then from the entire universe that centered around Dazau.

Mikh's muscles tightened and he forced himself to take deep breaths to relax. The bastard could be no threat to him now. Better yet—he might be a direct path to Riva. At the very least, he could tell Mikh exactly where Riva was now and what she was doing, make it easier for him to approach her. Because he meant to have that woman back. She might have been able to desert him on Dazau, but here there was no Bronze Bra Guild to protect her. She was a woman alone, his for the taking if only he could find her.

Mikh excused himself to Boatright, promising to return in a moment, and sidled around the reporters to the back of the room. "Great to see you again!" he said in a hearty undertone, mimicking the way he'd seen Paper-Pushers men greet each other. He thrust out his right hand to show that he bore no weapon or wizard's staff (the Leibniz was in his left sleeve).

He was gratified to see that Dennis looked blank. Mikh hadn't thought the man would recognize him without his wizard's robes and accoutrements; they'd only glanced at one another across a crowded arena. As long as Dennis didn't know him, he had the advantage. "We really must get together some time," Mikh continued. "Want to do lunch? I'll have my girl call your girl." An inspiration struck him. "Say, is that Riva chick still working for you? Gorgeous black-haired chick, built like a brick shithouse?"

A light of recognition came into Dennis's eyes. Oops. Not such a great inspiration after all, mentioning Riva right off. "You," he said, sounding as if he'd just found something nasty on the bottom of his shoe. "How did you get here?"

"The ways of wizards are not for common men to question," Mikh said loftily. At least he could drop his Rotary Club hail-fellow-well-met pose, now that Dennis had recognized him. He looked into Dennis's eyes with his best commanding stare. "You will tell me all you know of Rivakonneva and her child."

"Like hell I will," Dennis said without heat.

The commanding stare did work better with the appropriate mathemagical function.

"Okay, maybe this isn't the best time," Mikh agreed. Anyway, Boatright was making frantic signals at him; it must be nearly time for their act. "We'll do lunch some time and you can fill me in on things. I'd like to be sure she's making out all right here; fatherly interest, you know." He tried to look paternal, though it was a difficult pose to hold when every moment brought Riva's supple flesh and gleaming muscular thighs more to his mind.

"Fatherly," Dennis repeated, and something different—and much nastier—flickered behind his black-rimmed glasses. "Fatherly! So you're the sleazeball!"

"The what?"

"Riva told me about you. All about you," Dennis emphasized. "And I'm here to tell you that you can forget it. Salla's got a father now, one who'll take care of her instead of using her like a hostage to keep Riva under control. You come near either of them and I'll beat the living shit out of you."

Mikh drew back involuntarily. He was a wizard, not a man of violence.

But then, this tall dork didn't look as if he was up to much in the way of violence, either.

"I suspect," Mikh said with a venomous smile, "Riva would be better equipped for that particular task than you. And . . . are you absolutely sure that's what she wants?"

He left Dennis to think that over while he edged back around the reporters to join Boatright, who was already moving towards the front of the room to give his testimony.

"Brothers and sisters in Christ Jesus our Lord,"

Boatright began in ringing tones that carried through the crowded room, "it is time for decent Christians and heads of families to rise up with me and say: Lord, we've had enough of this malignant cancer in American society. No more pornography in our children's text-books! No more disguised witchcraft teachings of secular humanism, no more Satanic New Age symbolism, no more corrupting our children by telling them that they control their own lives and that they know what they feel!"

"Aaah, it's another religious nut," one of the camera-men said. He began packing up his equipment. "Never mind, we got plenty for the 6:30 out of the Scars and Mal Gainer."

Mikh was only half listening to Boatright's speech, which in any case he had heard far too often in the last twenty-four hours while Boatright rehearsed for his moment of glory. His mind was still on Dennis and his strange reaction. Evidently Riva was not exactly free for the taking; she must be Dennis's property now. Well, that could be fixed. He would have to dispose of Dennis somehow; then he would take over Riva's contract. And the child's, he decided generously. Women tended to get upset about leaving their children. In any case, Salla should be old enough to be useful by now, as a house servant if nothing else; then, if she'd inherited Riva's beauty, she could be sold at a profit in a year or two.

"The board is required to hear specific objections, Mr. Boatright," one of the people at the front of the room said. "Unless you can cite page and paragraph numbers, we will have to ask you to step down now."

"These books are riddled with corruption! You will never purify them line by line; they have to go entirely!"

"Er—did you wish to suggest an alternative line of textbooks?" the board member inquired.

Boatright drew himself up. "The Bible is God's textbook," he said, "and it's the only one we need. It's not just a good idea—it's God's idea."

Mikh recognized that phrase; it had been on one of the posters in Boatright's office.

"In witness thereof, I am asking you, Lord, to cause these salacious, sinful, and Satanist books to vanish utterly. Cut out this moral cancer from the body of our nation! May the Lord God Jehovah remove all sinful books from this room!" Boatright thundered, raising his hands above the table loaded with textbooks.

Mikh had drifted off into meditation, barely listening to Boatright. Exactly how to get rid of Dennis might be a slight problem. Perhaps Boatright could be persuaded to do it for him.

"I say," Boatright repeated, even louder, "May the Lord God Jehovah remove all sinful books from this room!"

That was it! He'd tell Boatright that Dennis knew about the Leibniz's disappearance function and would expose them for frauds unless Boatright had him . . . removed.

Oh. The Leibniz. Wasn't there something he was supposed to be doing at this point? As Boatright raised his hands even higher and thundered out his prayer for the third time, Mikh quietly slid his right hand into his left sleeve, pointed the Leibniz at the table full of books, and felt for the strip of masking tape that would allow him to identify function key F2 by feel.

"MAY THE LORD GOD JEHOVAH—"

So far, so good. Now for button A.

"—REMOVE ALL SINFUL BOOKS—"

And finally, the little green knob at the bottom of the Leibniz.

"FROM THIS ROOM!" Boatright finished triumphantly. The members of the Board looked incredulously at the empty place where *Families of Our World*, *Modern Health for Children and Teenagers*, and *Studying Society* had been stacked. On either side, the piles of math and science textbooks were intact, only emphasizing the swathe cut by the first pass of the Leibniz.

"Holy shit," someone breathed.

From the corner of his eye, Mikh saw Dennis edging out of the room. He decided to follow the man. He needed to know more about this person who was claiming ownership of Riva. He pocketed the Leibniz and sidled away from Boatright.

"Shit, shit, shit!" the cameraman who'd begun packing away his equipment mourned. "I didn't get it on tape. Say, buster, can you do that again?"

Mikh, moving steadily towards the door, kept his back turned on Boatright's furtive hand signals. After a few attempts to catch his attention, Boatright folded his hands with a sigh. "The Lord God Jehovah does not work His miracles like a computer receiving commands," he said. "When it pleases the Lord to work through me again, He will call me."

On that statement he strode from the hearings room. A path parted for him as people nervously moved out of his way. Behind him, Ronald Vranesik crossed himself. "It's a fucking miracle!"

"Fuckin' A," agreed "Mo" Molinares, joining Ronald. "This is big, man. Even bigger than that time the Blessed Virgin showed up on El Galindo's tortillas."

"Evidently," one of the other newsmen summed up the situation as Mikh left, "God doesn't object to math and science. Just to social studies."

"I can see his point," said the reporter with the packed-away camcorder. "Most boring subject I ever had in school. But why didn't you let me get it on tape, Lord?"

Chapter (3!)

Duke Zolkir's great hall would have been more to Mikhalleviko's taste than the public buildings of the Paper-Pushers' reality, although not quite up to Baron Rodo's standards. The hall was large and sumptuous, but there were no great swathes of red-and-gold tapestry here, no bare-chested slaves banging on gongs after the duke's every pronouncement, no house wizard generating illusions of flashing light around the duke's head.

But then, both Mikhalleviko and Baron Rodograunnizo had extremely bad taste.

Duke Zolkir's great hall matched his personality perfectly: rich without ostentation, powerful without overt threats, subtly luxurious in ways that distracted no one from the primary business of the duke's justice. The hall was large enough to hold a hundred petitioners and high in proportion to its length and breadth. The stone walls were softened by tapestries that hung from rafter-height to floor, but there was none of the garish coloring and flashy metal embroidery that Baron Rodograunnizo enjoyed; instead, subtly colored forest scenes, woven in the finest silk, gave the viewer the illusion of standing in a peaceful forest glade. Instead of generating a halo of smoke and lights behind Duke Zolkir's head, one of the house wizard's apprentices spent the hours of public justicing in maintaining the spells that filled the entire room with a soft, sourceless light almost as golden as afternoon sunlight falling through an autumn wood. If Zolkir wanted more attention from his people, a hand gesture told the apprentice to change the light quality to that of a bright morning in early summer. At the same time the mathemagical equations generating background sound changed from plucked strings and gently splashing water to muted hunting calls and a rhythm of pounding hooves.

At the moment, the hall held only the duke himself, his secretary, and three rather unhappy-looking ladies from the Bronze Bra Guild, all in full ceremonial armor. To accommodate this group, Zolkir had commanded the wizard's apprentice (whose name need not concern us; he doesn't even get a speaking part in this story) to brighten the lights immediately around his high seat while leaving the rest of the room dim. To match the duke's mood, the apprentice (who was quite quick on the uptake, and really deserves a bigger part in the story) had cooled the lights to resemble a frosty midwinter noon, while the mathemagical sound generator created a menacing rumble of low drumbeats and growling bass nyttovu horns.

"It was a simple assignment," Duke Zolkir said. "If Rivakonneva were still working for me, I would have sent her to handle it alone. Now would you ladies like to explain to me exactly why three of you were unable to break up Rodo the Revolting's latest scheme?"

Farmers along the ill-defined border between the duke's lands and those of Baron Rodograunnizo had sent a petitioner to Duke's Zolvorra the previous week. They didn't see why they should pay double taxes, they said, once to Zolkir and once to Rodograunnizo. The duke agreed entirely; they should pay him and ignore Rodograunnizo's demands. Yes, said the petitioner, but Things Happened to people who didn't slip Rodograunnizo's men a few zolkys when they came calling. Nothing official. Not, like, a border war or anything like that. But they tended to have accidents. One family had lost a barn full of grain in a fire that started in the small hours of the morning; another farmer had broken his ankle when a ladder collapsed under him; an old herb-granny who'd chased Rodo's men off had been beaten unconscious and her stocks of herbs trampled into the mud along with the shards of her pots. "Not that I haven't occasionally wanted to punch Granny Beerdouvou myself," the petitioner added, "the foul-mouthed old harridan that she is, but she was all we'd got for a healer barring Furo Fykrou, and we can't afford to pay Wizards' Guild fees for every sore throat or sprained ankle."

As the duke was now pointing out in acidulous tones, there should have been nothing in a minor protection racket like this that three warriors from the Bronze Bra Guild, one of them fybilka-trained, couldn't handle. Baron Rodograunnizo's assessor had come smirking back to collect protection money from Dozourdaunniko, the farmer with the broken ankle. Dozour told the man to get his money from Gredu, Lady of Ice and Wrath; Rodo's man hinted that accidents could happen to Dozour's entire household next time; and Dozourdaunniko paid the local wizard to send an urgent plea for help to Duke Zolkir.

It was as good as an engraved invitation. Zolkir sent the ladies off with instructions to put farmwife smocks over their armor and pretend to do drudgework in Dozourdaunniko's household until the inevitable attack came, then to mince Rodo's men into small pieces and send the pieces back in a basket as a subtle hint not to harass the duke's people this way again.

"If it was just muscle," said Sikarouvvana, the leader of the warriors' group, "we could've handled it. They were the usual kind of untrained lowlifes Rodo tends to hire because he can get them cheap. Riva could've taken them, sure. So could I. With one hand behind my back. You were the one who wanted to hire three of us."

"And you," said the duke frostily, "are the one coming back to report complete and utter failure."

"Not complete," Sika said. "Dozour's household wasn't harmed, and barring the bit of a fence that Kloreem here threw at one of the bravos, neither was his property."

"That's very nice," the duke said. Sarcasm dripped from his voice; the apprentice picked up on the change of tone and added the depressed splashing of a cold, sleety rain to the background sounds. "That's very, very nice. I didn't hire you to protect one household against one attack, ladies. I hired you to teach Rodo and his bravos a lesson that would stop this protection scheme once and for all. Well?"

"Well," Sika began, "see, it was this way—"

"I don't," the duke interrupted pointedly, "see a basket full of bravo parts. And neither, I gather, does Rodo. You already told me you let them get clean away.

Now you were going to explain how a fybilka-licensed warrior of the Bronze Bra Guild, with two assistants, manages to lose a mere half dozen of Rodograunnizo's men."

"Wizard's work, that's how!" Sika snapped. "If you'd sent your house wizard with us, there'd have been no problem. You didn't tell us there was mathemagics involved."

Zolkir leaned back against the furs padding the back of his chair. "The farmers didn't say anything about mathemagics," he said, feeling slightly defensive for the first time in the interview. "Rodo's house wizard disappeared a couple of years ago, and I hadn't heard that he'd filled the position. He's been using temporaries when he needs a bit of mathemagical work done."

Sika nodded. "That's what I heard, too. Actually, I heard he was too cheap to pay full rates, and he couldn't get another apprentice to work for him after Mikhalleviko took off in disgrace. That's Rodograunnizo all over. Always trying to get a special deal and cheating himself in the end. At least, that's what we thought, too. But there was some heavy mathemagics here, so maybe those stories were a ruse."

"What kind of magics?"

Sika shuddered. "Like nothing I'd ever seen before. Look, I don't mind having to hew the heads off a few mathemagical monsters—that's all in a day's work. But this stuff didn't have a head. It didn't have any shape at all. See, Rodo's bullies showed up right at noon, third day after we got there, bold as brass. And we were ready for a fight. We'd been blending in just like you said. Doing farmdrudge work." She shuddered again. "If I never see another nyttov again I'll die a happy woman. You know how when you're trying to milk them they swish their tails across and swat you in the face? And you know what's matted in their tails? And you can't tell them to cut it out or you'll cut them up, because they're too dumb to understand they ought to be afraid of you. And I don't even drink milk."

"Nyttovu, ha, you had it easy," said one of her assistants. "I was slopping the hogs. Put me off pork for life, seeing the way those animals live. And smelling them. I'll never be able to eat another fried sausage without thinking about—"

"Don't tell me," Sika snapped. "I don't want my taste for sausages spoiled, thank you very much."

"And the goats had it in for Kloreem. Remember that big black one with the twisted horn?"

Kloreem winced and rubbed her backside.

"Ladies," the duke said, "if you're finished with the farmyard reminiscences, do you think you could possibly tell me just what happened?"

"It was a real pleasure to finally meet an enemy we were allowed to cut on," Sika said. "We let 'em swagger into the barnyard. Kloreem here edged around behind them to block the way out, and Linnizyvv and I grabbed our swords out of the hayloft where we'd stashed them. Dozour's real farm servants scuttled for cover, I threw Kloreem's sword over their heads, she made a sweet left-handed catch, and we were all set. Hardly seemed fair, all three of us when there were only seven of them."

"Indeed," said the duke frostily. "Apparently I should have sent more of you."

"We would've taken them," Sika insisted. "But right then was when the mathemagics started. One minute it was clear day, the next there was this green fog-type stuff all over the farmyard."

"More like weed gruel," Kloreem said. "Thick and wet and sloppy."

"Talking weed gruel," Linnizyvv added. "Whining, really."

"Weird stuff," said Sika. "Some kind of mathemagical incantation, I expect. Anyway, what with this fog-type stuff that wouldn't stay in one shape long enough for us to get a handle on it, and the noises it made, and of course Dozour's people panicked and started running around in circles, screaming and getting between us and Rodo's bullies, and we couldn't tell who was who any more. And we didn't think you'd want us to hack a bunch of your own farmers to bits just to make sure we got Rodo's men," she finished with conscious virtue.

Duke Zolkir stroked the long green fur on the pelt that covered his chair. "So you let them get away."

"Guild rules state we're to have mathemagical backup whenever there's wizardry involved," Sika said. "Mind you, we don't necessarily need it for the occasional monster, like I said, but this stuff was in a different league. Rodograunnizo's got to have a major wizard working for him."

Zolkir frowned and snapped his fingers. "Get me Lavvu Lherkode!" he demanded.

The apprentice dropped his atmospheric mathemagics for a moment and sent an urgent call, transforwarded to the house wizard's quarters, where Lavvu Lherkode had been taking a little nap. A moment later, Lavvu appeared in the hall, surrounded by a cloud of glittering particles that dissipated slowly enough to cover his hasty attempts to smooth his hair and beard and shake out the wrinkles in his robe.

"From what these ladies were telling me," the duke announced, "Baron Rodograunnizo must have a new house wizard, probably a senior member of the Wizards' Guild. Why wasn't I informed?"

"Because it's not true," Lavvu Lherkode said at once. "I know where all the senior mages of the guild are working, and if one of them had changed House allegiances I would have heard of it." He looked at the dejected women warriors. "They're probably exaggerating the mathemagics they had to deal with to excuse their failure. Any really competent warrior should be able to take care of a few monsters. Now, Rivakonneva—"

"Is no longer an active member of the Guild," Sika interrupted, "and I don't think even Riva could have cut the head off a thing as doesn't have a head to begin with."

"I can't believe Baron Rodograunnizo could hire anybody strong enough to put up major mathemagics," Lavvu Lherkode insisted. "He's too cheap. If you were afraid to go up against his mathemagics with your swords, surely any competent mage could have dispersed the monsters. Why didn't you get local help instead of running all the way back to Duke's Zolvorra to whine about the problem?"

For the first time during the meeting, Sikarouvvana smiled. It was not a pretty smile, unless you consider that the bare metal jaws of a trap have a pretty sheen in the sunlight. "Oh, we did," she caroled sweetly. "We hired Furo Fykrou. Of course, by the time we got to him Rodograunnizo's boys were long gone, but the green gunk was still all over Dozour's farm and his household was upset about it."

"Don't see why they were so fussed about it,"

Linnizyvvana muttered. "Smelled better than the pigs, if you ask me."

"Nobody did ask you, Linnizyv. Anyway, Mage Lherkode can judge for himself. You see," Sika said sweetly, "Furo Fykrou tried to integrate the mathe-magical gunk back to the reality it had been dif-ferentiated from, but it wouldn't integrate. Then he cast it into matrix form, but he couldn't invert it . . . and the matrix kept shifting." She looked vaguely queasy. "He said he couldn't disperse the stuff without finding out which reality it had come from in the first place, and whatever universe it is, it's not one of the ones you wizards usually get monsters from, and in fact he's not even sure it is a monster. He's not sure what it is."

Lavvu Lherkode sneered. "I always said Fykrou was a half-trained hedge-wizard who never would have passed his Guild Mastermage trials if he hadn't bribed the judges with those differentiated nymphets."

"You think you could have done better?"

Lavvu Lherkode smoothed out the long sleeves of his robe. "My dear girl, there's no question of that."

"Well, that's wonderful," said Sika, "because now you can show us how it should be done. You see, Furo Fykrou couldn't disperse the mathemagical gunk, but he did manage to contain some of it and herd it back to Duke's Zolvarra with us. Mage Fykrou!" she called in a ringing voice that echoed the length of the hall. "Would you transform the stuff into the hall, please?"

" $Sin(x) = \frac{1}{cosec(x)}$," a voice responded from the door-way to the courtyard. A moment later, a shredded conglomeration of greenish-brown shapes, thicker than fog but thinner than pea soup, wobbled into the hall, wailing as they moved. "The lack of opportunities for people in the lower class can cause frustration, depression, and even despair," they moaned.

"$Tan(x) = \frac{\sin(x)}{\cot(x)}$!" Lavvu Lherkode snapped.

The greenish-brown shapes flickered and changed to a nasty purplish-orange that oozed into all the parts of the hall where the shape hadn't been and left the original space clear. "Yet, in an open society such as the United States it is . . . easy for a person to move from one class to another."

"Trigo Names won't get rid of it," Furo Fykrou said smugly, picking his way around low-lying blobs of orange-purple ooze. "You can make it shift form and you can nudge it along from one place to another, but you can't make it disappear that way. And," he added, "I'm not going to try any higher mathemagics until I get my fee for the work I've put in already."

"$Tan(2x) = \frac{2\tan(x)}{1 - \tan^2(x)}$," Lavvu Lherkode said.

"Sikarouvvana took it upon herself to hire you," the duke said. "Let the Bronze Bra Guild find your fee. I never asked to have this goop in my great hall."

"Your Grace!" Sika said sadly. "I never thought you were a chiseling cheapskate like Baron Rodograunnizo. Besides, we were on contract, and if you check the Bronze Bra Guild's standard contract, you'll see that the client is responsible for all extra magical expenses."

"Some human groups oppose other human groups because they may want different things," the goop wailed. Lavvu's latest attack had turned its purples to hazy lavenders.

"$Sin(2x) = 2\sin(x)\cos(x)$" Lavvu Lherkode called out. "Personally, I think Furo Fykrou shouldn't be paid at all. He didn't do the job he contracted for."

"Living in groups is different from living alone," the lavender haze whispered. "It is important not to judge ideas as good or bad. Statistics are figures that describe something."

Furo Fykrou's face turned a darker purple than the goop had managed. "I'd like to see you do any better!"

"You will," Lavvu replied. "Clearly all it requires is repeated invocations of the higher Trigo Names. $Cos(2x) = \cos^2(x) - \sin^2(x)$."

The orange parts of the goop faded to a sickly green-tinged tan. "Of course, if we have never perceived something before, it is difficult or impossible to conceptualize it accurately."

"Keep it up, Lavvy," Sikarouvvana cheered him on. "I think it's fading."

"$Tan(2x) = \dfrac{2\tan(x)}{1 - \tan^2(x)}$"

"Perceiving correctly is often not as easy as you think it is." The greenish-tan mist became more definitely green; it also glowed. Globules of it coalesced and pulsated with irregular flickering light.

"See? It's just changing form," Furo Fykrou said smugly. "You can't get a hold on it that way. I would suggest a Furry R transformation."

"Why would I switch formulae now?"

"If it came from another reality," Furo Fykrou said, "perhaps you can send it back that way."

Lavvu Lherkode took a deep breath and braced himself, feet planted solidly apart on the stone floor of the Duke's hall. He pointed his staff at the glowing, pulsating mists and thundered, "$\int e^{-st} F(t)dt$!"

"Self-actualization is a step which we never completely reach." The glowing lights faded and the mist slowly disappeared.

Drops of sweat beaded Lavvu Lherkode's forehead. "Takes a lot out of you, these Furry R transforms. I'll have to take several magical health days to replenish my mathemagical power. And I'm still not sure it was really necessary. Since the thing had no structure, all I had to do was keep throwing rigorous mathemagical logic at it until it dissipated into its own logical inconsistencies."

"That wasn't working," several people said at once, and then tried to look as if somebody else had spoken.

"Well," Lavvu Lherkode snapped at Furo Fykrou, "if you were so brilliant a mathemagician, why didn't you try a Furry R transformation on it in the beginning?"

"Takes a lot out of you," Furo Fykrou said mildly, "and as a contract wizard, I don't have a Great House plan to cover my magical health days. Who's going to pay me for herding the gunk down here?"

"Who's going to pay us?" chorused the three ladies of the Bronze Bra Guild.

Duke Zolkir looked sadly at the greasy ashes that the mathemagical gunk had left behind on every surface of the great hall. "Who," he asked, "is going to pay the cleaning bill?"

The offices of the American Values Research Center, although not nearly as luxurious as Duke Zolkir's great hall, had at least the advantage of not being covered with the residue of dissolving social studies textbooks. On the day after the great textbook hearings debacle, the only result of Mikh's actions in this reality appeared to be in Bob Boatright's mind. He was so excited he had been unable to sit still all day and only marginally disappointed that the news media had failed to capture his moment of glory.

"This is only the beginning, Mike," he told Mikhalleviko jubilantly as he strode up and down his office and barked directions over the speakerphone to his secretary. "We didn't set up the publicity properly yesterday; that was our mistake. And you can count on those liberal-commie Democrats in the government to hush up anything they don't like. Of course they wanted to see Mal Gainer's hired kids making a fool of him on the TV news, and of course they wanted to pretend my miracle never happened."

Whose miracle? Mikh thought, but did not say. In Dazau, the wizard who performed the mathemagics was credited with the work. In this reality, if he understood Boatright's prayers correctly, the man ought to be crediting somebody called Jesus Christ. He shrugged. As long as he was getting paid for the work, he didn't really care who got the credit, Boatright or Jesus.

Boatright punched the button on the speaker phone. "Sandra!" he barked. "Did you call Channel Seven and tell them to have a minicam at Bookstop this afternoon?"

"I called Channels Two, Five, Seven, Thirteen, Eighteen, and those public access nuts," Sandra's voice crackled back over the speaker. "But I don't think Two and Five and Seven are gonna send anybody."

"Why not?"

"They didn't ask which Bookstop. There's four of them in town now, you know."

"The new one, of course!" Boatright snapped. "The one that's having the grand opening today. Thirty-eighth and Lamar. Right next to that screwy grocery store that carries raw fish and doesn't sell paper towels. Call them back and get hold of whoever covered yesterday's textbook hearings, and tell them the Reverend Bob is going to have another miracle at five P.M."

Mikhalleviko wondered fleetingly whether this Jesus Christ had a publicity agent. It seemed to him the man needed one; Boatright was hogging more and more of the credit. It was something to look into if Boatright didn't pay him enough.

But, of course, he wasn't going to be around long enough for it to matter what Boatright paid. He would get Rivakonneva and Sallagraunneva back and they'd all get out of here, back to someplace where things were happening. Maybe not Dazau, but at least San Francisco.

And before he could get Rivakonneva back, there was one small problem which Boatright should be able to solve for him.

"It would be most unfortunate if anybody should tell these news people that the disappearance of the books is not a miracle," Mikh said when the speakerphone was turned off again.

An ugly look flashed across Boatright's round, jolly face. "You thinking of talking out of turn, Mike, boy? You forgetting who you work for?"

"No, no, no," Mikh said quickly, holding up his outspread hands. "But we do have a problem. One of the men at the hearing yesterday—he knows me. He knows what I can do." What he used to be able to do, before he transformed himself and his staff and spellbook to this worthless place. But there was no need to go into that now. "He may tell people that this is a simple mathemagical function."

"You mean he'd have the gall to accuse me—me, the Reverend Bob—of unnatural Satanic witchcraft practices?" Boatright's eyes bulged and his cheeks turned purple. "No, sir! The Reverend Bob Boatright does not meddle against the word of the Lord. The

Reverend Bob will stand firm against this moral cesspool. The Reverend Bob will even debate him on television if necessary."

Boatright seemed to be relishing the prospect of a controversy. That was exactly what Mikh didn't want. He briefly considered activating the F6 virtual function to give Boatright a good case of boils and an in-house demonstration of mathemagics. Satisfying, he thought, but in the long run counterproductive.

"The real problem," he said, switching tacks hastily, "is that he'll suggest I, not you, am causing the books to disappear. Once people notice that these miracles only happen when I'm with you, they may suspect it's not all the work of this Jesus Christ."

"The Lord sent you to me," Boatright said, "so it is too His work. And you suggest anything else, you're gonna be out of a job so fast you won't know it till your butt is on the street."

Mikh spread his hands placatingly again. "I would never consider such a thing. I am . . ." He groped for words that would be understood by this kind of man. How did the Paper-Pushers say, "loyal to my House?" "I am a team player."

Boatright nodded approvingly. "That's right, boy. We're all on the Lord Jesus Christ's team here and he's gonna drop-kick us right through the goalposts of life. That's the spirit!"

"But this man who knows me," Mikh insisted. "Dennis Withrow. A teacher—a respected person in the community. He is not on our team."

Boatright snorted. "A teacher? A nothing. Those who can, do; those who can't, teach." He frowned. "Still, we don't want him talking to the wrong people. You're right. Better do something about him."

Mikh relaxed. "Good. Can you have it done before this afternoon, or will that be too risky?"

"Risky?"

"It is usually safer to carry out assassinations at night," Mikh pointed out. That was Baron Rodograunnizo's preferred operating plan. Do everything at night, by means of hired bullies who couldn't be traced back to your House. He assumed Boatright was at least as bright as Rodo.

But the man was chuckling. That didn't seem the right spirit in which to plan removal of an enemy; unless he was more cold-blooded than Mikh had realized. "Assassinations? Where you think you are, boy, one of those spic countries where somebody gets 'disappeared' and nobody asks questions? Lemme tell you, somebody turns up dead around here, the cops ask plenty of questions! Besides, it's wrong to kill," he added in a belatedly moral tone. "Naah, we can fix this Withrow without doing anything illegal. My wife's kid goes to the school where he teaches. I've heard a few things about Withrow. He talks too much. I'll take care of him." He frowned. "Might take a few days, though. For today's action, we need to arrange a little distraction. Take more people, so nobody notices you. Sandra. She's plenty distracting. I'll tell her to go home and put on a shorter skirt."

From his glimpse of Sandra's legs that morning, Mikh seriously doubted whether such a thing would be at all possible, but he approved of the attempt and looked forward to seeing the results.

"Sure, I can go home, boss," Sandra's voice crackled through the speaker, "but whaddaya wan' me to do about these folks waitin' to see you? They said it's about your miracle yesterday," she added.

"What? Show them in at once! And don't let anybody interrupt us! No calls!" Boatright turned excitedly to Mikhalleviko. "I told you so! Reporters! The locals may've been too slow to figure out what was going on, but the national press must have had a stringer around. The *New York Times*," he said, pressing his hands together as if in prayer. "The *Wall Street Journal*."

"Looks more like the *National Enquirer* to me, honeybuns," Sandra's voice interrupted this paean of hope and thanksgiving.

Boatright scowled and flicked the switch on his speakerphone. "I keep forgetting to turn that thing off," he muttered. "Sandra should pretend she hasn't heard things that obviously aren't addressed to her. She certainly doesn't need to listen in to my. . . ."

The door opened and three muscular young men filed in: two Anglos and one Chicano. All three were dressed in T-shirts with the sleeves torn off and various logos of beer companies and heavy metal rock groups across the front. All wore red bandannas looped around their necks.

" . . . interview?" Boatright finished weakly. He drew a deep breath and swelled his chest out like a bullfrog preparing the croak of a lifetime. "And just who might you be?"

Mikh recognized the boy who seemed to be leading the group. "Reverend," Ronald Vranesik said. He nodded to the young men shuffling in behind him. "Me and Thunderhead and Mo, we seen you do that, whatchacallit, parable. Just like it says in the Bible like Jesus done."

"Mo" Molinares and the shaven-headed boy called Thunderhead nodded solemnly.

"So we figured, us Scars, we wanna be on the side of some righteous action for once. Man who can just snap his fingers and make things vanish, he's goin' places. And we goin' to go with you."

"Really," Boatright said, backing up a step, "I hardly think . . ."

"We're your bodyguard, man," Thunderhead said in a voice that resembled gravel going through a crushing mill. "Anybody mess with you, Rev, we gonna mess with him. Maybe beat his goddamn head off."

"I wanna see another one of them parables," said Mo.

"Miracles," Mikh said. Couldn't these cretins speak their own language? Of course they hadn't had the benefit of the transform spell that had given him the local language. Still, they had had seventeen or eighteen years to practice. One would think they'd have gotten it right by this time.

"Yeah." There was a general murmur of agreement. "Let's see it, Rev!" A few claps and cheers followed this.

"You wanted a distraction at Bookstop," Mikhalleviko murmured to his titular boss. "These should serve admirably." And they might be useful for other things, too.

"What? Oh—yes. Right!" Boatright raised his arms in an attitude of prayer, then dropped them again. "What are we going to do?" he whispered to Mikh. "Can you disappear anything on my desk?"

Mikh shook his head regretfully. "Only written or printed matter. Could you spare . . . " He gestured towards the shelves.

"No!"

"A diploma or two?"

"Absolutely not," Boatright said. "I know!" He flicked the speakerphone on again. "Sandra! Bring me the telephone directory."

"Okay, boss, but you got a call . . . "

"I said no calls!" Boatright snapped. "Just bring it!"

A moment later Sandra came past the Scars, holding the telephone book before her on outstretched palms.

He did wonder what Boatright could find to condemn as sinful in the telephone book, but it didn't really matter. His Leibniz didn't seem to care about the contents; it would perform F2-A on any printed stuff in this reality.

"In the name of our Lord Jesus Christ," Boatright intoned, "I command this book in which are listed the names of the sinful to begone."

Standing unobtrusively behind the desk, Mikh pressed the appropriate function keys and pointed his personal computer at the Austin telephone book.

There was a shimmering of mathemagics in the air, almost like a halo all around Boatright, and Sandra stared unbelievingly at her empty hands.

"What'd you do?" she demanded.

"Izza parable," Thunderhead announced.

"Miracle," Mikh murmured.

"You wanna talk to him now?" Sandra dropped her empty hands to her hips and nodded at the Reverend.

"Who?"

"Irving Dietz. *Austin Grackle*. That was him onna phone just now. He wants to interview you." Sandra smirked. "I told him you wasn't taking no calls, like you said."

"Is he still on the line?"

"Uh-uh."

"Well, call him back!"

"He din't leave no number."

"Look it up—oh." Boatright gritted his teeth. "Go next door and ask that chiropractor if we can borrow his phone book. No, never mind. I'd better do it myself." He gave Mikh a harried glance. "Take these good lads down to Bookstop, will you, and explain their first assignment as you go. I'll join you as soon as I can."

Mikh figured he could count on the Reverend Boatright telling this reporter everything he wanted to know and then some. It would probably be an hour or more before the man was off the phone.

Plenty of time for the Scars to carry out a little extra assignment on the way. It was a good thing Mikh had looked up this Dennis Withrow's address before Boatright asked him to make the telephone book disappear.

"There's a little errand we need to do on the way to Bookstop," Mikh said. "Just follow me."

He didn't explain the details until Ronald's battered pickup was parked a block away from Dennis Withrow's house. He was pleased to find that the Scars accepted his instructions without question. "Reverend B. wants this guy offed, we off him," Thunderhead said with a grin that exposed several broken teeth.

"Er—not exactly," Mikh said, remembering Boatright's comments on the difficulties attendant on actually killing someone in this world. "He's a mocker and a sinful man, but we don't believe in killing." Not until he could work out how to get away with it under the rules of this world, anyway. "It will suffice to—ah—persuade him that he should leave town for the sake of his health. You understand me?"

They understood him. Somehow Mikh had thought they would. The Scars were remarkably like the scum Baron Rodograunnizo hired to enforce his "tax collecting" efforts.

"I," Mikh said, "will be waiting one block over. I must not be seen in this matter. Officially, Reverend Boatright has nothing to do with this."

They understood that, too.

After Mikh pulled away to park out of sight, the Scars squeezed back into their pickup and drove the half block to Dennis's house. They didn't approve of unnecessary exertion.

"Nobody home," Mo complained.

"He's a teacher. School let out an hour ago. He oughta be home." It had never occurred to Ronald that teachers had anything to do after the school day ended.

A tall, bronze-skinned woman in sweat pants and jogging shoes rounded the corner and jogged towards them. Thunderhead and Mo watched her motion with appreciative eyes.

"Like to get a little of that action," Mo whispered.

"Maybe you can."

"Huh?"

"Look where she's going, ya dumb spic."

"I ain't as dumb as any three of you white trash put together . . . " Mo began his riposte, then watched with a growing smile as the dark-haired woman let herself in to Dennis Withrow's house.

"Put a scare into his woman, the nerd'll take her and run," Thunderhead said. "Easiest job I done in a long time."

They swung down from either side of the pickup and advanced on the house, moving as lightly as stalking cats.

Chapter 11$\frac{1}{2}$

By the end of the school day Ms. Margaret Fishbeck usually had a headache; anyone would, after six hours of giggling, whispering, note-passing kids. Today was worse than usual, probably because she'd put off hearing that brat Sally Konneva's report as long as she could. The little motor-mouth had a bulging folder of notes that looked like a solid hour of talking. Ms. Fishbeck had planned to thwart her by calling on other students until the hour was nearly up, but Orrin Pilkinton had let her down. He'd used up barely five minutes with his report on the Grail Quest. And she still had to read the written version.

Ms. Fishbeck's head throbbed. Why did a boy who couldn't spell English have to pick the Grail Knights, with all their peculiar Celtic names, for his report? She would have to look up every name in the report to make sure she marked all his spelling mistakes. It was all Cathy Harper's fault, really, for putting this outlandish material in the collection of readings. Grail legends and African stories and Polynesian "mythology"—as if a bunch of half-naked brown-skinned people with flowers in their hair could come up with anything to compare with the great literature of Europe! Ms. Fishbeck glowered at the selection of readings Cathy Harper had assembled by months of photocopying and typing. Just a bunch of dirty stories by people nobody ever heard of, that was all it was. If it weren't so much work, she'd make up her own course notes. Have the kids reading great literature—tales from Shakespeare and Bible stories and Norman Vincent Peale. Something uplifting and inspirational.

She turned the glower on Sally Konneva, who was bouncing up and down in her seat as if she knew it was her turn to be called on. Putting herself forward, just because everybody else in the class had given their reports! Pushy—those kind of people always were. Ms. Fishbeck wasn't quite sure what kind of people they were, because Sally's file said she was classified Anglo, but with that creamy brown skin and curly brown hair she certainly didn't look like the nice well-behaved white children Ms. Fishbeck was used to seeing at Cushman Middle School. A pity, the way *they* were getting into all the best neighborhoods these days. It hadn't been like that when she was a girl. . . .

Sally Konneva looked as if she were about to vibrate right out of the seat.

"Very well, Sally," Ms. Fishbeck said with a resigned sigh, "I can see you're eager as always to give us the benefit of your erudition and scholarship." She drew the last words out sarcastically and was rewarded by a titter from at least half the class.

Sally didn't seem to notice the sarcasm; she was out of her seat before Ms. Fishbeck had finished speaking, scrabbling at the untidy heap of papers that threatened to fall out of her folder and shoving the thick dark hair out of her face with her free hand. She tripped coming up the aisle and only recovered herself with a few quick trotting steps.

"Gently, gently, Sally dear," Ms. Fishbeck said. "A lady is never in a hurry."

Sally clutched the worn manila folder across her chest, tossed her head to get the mane of black curls away from her face, and said, "My paper is on the Woman's Quest. I got the idea from something Joseph Campbell said." She fished around in the folder, pulled out a sheaf of computer printout with the tractor-feed holes half ripped off, and read, "In the whole mythological tradition the woman is the place that people are trying to get to. When a woman realizes what her wonderful character is, she's not going to get messed up with the notion of being pseudo-male."

Ms. Fishbeck frowned and glanced down at the open notebook of class readings that Cathy Harper had photocopied from various sources. There were three pages of Joseph Campbell, but she didn't remember anything quite like that.

"He didn't say that," Orrin Pilkinton interrupted—without raising his hand, but Ms. Fishbeck decided to let it go for once.

"Yes, he did!"

"Nuh-uh. I read that section, too, and he didn't say anything like that."

Ms. Fishbeck had been rapidly skimming the photocopied pages while the children bickered. "I'm afraid Orrin is right, Sally," she said with a smile. "You really must not make up quotations, my dear."

"Oh, it's not in the readings," Sally said. "My goodness, Ms. Fishbeck, Joseph Campbell wrote books and books about mythology!"

"And which book is this statement in, dear?"

"It's not in any of them."

"Ha!" Orrin interrupted again. "I knew it!"

Sally gave him a withering glance. "As a matter of fact," she said, "he made that statement in a personal interview. Now, as I was saying," she went on loudly to cover Orrin's mumbled objections, "Campbell is only showing his typical male European bias here. Just because your stupid Grail Knights didn't let women in, Orrin, doesn't mean every culture has been that dumb!" She flipped through to another page of the computer printout, muttering, "If I had a laptop, this would be easier. Here we are." She put on her "quote" voice and read, "Among the Hopi Indians, for instance, Spider Woman creates the first people and goes on the first quest, when she looks for somebody who can give them the gift of speech."

Ms. Fishbeck didn't even have to check the readings this time. "Sally, dear, there wasn't anything about the Hopi Indians in the readings for this unit. You really mustn't make up stories." A female creator! Ridiculous! Blasphemous, too.

Sally turned to face her teacher, waving her sheaf of computer paper. "Who's making up references? Do you think there isn't anything in the whole world to read besides those pages somebody else copied so you wouldn't have to hurt your head making up lessons? As a matter of fact, the Campbell interview is quoted in Maureen Murdock's *The Heroine's Journey*, a very good book which I'm going to do my final book report on. And the Spider Woman story is in Frank Waters's *The Book of the Hopi*." She looked down at the page she'd been quoting from. "Viking Press. 1963. So there!"

While Ms. Fishbeck was still stunned by this gratuitous rudeness, Sally turned back to the class and attempted to pick up her report where she'd left off. "Anyway, I found lots and lots of folk tales where girls go on quests. But they're not like men's quests, where you always have the guys going off looking for the Magic Uzi or the Sacred Poker Chip or something else that'll make them boss of everybody else. Women's quests—"

"Girls," Orrin Pilkinton said loudly, "don't go on quests. Men go on quests. Heroes. You ever hear of a girl hero?" He gave a loud braying laugh which was echoed by half the boys in the class.

Sally flushed but stood her ground. "As a matter of fact," she said sweetly, "one of my references for this paper was a book by Tristram Coffin called *The Female Hero in Folklore and Legend.* So there!"

"What do girl heroes wear," Buddy Rylander called, "Maidenform Armor?"

"As a matter of fact," Salla started to say, then visibly changed her mind. She bit her lip and shuffled through her computer printout.

"It says in the readings that the quest is for warriors," Orrin insisted. "Women aren't warriors." He folded his arms and grinned at Sally.

"I'm afraid Orrin has a point, Sally dear," Ms. Fishbeck said. "You really should have chosen a research topic that had some basis in the readings for this unit, rather than going off on some wild chase out of your vivid imagination."

"Wait a minute, wait a minute!" Becky Boatright lumbered out of her seat. "What do you mean, women can't be warriors, Orrin? Don't you watch the news? Women are in the army now. Women fought in the Gulf War. We can do anything you can do!"

"Girls," Orrin said, "are physio—physic— Their bodies aren't suited to combat. My dad read in the paper where Newt Gingrich said it was a scientific fact that women weren't evolved to fight and men were, because we used to be the hunters in olden days."

"Yeah, he thinks you all used to go out hunting giraffes!" Salla jeered.

"I'll show you a thing or two about fighting!" Becky offered, advancing on Orrin.

"Children, children!" Ms. Fishbeck squeaked unheard.

"You can't take a single text as God's word, Orrin," Jason Tibbs pointed out at the top of his voice. "Personally, I'd like to hear what Sally has to say, so why don't you just keep yourself and your four-eyed nerd fantasies of being a Grail Knight out of this discussion!"

Orrin snatched off his glasses and swung a wildly unfocused punch at Jason.

"Booger brain!" he shouted.

"Butt-head!" Becky Boatright cracked her Language Arts binder over Orrin's head. The overstrained rings burst loose and showered the classroom with photocopied pages from Joseph Campbell, Benjamin Whorf, and *Jung for Juniors*.

The level of discourse went rapidly downhill from there.

Salla had pointed out more than once that she was not a little kid any more but a mature sixth-grader who could be trusted to walk home from school without having a mother waiting at the door for her. In principle, I agreed. In practice, I found myself scheduling my day so that I'd take a break from studying math about an hour before the end of the school day, go for a run around the neighborhood to loosen up, then work out in the backyard until Salla came home. I'd been building my life around the Paper-Pushers' school schedules too long to relinquish the habit just because Salla was apprentice-age in Dazau terms.

Today, though, was one of those October days that makes me homesick for the Great Fyrkozoul Desert at high summer—grass and leaves singed brown by the long summer drought going on into autumn, intense blue sky, shimmering waves of heat rising from the sand dunes. . . . Well, okay; the heat waves were actually rising from the asphalt street. All the same, by the time I finished my hour's run I definitely felt—and smelled—as if I'd been pulling caravan guard duty across the Fyrkozoul for all of a long hot summer. Working out could wait, I decided. First I was going to avail myself of one of the Paper-Pushers' luxuries and stand under a cool waterfall until I could no longer smell myself.

My best friend back in Dazau, Sikarouvvana, claimed bathing too often made warriors weak. While I lathered myself with scented soap and rinsed the suds out of my hair, I considered her theory for the umpteenth time and decided once again that Sika would change her mind if she were offered one of these devices called a shower instead of the cans of lukewarm water that we slopped ourselves off with in the Guildhouse. Still, there was no point in taking chances. I decided to do an extra-long workout after the shower.

Through the sound of running water I heard the screen door slam. Salla tromped across the living room like a charging nyttovu; I could never understand how one slender girl, built more like her willowy father than like a warrior woman's daughter, could make so much noise. Next would come the thump of her backpack hitting the floor . . .

It was like waiting for the other shoe to drop; I couldn't quite relax until I heard that thump. Instead, I thought I heard more footsteps, and voices. Male voices.

"Salla?" I called. "Salla, who'd you bring home this time?" The voice I'd heard was too deep to be Norah's kid. I envisioned some hulking eighth-grader who'd devour the chocolate cake I'd bought for dessert as an afterschool snack. I slapped the water faucet to off, grabbed my bathrobe, and stepped out into the living room, saying, "Now, you can have the peanut butter cookies and all the fruit you want, but that cake—"

Not one hulking kid, but three, and they all looked way too big to be in middle school. "Yo, mama," the big one with the shaved head said, "you offering cake, sweetcakes?"

The other two elbowed each other and giggled. I finished tying the sash of my bathrobe and wished that I'd taken time to dress. I tended to forget how seriously the Paper-Pushers took their nudity taboos. Still, the bathrobe covered as much of me as shorts and a T-shirt would have; the kids didn't need to shuffle and snicker like that.

"We come to talk to Mis-ter Dennis Withrow," one of the other boys volunteered, smirking.

"Oh, good!" They must be some of Dennis's old students come back to visit, not oversized middle-school kids. I wasn't supposed to know who they were.

"Hey, Mo, you hear that? Lady's glad to see us." The boys shuffled and giggled behind their big hands.

That was slightly overstating the case. I suspected I'd be violating several Paper-Pushers' taboos at once if I abandoned Dennis's guests in the living room and went out back to work out. Besides, knowing how Salla's classmates ate, I wasn't about to leave these even older boys alone in the house with a double fudge and mocha chocolate layer cake.

"Terribly nice of you to drop by," I said.

They elbowed one another and snickered again. I must be getting the Paper-Pushers' social formulas wrong. I fell back on Dazau stranger-greeting mode. "Our house is honored by your presence," I said. "My companion will grieve that his eyes have not had the delight of seeing you; unfortunately, he will not return until late tonight. Quite late," I added, stretching the truth slightly. Dennis had mentioned dropping by Bookstop after school to see if the new Sheri Tepper had come in, but even a thorough browse of the bookstore wouldn't keep him for more than an hour. The fact was, I didn't want to spend an hour making Paper-Pushers' social chitchat with these youths when I could have been working out and practicing my swordplay against the remote chance that Vordo would show up in my life again. I felt mean and inhospitable, so I smiled brightly as I waited for them to get up and leave.

"No problem, honey," the shaven one said. "We ain't in no hurry."

"Hey, Thunderhead," the one called Mo interrupted, "the man said he wanted us over at Bookstop, remember?"

"Me, I can always make time for a good-looking lady," Thunderhead said. He smiled at me, a proper smile showing all his teeth instead of the half grimace Paper-Pushers usually used. I smiled back. For some reason he looked startled.

The third boy got up and ran a hand along one of Dennis' cinderblocks-and-board bookshelves. "Lotta books here," he said. "You read them all?"

"No. They're my husband's. And as I told you, he's not here." Maybe they'd take the hint this time.

Mo's thin brown face stretched out in a sharklike grin. "Nice of you to invite us. We have some fun now, no?"

Oh, shit. I must have gotten the Paper-Pushers' social formulas completely scrambled. They thought I was urging them to stay! "No. I'm afraid you don't understand. Dennis," I said slowly and clearly, "is not here."

"Oh, we understand, all right. Ronald, you understand, doncha?"

The third boy pulled his attention away from the bookshelves and nodded. Thunderhead took a small black bar out of his pocket and pressed its side. A blade flashed out with a sharp click. Suddenly he had my complete attention.

"That," I said, "is a really nifty device." Most of the Paper-Pushers' weapons were either ineffective or dishonorable or both. But I didn't think a knife that flashed out of nowhere was quite dishonorable— granted, it was pushing the definition some—and it was a real pleasure to meet somebody who had a proper weapon in this universe.

Sort of.

"It is kind of small," I said, "but—would you mind telling me the name of the smith who devised it for you? I could use something like that, only bigger, of course."

"What I got gon' be plenty big enough for you, mama," Thunderhead growled.

The boy called Mo thought this was hilariously funny; their friend Ronald, like me, didn't seem to get the joke. His slight frown mirrored the confusion I felt on my own face.

Thunderhead flipped the knife up and caught it on his wrist. A quick swivel of his hand and he had the hilt again. The blade flashed too close to my nose; I blocked the move automatically and Thunderhead yelped in pained surprise as his knife fell to the floor between us. My own wrist throbbed with the force of our bones meeting. I knew from experience in sparring bouts that his would be hurting a lot worse, and his fingers would be almost numb. It's all a matter of getting the right angle; Sika and I used to work out the moves a half-day at a time, until neither of us could hold a spoon for the noonday meal.

Dennis would not be pleased if I accidentally injured some of his old students. "Sorry," I apologized. "I have this problem with my reactions, see. In Da—where I come from, you don't do something like that unless you want to start a fight." I thought of a way I could make it up to him. "Besides, the way you're shifting your fingers there at the end of the toss, you don't have a good grip on the hilt. See, you want to turn more like this—"

In Dazau it would be a deadly insult to demonstrate the trick with Thunderhead's own weapon, unless he offered it to me first. Did the same rules apply here? I had no idea. But Thunderhead was the first honorable fighter I'd encountered on Paper-Pushers', and I didn't want to give him offense if I could avoid it. I stepped two paces back, snaked an arm into the kitchen and retrieved the big chopping knife. It had a good balance for this kind of game, probably better than Thunderhead's clever little toy.

"Up, then flip over the back of the hand, reverse on the back of the wrist and it slides into your hand ready to thrust up between the ribs—see?"

Thunderhead stared at the broad triangular blade whose point rested between two knit loops of his sleeveless T-shirt.

"Hey, sweets, nice li'l lady hadn' oughta play with knives," Mo teased me, wagging one finger at my face. "Want I should showya some better games?" His hand darted like a snake's tongue, reaching inside the open V of my bathrobe—except, of course, that by the time it got there, I was somewhere else.

"That's rude," I told him. "In Dazau it's a mortal offense. I don't know exactly how your people react to that kind of gesture, but . . ."

"Smart ladies, don't wanna get hurt," Thunderhead rumbled, "they just lie back an' enjoy it. Now you give me that knife, little lady—"

I wasn't really listening to him; I was watching Ronald scoop an armload of books off the top shelf. "Some of these stories look like hot stuff," he said, waggling his thick blond eyebrows at a Frank Frazetta cover. "Think I'll take 'em home and have a read."

"You can't do that," I said, batting Thunderhead's reaching hand away with the back of the knife. "Dennis doesn't like to lend out his books."

"Dennis gonna have to put up with a lot of stuff he don't like unless he learns to stay out of other people's business," Mo informed me. "You take the message to him, pretty lady. Tell your man his health gonna be better someplace outa town. Long way outa town," he emphasized.

"Why would I do that?" I turned to Thunderhead, the only one of the three who seemed to make any sense at all.

"Lemme show you why," Thunderhead said, grabbing at the sash of my bathrobe.

Without thinking I flicked the chopping knife forward. The blade just grazed the tips of his knuckles. He snatched his bloody hand back and swore.

So did I. "Nauzu's tears! I didn't mean to do that," I said ruefully, looking at the blood spots sprinkling the front of my white terrycloth robe. "I think you'd better go away now." If I soaked it in cold water right away maybe the spots would come out.

"Go away? We just getting started," Mo said, and lunged towards me.

"Watch out, man!" Thunderhead said indistinctly through a mouth full of bleeding knuckles. "Goddamn! She's mean."

"I teach her to try mean with me," Mo said with a slow smile.

I sighed. Dennis was not going to be happy about this. But I'd tried to handle things the Paper-Pushers way, and obviously I just didn't know how to do it. Oh, well, back to the Dazau approach. "By your uncivil behavior," I said, backing away to give myself time to finish the sentence, "you violate host-right and lose guest-right."

"Huh?"

"Let me demonstrate," I said, sliding sideways out of Mo's grip. "As long as you were guests, it would be improper to do something like this to you." I caught Mo's wrist as he reached towards me for the third time, twisted so that his body pivoted on one foot, gave him a little nudge with my knee and let go. He tottered away from me and fell head-first into the picture window. The central pane shattered around his head.

"Gredu's wrath!" I said, "now look what you made me do! Those things cost lots and lots of zolkys—I mean, dollars. Go on, will you, don't bleed on the carpet. I don't want to have to replace that, too." I helped Mo on through the picture window. He seemed to be largely unhurt, despite the blood; at least, he managed to run quite fast after he landed on the ground.

"As for you," I said to Ronald, "you can put those books back where you—"

Instead of following my orders, he tried to scramble through the broken window after Mo, dropping Dennis's entire Eddings collection on the floor and yelping as the shards of broken glass sliced into his hands. I sighed and helped him through with a couple of whacks with the flat of the chopping knife.

I gave up trying to get any sense out of him. "Now, you," I said to Thunderhead, "being an armed warrior, I can dispatch honorably by the blade." He made an awkward swipe at me with his little toy knife; I flicked it out of his hand and stood waiting for him to retrieve it. Instead, the idiot dove out of the broken window and took off in the same direction as Mo and Ronald.

Naturally, I went after him. "Wait a minute!" I yelled. "We're not through yet!" He'd drawn a blade, he'd acted like a decent man; I couldn't believe he would deny me an honorable conclusion to our disagreement. I was halfway down the block, waving the carving knife and calling to him to stop, when he threw himself into a battered pickup truck and all three boys disappeared with a screech of tires and a cloud of noxious black smoke.

Across the street, some kids whistled and cheered. Among them I heard my daughter calling, "Way to go, Mom!"

I let the knife drop, tugged once again at the sash of my bathrobe, and turned to face Salla. "You're late," I told her.

She shrugged. "Fishmouth kept me after school. She says I'm gonna be kicked out of the G&T program for my bad attitude. But I didn't start the fight. He did." She jerked her head at Orrin Pilkinton. "You want to know what women warriors wear, Orrin? Sometimes they wear bathrobes. Hey, Mom, you want to soak the bloodstains out of that before they set?"

Kicked out of the Gifted and Talented program? We needed to have a serious talk about that. But not now. Not when I glanced up the street and saw, coming out of the clouds of smoke left by the pickup, far worse trouble than those three second-rate apprentice fighters could ever have given me.

"Well, Riva, light of my life," he purred, "we meet again."

The children who'd been accompanying Salla scattered like confetti on the breeze. I couldn't blame them. I'd have disappeared, too, if I knew the secret ways of cats and children . . . and wizards.

He was smooth as a cat, dressed all Paper-Pushers-style in a dark tailored suit and shoes whose polish reflected and rivaled the September sun. And I was sweaty again, despite my shower; wearing a bloodstained bathrobe, and clutching a kitchen knife instead of the sword I'd once meant to use to cut his heart out. Life is not fair.

"Gosh, Mom," Salla breathed, "you know him?"

She looked up at Mikhalevviko's smooth pale face, his dancing eyes under the dark sweep of brows as smooth as a butterfly's wing, and I could tell that she was forgetting to breathe. Mikh's good looks had had that effect on me too, once upon a time.

Twelve years ago, to be precise.

"Struck speechless with joy at the sight of me, I see," Mikh drawled. "And is this lovely young lady the offspring?"

I moved between him and Salla. That brought me closer to him than I liked, but it didn't really matter. Mikh couldn't have stood up to me in a fair fight twelve years ago, and he didn't look as if he'd done any exhaustive physical training since then.

But then, wizards don't fight fair.

"Salla," I said over my shoulder, "go inside and do your homework."

"I don't have any."

"Go. Inside. Now!" On the last word Salla scurried for the house and I let out a breath I hadn't known I was holding. The last thing in the world I needed was for those two to meet. If only I could keep Mikh away from her, I could—I could—what?

I hadn't the faintest idea; only that it would be fatal to let him know he'd rattled me.

"Why, it's Mikhalleviko the False, isn't it?" I said at last. "Do forgive my failure to greet you at first. The truth is, I hardly knew you. And in any case, I haven't much to say to you. Excuse me." I would have lifted the hem of my garment and swept past him with an air of freezing hauteur, but the bathrobe was too short to risk lifting it any. I followed Salla's path to the house. She'd shut the door, but the broken window made a gaping hole in the front. No doors are shut to a wizard, anyway.

"We have everything to say to one another, Rivakonneva." He fell into step beside me. I stopped at the door.

"I do not invite you in," I said. "I do not offer guestright."

He smiled, spread his hands. "You're still angry. I knew you still cared."

"I don't. I had completely forgotten you," I lied.

"Then you'll have no objection to letting me visit my daughter."

"By law and custom of Dazau, the parent who does not support a child has no rights in that child."

Mikh smiled again. I felt as if I'd stepped onto a stair that wasn't there; but I couldn't quite tell why. "But you," he said softly, "have chosen to live under the laws of this place. And now I am here, too."

The laws of this place. . . . I remembered Norah telling me about something called custody fights. Her ex-husband had wanted Jason to live with him, and the justicers of this realm had commanded her to send her son to his father's hall for one quarter of each year-turning.

Mikh couldn't take Salla away from me . . . could he? Surely not. These people believed what was on paper more than what was before their own eyes and under their own hands. On paper, I didn't exist, and presumably Mikh didn't either.

He was just trying to frighten me, like a warrior feinting before the battle is joined. The best thing to do is pretend you didn't even notice the feint.

"You're here too," I repeated slowly. "Gosh, there goes the neighborhood! Well, Mikhalleviko the False, I won't say it's been good talking to you. Let's not do this again." I put the screen door between us and pressed the thumb latch closed.

Anger flashed in Mikh's eyes, but he did not try to force his way into the house. "I must go to the Bookstop now. We will speak again, Rivakonneva."

My knees were shaking. I sat on the couch, staring at the paperbacks Ronald had spilled over the floor and thanking Nauzu that Salla had the sense to stay out of sight. After a long time Mikh's footsteps moved away.

Salla appeared right on cue. "Who was that gorgeous thing, Mom?"

"An old . . . acquaintance," I said weakly. "Not a nice person, Salla. If you see him again, you stay away from him, you hear?"

"Oh. Is he a dirty old man?" She sounded more interested than frightened.

"He is an evil man," I said. "He can . . ." I paused. "No, he can't."

"Can't what?"

"Mathemagics doesn't work here." As a human being, Mikh was a total loss. His only power came from his good looks and smooth talk, which I was now immunized against, and his wizardry, which he couldn't use here . . . I thought. The only mathemagical functions I'd ever been able to invoke from here were Call Trans-Forwarding and the transformation between this reality and Dazau's; and both of those were based on the link Furo Fykrou had created, allowing me to draw on his mathemagical power from Dazau. For a price, of course.

Salla frowned. "I'm not sure, Mom. It could be built into the computers. We had this lesson about how hard disk drives are made, see, and if that's not mathemagics . . ."

"Never mind," I sighed. "Of course it doesn't work

here, or Dennis would be a wizard. What was I worrying about?"

Suddenly life seemed bright and beautiful and simple. Mikh might be dangerous when he was using his mathemagical training, but in this reality it wouldn't work for him, obviously, or he would already have used it. All I had to do if he bothered Salla or me again was cut his liver out.

I sang all the way through my second shower of the afternoon.

Chapter $\int_{2}^{} 3x^2 dx$

Four-fifteen, and Mike still wasn't there. Bob Boat-right glanced at his watch again. It was still 4:15, and he was tired of standing in Religious and Inspirational, the only decent section of Bookstop Central. He paced up Mysteries, through Spies and Thrillers, and down Romance. This would be a good place to start, with this filth that had begun corrupting his own dear wife. He glared at the lifesized poster of a cardboard warrior embracing a busty cardboard maiden. Would Mike Levy's gadget work on something that was so much picture and so little print? Where was Mike, anyway? He should have been here before Boatright.

"Gonna have to go soon," said Irving Dietz, the reporter from the *Austin Grackle*. "Whyn'tcha go ahead and have your little prayer meeting, Rev?"

"The Spirit has not moved me," muttered the Reverend Boatright. "Now be quiet, will you? Try to look like an ordinary customer."

"You promised you'd pull off another miracle if I'd come along here with you," said Dietz. "I haven't got all day, you know."

Boatright sighed. "I am the servant of the Lord Jesus

117

Christ. When it pleases Him to work through my humble agency, you shall see His power revealed. Until then, remember, blessed are they that have not seen, and yet have believed. John 20:29."

"Yeah," muttered Dietz, "but they didn't make the paper with what they didn't see. Look, Rev—"

"Irving," Boatright interrupted, fixing the young man with his stare, "are you on the team with us? Are you going to take the field with Jesus Christ, or are you going to sit on the bench like so many who call themselves Christians?"

"Actually, Rev," Dietz said, "see, I'm Jewish, and—"

"You can still take Jesus into your heart," Boatright told him.

"I don't think that would go over so well with my mom. She's always bugging me about finding a nice Jewish girl to take into my heart. Now how about this miracle?"

"Irving," Boatright said, "God needs all of us on His team. See, He has documented all the plays we need to win. It's all in here." He held up his Bible and tapped the front cover. "Jesus is the quarterback, but He can't throw a winning pass unless we're out there to receive it. God can't save the world with most of his team still in the locker room. Are you ready to suit up, Irving? Are you on God's side? Are you going to help us clean up this cancerous plague of pornography and liberal-secular-humanist propaganda that is corrupting our women and children?" He flung out a hand and knocked over the advertising display at the end of the Romance aisle. Twelve copies of Zodiac Romances #1, *Capricorn Caress*, slid to the floor. The cutout cardboard figure of Vordo, romance male model extraordinaire, followed them.

"Can I help you find something?" A store clerk picked up the Zodiac display and smiled winsomely from behind Vordo's bulging cardboard thews. For a surrealistic moment the barbarian warrior appeared to have two golden-tressed heads, one sporting an armadillo tattoo on the cheekbone and three piercings in the left ear; then the clerk set Vordo back on his pedestal and stepped around the display. "Looking for something for your wife? What kind of romances does she like—sweet or spicy?"

"Spicy!" Boatright almost choked on the word. "Flagrantly salacious and evil!"

"Ah." The clerk took this as agreement. "She likes the longer, more sensual stories? How about the new Kathleen Fraser?" She slipped past Boatright and picked up a book from one of the carts that circulated the store, refilling shelves. "*Love's Tender Promise.* Just out this month; I can practically guarantee you she hasn't read it yet."

"So," muttered Boatright, remembering the singed cover and charcoal-fringed pages of Vera's contraband copy, "so can I."

"Well, then! The perfect gift! And look," the clerk pointed to a golden sunburst sticker on the front cover, "this one's autographed by the author. She's a local writer, you know."

"No earthly power could pay me to introduce this kind of smut into my home," Boatright told her.

"Oh." The clerk's smile dimmed for a moment; the tail of her armadillo tattoo drooped along her cheekbone. "Something in Religious and Inspirational, then? I thought I saw you browsing over there a moment ago. Just let me shelve this stack of Kathleen Frasers, and I'll help you out."

"Don't put that godless pornography out on the shelves where anybody can see it!" It would be just like Vera to sneak over here and buy herself another copy to replace the one Boatright had tried to burn.

The clerk sighed. "We aren't in the censorship business. I wouldn't read one myself, but these romance novels sell very well."

"Materialism is the devil's way into your heart!"

"Perhaps you'd like to speak to the manager?"

"The Reverend Bob Boatright doesn't need to ask anybody's opinion about this moral cesspool you call a bookstore," Boatright said. "God is against it, that's enough for the Reverend Bob."

"Spirit fixing to move you, Rev?" Dietz hinted.

Boatright's raised voice was drawing attention all over the store; customers' heads peered over the surrounding aisles of Mystery, Horror, and Science Fiction. Dietz backed off a few steps and raised his camera. "Reverend raps retailers," he murmured. "Preacher prays for prudery." It wasn't quite the story he'd hoped to get, but it might be better than nothing.

"You may be able to get by with words," said a voice behind him. "Channel 99 needs action pix."

Irving turned slowly. "Nadia," he said. "I might have known. You media vultures show up everywhere. How'd you know the Rev was acting up here?"

Nadia smiled sweetly from behind her camcorder. "He faxed news releases to everybody in town. *Long* news releases," she emphasized. "If you nineteenth-century print media types at the *Grackle* could afford a fax, it'd still be tied up with the Rev's press release; ours was printing out page 113 when I left. Everybody else was cursing him for tying up the machine, but I remembered Jody Klein saying he'd missed a good news bite at the textbook hearings."

"Real quick on the uptake," Irving said. "Took you until page 112 to remember? Typical brain-dead TV talking head."

"Gimme a break," Nadia protested, "the Rev didn't say where his next stunt was happening until page 110. I reckon that's why nobody else is down here."

"Nobody else is down here," Irving said, "because nothing is happening." He raised his camera again. "Come on, Rev baby, give us some photo action!"

As if he'd heard the reporter's murmured prayer, Boatright snatched the copy of *Love's Tender Promise* from the clerk's hand and waved it over his head. "No woman with a shred of moral decency would read this stuff," Boatright went on while the store clerk made frantic hand signals towards the manager's desk, "and this Kathleen Fraser who actually writes it ought to be—"

One of the customers browsing in Science Fiction was Dennis Withrow. "Before you get too wrapped up in that line of invective, Bobby," Dennis said from the science fiction side of the bookshelves that divided them, "I ought to warn you that Norah Tibbs is a good friend of mine and I find your present line of conversation offensive in the extreme."

Boatright floundered in midperoration. "Who the— who is Norah Tibbs?" he demanded.

"Kathleen Fraser to you." Dennis stepped around the corner of the bookshelves. His arms were full of new science fiction releases, but he freed a hand to point at the copy of *Love's Tender Promise* in Boatright's hand. "You may not like her stuff—frankly, I don't find endless courtship sagas all that interesting either—but there's a simple remedy. Don't read it. Go back to Religion and Inspiration, Bobby, like the nice girl suggested, and stop trying to tell the rest of us what to read."

Boatright narrowed his eyes. "You. I know you. One of those secular humanist perverts teaching sex and sin at my daughter's school."

"Right, Bobby," Dennis agreed amiably. "Satanic pentagrams and the Triangle of Trismegistus. Hardened sinners, the lot of us."

"Mike Levy was right about you," Boatright said. "I'm going to deal with you. I'm not having your sensual, godless, materialistic philosophy corrupting my daughter."

"You don't," Dennis pointed out with a grin, "hire and fire at the public schools, Bobby. And I don't have any connection with your phony foundation. Just what exactly do you think you're going to do?"

Before Boatright could answer, a friend pulled Dennis away. "You idiot," Jack whispered in Dennis' ear, "he won't have to do anything if you keep arguing with him. There's a reporter snapping pictures, and the manager's calling the cops. You want your picture on the front page of the *Grackle* with some caption about bookstore brawling?"

Dennis grinned. "How about, 'Pedagogue Punches Preacher'? You know how the *Grackle* is about alliteration. Anyway, they're not encouraged to distribute that paper near schools. Head of the school board thinks all those explicit personal ads in the back will make our innocent adolescents think about what they're already thinking about."

"You won't think it's that funny when Salla starts dating," Jack said darkly. "We had to get Judy-Lynn a separate phone line. With an answering machine! I don't have an answering machine, but my teenager needs one to keep her social life—well, never mind. Let's just pay for our books, okay?"

"Okay," Dennis agreed. "Just a minute, though. I see one more I need." He took the copy of *Love's Tender Promise* from Boatright. "Do you mind, Bobby? You're so het-up about this book, I guess it's time I read one of Norah's sagas all the way through. Want me to mark the good parts for you?"

Muttering darkly, Jack took Dennis by the elbow and steered him forcibly towards the cash registers at the front of the store. As they made their way to the line of customers, the Scars swaggered into the bookstore. On the short ride from Dennis and Riva's house to Bookstop they had managed, without actually saying so outright, to work out a version of events that salvaged their pride without quite contradicting what had happened.

"About time!" Boatright bustled over to the boys, meeting them halfway down the shelves where Horror mingled with Spy/Thriller. "Where have you been? And . . ." His voice trailed off as he noticed one conspicuous absence. "Where is Mike?"

"Who's Mike?" asked the reporter.

"My personal assistant. Never mind. None of your business."

"And these boys?"

"Members of the faithful," Boatright said, "come to witness to the Truth today."

"Names? Addresses?"

"Go away, go away," Boatright flapped his hands at the reporter. "I'll tell you when it's time."

Up at the line of cash registers, Dennis and Jack

watched the byplay with mild interest. There wasn't much else to look at: the blonde with the earrings was working one cash register while the other six stood idle. There were three people ahead of them in line. And the stand near the counter that usually held new paperback releases was filled with the twelve Zodiac romances.

"Where have you been?" Boatright repeated in an agitated whisper when the reporter had retreated a few paces. "And where's Michael Levy?"

"We done that other little errand for you on the way over, like he told us to," Ronald said with a sickly smirk.

"What errand?"

"You know. Discouraging that wimp teacher who's been giving you trouble."

Thunderhead rubbed the bump on his bald head. "Yeah. No big deal. Busted a few windows."

"Spilled some books on the floor."

"But he wasn't home," Mo finished, "only his old lady. We don't slap girls around, right, guys?"

"Right," Ronald and Thunderhead chorused with great conviction.

"So we left."

"Idiots . . ." Boatright stopped himself. So these boys had left a little surprise waiting for Dennis at his home? What was he complaining about? He might not have ordered it, but at the moment he couldn't think of anything he'd like better than to see Dennis pushed around by the Scars. "Of course he wasn't home," Boatright said more cordially. "You couldn't know it, but he's here right now." He nodded at Dennis, who was by now bored enough to be reading the back cover blurb on *Pisces Passion*.

"Second cashier to the front," the harried clerk

said over the store speaker system. She put the microphone down and turned back to the customer at the front of the line. "What book were you looking for? Oh, you aren't sure of the title, but it had Codependence in the title? And you don't know who wrote it, but you think it was a psychologist?" She sighed. "Addiction and Recovery is Aisle Thirteen. You could go look over there and see if you recognize it."

"Couldn't you just check in your computer?"

"We carry," the clerk said, "several hundred books with the word 'Codependence' in the title. Just go and look on the shelves. Please?"

The man turned away. Dennis put down *Pisces Passion*, picked up his stack of science fiction topped with Norah's latest romance, and reached into his pants pocket for his wallet.

"A Bookstop discount card?" repeated the woman in front of him. "Ah, no, I don't have one. How much did you say it costs?"

"Nine dollars, ma'am, but you'd save nearly that much on what you're buying today alone."

"How much exactly would I save today?"

The clerk picked up her calculator. Dennis set down his science fiction stack and reached for *Smouldering Scorpio*.

"This your friend?" the reporter called.

Mikh was making his way between New Age/Magic and Addiction/Recovery. He sidled past a man balancing copies of *Codependent No More* and *The Codependent Executive* and nodded over the bookshelves to Boatright.

"Friends," Boatright announced, "the spirit is moving me to pray that these filthy books be returned to the darkness from whence they came. Lord, bless Thy servant and cleanse this bookstore!"

"That's the man you were supposed to take care of," Mikh said to the Scars, jerking his head towards the cash registers. "I didn't tell you to bother the woman."

"All cashiers to the front, please," the clerk called.

"Believe me," Ronald said very sincerely, "we'll stay away from that woman."

"A-men," Mo put in, unluckily in the middle of Boatright's prayer. Boatright gave him a dirty look and tried to recapture his stride.

"That filth and corruption be removed from the earth, that the purity of womanhood and the innocence of childhood may no longer be defiled by these foul books, Lord!"

There was a brief silence. Boatright stretched out both hands towards the shelves of Romance and repeated, "These foul books," with a pointed look at Mikh.

Mikh sighed, slid the Leibniz from his sleeve to the palm of his hand, and turned towards the Romance shelves. He pressed function key F2, button A, and the little green knob at the bottom of the Leibniz. Romance (A–M) disappeared.

"Holy shit," breathed Irving Dietz.

"'Nother parable," Ronald said with a grin.

"Miracle," Mikh said.

"Hey, people, get out of the back room. I really need another cashier up here," said the harried clerk at the cash register.

"Hey, Mike, the Rev say that guy you wanted us to talk to up front right now," said Thunderhead. "Want we should finish the job now?"

"Lord Jesus Christ, smite these shelves of corruption

and pornography!" Boatright stretched out his hands to the shelves opposite the now-empty Romance shelves.

Mikh sighed, thumbed the green button on the Leibniz again and saw Science Fiction (H–Z) vanish. "Where?" he asked Thunderhead.

"I got that on tape!" crowed Nadia.

"All cashiers to the— Manager to the front, please. Manager to the front," the clerk changed her announcement in midstream.

"Did you see that?" Jack breathed. "Sheesh. If the Reverend Bob can really do miracles, I'm gonna have to rethink my entire theological stance."

"Not a miracle," Dennis said, "only a wizard. Damn! I thought mathemagics didn't work here."

"What are you talking about?"

"Never mind. I know that guy with Bobby Boatright," Dennis explained. "Come on. I want a closer look at his hands."

"Call that an explanation?" But Jack picked up his books and followed Dennis. "And we were only one customer from the front of the line, too," he murmured plaintively.

"Finish these next," Boatright said, striding around to Science Fiction (Series Books and A–G). Mikh followed him. "I mean, now I will pray that the Lord removes the rest of these Satanic fantasy books."

"I can see why you don't like the bodice-rippers, but what you got against fantasy and sci-fi?" Nadia demanded.

"Science fiction," Irving said. "Only geeks call it sci-fi."

"You should know!"

"Look at this!" Boatright pointed to a book with a

unicorn on the cover. "Don't you know that the unicorn is the New Age symbol of the Antichrist? And this!" He waved at a popular series with the word "dragon" in every title. "Dragons are mythological creatures and contrary to God's word."

"But they sell books," Irving said. "There's a dragon on the cover of the book," he chanted under his breath, "he is green and he has scales, and he's nowhere in the tale, but there's a dragon on the cover of the book!"

Mikh touched the green button again and Science Fiction (Series Books and A–G) disappeared.

"Not anymore, there isn't," Jack murmured. "No dragons, no books."

"Hey, that guy you wanted us to talk to? He's right there now," Thunderhead said to Mikh.

"Where? Up front?" Mikh pointed towards the cash register.

"No. Behind you."

Mikh started and whirled round. The Leibniz whirled with him. His thumb was still on the green button at the bottom of the device. Dennis's hands were suddenly empty. Mikh's rapid movement caught Jack's books, as well, not to mention a small conic section of *Addiction and Recovery* (S–T).

"Got it, got it, got it!" Nadia cried exultantly. "Film at six!"

"Damn media geeks," muttered Irving Dietz. "Oh, well." The *Grackle* was a biweekly; he was used to being scooped.

"Manager to the front," the clerk chanted. "Manager. Police. Somebody!" She dropped the microphone and headed for Science Fiction herself to see what exactly was going on.

In the brief silence that followed, Jack exhaled loudly. "Rev, you planning to hit all the other book-stores around here? Gonna be a real bitch, driving all the way to Waco for science fiction."

"He'll never find Willie's store," Dennis said, tugging Jack by the arm. "Come on. I need to tell Riva about this."

"Why?"

"Nobody can find Willie's store. He keeps moving."

"No, I mean why Riva?"

"It's a long story." Dennis glanced back at Mikh. "I'll be seeing you again."

"Indeed you will," Mikh agreed with a slight bow.

I was singing to Sasulau and apologizing to her for having left her out of the fight when Dennis stomped into the house. "Nice to see somebody's feeling happy," he said between clenched teeth.

"Forgive me for abandoning you yet again, Sasulau," I sang, sliding her back into the scabbard. It looked as if polishing her was as close as I was going to get to a proper workout this afternoon.

Dennis glowered at the sword. He doesn't scowl often; it gave me a funny feeling to see him looking as grim as a rising sand-demon storm in the middle of the Great Fyrkozoul. "If I knew ki-Dazau," he said, "I'd think you were talking to that damn sword like a person."

"She—" I stopped myself midsentence. Now was not a good time to explain to Dennis about the lengthy process of forging part of the owner's soul into the steel of her sword. Sasulau was a person; a part of my self.

"Is something wrong?" I substituted at last. Dumb

question. Even as I spoke, my brain started working. Dennis had meant to go to Bookstop after work. Mikh had mentioned Bookstop. Dennis had come home in as foul a mood as I'd seen him in since the principal of Cushman Middle School had announced that as a matter of school policy, all students were to function above their grade level on the math section of the TAAS tests. That had produced scowls, thumped fists, and ironic queries as to whether the principal also meant to legislate the value of π.

"Didn't you play with dolls when you were a little girl?"

"Why would I do that?" I slid Sasulau back into her box under the bed and sat down. "Come on, what's the matter?" Belatedly something occurred to me. "You're upset about the window? Look, I can get it fixed—"

"What window?"

If Dennis had managed to drive home and stomp up the sidewalk without even noticing the hole in the front of the house, he must be really upset. "The man's got to be stopped," he said now. "He's a maniac. He's going to destroy the First Amendment singlehanded. Not to mention that I will never be able to find anything decent to read again. The books just go poof. Thin air."

"Gredu save us!" I sank back onto the bed. "He's figured out some way to make mathemagics work here after all."

"How did you know?" Dennis glared at me as if he thought I were personally responsible.

"He said something about an appointment at a bookstore," I said. "I wasn't really paying attention; there's been a lot going on this afternoon."

"That wizard was here?"

"Well, yes—"

"All afternoon?"

"Not exactly. At least, he may have been here, but I didn't notice until after . . ." I really didn't want to tell Dennis exactly how the window got broken. He got so upset when I tried to settle disagreements honorably; I'd promised not to draw Sasulau on anybody without his permission. Of course, I hadn't actually used the sword, just a chopping knife, and I hadn't really used that, not to get blood on it or anything. But if I told Dennis the whole story, I'd have him and Sasulau both mad at me.

"I suppose it would be too much to hope that you broke the window throwing him through it?"

"If that would be okay with you," I said cautiously, "then that's how the window got broken." It was half true, anyway; I was throwing somebody through the window. What difference did it make whether it was Mikhalleviko or somebody else?

Dennis sat down beside me. "Riva. I have had a very bad afternoon. That bastard destroyed half the fiction in Bookstop, including the new Sheri Tepper I was just about to buy, and I have a feeling he's not going to stop there. The last thing I need is to come home and find out he's been sneaking around with my girl—and she's being evasive about it."

Dennis was really being impossible. I'd put up with the first scowls and growls because I felt guilty about breaking my promise not to fight anybody, but this was ridiculous. It wasn't my fault Mikh had figured out a way to apply mathemagics. It wasn't my fault he'd used it to destroy the book Dennis was about to buy. And furthermore . . .

"I am not," I said, slowly and clearly, "your woman."

"If you'd married me when I asked, you would be."

"I. Am. Not. Property."

"And I suppose it's none of my business what Mikhalleviko was doing with you this afternoon?"

"You suppose exactly right!" I badly needed Dennis's advice on how to stop Mikh from getting at Salla in this world, but how could I ask somebody who was being such a jerk? "I am a free person," I told him. "So is Salla. If that's not okay with you, we will be perfectly happy to move out."

"It's your house," Dennis pointed out.

"Fine! You move out, then. And what's more, you can carry your own damned boxes of books when you do."

Dennis gave me a disgusted look and stalked out of the room. A moment later I heard his car coughing to life.

He wouldn't just walk out like that, would he? Over nothing? Not without his books, I thought. I looked at the shelves of tattered paperback books with their garish covers. Dennis said it was a world-class collection of classic science fiction. It had taken him years to assemble. Many of the books were out of print.

"He might leave me," I said under my breath, "but he'd never abandon his books."

A few minutes later I heard the distinctive rattle of Dennis's car returning. I felt a moment's intense relief, then wondered if he'd only gone out to get boxes for his books. Nauzu could take him before I'd run out and check! I sat cross-legged on the bed and waited to find out what was going on.

He didn't come inside at all. He dropped something heavy on the front lawn, then went around to the minuscule garage that we used as a catch-all and storage space. On the way back he was carrying the stepladder. An assortment of thumps, bangs, and muffled curses followed. Probably he was nailing something over the broken window. I supposed I ought to go and clear things up with him. But was that possible? He wouldn't be exactly overjoyed to hear that I'd been throwing Paper-Pushers through the window; I'd promised him to seek nonviolent solutions to problems here.

The screen door slammed and the floor quivered. Salla? Hastily I pushed my hair back and wiped the back of my face. Salla didn't need to know anything about the quarrel with Dennis—not yet, anyway. If he moved out, I suppose I'd have to tell her something; she was bound to notice.

But it wasn't Salla; it was Norah, in a purple sweatsuit that made her look like a cheerful grape.

"We're going jogging together," she said. She bounced up and down on her toes as she spoke, like a Serious Runner waiting out a traffic light.

"We . . . are?" I couldn't remember making plans to go running with her.

"Come on," Norah said. "Get your shoes on."

"I don't like to run in shoes," I grumbled, but I reached for the Reeboks anyway. Where was my mind going? The last time I remembered discussing exercise with Norah was the evening she'd come over for dinner to explain to us how Vordo landed on the cover of her latest bodice-ripper. She'd said something about wanting to work out with me, but we hadn't made a firm date . . . had we?

I asked her about it after we rounded the first corner. "Where are we going? And how come I don't remember anything about a jogging date?"

"Oh, we didn't—*puff*—really have—*pant*—firm plans," Norah wheezed. She stopped and bent over in a sort of approximation of a hamstring stretch. "I don't have a firm anything," she said ruefully when she'd recovered her breath. "Gotta start some sort of regular exercise program. Let's go up to the track behind the school. It's a better running surface than asphalt."

I slowed my pace to match hers. It wasn't easy; I felt as if I were walking on tiptoe, not running. But I didn't want her too out of breath. It had not escaped me that she hadn't answered my other question. "Norah. What exactly is going on?"

We crossed the street and swerved in opposite directions around Mr. Siegel and his two yappy little dogs. Fluffypoop and Dustball strained their leashes to get at us, doing their best to strangle themselves and pull down old Mr. Siegel simultaneously. Fortunately, since they were pulling in opposite directions, they kept Mr. Siegel nicely balanced between them.

When we joined stride again, the empty school playground lay before us, green and soggy, with a sandy jogging track laid out in a meandering course around trees and temporary trailer buildings and the basketball court. I couldn't tell whether Norah was blushing or just red in the face from unaccustomed effort. "Okay, we didn't have a date," she admitted. "Dennis stopped by on the way back from the hardware store. He said you were upset and he was afraid if he tried to talk about it you'd throw him out."

"Ha! He was the one threatening to move out! I think." I couldn't remember exactly how the fight had gone now.

"Whatever," Norah said pacifically. "Anyway, he wanted to send Salla over to finish her homework with Jason."

"Oh." Now I could feel my own face going red. "That bad, huh?"

"So I thought—some exercise—would help us—both." Norah wheezed to another stop beside a gnarled live oak. "Wait up, I gotta tie my shoe." She braced one foot on the trunk of the tree and played with the shoelaces while gasping for breath.

"It's been a weird day," I said. "Dennis is acting weird, too. He seems to think it's all my fault Mikh showed up. Gredu take him!"

"Who?"

"Both of them. Well, Mikh, I guess. I could have lived quite happily without ever seeing the man again! In fact," I said gloomily as Norah tried another hamstring stretch, "at the moment I think I could live quite happily without seeing any men again."

"Ha," said Norah. She leaned against a tree and breathed deeply. "Wait till you've been celibate as long as I have. After my ex took off for California I cried and ate chocolates until I looked like this, and now I can't have a meaningful relationship because I'm not willing to take my clothes off in front of another adult."

"You have to take your clothes off to have a meaningful relationship?" I asked, momentarily distracted.

"The kind I'd like to have," Norah said, "yes. Unlike my Kathleen Fraser fans, I do not find reading about it a satisfactory substitute. Or," she added, "writing about it."

"At least you've got a career to fall back on. Of course, I do too, sort of. I don't need Dennis. I took care of Salla and me before and I can do it again.

I don't have to finish my studies; I can always go back into my old line of work." Perhaps, I thought, that was why I'd been working out regularly, going through my boklu routines and singing to Sasulau. Maybe something had been telling me that the time of living quietly with Dennis was over, that I was going to have to move on.

"What's that?"

"What—oh, my old job? Er. Um. I'm not quite sure how you would say it. Mercenary? Soldier of fortune?"

From the look on Norah's face, I hadn't gotten it quite right. I tried again. "Private security guard."

"Riva, you're too smart for a job like that! You know what your trouble is? You should have stayed in school. You should have gone to college. You didn't think ahead when you were younger."

"I'll say," I agreed, remembering that big dumb mountain girl who'd gotten herself mixed up with Mikhalleviko the Sleaze. But out of that had come Salla, so how much could I regret it?

"That reminds me," Norah said, "I wanted to talk to you about something anyway. Out of the children's hearing. So this is as good a place as any."

"You," I said, "just want an excuse to lean on that tree for a while longer."

"Yeah. I'm poorly coordinated; I can't talk and wheeze at the same time."

"So what's the problem?" I was glad of an excuse to think about somebody else's troubles for a change.

"Careers Day," Norah said.

I grinned. "They got me on that one two years ago. What did you agree to do, lead the class on a guided tour of your study? They could analyze it by archaeological strata." Norah's study had piles of paper dating back, she claimed, to something called the Second Punic War. (Which was not, confusingly, anything to do with the Second World War—the Paper-Pushers seemed to have more wars than names to give them. Strange, considering how hard it was to get them to stand up and fight as individuals.)

"I couldn't risk it," Norah said. "They might move things around and then I'd never find anything again."

"I don't see how you find anything now!"

Norah sighed. "Look, Riva. I'm trying to be the romance writer Kathleen Fraser, the SF writer Norah Tibbs, and Jason's mom who pays the bills, all in the same room, and—why am I apologizing to you about the state of my study, anyway? The point is, I didn't dare let the little monsters, I mean our darling children and their friends in the sixth-grade Gifted and Talented program, into my study, because if one of them knocked over a pile of paper it would destroy my entire filing system. Besides, there's not room for them all. So I offered to give a talk to the class instead. On Writing As a Career."

"So?"

"Well, nothing really. I mean, it was just like giving the same talk to adults. Three of them were worried about how to keep a publisher from stealing their ideas and two of them wanted to know if they really had to learn to type before they sent in a manuscript and the rest wanted to hear about the publicity tours, champagne parties, movie offers and other glamorous parts of an author's life."

I perked up. "You never told me about those parts."

"That," said Norah, "is because the farthest my publisher has sent me on tour is to a signing in San Marcos, and I had to pay my own gas mileage for that."

"Oh."

"That's more or less what the kids said when I broke the news to them. Anyway, after that they sort of lost interest in becoming writers, and we got into this general kind of discussion about what they wanted to do when they grew up." She giggled. "My Jason and your Salla are planning to found a company together, but they think they'll have to wait until eighth grade because no venture capitalist will talk to sixth-graders. They want to be software wizards."

"What?" I grabbed the tree trunk. "Oh, no. No. And here I thought I was going to relax and hear about somebody else's problems for a change. What were you doing, breaking it to me gently? She's taking after her father; I should have been watching for it."

"Riva, you're babbling," Norah interrupted me. "What's so terrible about Salla and Jason wanting to be computer programmers? They'll probably be rich and support us in luxury in our declining years."

"You said they wanted to be wizards."

"Software wizards. That just means they plan to be real hotshot programmers," Norah translated.

"Oh. Well." My heart rate slowed down. "So if that's not the problem you were leading up to, what are you worried about?"

"Becky Boatright," Norah said. "All the other kids were going wild with plans to be everything from software wiz—er, experts to alien language translators in case we ever encounter any aliens, and she just sat there like a lump of underdone oatmeal. Finally I asked her point-blank what she wanted to do when she grew up, and she said it didn't matter."

"So?"

"You didn't hear her." Norah shook her head. "She was talking in this kind of dead voice, no expression. And she said, 'It doesn't matter what I want. They make you do what they want.'"

"Her parents are pretty strict fundamentalists." I recalled Vera Boatright's protests against Satanism in the textbooks. "Probably whatever she says she wants, they tell her God wouldn't like it."

"Maybe." Norah sounded doubtful. "I hope that's all. She's got this weird rash on her arms, too. Sort of thing kids show when they're really stressed about something. I'm worried about that child, Riva."

"I will be worried, too," I promised her, "as soon as I quit worrying about my own kid and whether I'm going to get to keep her. Let's jog some more. I can't think standing still."

"Your ex making trouble?" Norah panted a moment after we set off.

"Yeah. Custody."

"Exes," Norah offered in between gasps, "are the scum of the earth. Mine thought he owned me."

"Exactly," I said as we rounded the curve of the track and turned back towards home. "Exactly."

Chapter $3\left(\lim_{t \to 1}\frac{t^3-1}{t-1}\right)$

Dozourdaunniko's farmstead on Weariefauld was shaped like three sides of a square. The centerpiece was the house and kitchen, facing the courtyard and with its back turned to the high bleak hills of the border country. Along one side of the courtyard ran a long, low stone building divided into turnip shed, dairy, and a byre for the sweet, stupid, long-horned nyttovu. Along the other side was a two-story building, stables below, hayloft and bothy for the horsemen above.

Kurdy the orra boy slept above the stables with the horsemen Zido and Kimoc, but his place after the bell rang was in the main house with Dozour himself and silly Gaubi the kitchenmaid. Kurdy had rung the bell himself, it being his turn to watch in case Baron Rodograunnizo's men came back for another try at extortion. It was usually his turn to watch. At least he'd been paid for days of shivering on the ridgepole of the hayloft by being the first to see the three swordsmen sneaking across Three Stones Ford. One of them slipped on the wet rocks; Kurdy could see his arms flailing as he went down, but he heard neither splash nor swearing. So he reckoned they were too far away to hear his bell ringing, just like Master Dozour had said they would be.

There'd been plenty of time for them all to scatter to their assigned places: Zido and Kimoc over the stables, the dairymaids and the bailie loon in the turnip shed beside the nyttovu byre, and Kurdy in the kitchen with Dozour and Gaubi Scatterbrain.

The only thing that hadn't gone according to plan was that Granny Beerdouvou was there, too. She'd hobbled over to check the bindings on Dozour's broken ankle and to smear one of her foul-smelling salves on the foot. All totally unnecessary, in Kurdy's opinion, and just an excuse for her to help herself to a pail of milk or one of the golden rounds of nyttovu cheese every time she came; but nobody asked his opinion.

Anyway, she was with them now, telling them all what a nasty little boy Rodograunnizo had been, nagging poor Gaubi to tears, and criticizing Dozour's plan to defend the farmstead. And nobody was going to turn out the only healer between here and Gowanlea for Rodo's swordsmen to slaughter, no matter how irritating she was.

"Call that a plan?" Granny Beerdovou grumbled for the fourth or fifth time. "All hide, then leap out and whack them over the head with harrows and tie them up with broken harness bits? And who's going to leap out first to be sliced up by the swordsmen? The dairymaids or the horsemen? You're daft, Dozour."

"We'll all fall on them together when Kurdi here rings the bell again," Dozour said. "It's an agreement between us. Fight them off or die trying."

Kurdi sighed and squinted through his peephole in the shutters at the empty courtyard. In a few minutes, if their plan went aright, the swordsmen would come into the courtyard, surprised by the silence and inactivity of the farmstead. Once they were all in, he was to ring the bell. Zido and Kymoc would jump down from the bothy over the stables and block the open side of the courtyard, while he and Pauvi and Suferi and Rumau ran out to attack them from the other sides. Granny Beerdouvou was right; it wasn't much of a plan. But he wished she wouldn't keep pointing that out. He had agreed to die defending Weariefauld; it was the only home he'd ever known, and he knew who would be taken first to fight in the baron's wars if they ever knuckled under to Rodograunnizo. He had not quite so much appetite to die defending Granny Beerdovou.

"I'm no' afeard of the swordsmen," Gaubi declared with a sniffle. "It's that wizardly mist they call up."

"No such thing," Dozour said firmly. "There was a heavy fog last time, that's all."

"A fog that needed Furo Fykrou to disperse it?" Kurdy demanded. "A fog that talked?"

"Wizards, aye, come in handy to manage the ill weather," Dozour said. "As for the voices, it's well known that fog will distort sounds and make you hear folk speaking from the next hill over, or even farther. There was no wizardry involved last time, and furthermore, it won't happen again."

"Hush!" Kurdy flapped his hands behind him to shut them all up. "They're here. They're quarreling."

He strained his ears to pick up the voices of the swordsmen who swaggered into the courtyard. The wet one looked unhappy. There was a sharp wind from the east today; Kurdi had felt it on the rooftop.

"I don't like it," the wet one said.

"You haven't liked anything since you fell on your arse in the river," sneered the one with the bushy beard. "Piece of sweetmeat, y'ask me. Fire the byre—"

"Nobody did ask you, Fuzzface," the wet one interrupted. "If y'ask me, there's something amiss here. Where's all the folk?"

"Hiding from us." Fuzzface grinned. "Wanna hide with them, Tenthumbs? 'Bout all you're good for, if y'ask me."

"Could be another ambush," whined Tenthumbs. "Them ladies of the duke's what ain't no ladies, if y'ask me—"

"Sharrup!" roared the third man, the one who'd been silently checking out the featureless stone walls and shuttered windows all around them. "Didn't I tell you already, you feckless loons, those tarts from the Bronze Bra Guild went back to Duke's Zolvorra. You think the baron doesna' have his eyes and ears on the highroad south from here?"

Now that, Kurdy thought from his listening post, was something to tell the duke. Assuming any of them lived to tell the duke anything. For a moment he was blinded by the image of himself, Kurdy the Orphan, Kurdy No-Clan-Name, marching into the grand hall at Duke's Zolvorra to present his prisoners and his information about the baron's spies on the northern highroad.

"What are they sayin' now?" hissed Gaubi. "Lemme see."

Kurdy shouldered her out of his way and fastened his eye to the peephole again. He'd missed a few words; now the one called Fuzzface was fretting about the possibility that the green fog might come back.

So Rodo's men weren't the ones who'd called up

the wizardwork! That was something else to tell the duke about. But then, who *had* called up that fog? Because it hadn't been natural, no matter what Dozourdaunniko said about weather and voices carrying from a distance.

"You're scaring your worthless selves wi' your ain shadows," the leader of the group said firmly. "There wasna' wizardry in it last time, and anyway yon wizard's gone back to Duke's Zolvorra, too, so it'll no' happen again."

Kurdi suppressed a snicker at this echoing of Dozour's views. *Folks on top, aye, talked the same line,* he thought. *It didn't happen, don't worry about it, just go out there and stick your neck out for us and never mind if you get eaten by . . .*

There was something white obscuring his view. Fog, after all? And not a natural fog, either; it was too white, too solid.

It moved away from the peephole, and Kurdy caught a glimpse of shape: barbed backbone, massive haunches bent over white talons.

"Nauzu's Blood and Tears!" he whispered.

One of Rodo's men shrieked. The scream ended abruptly. Kurdy couldn't see past the white blob.

"What is it, what is it?" Gaubi clawed at Kurdy's shoulder, trying to drag him away from the peephole.

"Hush," he said without moving. "I can't see . . ."

He could see, now. But he didn't want to put it into words. If he said it, it would be real. And where had it come from, anyway? Not through the open side of the courtyard; he'd been watching that way, behind Rodo's men, in case there were more hiding out of sight. Over the roof, then. And if he'd still been sitting up there, he might have been its lunch instead of . . . was it Fuzzface? Yes, he recognized the boots and the top of the leg. The other two men were trying to burrow under a pile of turnips.

Behind him, Dozour whispered curses and demanded to know what was happening. Granny Beerdovou snuffled around the kitchen, thrusting her long nose into the air, and told Gaubi to stop crawling all over Kurdy and get her some bitterweed tansy leaves from the stillroom.

"I'm afeard to leave the room!" Gaubi whimpered. "What is it, Kurdy?"

Kurdy could see it clearly now. It didn't look anything like the pictures on the shrine walls. No gloriously shining colored scales, no sharply etched outline of jagged backbone and webbed wings; just a vaguely dragon-shaped white form with a patch of dark stripes on one haunch. It was snuffling around the courtyard just like Granny Beerdovou in the kitchen, lifting its long scaly head and then sighing out a wavering gust of blue-tinged fire.

"It's . . . a dragon," Kurdy said reluctantly. It had nosed out one of the men hiding under the turnips now; the indistinct jaws were strong enough to drag him out by one booted foot. Hisses and squawks drowned out Tenthumbs' screams; two more fuzzy white heads appeared and made darting pecks at the man and the first dragon simultaneously. More shapeless wings fluttered by the stables.

"Lots of dragons."

"Lemme see, lemme see!"

This time Kurdy was more than willing to surrender his place at the peephole to Gaubi. The first three dragons were pulling on different portions of Tenthumbs. He felt sick.

"Told you so!" Granny Beerdouvo cackled. Kurdy didn't remember the old harridan saying anything about dragons, but he felt too queasy to argue with her. "Quit gaping through the shutter, you gormless chit, and fetch me those tansy leaves!"

But Gaubi had fainted, so Kurdy wound up going to the stillroom for tansy leaves and dried caumopi and eels' tongues.

"Eels' tongues?" he repeated on that last demand. He paused to peek through the shutters. The dragons had finished off all three swordsmen now. Bits of swords and armor, mangled as though the dragons had had some trouble mouthing them free of the bodies, lay about the courtyard. The dragons were sniffing interestedly at the byre. The nyttovu wailed plaintively, but so far the dragons hadn't figured out how to get through the good solid stone walls and the triple-planked door that guarded the nyttovu against wolves and thieves.

"My woman Savra had some skill as a herb-woman," Dozourdaunniko said. "She laid down a goodly store of all we were like-to need before the sweating fever took her. If it hadna' been for that pestilence, we'd no' need to suffer this one." He jerked his head at Granny Beerdovou where she stooped over the hearth-fire, muttering and poking at a slimy, stinking mass that heaved and glopped inside the farm's biggest cooking pot.

"Keep a civil tongue in your head, Dozour, or I'll tell the halflin here the tale of how you went a-raiding for nyttovu and came back with Savra riding atop the bull nyttov and ruling you like she'd had a ring through your nose as well as the bull's," Granny Beerdovou threatened.

Kurdy's eyes widened, but he had to go for the eels'
tongues after all, and when he got back Dozour and
Granny Beerdo had made a sort of edgy peace. Outside,
as well as he could tell from a quick peep through the
shutters, nothing had changed. The dragons were still
snuffling around the stone walls that protected the
nyttovu in the byre and the horses in the stables. The
nyttovu were still uttering their long, plaintive moans.

There was no sign of the other farm workers.

"Uh—they didn't get anybody else, did they?" he
asked.

"No!" Granny Beerdovou said sharply. "And they'll
no' hurt any of us, if you've the sense to follow my
orders. No, lad, all's quiet because the dairymaids and
horsemen have more sense than to make a noise that'd
maybe get the dragons interested in them as well as
the stock. First time I ever allowed as how that thick-
legged Zido had more sense than a nyttov," she added,
"and could be wrong, at that. Could be he's fainted.
Is that all the eels' tongues you've got? Not enough
to do more than half the ointment. Not proper. I
wonder, should I pour out half of it to finish later,
or just mix in what eels' tongues you've brought and
hope it'll be strong enough."

"Strong enough for what?"

"To keep the dragons off, of course. You didn't think
we were going to stay in here until they wandered
off, did you?"

That was more or less what Kurdy had had in mind.

"Could be days," Gramy Beerdovou said, "and the
nyttovu need to be milked. A pity you didn't tell the
dairymaids to hide in the byre instead of the turnip shed,
Dozour. Ah, well, you're a lucky man that I'd come to
tend you the day. Nauzu must hold you in his favor."

Kurdy was of the opinion that the nyttovu could just wait to be milked until those bland white dragon-shapes did go away. But Dozour swore and talked about udder-blight, and the moans of the nyttovu got longer and louder as the day wore on.

"Dozour can't go," Granny Beerdovou pointed out, "not with his ankle broken. I'm too old and frail to hobble around dragons; they won't eat me, but they could still step on me. If you're afeard to go, Kurdy, we'll just have to put the ointment on yon feckless kitchen wench and send her."

At this suggestion Gaubi set up a wail louder than the nyttovu and threatened to faint again.

"Oh, all right, all right," Kurdy said. "I'd rather be outside with the dragons than inside with a nagging witch and a whining kitchenmaid, anyway."

Following Granny Beerdovou's instructions, he smeared the still-warm ointment over every inch of his exposed skin, and for good measure rubbed it over his tunic and trews—ruining a perfectly good set of clothes that hadn't been worn but two seasons, but so what? If this stuff the old witch had brewed up worked, Dozour would owe him a new outfit. And if it didn't, the stinking stains on the clothes wouldn't be his biggest problem.

He did wish the stuff didn't smell quite so much like a privy that was ten years overdue for shoveling out and didn't have quite so much tendency to run down his forehead into his eyes and nose and mouth. And most of all, he wished that he had encouraged Granny Beerdovou to put aside half the ointment and mix the other half full strength with the eels' tongues.

"I should have guessed what she meant to do with it," he grumbled while the women circled him, slapping on handfuls of gloppy green ointment wherever they saw a dry spot. "Always the same story. Who gets to sack the nyttovu droppings and spread them on the fields? Kurdy. Who gets to sleep under the leak in the bothy roof? Kurdy. Who gets sent out to be eaten by dragons? Kurdy, who else?"

"You'll do grand, lad," Granny Beerdovou assured him. "My great-granny Seenkdovou swore by this ointment. Seenk's Special Mix, they used to call it back in the days before the old Duke's father's cousin cleared the dragons back into the highlands where they belong. Or was he Zolkir's good-uncle's stepson?" she mused. "Let's see, the old duke's aunt wed a man with three sons by some foreign wife nobody ever saw, and there was something unco' strange about all three of them, but 'twas the middle lad the power descended through. Or was it the third one?"

"When I open the door a crack, you slip out," Dozour told Kurdy.

"They should have called it Stink's Special," Kurdy muttered as Granny Beerdovou slopped a final stinking handful of the stuff on his head. It ran down into his eyes and nose and blinded him for a moment so that he didn't know to duck when Granny Beerdo smacked him on the side of the head. Ears ringing, he swiped the back of one wrist across his eyes and saw Granny Beerdo with hands curved like talons, shrieking about impudence and ingratitude and disrespect to her great-granny.

The crack of the barely opened door looked, for a moment, like peace and freedom. Kurdy slithered through and heard it slam behind him. The noise gave him a surprisingly hollow feeling.

"Better the dragons outside than the old witch

inside," he muttered. Actually, the dragons didn't seem to be outside any longer. There were some mangled bits of bloody stuff strewn carelessly about the court- yard. Bones, gristle, half a boot . . . Kurdy gulped, averted his eyes, and sidled along the farmhouse wall towards the byre.

Something warm and wet slapped his legs, tangling them so that he fell hard on the packed dirt of the farmyard. He curled up like a baby, keeping his face covered. For some reason he couldn't bear the thought of a dragon biting at his head. Images of the torn leather and bloody bones on the ground flashed through his mind. All right, so he was as good as dead anyway, but couldn't he start dying at the other end?

The warm wet thing followed him, rolling him over the stones like a ball; then after an especially vigorous shove that knocked him into the stones of the byre, it withdrew.

After a moment Kurdy uncovered one eye. A round dark eye the size of his own head stared back at him. The white dragon-shape surrounding it was too smooth, almost featureless, like a child's outline scribble in the dust. But the eyes and teeth were real, and the tongue like a wet red blanket hanging half out of his mouth.

The tongue moved and slapped against the dragon's horny mouth as though the beast were trying to scrape away a bad taste. Kurdy had seen a nyttov in pasture acting that way, when the stupid beast bit off a piece of bitterweed tansy.

Bitterweed . . . "By Nauzu," Kurdy said, hardly daring to believe his good fortune, "it works! It really works!"

He uncoiled himself with aching slowness. The dragon came no closer. Its nostrils were pinched; looked like old Dozour telling him it was time to clean the privy.

Two more smooth white heads appeared behind the first one, inspecting Kurdy with lively interest. They squeaked. The first dragon squeaked back, ending with a long retching noise. The two other heads sank down, looking disappointed.

"It works," Kurdy announced after he'd milked the nyttovu. "It really works! Give me a bucket of that glop to take to the stable hands, Granny. And the dairymaids. They're all scared witless and gibbering for fear the dragons will come through the walls at them. Besides," he added righteously, "I can't do all the work around here."

"Doesn't look as if you've done much," said Dozour, inspecting the pale wash of milk at the bottom of Kurdy's bucket. "Is that all you took from six nyttovu?"

"I filled the bucket," Kurdy said indignantly. "But the dragons like nyttovu milk. If you think you can keep them out of it, you do the next milking!" He closed his eyes for a moment, reliving the terror when they'd attacked him coming out of the byre, sure that Granny Beerdovou's stinking charm had worn off; the intense relief of sitting up, bruised but not chewed on, to see three dragons lapping up the puddles of spilled milk like three outsized white kittens.

"There, there, lad," Dozour said, "no need to get huffy with me. Give him enough ointment for the rest of the hands, Granny, and let's get back to work!"

But it wasn't quite as simple as that. Apart from the stench of the bitterweed ointment that permeated the air and the wet gloppiness of the stuff squelching in their hair and clothes, there were a few problems.

Granny Beerodovou complained of a shortage of ingredients, so Dozour sent Kimoc the second horseman to scour the neighborhood for more. Kimoc's horse had to be anointed, too, and it didn't like the stuff. Neither did the nyttovu; they kept licking it off and then lowing indignantly at the sharp taste of the bitterweed in their mouths. But being even stupider than dragons, they didn't learn not to lick off the next batch of ointment the dairymaids slapped on their thick hides.

And Kimoc reported that as soon as the neighboring farmers learned what he wanted their stocks of dried caumopi for, they started working on their own ointments and refused him any of the roots. As for eels' tongues, nobody except Savra and Granny Beerdovou herself had laid in a supply of those; Kimoc stopped by the herb-granny's cottage and helped himself to her supplies on the way back. Fortunately, there was plenty of bitterweed tansy available for the pulling; it just needed somebody to cover himself with ointment and get past the dragons into the worthless corner of the north field where the weeds grew.

"Let me guess," Kurdy said with resignation when they reached that point. "Kurdy can do it."

"I need Kimoc to keep the horses safe," Dozour pointed out, "and the lasses have their hands full carrying Seenk's Mix in buckets and slapping it on the nyttovu."

"What about Zido?" Kurdy muttered sulkily. He knew better than to think the first horseman would lower himself to pulling bitterweed, but he was so tired of being stuck with all the worst chores!

"Zido's away," Dozour said. "As soon as he got some of the ointment on himself and his horse, he volunteered to ride for Duke's Zolvorra."

"I could have done that," Kurdy grumbled.

"The duke might not be just so willing to send his soldiers out on the word of a young lad like you," Dozour pointed out. "Now Zido, he's got, what-you-call-it, presence. The ladies of the Guild will come back here if Zido tells them about the dragons."

"Let's hope," Kurdy said, "they're not too distracted by Zido's, what-you-call-it, presence."

Chapter $3^2 + 1$

He was in a good mood when he came home that afternoon. Not *he*, Becky corrected her thoughts. Daddy Bob. That was what they'd agreed she would call him, when they had a family discussion right after he married Mom. Well, not exactly a discussion. Daddy Bob did all the talking. He'd said he wouldn't expect Becky to call him "Dad," not right at first, but he wanted them to know he intended to be a good husband to Vera and a good father to Vera's sweet little girl and he wanted his little girl to stop calling him, "Mr. Boatright," like some stranger.

That was three years ago, just before they moved to Austin and Mom told Becky never to talk about the fact that she'd been divorced because it would embarrass her in the church here. But Becky still couldn't bring herself to say "Daddy Bob." Mostly she called him "You," or "Sir."

"Sir" was all right. He liked that.

Now she hunched her shoulders over her Language Arts book and hoped he wouldn't come upstairs to check on her. He was whistling. That meant he was in a good mood. Something good had happened, he'd converted another soul for the Church of Living Salvation, or some big businessman had promised a donation, and he'd want to tell somebody about it. Becky wished Mom were back from the Save Our Schools Christian League meeting, so he could tell her all about whatever it was instead of coming upstairs to hassle Becky.

Heavy feet on the stairs, making the house shake; big heavy hand on her shoulder. "How's my sweet little Becky-beck doing this afternoon?"

"Homework," Becky mumbled, twisting around in her chair so that his hand was more on the back of her neck than her shoulder.

"Your Daddy Bob has won a great victory for the Lord today," he said, his voice deep and vibrant as though he were preaching to the whole church. "The forces of Midian have been routed, yea, verily, and with any luck it'll be on the six o'clock news. Why don't you come downstairs and watch it with me, Becky-beck?"

"I really gotta finish this paper," Becky said. "It's late already, but Ms. Fishbeck gave me an extension because I explained to her about not being able to work over Church Camp Weekend."

"And very right and proper," he said. "The work of the Lord comes before worldly learning. Now come on, Becky-beck. You want to see your dear Daddy Bob on television, don't you? You're not like your mother, gadding about and leaving her loved ones alone."

"Mom's at the Save our Schools Christian Decency League meeting," Becky reminded him. Did she dare add that he had told Vera to join the league? Probably not. She wished he would take his hand off her neck. It was like a weight pushing her down into the chair, making her head all fuzzy. She couldn't think properly when he was standing so close to her.

"Becky-beck." He stroked the curve of her neck, and Becky wished she hadn't thought that about him moving his hand. It was like she was making him do it that way, so his fingertips just grazed the mounds under her T-shirt that had been embarrassing her ever since she was the first kid in fourth grade to really need a sports bra.

"I wish you wouldn't call me that," she said. "It's a dumb little kid nickname. I'm not a little kid anymore." She'd already been old enough to be embarrassed by the Becky-beck and Daddy Bob crud when he married Mom, when she was in third grade. Now that she was in sixth grade it was positively revolting.

"My little girl is growing up," he said. "Bet you're not too big to sit on Daddy Bob's lap and watch the news, though. If I give you a Snickers Bar? Huh?"

Becky felt her mouth watering. Mom was always on her case about losing weight. She practically lived on salads and sprouts, but it didn't do any good; she was a big girl and she had a big body, the kind of body the high school boys whistled at. And he wasn't about to give up. She was always going to be too big, and she was going to do what he wanted like always. She might as well get a candy bar out of the deal.

"Your mother doesn't have to know," he added. His hand moved lower. Becky felt her neck getting hot.

"I have to get right back and finish this paper," she said as she pushed her chair back and stood up. His hand cupped her elbow, like one of the high school boys steering his girlfriend around. "As soon as the news is over." How long could it last? She could leave as soon as they'd watched the bit about him, couldn't she? Maybe she'd get real lucky and they'd do the local color news first thing. Sometimes they did that if there wasn't anything interesting like a war or a bombing to talk about. Ten minutes. She could stand ten minutes; she could go into her secret place, the place nobody else knew about where there was glittering sand and tall brave women in bright armor who didn't have to do what anybody said.

More likely it would be the last thing, though. Thirty minutes would be too long. She couldn't stay in her secret mind place for that long.

"Why don't you call me when you come on, Daddy Bob?" she said. "I'll just work until then."

"You can bring your book downstairs and work while we watch."

No! Becky cried inside her head. *I can't think, it's not safe to think, I have to always be ready to get away.* Get away from what? She wasn't making any sense. This always happened to her when he was standing by her, stroking her arm and trying, she guessed, to act like a Real Father.

"It's a lot of books," she babbled, pointing at her desk. "See, this is a real research paper with references and everything, just like the high school kids do, because I'm in the Gifted and Talented program and we have to do more, you know? And I'm doing the African roots of voodoo, you know, how the slaves brought their gods over here and it turned into a kind of folk religion . . ."

"African idols?"

"Not idols," Becky said, "gods."

"Thus saith the Lord: Thou shalt have no other gods before Me!"

"Well, I guess they weren't gods exactly. Or maybe they thought they were gods, but of course they were wrong."

Becky tried to appease him. "Nature spirits. Orishas and like that, you know? Look, it's in the textbook."

He let go of her arm to take the looseleaf binder of photocopied readings that they were using in Language Arts for the folklore and mythology section. He needed both hands to steady the binder and flip through the pages. Becky felt shaky with relief.

"Heathen stories, idolatry, devil worship," he muttered. "Why didn't you tell me you were being made to study this sort of thing?"

Becky closed her eyes in despair. She hadn't told him because she didn't want her parents to write one of those letters of exemption and have her reading Tales from Shakespeare while everybody else got to do Africans and Indians and all kinds of neat stuff. She'd been really, really careful not to let him find out about the Language Arts curriculum this year, and now she'd blown it. She should have just gone downstairs and watched the dumb show. What harm could it do? Just because he liked her to sit on his lap and pretend she was still a little kid and she got embarrassed.

"Something should be done about it," he announced. "I will do something."

"I know. You're gonna write one of those letters." She was resigned now. They took everything bright and beautiful away and made the world gray. The only good place was her secret world, because they didn't know about that.

"Better than that." He was grinning like a kid with a new toy. "Oh, much better than that. The Lord shall smite these idolatrous books, just like I smote the junk fiction at Bookstop. Come on downstairs and see!" He pulled her by the hand, and Becky gave up and followed him, curious in spite of herself.

She perched on the arm of his big recliner while the news anchors droned through the usual catalogue of disasters and politics. (Jason's mom had said that living in the state capital, as they did, sometimes it was hard to tell the difference between the two.) A tractor-trailer had spilled two hundred live turkeys on I-35. The state legislature was considering a bill to require parental consent for minors to get abortions, have parts of their body other than earlobes pierced, or stay out after 10 P.M. The rumors of a sword-wielding lunatic in the neighborhood of Cushman Middle School had not been substantiated, but they showed footage of reporters inverviewing the neighbors anyway.

"Get on with it, get on with it," he muttered. Becky felt his arm sliding around her. "Come on, Becky-beck, let's get comfortable. No telling how long they'll take to get to the real story."

"Wait a minute," Becky said crossly, "I want to see this." Wasn't that a piece of Salla's mom's front porch in the corner of the screen, right behind the old guy with the two little lap dogs who was telling a reporter that his Fluffy and Muffy would take care of any loonies that came around this neighborhood? Maybe they'd interview Salla's mom next. Maybe they'd interview Salla. That would be cool, being on TV. It would even be cool for Becky, knowing someone who'd been on TV.

"And now for a look at the lighter side of things in the capital city," said a man's voice. You could tell he was trying not to laugh, but not trying real hard. A picture of the Bookstop at 38th and Lamar replaced the neighborhood street scene with a corner of Salla's house. Becky slumped back just as

Daddy Bob sat up straighter and quit trying to pull her down into the chair.

"Chaos and confusion reigned at a local bookstore today as a self-appointed censor apparently censored much of the store's stock." There was Daddy Bob on the screen, raising his arms and moving his lips, but you couldn't hear what he was saying; the man who'd introduced the story kept talking instead.

"Some people might describe Bookstop's science fiction section as 'out of this world,'" the man chuckled. The camera zoomed in for a close shot of the books behind Daddy Bob: rows and rows of Dragonspatula and Star Trek books. Becky sneered. Jason had recently introduced her to real science fiction. Heinlein and like that. "And that, apparently, is where it is now," continued the anchor's smooth voice, "out of this world." A long shot now, showing Daddy Bob again, and the books vanished behind him.

"No, folks, this isn't a trick shot," the anchor said. There was a brief snatch of sound from the film: a customer screaming, and a clerk's voice over the PA system calling, "Extra cashiers to the front. Manager to the front. Police to the front! What's going on there, anyway?"

Then they were looking at the anchorman's smiling face again. "No tricks, folks, or at least not on the part of Channel Six News. As far as our cameraperson-on-the-spot could determine, Bookstop's displays of romance, science fiction, and self-help mysteriously vanished into thin air just moments after a local preacher invoked the Lord to cleanse the store of impure and evil writings. Bob Boatright, interviewed immediately after his impressive prayer, gave God the credit and insisted he did not know where the books had gone. The police said they could not hold Boatright as a material witness; he obviously did not have the books on his person, and there was no physical evidence linking him with the apparent crime. But our crew of top-notch investigative reporters is still on the story, folks. Have we just seen a clever publicity stunt from the largest bookstore chain in Austin? Or have we seen a true 'Miracle on 38th Street'?"

A commercial for Texas Orange Pop, "the patriotic soda that tastes as orange as it looks," replaced the anchorman's face. Daddy Bob clicked the remote control and turned the TV off.

"The unbelievers see and still do not believe," he announced.

His face was getting purple. That was always a bad sign. Becky thought quickly. "I believe, Daddy Bob," she said. "You always told me that the Lord God answers prayers, so why wouldn't I believe that He answered yours?"

His face cleared slightly. "That's my sweet little Becky-beck," he said. "'And a little child shall lead them.' I guess the Lord just wants me to work a little harder at getting His message out to the people that He will no longer tolerate filth and violence masquerading as literature. Now you know what I'm going to do about that book your Language Arts teacher gave you, Becky. We don't have to bother with letters and censorship meetings anymore. The Lord God is just going to make it disappear, just like all those trashy books at the store."

"Right now?" Becky breathed. "But I haven't finished my-"

"No, not now, of course not! Mike isn't—I mean, the Lord doesn't just whip up miracles like your mother makes a cake." Daddy Bob was striding up and down the living room now, not even bothering to stay on the strip of clear plastic that protected the carpet, and striking his hands together with each step. "Prayer and fasting and preparation. Especially preparation."

"Who's Mike?" Becky asked.

Daddy Bob scowled at her. "Nobody! Nobody important, that is," he amended hastily. "Just a young man who's working with me. I want him along when we clean up your classroom; it'll be good experience for him."

"Oh, Daddy Bob," Becky said, clasping her hands and looking up at him adoringly, "could you possibly do your miracle during my Language Arts class? That's fourth period, 1:17 to 1:42, except on Thursdays, because we have Peer Counseling then."

"Friday, then," he said. "That'll give me time to call the—I mean, to pray and gather strength for the next miracle. They will believe me yet," he muttered, "they will. How long, O Lord, how long? How many times do I have to show them?"

"Oh, goody!" Becky squealed. "Can I go call all my friends and tell them to be sure not to miss class on Friday?"

"You do that, Becky-beck," Daddy Bob said. "You just do that little thing."

So she got away with just a fatherly pat on the bottom and no more cuddling in the recliner.

Becky had only said that about calling her friends as an excuse to get away, but by the time she reached the top of the stairs she realized there was one person she really did want to forewarn about Friday's class.

The Old Town of Duke's Zolvorra was a winding maze of stone houses piled upon houses, with tunnels through the lower levels of houses leading to flights of spiraling stone stairs and narrow cobblestoned lanes. The houses tended to be divided into dark one-roomed apartments with only a slit of window for each section, and the residents tended to dispose of their household trash through the windows; which did not improve the cobbled lanes significantly.

After her height and her sheer raw ferocity as a fighter won Sikarouvvana a place in the Bronze Bra Guild and the training to use her size and muscles effectively, she had vowed never to return to the odorous mazes of Old Town. It was a vow she'd been able to keep for some years; the residents of Old Town mostly settled their differences among themselves, with knives and cudgels, and preferred not to invite the duke's personal guard into their quarrels.

But this, said the old hag who'd hobbled up to the duke's own hall and demanded aid, this was different. Foreign trouble, this was, and none of Old Town's making, and in the days of young Zolkir's da as was a proper duke them sort of hussies wouldn't never of been allowed to go disturbing the peace and ruining trade, but then what could you expect of a duke as went off hunting for pleasure when his own people in his own town of Zolvorra were in dire need, and—

"Hold your tongue, you horrible old woman," Sikarouvvana interrupted. "The duke's hunting is none of your business." She herself wasn't even supposed to know why Zolkir had left Duke's Zolvorra in such a hurry, with his house wizard and half the ducal guard; if she let the real reason slip to some jabbering old woman like this, half of Duke's Zolvorra would be in panic while the other half looted them. She sighed and waved Linnizyvvana over.

"Call out two hands of trainees, Linnizyvv," she ordered. "Whatever this fuss is, I suppose it'll be good practice for them. And you'd better come along. Kloreem, too." No use disturbing the whole fighting strength of the Guild for some minor disturbance in Old Town; on the other hand, Sika wasn't about to go down into that stinking labyrinth without a couple of experienced lieutenants to guard her back. A double-hand of trainees, plus Linnizyvv and Kloreem, seemed a reasonable compromise.

They could hear the noise from three wynds above the old Market Cross, where the crone had said the trouble started. Women's shrieks and hysterical laughter mingled with a low, troubled murmur like a hundred hives of bees swarming at once, or half a hundred husbands saying, "Now, dear, now, dear, don't take on so."

"Nauzu klevulkedimmu," Linnizyv grumbled. "I hate breaking up family fights."

"No family of ours!" the old wife who'd demanded their aid said. "Foreign trollops, that's what they be. Probably some wizardry of that there Rodograunnizo, stirring up trouble again."

They ducked to pass through a narrow, low tunnel that stank of slops and worse: dead cat, Sika decided, trying to breathe through her mouth and think of other things. The air at the end of the tunnel seemed rich and fresh by comparison. She straightened and took a deep breath. Something bright red hurtled towards her; reflexively Sika drew her shortsword. It slid through the crimson form as easily as through a tattered parchment. Frail arms clasped Sika's neck.

"Oh, have you come to save me? I am in sore distress—"

The slight touch of the thing's fingers sent chills through Sikarouvanna's body. But it withdrew almost at once, slipping off the blade of her shortsword like a wraith. "Why, you're only a girl!" it cried, stamping one foot and tossing its mane of raven curls. "Where's the Hero? He's supposed to appear by Chapter Two at the latest."

"We're being cheated," cried an auburn-haired beauty behind her. "I haven't had any scenes with my Hero yet! How can we develop a meaningful relationship, let alone a passionate sex scene in the first five chapters, if he's not even in this story?"

"I won't have it," declared a third wraithlike form. "I didn't flee my wicked uncle and the degenerate lord to whom he would have wed me just to stand around in this—this dunghole!" And she tossed her mane of silver-blond curls.

"We need our Hero," all three wraiths chorused. "Our lives are meaningless without a Hero. We demand a Hero!" Three tiny feet stamped in unison; three manes of raven, auburn, and silver-gilt curls flopped backwards and forwards; three sets of bosoms heaved beneath tight low-cut bodices. Behind them, a horde of similar figures pressed forward, shrieking their own claims.

"Now you just wait your turn!" cried the first raven-haired beauty, half turning to scream at the others. "I was here first, and I get the first Hero, or my name's not Kimberley de Kevin!"

"You're not even noble," shrilled the auburn-haired beauty. "I am Brigiditta, Queen of the Celts, and I take precedence over you in this matter of Heros!"

"Personally," cried Silver-Gilt, "I vow an honest English title such as mine own, Lady Sybilla Ravensthwaite, doth outrank any mere Irish claim!"

"You see?" muttered the old hag. "Now will you clear them out of here so we can have our market day?"

"Should be easy enough," Sika said. She had noticed something during all the twisting and turning that accompanied the altercation of the three feisty heroines. "Look, they may look real enough from the front, but they're all as thin as parchment. Cheap parchment," she added thoughtfully, "old and scraped down too many times. They should stack neatly enough." She grasped the raven-haired beauty by the waist and swung her parallel with the auburn-haired Queen of the Celts. "All cut from the same pattern, too," she commented as Kimberley de Kevin's upraised arm and tiny waist fitted perfectly against Brigiditta's arm and waist. "I bet we can stack them fifty deep in the duke's warehouses. You could have done this for yourselves; why did you have to call out the Guild over such a trivial matter?"

"Huh," said the old crone darkly. "Go ahead and try. There's a lot more where those came from, and it's not so easy keeping them in a stack."

"All in all," Sika said, rapidly capturing Lady Sybilla Ravensthwaite and adding her and three more beauties to the armload she held, "one of the easier manifestations I've had to contend with in the last couple of days. Put these in a corner, Kloreem. Linnizyvv, you organize the trainees and set them to catching and stacking."

"Didn't join the Guild to move furniture," one of the trainees muttered, but under Linnizyvvana's cold eye she joined the rest and moved forward in a line, hands outspread, catching parchment-thin heroines as they dashed and sobbed and stamped their feet.

"You can't treat Kimberley de Kevin like a common peasant!" screeched the raven-haired beauty, rising from her stack.

"Nauzu's fingernails," Sika said, "I should have put something on top to weight them down. Give me a rock, somebody."

Brigiditta, Queen of the Celts, and Lady Sybilla Ravensthwaite arose from the stack and darted around Sika, screaming, "Help! Help! Where is a Hero!"

"You see?" said the old woman. "Told you it wasn't so easy."

Sika caught Lady Sybilla by the wrist. "Back into your pile," she warned, "or I'll scrape you off and use you to write sheep-dip records on."

"No!" Sybilla shrieked, flopping in Sika's grasp. "Not that! No more editing! No more rewrites, please!"

"What is she talking about?" Kloreem demanded.

"Nauzu take me if I know," Sika said. "Better yet, Nauzu take all of these—these—"

"Hussies," the old woman suggested helpfully. "Trollops. Strumpets, trulls, baggages, doxies—"

"My Hero!" cried Brigiditta, Queen of the Celts.

"No, mine!" chorused the other wraiths, rising from the neat pile in which Sikarouvvana had stacked them.

"I am too delicately bred for this clamour," Lady Sybilla announced. "Obviously the Hero must rescue me, as I am in the greatest distress of all of you." She fainted, bending neatly at the waist until she flapped like a banner over Sikarouvvana's arm.

"Idiot," snapped Brigiditta. "She doesn't even know where to faint." The Queen of the Celts went limp and draped herself over the tall, dark, mud-spattered Hero who had come clomping through the wynd while Sika and her trainees tried to collect beauties.

"At last," breathed Kimberly de Kevin, plastering herself against the Hero's other arm. "You have come to set your seal of possession upon my lips!"

"Brand my soul with your burning kisses!" cried a second raven-haired beauty, this one in a green gown whose laced front looked in danger of giving way from the strain of her heaving bosom.

"Ravish my heart and honor!" pleaded a violet-eyed blonde in a wisp of lavender silk.

"Be these leddies for real?" Zido, the first horseman of Dozourdaunniko's farm, asked Sikarouvvana.

"Well . . . yes and no," Sika replied. "They certainly mean it. I gather they've been whining for a Hero ever since they appeared."

"Well," said Zido with a broad grin, "always happy to oblige. . . ." He clasped Kimberley de Kevin in one arm while reaching out for the tempting pink mounds displayed under the blonde's lavender silk negligee.

Kimberley crumpled.

Zido withdrew his hand from the blonde's chest and dropped Kimberley. She fluttered to the ground.

"They be flat as walls!" he said indignantly.

"And not quite as solid," Sikarouvvana agreed. "But they seem to like you."

Zido batted away swarms of advancing beauties. They whirled and shrieked in the air around him like demented, outsize bats.

"Help!" he cried, ducking under the onslaught.

"You seem to be doing admirably on your own. They didn't like me half so well." Sika restrained her chuckles with an effort. Linnizyvv and Kloreem were not so dignified; they leaned against a wall and laughed till the tears came, while the squadron of trainees backed well away from the action. One of them made occasional slashing motions with her sword until Linnizyv called, "Don't do that, Dypti! You'll only tear them!"

Zido grasped a double armful of feisty heroines and stepped on a half dozen others. "I didn't mean," he said with dignity, "help for me. I been sent by Farmer Dozourdaunnivo to request the duke's help in driving away a plague of dragons."

"Dragons?" Sika repeated. Her eyes lit. "Real dragons?"

"As real as these leddies," Zido said.

"Oh, well, parchment dragons—"

"Nay, 'tis more other way round," Zido interrupted her. "These here leddies look pretty but they'm not good for nothing, at least nothing you'd want to do with a woman, get me? Them dragons don't look right, but they do dragon stuff all right." He shuddered at the memory. "No proper flashing colors. No bejeweled eyes. Just horrible big white shapes with black stripes."

"What, all over?" Sika asked. "Like zebras?"

"What's a zebra?"

"A mythological beast. That means," she translated for Zido, "they don't really exist. At least nobody thinks so. But if these beasts of yours are striped black and white all over—"

"They aren't," Zido told her. "All white except for a little square shape on one flank. That's got stripes all different thicknesses, and numbers over the stripes."

"Ha! Mathemagical creations. What numbers?"

"Only ones as got close enough to read them," Zido said gloomily, "was a couple of bandits, and they can't tell you, less'n you want to raise their shades. See, these dragons, they may not look real, but they sure's

Nauzu Wept act real. Eating people and crunching bones and strewing the waste bits all over the courtyard, not that there's much goes to waste. We got an old herb-granny cooking up dragonbane ointment, but the supplies won't last forever. Besides, the stuff smells something ferocious. So my master says, Zido, he says, just you take the fastest horse in the stables and get along down south to warn the duke of this here plague of dragons."

"Dragons," Sika said with an edged smile. "You know, I don't believe I've ever slain a dragon. Except for those little poison-spitters in the Fyrkozoul Desert, and they hardly count; not much bigger than a horse." She glanced behind her at Kloreem and Linnizyvv. "What do you say, ladies? Want to give these trainees a chance at some real action?"

"Marching formation, ladies!" Kloreem called. "We'll double by the Guildhouse for supplies and arms," she suggested to Sikarouvvana.

"Good idea," Sika agreed. "Duke Zolkir's got this foolish prejudice against eating off the countryside. Says it annoys the peasants. Soft, he is."

"Waitaminute, waitaminute!" screeched the old woman who'd called for the Guild's aid. "You can't just march off and leave us with this—this—"

"Heap of hussies?" Kloreem suggested.

"Swarm of strumpets," Linnizyvv added helpfully. "Drove of doxies, troop of trollops—"

"Horde of Heroines," Sika said. "Don't worry. Zido here can help you stack and store them."

"Ma'am?"

"It'll be much easier for you than it was for us," Sika assured him. "They like you. Convenient. Ladies, right face, march!"

"Wait! Stop! You can't do this!" Zido cried as a new wave of Heroines appeared, demanding burning kisses and passionate embraces.

One of the trainees, last in the line of march, turned and blew a kiss at him.

Chapter $\sqrt{121}$

Becky was almost late for Language Arts on Friday, because the counselor hauled her out of Social Studies (which was no loss) and spent half an hour telling Becky that she understood how she felt and that it was good to talk about feelings. Becky didn't think Stinky Wits knew anything, and even if she did, she wouldn't do anything. Grownups never did. At best she'd get in trouble for making up dirty stories about Daddy Bob, at worst— Becky couldn't imagine worse than that, and she didn't want to find out. So she played dumb. It wasn't hard. She just went away in her mind. She was getting pretty good at that after three years of practice. Stinky Wits told her how hard it was for some girls to cope with early puberty, and Becky told herself that she wasn't in a school office but in a place of golden sands and blue skies, a place where evil looked like spotted purple monsters and the only coping anybody needed to do involved a nice long sword. Stinky Wits asked if the math teacher had done or said anything to upset her, and Becky stared out the window and imagined the purple monsters coming through it to spit acid on the counselor.

But the bell had already rung by the time she got out of the counselor's office, so she didn't have time to grab Jason in the hall. And Fishbeck made them enter her classroom and sit in alphabetical order, which meant that Becky (Boatright) didn't get a chance to ask Jason (Tibbs) if he'd remembered her phone call on Wednesday. Fortunately, the way the rows lined up meant that Jason's desk was just two seats behind Becky's. To communicate with him, she only had to pass a note by way of Emily (Hoover) and Orrin (Pilkinton). Fishbeck was handing back their written reports from the Folklore and Mythology unit and going on about proper composition structure; nothing that required attention or answers.

"Some of you followed the rules for compositions very well indeed," Fishbeck announced. "Emily Hoover's report is a model the rest of you would do well to emulate."

Emily was the kind of kid who wore dresses and always had her blond hair pulled back in a French braid. Her report had been a terminally dull list of Indian tribes with a snippet of information straight out of the *World Book Encyclopedia* on each tribe. In alphabetical order.

She smirked as Fishbeck handed back her report. Becky wrote, *Did you remember to stop taking your Ritalin?* and slipped the note under Emily's report for her to hand back to Jason.

"Orrin, you need to work on your spelling, but at least you followed the composition format," Fishbeck announced. "The rest of you need to review the basic rules of good writing. Remember that a composition has five paragraphs."

Emily slipped a folded note back to Becky. *Don't worry*, it said. *Everything's cool*.

Did that mean yes or no? Becky was so worried about it that she didn't realize Fishbeck was asking her a question.

"Very well, Becky, if you can't or won't answer, I'll call on somebody else to tell us the structure of a paragraph."

Emily Hoover's hand shot up. "A paragraph has five sentences!" she announced.

"What if you have more to say than twenty-five sentences?" Salla Konneva demanded.

Emily looked confused. "Who said anything about twenty-five?"

"Five paragraphs," Salla said patiently. "Five sentences. Twenty-five sentences, total. Some people have more to say about a topic than that. Those who have anything to say in the first place, that is."

Becky wriggled in her seat and gazed anxiously at the classroom door. The big clock above the door read 1:27. Ten minutes into the period, and her stepfather still hadn't shown up. Had he forgotten? Or changed his mind?

"Sally, I didn't see you raise your hand," Fishbeck reproved her, coyly wagging one finger. "But speaking of topics, can anybody tell me what the first sentence of a paragraph is?"

Emily Hoover's hand shot up again. "It's the topic sentence," she announced.

"Very good, Emily dear. I'm glad to see that at least some of you have been paying attention. Sally, your report was so poorly structured that you hardly deserve a grade at all." The large red "D–" scrawled across the front of Salla's paper was visible to the whole class as Fishbeck handed it back.

Salla's face turned red and she scowled at the paper. "What's wrong with the structure?"

"I'm sure you can read my comments," Fishbeck said, "since you love reading so much."

"Too many paragraphs," Salla read aloud, "ten points off. Too many sentences in each paragraph, ten points off. Citing references you haven't read, twenty—I have so read them!"

"Don't be silly, dear," Fishbeck said, "those books aren't even in our library. I checked. And I'm sure they are well above sixth-grade reading level."

"So," said Salla, "am I. And Austin has a very good public library system. Would you like me to tell you what else is in those reference books you say I haven't read? Go on, ask me a question about them! Ask me anything!"

Fishbeck's face turned as red as Salla's. "I hardly think that will be necessary," she said coldly.

Salla was half out of her seat. Becky scrunched down and tried to make herself invisible. Salla was going to get detention again. She didn't understand. It was no use fighting them; they always won. But Salla kept fighting anyway. Becky admired that. She might have given up for herself, but Salla's standing up to Fishbeck made Becky feel that somehow, some day, she might be able to fight back, too.

But she hated seeing Salla lose.

1:42. Twenty-five minutes, half the period over. He wasn't coming, and Salla was going to get detention for talking back to the teacher, and Jason was probably stuffed so full of Ritalin he didn't know what day it was, not that it mattered since nothing was going to happen after all. Becky slumped down in her seat and called up an inner picture of the secret world. She could go there in her head, striding the dusty tan streets and visiting square courtyards where women in bright armor didn't let anybody push them around, and at least she wouldn't have to witness Salla's humiliation.

"Go on," Salla insisted. She was standing up now. "You can't call somebody a liar and not give them a chance to defend themselves. It's—it's—"

"Unconstitutional," suggested Jason.

"Class! Quiet!" Fishbeck snapped. "The folklore and mythology unit is now finished. Please turn in your folklore readings collections. Pass them forward to the front row."

At last the door opened. Becky's stepfather walked in, followed by a sleek young man and some big kids from, like, high school or somewhere.

"Is this Language Arts for the Gifted and Talented group?" her stepfather demanded. "Oh, okay, there you are, Becky. You wouldn't believe how confusing this place is. Why didn't you tell me the room number?"

"Are you a parent?" Fishbeck asked. "I'm sorry, but we discourage interruptions during class. If you want to observe, you need to go to the office and register."

"I have already," Daddy Bob said, "observed more than enough."

"You can't stay without a visitor's badge."

"The law of God supersedes the laws of sinful man," Daddy Bob announced. "Children, stay in your seats. Everybody stay exactly where you are."

Two of the high school boys leaned against the door.

The handsome dark man with Daddy Bob murmured something. Becky strained her ears but could only catch disjointed phrases. "Easier . . . all in one stack . . . accuracy . . . distance . . ."

"Right," Daddy Bob said. "I want all those Satanistic books brought up to the teacher's desk."

"Huh?" said Orrin Pilkinton.

"I think," Becky said, "he means our folklore and mythology notebook binders with all the readings."

"But we were already passing them up," Orrin pointed out.

One of the big kids grinned. His teeth gleamed. So did his shaved skull. "Then keep doin' it, kid."

When the stack of binders covered Fishbeck's desk, Daddy Bob raised his hands in prayer. "Dear Lord Christ Jesus, these innocent lambs have been corrupted by filthy books. Please restore their innocence and remove the teachings of Satan from this classroom, as they should be removed from every place, by the grace of our Lord Jesus Christ, amen."

The dark man was moving his hands while Daddy Bob prayed. Becky could see something shiny in one hand. A gun? Then Fishbeck's desk was empty. You could even see the bare wood.

"Awesome, dude," breathed Orrin Pilkinton.

Emily Hoover screamed.

"Cool!" said somebody at the back of the room.

"Waaaaay cool," concurred somebody else.

Fishbeck's eyes rolled up in her head and she sagged towards the floor. One of the high school kids caught her before she hit the tiles. "Hey, lady, hey, lady, it's okay," he said.

"Children, remember the power of the Lord and

walk always in the ways of Christ Jesus," Daddy
Bob said. He rested one hand on Becky's head;
heavy, pressing down on her. *You owe me*, the
pressure said.

Becky tried not to think about that. She did owe
him. And he would collect. But he would've done that
anyway, so what difference did it make? And maybe,
just maybe, Jason had seen something.

While most of the kids were crowding around
Fishbeck and making suggestions for reviving her,
Daddy Bob and his friends marched out of the
classroom.

"Put a damp handkerchief on her forehead," Emily
Hoover said.

"So who has a handkerchief?"

"I do," Emily said, "and it's clean, too."

Becky sidled back to stand beside Jason. "Did you
stop taking your Ritalin?"

"Naah, you're supposed to burn something," somebody argued with Emily. "Feathers or like that."

"How about we burn the dumb reports?"

"We ought to get the school nurse," Emily Hoover
said. "I'm going for her right now."

Jason grinned. "I haven't been taking it for two years.
I told Mom it made me feel sick. It did, too," he
added.

"But every morning Fishbeck asks if you've taken
your medication."

"The doctor gave me some sugar pills. I take one
every morning. So then I can say yeah, I took my
medication. So she thinks I'm still on Ritalin. So if
I'm on Ritalin, I'm not hyperactive. So she puts on
my report card that the medication is really helping
me control my behavior."

Becky thought this over. "But if you're not taking it, what is helping you control your behavior?"

"Not wanting to take Ritalin again," Jason said tersely. "You wouldn't believe the headaches. Mom said as long as I stay out of trouble at school, I can stay on the sugar pills. So I'm like *motivated*."

"Take her shoes off and tickle her feet," Orrin Pilkinton suggested.

"So did you see anything?" Becky returned to the main point. "How did he do it? Is it really a miracle?"

A nurse, the assistant principal, and several counselors all tried to get through the classroom door at once. "What's going on here? What happened to Margaret Fishbeck? Is everybody all right?"

Erica Stankewitz's voice rose above the babble of adult questions. "These children have been severely traumatized. I must insist on counseling them at once."

Jason winked at Becky. "In other words, she wants to find out what really happened."

"So," said Becky, "do I. What did you see?"

"What makes you think I saw anything you didn't?"

"You notice everything when you're not on Ritalin," Becky said. "It worked before—I mean—"

Jason grinned. "Fourth grade. Careers Day. Field trip. Salla's mom called it Dazau, that place we went to, but everybody else said it must have been a theme park."

"It *did* happen." Becky had never been sure about that day when she'd found herself and the rest of Miss Chervill's fourth grade class in a place of sandy streets and tan-colored buildings and bright silks: a place where Salla's mom Riva turned into an Amazon warrior in glittering armor. By unspoken consent, none of the kids had talked much about that field trip, and over the years it had gradually become unreal to Becky: a secret world where she could go in her head when she didn't like the way Daddy Bob was touching her, but not a real place, a real experience. She was almost afraid to press Jason further. If Dazau was real, then anything was possible. Escape was possible. A whole different world was possible, and she could be in it. "You remember it, too?" she said at last. "Dazau?"

"Mom said if I talked about it they'd probably send me for counseling," Jason said.

"Yeah," Becky agreed. Besides, she didn't want to talk about it; not just yet. It would take some time to assimilate the glory of knowing Dazau was real before she started anything practical, like figuring out how to get there. "I can just see trying to explain to Stinky Wits about Dazau. Anyway. If it was real and you remember it, then so do I," she said firmly while inside her a joyful voice was crying, *It wasn't a dream! it wasn't a dream!* "And you forgot to take your meds that day and you saw how that wizard was giving the other guy a magic shield and you probably saved Salla's mom's life. Because you notice things. So what did you notice this time? Is it a real miracle or what? What's the trick?"

"Children! Back to your seats!" the principal shouted. "We'd better get in a substitute for the rest of the period," he said more quietly. "Can you take over for a few minutes, Ms. Stankewitz?"

"I need to counsel the children. They've been traumatized."

"The books just went poof," said a revived and tearful Ms. Fishbeck. "Into thin air. I saw them! I mean, I didn't see them, they weren't there anymore. . . ."

The principal and Erica Stankewitz exchanged looks over Fishbeck's head. "Maybe I'd better find somebody for the rest of the week," he said. "Semester. Whatever. Poor Ms. Fishbeck."

"Come and lie down," the nurse urged Fishbeck.

"Children," Stankewitz said as Fishbeck left, "it is important for you all to talk freely about what just happened. I know it must have been a very frightening experience, but you must be sure to separate reality from imagination. We all know that books cannot just vanish into thin air."

Emily Hoover nodded solemnly. Orrin Pilkinton's hand shot up. "Is Becky's father gonna go to jail for making the books disappear?"

"Nothing disappeared," Stankewitz snapped.

"So what did you see?" Becky pressed Jason.

"Becky Boatright, return to your seat, please!"

Jason winked. "Later," he promised. "I know the trick—some of it, anyway. Tell you later."

After she heard Jason's story, Salla insisted that he had to come home with her after school. "Sounds like Dazau magic to me. Mom has to do something to stop it. If somebody's found a way to make mathemagics work here, we could all be in trouble like you wouldn't believe."

Jason shrugged. "Okay with me if all they do is make textbooks disappear. Think we could get Becky's dad to visit our Social Sciences class next?"

"That is not," Salla said, "all he's up to. They disappeared all the science fiction at the Bookstop on Thirty-Eighth."

"What?"

"Don't you watch the news?" She turned to Becky. "Well, are you coming with us, or what?"

"I can't," said Becky. "I have to go home."

"Jason's supposed to go straight home too. He's gonna call from my house to let his mother know where he is."

Jason shrugged. "I may not even do that. Mom's finishing a book. As long as I'm home before dark, she'll never know the difference."

"He will," Becky said. "My stepfather. He'll be expecting me home."

"So call from my house. Come on, Becky. It's really your story. Your Quest," Salla added on a sudden inspiration. "We have to track down the evil wizard and take away his magic staff."

"You mean his Leibniz Personal Assistant," Jason corrected.

"How do you know what brand it is?"

"Leibniz puts that green band on the end of all their stuff. Didn't you see it?"

"Nope," Salla said. "That's what you're for—to notice the important details. Anyway, I bet it is a magic staff really. Come on, let's talk to Mom."

"I can't," Becky said. Her face settled into the doughy mask that made her look like a big dumb fat girl instead of a big strong smart kid. Salla hated that look. "He'll be waiting. Especially now."

"Why especially now?"

Becky didn't answer, just turned and plodded down the long treeless curve of Forest Brook Drive. Salla shrugged and turned the other way, down Babbling Brook Drive. "C'mon, Jase."

Riva's car stood in front of the house on Willow-brook, and the screen door was unlatched. Salla tossed her books on the sagging sofa in the living room and yelled, "Mom!"

"She's gotta be around somewhere," she said a moment later. "Let's look."

The search took them through the kitchen, where Salla flipped open the lid of the cookie bin and grabbed a handful of cookies without pausing. Jason followed her example.

"Ugh," Salla said indistinctly. "Whole wheat oatmeal raisin bran with carob chips. Mom's been to the health food store again." She swallowed with an inelegant gulp. "Oh, well, they'll do to sustain life in the weary Knights of the Leibniz until something better comes up. Mom! Where are you?"

"Knights of the Leibniz?"

"The Grail Knights were looking for a grail, right? We're looking for a Leibniz. And if you were going to say anything about girls not being knights—"

"Never crossed my mind," Jason said hastily.

"Mo-om!"

Salla cocked her head, listening. "I hear her in the backyard."

All Jason could hear was a dog panting in the late-September heat, but he followed Salla anyway.

The panting turned out to come from Salla's mother, who was wearing nothing but a very thin T-shirt and gray shorts, both soaked with sweat and clinging to her body. She was going through a complicated series of whirls, kicks and leaps, like some kind of ethnic dance or something.

"Mom, you shouldn't leave the door open when you're working out," Salla chided her. "Like anybody could walk in."

Riva came down from a particularly spectacular leap and leaned against the tree, gasping for breath. "Looks like anybody just did. I'm not through yet. Go have some cookies, I bought new ones today."

"I noticed," Salla said, making a disgusted face. "Mom, Jason and I have something to tell you. See, what happened in school today—"

"Later," Riva said. She did something with one hand on a branch of the tree that propelled her up and over the branch in a whirling arc, coming down on the hard-packed earth with a thud. "Nauzu klevul-kedimmu, but I'm out of shape. And I haven't even started the full-armor practice yet." Her eyes slid towards Jason, and Salla noticed the neatly stacked armor by the back steps.

"Don't worry about Jason," she said, "he remembers the field trip to Dazau. And no, he didn't decide it was just a dream. I think most of the other kids did, but not Jason. He notices things, you know."

"I know," Riva said, contorting herself into a pretzel and leaping out of it with a spring that carried her feet well above the tallest weeds in the unkempt lawn. "I owe you a debt of blood, Jason." She bent one leg and began rhythmically kicking out with the other.

"You may," Salla said grimly, "get a chance to pay it. There's a Dazau wizard loose in this reality."

"I know," Riva panted between kicks.

"With a magic staff," Salla said. "That works. Here."

Riva's supporting leg wobbled and she kicked the tree instead of the air between the branches. "Ow!" She stopped and looked straight at Jason for the first time. "How did you figure that out?"

"It's not a magic staff," Jason said. "It's a Leibniz. One of those palm-sized computers that costs like a fortune, you know? And I don't know how he programmed it to make things disappear—"

"Mathemagics," Riva and Salla said in unison.

"—but Mr. Boatright made a bunch of notebooks disappear out of our classroom today, and I noticed that he was real careful not to start praying until this other guy—"

"Mikhalleviko," Riva said.

"Whatever. Anyway, first he told Mr. Boatright that he could do it better if all the notebooks were in one stack—we weren't supposed to hear that," Jason said, "and then Mr. Boatright moved to one side so Mik—what you said—could get a clear shot of the books, and he was pointing his Leibniz at the books and pushing buttons while Mr. Boatright did his prayer number."

"A *disguised* magic staff," Riva said. "How fiendishly clever. No wonder Dennis couldn't figure out how he did it."

"Dennis wasn't there," Salla said, "this was Language Arts, not Math."

"Bookstop," Riva said absently, without explaining. "I wonder what his grimoire looks like. Well, that explains how he managed to use mathemagics in this world. He brought his staff with him. He's drawing on the magical power he stored in the other reality."

"So you gotta go take it away from him, Mom, before he disappears all the books in the world!"

"That'll take a while," Riva said. "Go have some cookies. I can't think when I'm working out. And I want to be in top condition before I take on Mikhalleviko." She pinched her middle and looked disgusted at the minuscule roll of fat that appeared. "We'll need Dennis, too. And I need to put you somewhere safe where he can't find you, Salla."

"Why? It's my Quest," Salla protested.

"Go eat some cookies." Riva turned and crouched

before the tree as if it were an enemy waiting to attack her. She grasped one branch and twirled herself around it. "Go away. I'll think about it later!"

When Salla and Jason went back inside, they found Becky sitting at the table, her mouth full of oatmeal cookies. "I thought you had to go home," Jason said.

"I did," Becky muttered indistinctly through the cookie crumbs.

"Those cookies aren't any good," Salla said.

"I noticed." Becky swallowed hard. "It doesn't matter. I don't care. Do you have any milk? I'm thirsty."

Salla poured a glass of milk. Becky drank it in two long gulps. "That's good," she said. "Mom won't buy anything but that thin blue stuff."

"Two percent?"

"Skim. Like she thinks if she keeps me on a total no-fat diet I'll get small and pretty."

"You're not fat," Salla said. "You're big."

"Yeah. Big girl. Big girl . . ." Becky wrapped her arms around herself and hunched over.

"What's the matter?"

"Nothing. I thought you wanted to go on a Quest. When do we start?"

Salla pulled out a chair and slumped down on the other side of the plastic-topped table. "I don't know," she admitted, tracing patterns with her finger on the shiny top of the table. The blurred lines shimmered and evaporated almost as fast as she could trace them. Mathemagical symbols, only they didn't work here. Not for her. They did for this wizard, but he had his own source of power. "I thought we'd ask Mom, but she's busy. I guess we could start by going back to your place."

"No."

"We have to find that guy who was with your stepfather. Wouldn't your house be the logical place to start?"

"It might," said Becky, "but I'm not going back there."

"Huh?"

"I'm not going home ever again. I can't. Are there any more cookies?"

"Becky, what happened?"

"Never mind. I'm not going back, okay? I told him so. I told him I was going to live with you. Can I?"

"Nauzu's Tears," Salla said. "You told your stepfather you were running away from home? And then you told him where you were going? Becky, did it occur to you that wasn't real smart?"

Becky picked up an oatmeal cookie crumb and stuck it on the end of her tongue. "It doesn't matter," she said. "I knew your folks wouldn't really let me stay here. I thought we could go on the Quest and I wouldn't be here, so your folks wouldn't be in any trouble, and he wouldn't find me."

Jason picked up a sponge and wiped the table clean. "Becky, it won't work. They get upset if you don't come home eventually. This is going to be hard enough without having your parents call the cops on us. Besides, we might need Mr. Boatright's cooperation to find that other guy."

"Mikhalleviko."

"Whatever. Look, why don't we all go over to your house and talk to Mr. Boatright—"

"*No*," Becky said.

"If we don't," Jason pointed out, "he'll just come here for you."

Becky hunched her shoulders and stared down at the table top. Salla felt something twisting inside her. She hated to see people cry. Becky wasn't crying. But it was worse, somehow, because she wasn't.

"He won't find her," she said. "I know what to do. Becky, I know a place you can stay and be safe and nobody will ever find you. But we gotta hurry. I don't know how long Mom will be working out."

"She just put her armor on," Jason reported.

"How do you know? You've got your back to the window."

"I heard the jingling noise. Just like before. Just like Dazau." Jason looked smug.

Salla peeked out the kitchen window. "Okay, good, she usually works about half an hour in full armor. We've got plenty of time. Come on. I need the computer to set up the transfer function to Dazau. And I'd better go with you, just to make sure you're all right. I'll have to diddle with the program to make it take two people instead of one; they should have made that an input parameter to begin with, but of course they didn't ask me. I'm not even supposed to know about it."

"You'd take me to Dazau?" Becky looked as if somebody had just offered her a free pass to Disneyland with unlimited rides.

"Three," Jason said.

"What?"

"You have to change the program to accept three people, not two." Jason pointed to himself.

"You don't need to come along."

"I want to. Anyway, this is an equal opportunity quest, right?"

Salla sighed and threw up her hands. "All right, but remember, the real Quest is here, not on Dazau."

"How's it work?" Jason asked a few minutes later, when the three of them were kneeling around a small leather-bound box attached to the computer by a tangle of wires. "What's this little knob do?"

Salla slapped his hand away. "Don't change the settings! You want to wind up in Outer Yark?"

"Don't know. What's Outer Yark like?"

"It's the reality wizards draw monsters from," Salla said. "At least, they're monsters when they appear in Dazau. I don't know what they're like when they're at home in Outer Yark, and I don't particularly want to find out." She sat in front of the computer and tapped in a series of numbers and code symbols. "They should never have hooked this thing up to the computer if they didn't want me to use it," she said over her shoulder. "That was Dennis's idea, putting all the mathematical equations into a program so Mom could use the system by just running a program instead of doing all the mathemagics by hand."

"I thought mathemagics didn't work in this world," Jason protested, "unless you've got, like, a magic Leibniz or something."

"Yeah," Salla said, typing with two fingers. "You have to draw power from somewhere. Dennis and Mom don't know I can get into this program. I guess he thought double-encrypting the program and putting it in a hidden file would keep me from noticing."

"Grownups," Jason said, "are really dumb about computers. Most of them don't even know how to get into the configuration files. What's your power source? Does mathemagics run on electricity?" He pointed at the yellow bar of the surge protector on the wall outlet.

"Of course not, dummy, or this reality would be lousy with magical effects! You have to have magical power.

Which only exists in the other reality. You're as dumb about mathemagics as my mom is about computers," Salla said scornfully. "She can't do anything unless it runs under Windows and all she has to do is point a mouse and click. Typical naïve user. There, I got the transfer menu. It's set to take whoever's in this chair. Can you guys sit on the arms?"

After a bit of squashing and rearranging and people's elbows getting into other people's eyes, they worked out an unsteady arrangement with Becky sitting in the chair, Salla perched on her knees, and Jason leaning over one arm with his feet on the swivel wheels.

"Here goes nothing," Salla muttered, and selected Option 1 (Fast Wizard Transfer).

The computer screen shimmered; the menu vanished, to be replaced by a swirl of colors and jagged lines which gradually translated into a narrow face with deep-set eyes and a long sharp nose.

"Three of you," Furo Fykrou said through the screen. "There'll be a surcharge for that."

"I think I'm going to throw up," Becky said.

The chair went soft and Salla's stomach leapt in protest. "Don't say that, okay?"

There was nothing under them then, and they fell in a tangled heap onto a stone floor. Furo Fykrou looked down at them with interest. "About my fee," he began.

"We're not staying," Salla said quickly. "Just this one. Jason and I have to get back, but Becky needs a place to stay for a little while."

"And how," Furo Fykrou asked with a smile that made Salla feel cold, "were you planning to pay the return fare?"

"My mom. . . ."

"Oh-oh," Jason murmured. "I think I just figured out where the mathemagical power was coming from. And it wasn't free. Was it?"

"Were you aware that by Dazau law, use of a wizard's powers without the means to pay his or her fees is considered major theft?"

"My mom will pay you!"

"She certainly will," Furo Fykrou agreed. "And until she does, you aren't going back. In fact, you aren't going anywhere. Dazau law permits me to keep the three of you as bodyservants until your outstanding debts are settled. I'm sure your mother will pay to get you back, if not the other two."

"Pay what?"

"Whatever I ask of her, dear child. Whatever I ask. Until we've negotiated the ransom terms," he said, still smiling, "you three may as well make yourselves useful around here. It's time I took on some new apprentices."

Chapter 20₆

As a matter of principle, Sika led her troop from the Bronze Bra Guild across country towards the northern farmsteads where dragons had been sighted, rather than taking the north road. One could be sure that Baron Rodo had spies along the north road, whereas he couldn't possibly be covering all the hills and fens and windswept moors and deep glens that lay between Duke's Zolvorra and the border. Even a wizardwatch could only observe one place at a time.

Her lieutenants were not entirely happy with this principle. "Why shouldn't Rodo the Revolting know we're on our way?" grumbled Linnizyvv after they had splashed through a particularly odoriferous bog.

"Use your head," Sika said patiently. "First he sent his bravos to intimidate the border farmers. Then when we drove away the bravos, he sent that wizardly mist, remember? Obviously the dragons are the next step in his attempt to take over the high farms. And if you don't mind," she said, "dragons are quite enough to fight without also having to deal with whatever Rodo might send as backup to the dragons."

193

"I think something died in this bog," Kloreem said.

"Recently?"

"Not recently enough."

"Breathe through your mouth," Sika advised.

"If Baron Rodo has a wizardwatch on this bog, will it pick up the smell as well as the sights?"

"No."

"Figures."

The trainees behind them picked their way in single file, trying to step on the more stable parts of the bog. Rhythmic squelching sounds announced their failure; there weren't any solid parts.

There were stingflies, though. Slapping sounds added a light counterpoint to the regular, slow squelching noises. A few curses floated out of the clouds of stingflies.

"Rather more inventive than one would have expected," Kloreem commented approvingly after one of the trainees invoked the curses of four of five minor deities, the bodily excrement of Nauzu, and the death by fybilka on all stingflies and their progeny. "This new bunch may shape up well."

"This new mob," said Sika, "grumbles too much. They've already been complaining that wizardly dragons should be fought by wizardly means, instead of by honest swords. That's the trouble with taking in recruits who're already grown women; you don't have the chance to toughen them up like you do raising apprentices."

"Rivakonneva started when she was nineteen. And she had a kid already."

"Riva," said Sika, "was exceptional. Besides, Vleenacottara was Arms Mistress then. Anybody would've toughened up under basic training with Vleena. I still say, to make good swordswomen out of average girls, you have to bring them up in the life. Sharrup, you lot!" she shouted to the mud-covered figures emerging from the bog. "Look at it as a training exercise, all right?"

"Dragons," said a disgruntled voice, "is one thing. What else that Rodo and his wizard may send on us is another story."

"She's got a point, Sika," said Kloreem. "We could use mathemagical backup."

"According to Zido," Sika pointed out, "these dragons eat bandits. None of the manifestations we've encountered so far are anywhere near solid enough to do physical damage."

"They could still be wizard-work. Sometimes wizards call monsters from Outer Yark."

"I never heard of white monsters with black stripes coming from Outer Yark."

"Exactly," said Kloreem, "so these are probably manifestations from the same wizard what called up all the other stuff we never heard of. Green mists and paper ladies and that singing metal tower Duke Rodo's got just over the border. Bet you a zolky they're part of the same lot."

"A whole zolky? It'd be stealing your money, girl. Anyway, even if they were manifestations, what would we do different? Duke Zolkir took his house wizard with him. Remember?"

"To reach Weariefauld and the other border farmsteads," Kloreem said, looking across the river before them and up at the line of rolling hills they would have to cross next, "we have to pass within a quartermarch of Furo Fykrou's tower."

Sika was also squinting at the horizon. Small stick-figures moved aimlessly about, barely visible against the windswept clouds. "If those are some of Rodo's spies," she muttered, "what are they thinking of to let themselves be skylined like that? And if they aren't Rodo's spies, what are they doing here? This land isn't good for anything, even grazing."

"You can say that again," one of the trainees agreed, shaking herself until bog mud flew in all directions.

Sika glanced down at the river. "Go wash yourselves. No, not there, idiots! Behind the trees, where those spies won't see you. I'm going to find out what they're up to."

Three clumps of bushes, a stream, and two trees later, Sika was within earshot of the mysterious strangers. If they were spies, they had to be the most inept ones she'd ever encountered, letting her get this close to them in country with so little cover. Either that, or they were exercising some fiendishly cunning plot of their own that involved letting her sneak up and then overpowering her with—what? From her inadequate cover behind a spiky motherthorn, Sika studied the strangers curiously. Their soft, stretchy clothes covered bodies equally soft and stretchy by the standards of the Bronze Bra Guild. One of them, the one who seemed to be the leader by the way the other two deferred to him, was downright pudgy. One of the others had funny-looking ears. None of them were armed, unless the black boxes on their belts were some kind of foreign weapon. Sika watched while one of them lifted his box to his lips and spoke to it. The demon inside, if there was a demon, didn't answer.

"I canna' raise the ship," he told the others.

"I have this funny feeling," the pudgy one said, "that the ship isn't here. I think we're on our own this time."

The one with the funny-looking ears frowned, brows drawing together in a sharp V. "That is not logical. The ship takes us wherever we go. Therefore the ship took us here. Therefore the ship is nearby."

"I sure hope so," said the pudgy one. "I don't feel quite real without my ship, you know what I mean?"

"She'll be comin' to get us," said the one who'd attempted to talk with a demon in a box. "I only hope the engines will stand the strain."

"Always worrying about your engines," snapped the pudgy one, "what about me? Do you have any idea how many movie sequels they've dragged me through by now? And I never get a chance for a nap, and the blondes never stay in the story. It's not fair."

Sika sighed and stood up. The motherthorn was a very uncomfortable hiding place. And clearly these poor lost souls were not working for the baron. "Are you manifestations?" she asked.

The one with the funny ears nodded slowly. "Now this," he said, "is entirely logical, predictable and reasonable. A blonde always shows up for him."

The pudgy one's eyes lit up. "On the other hand," he breathed, reaching out both hands towards Sika, "it is our mission to boldly go . . ."

Sika sidestepped him and hooked her heel behind his leg, bringing him down with hands still outstretched. "You're awfully solid for manifestations," she said. "Who sent you on this mission?"

The other two looked at each other.

"I dinna' know," said the one who talked funny,

"It just is," said the one with the pointed ears, "our mission. There's no reason for it. Wait a minute. That's not logical. There must be a reason for everything. What is the reason for our mission?" he appealed to the leader, who had made it up to his hands and knees and was catching his breath.

"How can you look at this lovely creature and ask a question like that?" the pudgy one panted. He stood up, brushing the mud from his stretchy garments. "We exist to explore, to learn, to seek out the new, to boldly go . . ."

"Are you lost?" Sika asked.

The two relatively sane ones agreed that yes, indeed, they were lost, while the pudgy one asked, "Are there any more at home like you?"

Sika put two fingers in her mouth and whistled. A moment later, Linnizyvv jogged into view, followed by a double file of dripping-wet trainees.

"I think I've died and gone to heaven," the pudgy man murmured.

"Linnizyvv, detail two trainees to escort these manifestations back to Duke's Zolvorra," Sika said.

"Oh, can't we come with you ladies?"

The last thing Sika wanted was a bunch of manifestations getting in the way while her soldiers disposed of the mysterious white dragons.

"You will be much happier in the city," she told them firmly. "There are, er, more of your sort of people there."

"Oh, but—"

"Including," Sika said, "many beautiful women."

The pudgy man tried to square his shoulders. "Well, then. I suppose it's our duty to investigate. Lead on!"

After the strangers had been dispatched, Sika fumbled in her pouch and tossed Kloreem a gold zolky. "You win. Manifestations can be solid enough to hit the ground with a thump." She tried not to think about what this implied about the trouble the duke had gone

off to settle. All that sand . . . if it was real, the
smothering tons of it overlying what had been a fertile
river valley . . . Well, it didn't have to be solid, did
it? Some manifestations were misty, some were thicker.
She'd just have to hope that Duke Zolkir wasn't trying
to shift real sand. And there was no point in mentioning all this to Kloreem and Linnizyvv. Just get the
trainees all upset about something they couldn't do
anything about. And neither could she. "Therefore,"
Sika said after a pause and a gulp when she thought
about all that sand, "therefore, the dragons could also
be manifestations. Therefore, we will consult with Furo
Fykrou on our way to Weariefauld. Not," she emphasized with a scowl at the trainees, "because of this
lot's eternal grumbling and moaning. Only because it
is the logical thing to do."

"You're beginning to talk like that one with the funny
ears," said Kloreem.

After all the unpredictable and mildly insane manifestations she'd encountered recently, Sika found the
commonplace atmosphere of a wizard's tower quite
restful. Furo Fykrou was a traditionalist in matters of
decor; the collection of small monster skulls and horns
that ornamented the top shelves of his tower sanctum
looked exactly like those in the duke's wizard's chamber.
Those delicate white bones, and the bottles of herbs
steeped in oil, brought back comforting memories of
being taken to the old duke's house wizard to have
her bad tooth fixed up after she won a place as a
Bronze Bra Guild apprentice. The thick mathemagical
texts piled higgledy-piggledy on the lower shelves
reminded Sika of lazy, hot afternoons in the Guild
lecture room, yawning through the compulsory talks

on elementary mathemagics and monster-fighting strategies. Afterwards, there was usually a practical demonstration, a chance to show one's sword skills on a small monster brought from Outer Yark for educational purposes, but only the girls who sat through the whole lecture with their eyes open were allowed to throw dice for a chance to dispatch the monster.

"Of course, if the matrix of transformation is inverted, the beings involved will be horribly distorted and possibly nonviable upon arrival," Furo Fykrou said.

Sika nodded as if she understood what he was saying. She felt truly grateful for what she'd learned during those compulsory Guildhall lectures. True, not a single mathemagical equation had stuck in her thick head, nor had anybody really expected that. The wizard hired for the lectures always began by announcing that anybody with true mathemagical talent belonged in the Wizards' Guild, not in a bronze-bra job, and that he didn't expect any of the current crop of apprentices to understand anything he had to say. Sika and most of her friends took this as license to turn off their brains during the lectures.

"You want to be careful about your reducing terms, too," Furo Fykrou was saying now. "Of course you know what happens if the divisor is zero. That's basic Al-Jibber."

Sika nodded and hoped he wouldn't demand that she produce the answer on her own.

"Disaster," Furo Fykrou said with relish. "The equation isn't solvable in our mathemagical reality, so it transforms the text and possibly the wizard himself into a mathemagical reality where it is possible to divide by zero."

"Oh, really? That must be quite . . . upsetting."

"I wouldn't know," Furo Fykrou said with a smirk. "It's never happened to me, of course."

"Of course."

"But then, I've specialized in Al-Jibber and K'al-Kul. The real trouble starts when you get some of your herb-grannies who know a few catchwords from Jomtrie thinking they're qualified to handle higher mathemagics."

Sika nodded again. The one thing she had learned to perfection from Guildhall lectures was the art of simulating wide-eyed attention to a wizard's discourse while her mind drifted lazily off on its own currents. And that came in quite handy when one was seated on the cushioned benches in Furo Fykrou's sanctum, being told everything the wizard knew or thought or guessed about manifestations while waiting for his apprentice to bring in the sweetea and small cakes he'd offered them.

The trainees, of course, were outside, squatting on the shady side of the tower and washing down their marching rations with buckets of good cold water from the wizard's well. Lucky trainees. Sika wished she were out there, cracking jokes and polishing her gear and waiting for a nice straightforward fight, instead of being polite indoors while she waited for Furo Fykrou to come to the point.

"So you see," Furo Fykrou said, "whether manifestations, monsters, or natural deformities, once these dragons have acquired a full three dimensions in this reality—if not more—then they naturally become a task for warriors rather than for wizards. A case where the sword is, for once, mightier than the pen—ha, ha!"

Sika laughed too, for once without forcing it. Wasn't

it just like these scholars to fantasize a battle in which they opposed swordswomen with their fragile quill pens?

"Even if the dragons were still at Weariefauld, therefore, I could be of no help to you whatsoever." Furo Fykrou nodded firmly. "The problem is squarely in the practical realm now."

"What?" Sika leapt to her feet. "They're not at Weariefauld?"

"Why, no. It seems Granny Beerdouvou's potion was indeed remarkably effective. Of course, she had the simple wisdom of the people—she stuck to herbal remedies and did not dabble in mathemagical formulae which she wouldn't have understood anyway. In any case, the dragonsbane ointment served its purpose. After the dragons had polished off the remains of the bandits, they lingered for a day or two in the hope that some member of the household would forget to apply the ointment. At least, one supposes they were hoping that. One cannot really be sure what goes on in the minds of beasts. They snuffled together this morning, presumably taking counsel in their own way, and then moved off down the north road towards Duke's Zolvorra. If only you'd marched that way, you would have encountered them by now."

"Why didn't you tell me this at first?"

Furo Fykrou smiled. "Dear girl, you did not ask me where the dragons were. You asked whether they could be manifestations like the ones that appeared in the city, and whether I could help you to deal with them. One should always be careful to ask a wizard precisely what one wishes to know. And besides," he added, "I really did not expect my apprentices to be so long in making the tea. I can't think what can be keeping them."

"If that's your apprentice," said Linnizyvv, pointing towards a dark loft at the far end of the sanctum, "she hasn't been doing anything about tea. She's been reading all the time we've been here."

Furo Fykrou waved his hand dismissively. "One of my more advanced apprentices. A man of my standing has many servants. Another one is bringing the tea."

There was a crash from the stairs. A young voice cried out in dismay. Furo Fykrou opened the door to the stairs and looked down unhappily. "Was bringing the tea," he corrected his statement. "Boy! Clear up this mess and start another pot of sweetea brewing. And you, girl, stay here where you can't do any more damage. Just sit on the steps and stay out of trouble. You're completely worthless for the simplest tasks."

"That kid in the loft reminds me of Riva when she was young," Kloreem said as the wizard slammed the door on the other apprentices. "Maybe you're right, Sika. We should be bringing in more young girls for early training. I wonder how she'd be with a sword?"

"She is already apprenticed," Furo Fykrou said. "To me."

"Never mind the wizard's apprentice," Sika snapped. "Kloreem, Linnizyvv, tell the trainees to stand to. Gracious Wizard, I am afraid we will not be able to stay for tea after all. Many thanks for your hospitality, and—how far did you say the dragons had gone?"

"I didn't say." Furo Fykrou smiled and shook out his long sleeves. "There will be a small fee for that and any additional information."

Sika held out her belt pouch and jingled it. "Fresh-minted zolkys, never clipped. But only if you tell us something useful."

"Twenty zolkys and I'll give you their longitude, latitude, heading and astromagical signs."

"Too much. We can just follow their trail down the north road."

"Ah, but what if they've turned off the road?"

Sika hesitated. "Ten zolkys. I'm not authorized to pay more than that for a single transaction without the duke's seal on it."

"Make it twenty," Furo Fykrou said, "and record it as two separate transactions."

"I do not cheat my duke!"

"All right, all right. We'll make it two separate transactions. Ten zolkys for information, and ten zolkys for an apprentice released from me to your Guild."

Sika's glance flickered up to the dark-haired, leggy girl child in the loft. Damn it, she did have a look of the young Rivakonneva. There was promise there. If the Duke didn't agree, the Guildhouse would cover the fee. "It's a bargain."

So far, being a wizard's captive hadn't been anything like Jason had expected. Where were the dismal dungeons, the bats, the creaking stairs, the ghosts, the manacles, the mysterious riddling messages whose answers would lead them to escape and success?

Well, all right. The riddles were there. But they reminded Jason more of the TAAS tests than of anything in the Defenders of Doom game trilogy. Furo Fykrou's very first move had been to set all three children to do something he called a Normalized M.E.T. At first the illuminated borders on the papers amused Jason, with their complex tracery of impossible beasts and flowers. But when he'd finished admiring the decoration, the questions inside the borders were just—dull. Dull and, for the most part, meaningless.

"The algebra part isn't so bad," he whispered to Salla, "but the rest of the questions don't make any sense at all."

Becky Boatright wiped her brow. "Since when does algebra make any sense?"

"*No talking,*" said the three-headed bronze statue the wizard had left to watch them.

Jason shrugged and went back to the Normalized M.E.T. He'd zipped through the straight math and was now struggling with the section headed, "Para-Comprehension and Listening Spells." There was a paragraph out of a fairy story or something, all about how a dragon had helped Nauzu solve three riddles. But the answers to the riddles weren't in the paragraph, and he was expected to somehow guess them and write them underneath the text. "I don't see what this has to do with reading comprehension," he muttered. "I read at ninth-grade level. But that doesn't help if the answers aren't there."

Something hissed on Salla's side of the table. Startled, Jason looked up and blinked. A real little dragon, shimmering with blue and green scales, was sitting on her paper. She was alternately scribbling and looking into the dragon's eyes as if she were reading the answers there.

"*You have been warned. No talking,*" said the middle of the three bronze heads. A mist descended between Jason and Salla. When he twisted his head to the right to look at Becky, there was only more mist.

He sighed and discarded the sheet of riddles to concentrate on one headed, "Elementary Mathemagical

Transformations," but could make no sense out of this, either.

"Using a system of three to ten vectors, construct a subspace and place in it as many of the provided beings as you can locate without dimensional overlapping. N.B.: Extra credits will be given for maintaining metric relationships in the subspace transform."

"Subspaces is linear algebra," Jason muttered. "I haven't had that yet. And . . . what beings? I don't get it." He glared balefully at the illuminated border with its tangle of legged snakes, winged hares, and other monstrosities until the mist lifted as suddenly as it had descended.

"Did you get any of that, Becky?" he asked.

The papers slipped to the center of the table and arrayed themselves in a neat stack with Salla's uppermost. Jason noticed that the painted border around her last page was oddly faded. It looked as if somebody had erased all the pictures of mythical animals, leaving only the supporting framework of vines and curlicues.

"What happened to your paper?" he demanded.

This time the brazen heads didn't object. Jason guessed the test was over.

"I transformed the beasts into a subspace, like it said," Salla answered.

"But I notice," said Furo Fykrou, leafing through the papers, "that you failed to maintain metric relationships."

Salla blushed. "I haven't had linear algebra yet."

"No matter, no matter. Considering your poor preparation, being raised in that backwater reality of the Paper-Pushers, you've done very well indeed, my child. Indeed, I could expect no less of Rivakonneva's daughter. You have some weaknesses in pure mathemagics, but your M.E.Q. is quite satisfactory." The wizard's smile faded as he looked rapidly through the remaining papers. "Mathemagics—WNL," he murmured at Jason's work. "M.E.Q., too low to measure with this instrument." Becky's paper came in for even more disparaging comments. "No mathemagical ability whatsoever, and severely magic-challenged."

"What's WNL?"

"Within normal limits," the wizard said.

"I'm very good at math," Jason said.

"You made three errors in the simple algebra section."

"I can fix those. I just wasn't paying attention."

"A wizard who is not paying attention," Furo Fykrou said sternly, "may be consumed by the forces he would control. You omitted the infinity sign in this summation; a small error here, but the same mistake in a Furry R transform would send your object to Outer Yark instead of to the reality of your choice."

"Oh. Well, what's an M.E.Q.?"

"Magical Eptitude Quotient, of course. Rivakonneva's," the wizard said wistfully, "was very high, but some idiot lied to her about it when she was a girl, so she never studied seriously. And of course, without higher mathemagics, you can't do much no matter how much native magical eptitude you may have. . . . Not that it matters to you two," he finished, scowling at Jason and Becky. "Neither one of you has any potential for wizard's work. If I were responsible for your schooling, I'd recommend that your parents enroll you in one of the less challenging guilds immediately— Street Sweepers', perhaps. As it is, you'll have to make yourselves useful with some menial tasks until ransomed. Sallakonneva here will come up to my sanctum for special studies. If she's not ransomed, I may be able to train her into quite an able assistant. What I'll do with you other two, I really don't know."

"Wait a minute, waitaminute!" Jason grabbed Salla's hand. "You can't separate us. Besides, it isn't fair. You can't vocational-track us on the basis of a single test. We don't have the cultural context. We don't know how to take this kind of test. We—"

"The Normalized Magical Eptitude Test is a bias-free instrument which automagically corrects for deficiencies in your previous education," Furo Fykrou said. "You can start by cleaning up the kitchen. Come, Sallakonneva. You have some remedial reading to do, to make up for all that time you wasted in the Paper-Pushers' universe."

The kitchen was huge, dark, cold, and filthy. Small dark insects scattered into its shadowy corners when Jason and Becky came down the stone steps; something larger, with green eyes, hunched protectively over a pool of congealed fat and rattled its tail claws in a warning manner when they came closer.

"I don't like this," Jason said.

"I don't like it either," said Becky. "Where's that broom?" She reversed the twig broom and swung the handle low over the floor, catching the large bug square between its diamond-shaped green eyes. The rattling sound rose to a fast, furious patter, then stopped abruptly. Becky turned the broom around, wiped the handle with a greasy rag she found hanging from a hook on the wall, and swept the remains of the bug towards the door at the far end of the kitchen.

On the other side of the yard was a crazy-paved courtyard with weeds growing through the grass. A small pool in the center of the courtyard was crowned by a fountain that burbled and chuckled merrily to itself.

"Good," Becky said with satisfaction. "Water."

"Now if it was hot, and we had soap, we could get somewhere with this mess. If we wanted to," Jason grumbled.

Furo Fykrou leaned over a balcony, three teetering stories above their heads, and called out, "Let $\xi = t(\beta) + (1-t)\alpha_m$!"

The fountain's tune changed slightly. Steam rose from the surface of the water, and a white froth of soap bubbles appeared.

"Hey!" Jason called up to the balcony. "If you can do that, why can't you clean the kitchen by magic?"

"You two need something to do while I instruct Sallakonneva in the Great Science," the wizard called back.

"As if we couldn't think of something better to do than scrubbing a filthy kitchen," Jason grumbled. "I've a good mind to run away."

"I suspect he's thought of that," Becky said. "They always do. We'd better do what he wants or he'll get mad. Stack up those dishes and help me carry them out to the fountain, okay?"

"So who cares if he gets mad? It's not the end of the world." But Jason helped Becky wash the dishes anyway. After all, one didn't know exactly what a wizard might do when he got mad. And it was only for a couple of hours, right? Just until Salla's mom got the ransom note and came for them.

He wondered uneasily just how much Furo Fykrou was asking for them. Perhaps he'd better go upstairs and explain that writers didn't make very much money, especially if they'd rather write science fiction than romances. His mom might have to write a whole extra romance novel just to pay the ransom. She wouldn't like that. Better not get any more grownups mad at him just now. Jason put his worried energy to use in helping Becky to carry in buckets of hot soapy water and mopping the immense kitchen floor. And he only grumbled once or twice that the wizard could just as well have magicked up hot and cold running water right there in the kitchen.

They were just rinsing the soap off the floor when Furo Fykrou's face appeared inside a glowing bubble of light over the stove. "Sweetea and cakes," he said. "For four. Myself and three guests. You'll find supplies in the pantry and the good china on the top shelves."

The pantry, which had contained nothing but boring sacks of grain and dried vegetables last time they looked, now held a glass jar of dried leaves and a basket of sweet-smelling pastries. "About time," Jason said. "I'm starving."

He took a huge bite out of one of the pastries. Flaky crust crumbled all around him.

"My clean floor!" Becky cried.

"Master, master!" the pastry shrilled.

The glowing bubble reappeared. "Upstairs. Now," said Furo Fykrou's scowling face.

"The tea's not made," Becky said. "We don't have any way to heat the water."

The wizard reeled off another long string of algebraic formulae. "Fill the teapot from the fountain," he said. "It is now hot."

"And soapy?"

"And not soapy. If you had any mathemagical

eptitude whatsoever, you would have noticed that I changed the last term of the equation."

"I'll take the pot of sweetea," Jason said when they had tested the truth of Furo Fykrou's assertion. "It's heavier."

Becky looked down at him. "I'm stronger. But you better take it anyway, I don't trust you with the pastries."

"What's the matter," Jason grumbled as they hiked up the narrow, twisting stairs to the wizard's sanctum, "do you want to please this guy?"

Becky's shoulders slumped fractionally. "There's no way out," she mumbled. "There never is. You always wind up doing what they want."

"Not necessarily," said Jason. "Haven't you learned to work around your parents any better than that by now?"

"No!" Becky almost shouted. "And I don't want to talk about it."

"Okay, okay, this isn't about your parents anyway. But think. He made us kitchen drudges because his dumb tests showed we didn't have any talent for magic, right?"

"So?"

"So I, personally," Jason said, "don't have any talent for kitchen drudgery, either. My mom's always complaining that men do a lousy job of household chores so nobody will ever ask them to do any. Maybe it works here, too." And just as they arrived at the door to the tower room, he dropped the tray with the pot of steaming sweetea. The hot liquid splashed up between them, steaming and weeping, "Master, master, they're wasting me!"

Becky gasped and dropped her platter of pastries in the middle of the steaming puddle.

The door flew open.

And after all that, Jason didn't even get out of doing the work over again. You'd think the old guy knew he'd done it on purpose. Becky got to sit on the steps and rest; he had to go down to the kitchen for water and a mop to clean up the mess they'd made. Becky got to stay on the steps, eavesdropping on the conversation inside; he had to go back down to the kitchen and prepare another tray of tea and cakes. This time, to save trips, he crowded everything onto one tray. It didn't make the task of lugging the stuff up to the top of the tower much easier: the tray was so heavy that he had to put it down and rest after every three or four stairs. At least he was building muscles. Maybe he'd do better in P.E. when he got back home.

If he got back home. It sure was taking Salla's mother a long time to get together the ransom.

By the time he made it up the stairs again, Becky was nowhere to be seen. She must have been invited into the sanctum with Salla, to loll around reading magic books while he did all the work. His plan of demonstrating serious incompetence had worked, all right—only it got her out of the kitchen, not him.

It wasn't fair.

And after all that, the wizard just opened the door a crack and told him he was too late, the visitors had just left. "Take that stuff back to the kitchen, I never eat in midafternoon. And start polishing the fireplace brasses."

Jason would have been perfectly happy to eat in midafternoon or any other time, but the pastries squeaked in protest when he merely pinched off a crumb of crust that was about to fall off anyway. He checked the pantry hopefully, in case Furo Fykrou had magically supplied a snack. A couple of hamburgers and a large order of onion rings would just do to sustain him until dinner.

Fat chance. There was nothing in the magic pantry now but the same old jars and sacks and strings of unidentifiable, unappetizing dried stuff. And a pile of rags and a bowl full of something which Jason deduced to be brass polish.

"I won't do it," he said aloud. "I'm gonna explore instead."

The trouble was, there wasn't very much to explore. When he pushed on the door to the tower stairs, it refused to move; apparently Furo Fykrou didn't intend to let him out of the kitchen until he was wanted to carry something upstairs again. The other door, the one leading into the miserable little courtyard, was still open. But there wasn't much to do out there. The walls were too high and too slippery with moss for Jason to climb. The fountain, probably exhausted from all the magic it had done, was reduced to a morose burble that barely stirred the water in the pool. For a while Jason amused himself by floating twigs round in the slowly moving water, but that was a kids' game.

Finally, in extreme boredom, and after checking every shelf in the kitchen for something interesting to eat, he took the fireplace brasses out by the fountain and began polishing them.

The sun was sinking behind the high walls of the courtyard when the glowing bubble appeared again and Furo Fykrou commanded him to come upstairs.

"What do you want me to bring this time?" Jason asked wearily.

"Nothing. Just yourself. Which is, now I think of it, almost the same thing."

Jason was not particularly surprised when the door to the stairs swung open without a touch of his hand. This place was obviously lousy with magic. But what fun was it, when all the magic belonged to somebody with a personality like Ms. Fishbreath?

Salla was curled up on a cushion at the edge of the loft, arms wrapped around her knees. She was scowling. The wizard, by contrast, was wreathed in smiles.

"You will doubtless be relieved to hear that I've concluded my negotiations with Rivakonneva. She has promised to meet my demands in full, and in person, within the hour. As soon as the ransom is delivered, I shall return Salla to that strange reality where Riva chose to have her reared. And since I am a generous man, you may go with her, boy. You're not worth anything to me anyway. For now, though, I wish you two to get out of sight. Wouldn't do to let Riva get her hands on you before I have my payment properly bonded, would it now?"

"What about Becky? Where is she?"

"Go on, now, go on." Furo Fykrou made flapping motions with his wide sleeves. "Shoo!"

"Not without Becky."

"GO!" shouted the wizard. "Let $\lambda = \sum_{i=1}^{n} a_i$!"

A fiery wind pushed Jason up the stairs to the loft where Salla was crouched. The back wall opened and he fell into a dark, musty space. A moment later Salla fell on top of him and the wall slammed shut, leaving them in darkness.

"Salla?" Jason whispered when he had caught his breath. "What did he do with Becky? Did he, like, turn her into a frog or something?"

"Worse." Salla sounded as though she were trying very hard not to cry. "He sold her. They thought they were buying my contract from him, but at the last minute he produced Becky and said an apprentice is an apprentice and he never specified which one they were going to get."

"Well, then," Jason said, trying for his part to sound perfectly confident, "as soon as your mom gets here and pays the ransom, she'll have to help us get Becky back."

"She won't be able to," Salla said. This time a sob broke through. "My mom is the ransom. Now that she's learned mathemagics, Furo Fykrou wants her to work for him. Forever!"

Chapter $\left|\lim_{x \to 3}(x^3 - 5x^2 + 2x - 1)\right|$

Dennis missed all the excitement in Ms. Fishbeck's fourth-period English class. Fourth period was his class preparation time, and normally he spent it working out some complex algebraic riddles for the eighth-grade Gifted and Talented math groups that came to him during fifth and sixth periods. On this Friday, however, his preparation period was interrupted by a summons to the counselor's office.

Erica Stankewitz was sitting at the head of the long table in her office, flanked by the principal and the assistant principal. Before Dennis could ask what she wanted, she launched into an obviously prepared speech.

"We thought it would be best to give you a chance to explain yourself in private," she said. "Cushman Middle School does not want a scandal."

"Neither do I," Dennis said. "What—"

"It would probably be best if you resigned," Ms. Stankewitz interrupted him.

"What are you talking about?"

"There have been Complaints," Ms. Stankewitz said in a grave voice.

The principal shifted uneasily in her chair. "Is it

217

necessary to go into that? We have grounds for dismissal without bringing up, um, controversial matters."

Dennis cleared his throat. "Excuse me. I don't think you have any grounds for firing me. Anyway, you can't do it this way. I'm entitled to a hearing and—"

"Even if you don't mind having your name dragged through the mud," the principal interrupted, "Cushman Middle School doesn't need this kind of publicity."

"What kind of publicity?" Dennis nearly shouted. "Will you for God's sake tell me what you're talking about?"

"We've had Parent Complaints." Erica Stankewitz flipped open the manila folder in front of her and handed Dennis a pamphlet. The title read, "Is HUMANISM ABUSING YOUR CHILD?" in red capitals, and scribbled above the title were the words, "Dennis Withrow is a Satanic abuser."

"Oh, for—" Dennis shook his head. "Let me guess. Bob Boatright."

"I find it interesting," said Ms. Stankewitz to the other two women, "that Mr. Withrow could identify his accuser so readily."

They nodded.

"Of course I can guess who it is," Dennis said. "We had a run-in at Bookstop the other day. He said then he was going to get me. Besides, who else in town peddles this kind of garbage?" He tossed the pamphlet back to Erica Stankewitz.

"Cushman Middle School does not take allegations of child abuse lightly."

"Have you read the pamphlet?" Dennis hadn't, but he had scanned the opening paragraphs when Erica handed it to him. "It's not about child abuse—not in any real sense. They're claiming that anybody who doesn't go along with their fundamentalist religion is an evil person who is probably teaching the kids bad things."

"I have just counseled Becky Boatright," Erica said. "She was afraid to tell me anything about you—"

"There wasn't," Dennis said between tight lips, "anything to tell."

"—but it was clear she'd been traumatized," Erica continued as though Dennis had not spoken. "Shame, guilt, fear of adults, silence, pathological apprehension of giving away some ugly secret. And she's been cutting her arms. Self-mutilation is part of the classic syndrome."

"There is something wrong there," Dennis agreed. "I've been concerned about her for some time."

"Worried that she would tell on you!" Erica leapt on his words like a cat pouncing on a lizard.

"That's not what I meant, dammit!"

"How did you terrorize her into silence?"

"I didn't! And there wasn't anything to be silent about."

"She's visited your home."

Dennis sighed. "Yes. She's one of my daughter's classmates, you know. A lot of Salla's friends come over after school." It probably would not be a good idea to mention that Becky Boatright tended to hang around their house as much as she could, lingering until a phone call from one of her parents yanked her away. It was usually, now that he thought of it, Bob Boatright who called.

"Listen, if you think somebody's abusing her, you ought to take a look at the Reverend Bob."

"Wild accusations will not help your position."

"I think," Dennis said, "I want my lawyer. Maybe he can talk some sense into you people."

"This is not a formal hearing," the principal said. "You're not entitled to bring in anybody from outside the school."

"But you're entitled to sit there and insult me on the basis of a crazy preacher's pamphlet that you can't even read accurately?" Dennis took a deep breath, knowing he was about to say things he'd regret later. But before he could start, the assistant principal jumped up and opened the door to the hall.

"No running in the hall!" she snapped at the child who skidded in through the open doorway.

The kid came to a halt and smoothed down her neat blond braids. "Where's the nurse? Ms. Fishbeck's fainted. And they're trying to revive her with burnt feathers, and the men went away, but so did all the books, and——"

"Intruders," said the assistant principal. "I'll call the police."

"Get the nurse."

"Trauma!" Erica Stankewitz's face brightened. "The children are traumatized. I will counsel them!"

She and the assistant principal trotted out of the office, leaving Dennis facing the principal.

"I'm not going to quit because your tame psychologist got a bee in her bonnet, you know," Dennis said to the principal. "Now that I think about it, the Boatright kid does have some problems, and it probably would be a good idea to check it out. But whatever her problems are, they're nothing to do with me."

"We can't let a suspected child molester go on teaching here," the principal said. "I'm thinking of the good of the school. It doesn't matter whether it's true or not."

"It matters a hell of a lot to me," Dennis said, "and I have a legal right to a full hearing."

The principal picked up the manila folder that Erica Stankewitz had been holding.

"I didn't want to do this," she said, "but you're forcing me to it. You have no legal right to be teaching here at all. The Reverend Boatright did not just send that pamphlet; he also suggested that we should look into your teaching credentials. It appears that you are not qualified to teach here or in any other Texas public school. You don't have an education degree."

"Of course not," Dennis said. "I have a mathematics degree, which in my opinion is a lot more relevant to the business of teaching math. And I got an emergency teaching credential ten years ago, when there was that shortage of teachers."

"Conditional," the principal said, "on your completing forty semester-hours of education classes. I see no record that you ever fulfilled that condition."

Dennis sighed. "I've been meaning to get around to it."

"For ten years?"

"Okay, okay. I'll sign up for something next semester."

"Not good enough," the principal said. "Especially considering—"

"If you're trying to fire me because you think that idiot Boatright accused me of molesting his daughter," Dennis said, "I want a lawyer, and I'm entitled to a formal hearing."

"But if I'm suspending you for failure to complete your teaching certificate requirements," the principal said, "you're not entitled to anything. Until you come back here with proof that you've completed the required courses. It shouldn't take more than two years. See you then. Oh, and Mr. Withrow—"

Dennis stopped at the door. "Yes?"

"Stay away from the children on your way out," the principal said. "I'm only advising it for your own good."

He couldn't go home and tell Riva about it yet, not while the steam was still coming out of his ears. So he drove downtown to spend a calming hour or two browsing at Adventures in Crime and Space. "I still don't have the new Sherri Tepper, anyway," he told Willie. "And come to think of it, that's Boatright's doing, too. Dammit, somebody's got to stop that man before he does serious damage!"

"Getting you fired isn't serious?" Willie asked. "Never mind, you can always come work here. I could use a bookstore clerk who knows every SF title published since 1940."

"I like teaching," Dennis said. "Besides, you probably won't have a bookstore once Boatright finds this place. Did I tell you what he did at Bookstop?"

"Publicity stunt."

"Yeah? They had to reorder the entire SF, romance and mystery sections, and the books haven't come in yet. The shelves are still bare. You think they'd lose all that money for publicity? Those books have to be somewhere," Dennis fretted. "If I could find them, maybe I could figure out how Boatright worked it. Looks like I'm going to have plenty of spare time to look into it, anyway. Did the Leiber reprints come in yet? I need to replace my copy of *Conjure Wife;* the pages are falling out of the binding."

When Dennis finally got home, an hour after school let out, he was rather relieved to find nobody in the

house. He wouldn't have to tell Riva about being
suspended right away. And he wouldn't have to take
any teasing about having brought a dozen more
paperback books into a house where every bookshelf
and every flat surface was already stacked with books
he'd read and wanted to keep forever, books he'd read
once and thought he might want to reread some day,
books that had been autographed by friends so that
he couldn't decently sell them to Half Price Books,
and books he meant to read someday. He stacked ten
of the new purchases on a table already groaning with
books in the last category, shelved the reprinted Fritz
Leiber in the L's in his permanent collection, and
stretched out on the couch with the new Sherri Tepper.

A pounding on the door disturbed him as he savored
the first scene-setting paragraphs, with their promise
of mystery, intrigue, and something to think about in
the next few chapters.

"Yeah? Wait a minute." Sighing, Dennis closed the
book over one finger to mark his place and swung
his feet to the floor. He was almost standing when
the door burst open.

"Where is she?" Bob Boatright demanded.

Three unpleasant-looking young men crowded in
behind him, making the small living room uncom-
fortably full. Boatright shoved Dennis in the chest and
he sat back down on the couch.

"Where is who?" he asked. "And didn't you ever
hear about waiting for people to answer the door?"

"You know," Boatright said. "Becky. You've got her
hidden over here."

"The hell I have!" Dennis started to get up again,
but this time one of the young men behind Boatright
moved forward and put a hand on his shoulder. "Take

it easy, pops," he said. "We don't want nobody to get hurt here."

"We don't?" asked the dark-haired teenager beside him.

"All depends," said the third boy, the one with the shaved skull and the lightning-bolt earring. He grinned at Dennis, showing an impressively broken front tooth. His shoulders and biceps bulged out of his muscle T-shirt.

"My daughter told me she was leaving home to move in with you!"

"Well, she didn't tell me," Dennis said, "and she's not here now, and I would like you and your friends to get the hell out. Now." He grabbed the first boy's wrist as he spoke and twisted it sharply, breaking the hold on his shoulder long enough to let him stand up. He felt better standing, looking down at the pudgy figure of the Reverend Bob. "I've had about enough of your accusations today. Get out or I'm calling the police."

"Naah," said the dark boy, "you don't wanna do that, mister." As he spoke he picked up the telephone and yanked the cord out of the wall.

"Was that supposed to impress me? Okay, you've had your fun, and I'm tired of it. Now, out. All of you." His stomach was quivering, but he used the voice that could shut up thirty rowdy eighth-graders on the last day of school, and for a moment the boys looked cowed. Then the shaven one grinned again.

"You want impressive," he said, "we'll give you impressive, buddy." He dropped a paperback book on the floor, covers splayed open, and squashed it under his boot. "You want to let the Reverend's little girl go, or you want me to step on you next, huh?"

Dennis hit him with the Tepper. It was a hardback book, six hundred pages of wonder and adventure and a little preachiness mixed in. It made a very satisfying thud against the big guy's nose.

Bob Boatright backed out of the way, but the other two boys came at Dennis at once, grinning as if they'd only been waiting for this excuse to let go. One of them got his left arm. He dropped the Tepper and grabbed for a bookcase, trying to stay upright. The bookcase wobbled and leaned to the left, then gave way with a creaking of nails and boards and collapsed in a heap, burying Bob Boatright in the collected works of Roger Zelazny.

"Hey, mister, you don't wanna get rough," said the dark boy. He grabbed Dennis by the shoulder and tried to push him into the bookcase. Something banged into Dennis's knees at the same moment and he went down. Mistake, he thought as a foot caught him in the ribs. He struggled to his knees, trying to ignore the lance of pain in his side, and butted forward. The dark boy squealed and bent double, and Dennis got up on one foot. A plank from the fallen bookcase was conveniently near, and he didn't mind in the least that one end of it was studded with nails.

"I really don't like—having my reading—interrupted," he panted, and swung the plank at the blond boy's head.

The next few minutes were almost satisfying, in a grim and desperate way. There were three of them, all bigger and younger than he was, and he really didn't have a chance. But he'd been wanting to hit something, and the three teenage thugs were ideal targets. Sheer rage kept the fight going for minutes longer than it should have lasted, and also kept Dennis from feeling some of the pain from the blows he took back. But after a few strenuous exchanges somebody kicked his feet out from under him, and he was on the floor again, amid blood and paperback books, watching the big black boots coming towards his face with the inevitability of a train wreck.

Something else was coming faster than the boots; he heard footsteps and then a whistling sound, and the boots jumped backward out of his line of sight. A glittering arc swept through the air where they had been.

A full-armor workout in a Texas September is about as much fun as the same workout under Dazau's sun. And without Vleenacottara the arms mistress to keep me up to speed, I had to do it myself. I was trying so hard to make sure I didn't slack off that most of the time I couldn't hear anything but the blood drumming in my ears, the thud of my own feet hitting the hard-baked dirt, and—okay, let's admit it—my own gasps for breath. That's a pitiful state for a swordswoman to get into. What little neural capacity remained to me was ruminating on how soft I'd allowed myself to get during two years as a student, and wondering how much of the decay was because I was, Nauzu take it, getting older.

None of which is any excuse for the even more pitiful mistake I had made: getting so wrapped up in the workout that I didn't notice the sounds of a fight in the house. Any swordswoman who doesn't notice danger behind her won't last long in the Guild. Oh, they wouldn't expel me. They'd wait for the inevitable to happen and then give me a very nice funeral.

All of which is just to explain that when I heard people crashing into the walls and knocking down furniture, I was not only hot, sweaty, and annoyed with the people in question. I was also seriously upset with myself for having missed the first sounds of trouble. As a result, I may just possibly have been overly testy when I dashed in to stop the fight.

One glance showed me blood and paperbacks and Dennis sprawled all over the floor, while one of the cowardly punks who'd refused to fight me before drew back a booted foot to kick him in the face. I left the doorway and came down straddling Dennis in time to block the kick. Sasulau sang joyfully in my hand.

"Nauzu klevulkidimmu!" I spat at the boys who'd attacked Dennis. "You touch my man—my house— my honor!" With each phrase I lunged forward and let Sasulau take a strip from one of them. Not much; just a little slice through the fronts of their baggy shirts and a scratch down their soft chests. I am not, you understand, claiming that this was a sign of self-control. I planned to try a three-way fybilka execution as the culmination to this workout. I was seriously pissed.

"Holy shit, man, you din't tell us she was here again!" somebody whined, backing into the nearest wall.

"Not. One. Step," I said. "I'm not through with you yet." I grinned. "You don't want to annoy me any more. Do you?" Not that it really mattered; I had already decided, as I said, on a triple fybilka execution. But they didn't know that yet.

"Woman!" said a rich baritone voice somewhere to my right. I glanced that way without lowering Sasulau. Bob Boatright was standing in the hall doorway. "Woman, your attire is an offense against the Lord Jesus Christ. Go and cover yourself!"

I took two steps sideways, slid the little knife out

of my boot, and jabbed an elbow into Boatright's chest. He fell back against the doorframe and I had the point of the knife pressing into the soft flesh under his chin before he could get his balance. And I still had Sasulau poised to slice through the other three. Neat work, if I do say so myself. Perhaps I hadn't entirely lost my old fighting skills after all. I began to feel a little better. Not enough to give up my plans, though.

"Your whole existence," I told Boatright, "is an offense against me. And in case you haven't noticed, I'm a lot closer than Jesus."

Boatright gurgled something, but whatever it was didn't sound as impressive as usual. He couldn't open his mouth without impaling his fat chin on my boot knife. An entirely satisfactory state of affairs. I turned my attention to the three boys, who were trying to shuffle towards the door in steps small enough not to attract my notice.

"The thing I don't like about Chinese cooking," I told them, "is all the chop chop chop, dicing everything into tiny pieces. On the other hand, I've had a lot of practice at chopping things into tiny pieces. It's a popular method of execution where I come from. I think I'll practice it. Go ahead. Try to run away. I promise I won't throw any of you out of the window this time."

I smiled brilliantly and the boy with the lightning-bolt earring turned pale green.

"Riva, I've told you how people here feel about violence," Dennis said. He sat up and began feeling around on the floor for his glasses. "You really mustn't kill them."

"These particular people," I pointed out, "seem to be all in favor of violence. And I really need some live opponents to train on. There's only so far you can get sparring with a tree. Can't I have just one?"

"No," Dennis said. "Let's just call the cops."

"You can't," Boatright pointed out. "We took care of the phone. We'll just go peaceably—"

"Oh. No. You. Won't. See, Dennis, they don't want us to call the cops. They want to settle it among ourselves, honorably. Can I start now?"

"Oh, hell, Riva, they only pulled the plug out of the module." Dennis pulled himself up and sat on the couch. He was moving cautiously; I wondered how much damage they'd done to him before I got there. "I can plug it back in and call right now."

A beeper went off in the back bedroom. The punks twitched and looked at each other nervously.

"Oh, Nauzu!" That was the beeper Furo Fykrou had sold me to keep in touch with Dazau by Trans-Universal Call Forwarding. And he had set it to the highest frequency, meaning death, destruction, and pissed-off wizards if I didn't answer. "You kids. Wait right there. I can see through walls," I lied, backing past Bob Boatright to take the call.

It turned out to be a prerecorded message, trans-forwarded an hour ago and set to repeat at fifteen-minute intervals. I almost left to catch it on the next repeat, figuring that anything that had been left for an hour could wait the ten minutes it would take me to slice those punks into stir-fry; but while I was reading the "PREVIOUS CALLS ATTEMPTED" display, Furo Fykrou's image formed on the screen. (One advantage of the way Dennis had hooked my beeper up to the computer; I got full video now instead of just voice trans-forwarding.)

Thank Gredu I didn't put off taking his message.

I was shaking when I got back to the living room; the euphoria of a good fight was drained off. I felt sick at my stomach.

Not too sick, though, to notice that the kids had disappeared. Only Bob Boatright was left.

"Hey," I said, "what happened to our prisoners?"

"They left," Dennis said, "as soon as your sword wasn't pointed at them."

That accounted for the whining noises Sasulau had been making while I took Furo Fykrou's message. She knew we weren't going to get any blood-revenge today.

Somehow, though, that didn't seem as important as it had a minute ago. I looked at Boatright. "And what's keeping you?"

He started sidling towards the door. Dennis stood up, favoring his left side. I made Sasulau a promise that we'd hunt those boys down and take our revenge. Later. When the immediate problem was settled.

"No," Dennis said. "You're not going anywhere yet."

"Did he hurt you?" I was perfectly willing to start the blood-payment with this pudgy preacher.

Dennis shook his head. "He didn't hit me, if that's what you mean. But he thinks Becky is here. I don't want him to leave until he sees that she isn't."

Becky. I could feel the color draining from my face. I took Dennis's arm. "Dennis, I need to talk to you."

"Er—we aren't hiding the kid, are we?" Dennis whispered.

I shook my head.

"All right, then. I want the satisfaction of making him admit it."

It didn't take long. There weren't that many places to look: the tiny bedroom Dennis and I shared, the somewhat larger one that Salla shared with the

computer and VCR and TV, a long narrow kitchen
full of strings of dried chile peppers, and a bathroom.
Dennis even pulled back the shower curtain with a
flourish. "See? She's not hiding in the bathtub.
Satisfied?"

"Now," I said, "go away." Boatright hovered uncertainly, burbling about reasonable suspicions and rights
and a lot of other Paper-Pushers nonsense. Under the
circumstances, I could hardly tell Dennis about Furo
Fykrou's message in front of him. And my adrenaline
rush was over; I was, unfortunately, calm enough to
remember how much Dennis disliked it when I took
the obvious solution to problems. Boatright didn't know
about Dennis' strange aversion to killing people,
though; I could probably scare him off.

"My sword is thirsty," I remarked. "She deserves
better than a pious lardbucket like you, but since your
friends have left . . . "

I bared my teeth at Boatright and he backed out
the door without a word.

As soon as he was gone, Dennis gave me a dirty
look. "You know something about Becky, don't you?"

I did think he could have started with a few words
of thanks for saving his life, not to mention his glasses.
But we didn't have time to quarrel about little things
like that right now.

"Becky? Yes. I know where she is." I felt dead tired,
too tired to go on; as soon as I told Dennis, it would
be real. It would be the end of our life together.
Funny, I hadn't expected to mind this much. "Salla's
there, too. And Jason."

"Well?" Dennis still sounded mad at me, instead of
grateful.

No way to put it off any longer.

"Furo Fykrou's got them. The three of them figured out how to use my beeper to make a transuniversal connection to Dazau. I will kill Salla when she gets back."

"So let's go get her back," Dennis said.

"It's not that simple." Nauzu knew, I wished it were! "The transporter draws on Furo Fykrou's magic at the other end to power the transfer. He claims the children are in debt to him for the cost of the transfer."

"We can pay him. I don't know how you transferred credits before, but—"

"He doesn't want zolkys! By Dazau law, anyone who incurs debt to another without the means to pay it becomes the property of the creditor."

"But we've got the means to pay it."

"The children didn't. Legally they are now his slaves."

"Riva. Relax. He doesn't really want three sixth-graders. Nobody in their right mind would."

"No," I agreed. "There was a ransom demand."

"See?"

"He wants me."

"What?"

"I've been studying mathemagics for two years now. You know I always planned to go back to Dazau and apprentice to a wizard when I'd learned enough. Furo Fykrou thinks this would be a suitable time. He probably thinks I've learned all your mathemagical secrets."

Dennis shook his head. "Even somebody with a gift for math couldn't learn everything in two years, let alone— I mean, I don't want to insult you, but—"

"I'm not insulted," I said wearily.

"You could learn higher math. If you'd just pay

attention." This was drifting into an argument we'd had before.

"It bores me, all right?" I snapped. "Anyway, that's not the point. The point is, Fykrou won't free the kids until I go in their place." I felt perversely impelled to explain to him just how right and logical the whole arrangement was. "It's probably the best thing all around. I'm running out of money; I'm not qualified for any job I can think of in your universe; and although the Guild would probably take me back, the fact is I'm getting kind of old for a bronze-bra job. I'm over thirty now, you know. A nice quiet apprenticeship to a wizard is probably the best work I can get in Dazau's reality. I would've had to move back soon anyway; it's just a little sooner than we planned on."

I'd sort of expected Dennis to argue with me, but he just said, "What do other swordswomen do when they get older?"

"The smart ones save enough to retire on," I said, "but with commuting here and keeping up two households, I never did that. And the others . . . well, mostly they don't get older."

"Umm. You don't look all that aged and decrepit to me," Dennis said, "but if you think a Guild job would be too much for you, you're probably right. The only thing is . . ."

The only thing is, I don't want you to go back to Dazau. The only thing is, I can't live without you. The only thing is, I love you.

Any of those would have been a totally acceptable way to finish that sentence, even if they didn't constitute a logical solution to our present problem. Instead Dennis went on after a pause, "The only thing is, I think practical mathemagics would be too much for you too."

"I've been studying," I reminded him.

"Yes, but you keep trying to do it by rote memory. I don't think you have any real feeling for the theoretical basis." Dennis picked up my Al-Jibber notebook, which had landed on top of some of the paperbacks Boatright's little friends had thrown around the room, and flipped through the pages. "Look at this!"

It was a page-long equation, and it looked like perfect mathemagical Jibbrish to me: all full of x's and y's and slashes and parentheses and other occult symbols. And I'd spent an entire day deriving it. "So what's wrong with that?"

Dennis sighed. "If you reduce all the terms, you'd end up dividing by zero."

"So? Oh—that's against the rules, isn't it?"

Dennis slammed the notebook shut. "My point exactly. You don't have any feeling for mathematics. You try to memorize all the rules, but you don't notice when your equations aren't making sense. No intuition. Furo Fykrou doesn't know what he's asking for. Turn you loose in a reality full of mathemagical energy? You're liable to turn the entire population of Dazau into armadillos with one misplaced term!"

I could have stood being argued with on the grounds that he loved me madly and didn't want me to leave this reality. It wouldn't have fixed anything, but at least I could have gone off feeling noble and tragic.

But I wasn't in the mood to hear how hopeless I was at math. "Look," I said in what I thought was a reasonably calm tone, all things considered, "I really don't need you making me feel incompetent just before I trade myself to Furo Fykrou for the children. If he finds out how weak my mathemagics are, he just might decide to keep them instead of me—have you thought about that? Of course," I added, "I guess Salla might as well stay there. She needs to be in the same reality as her mother. But not as Furo Fykrou's slave!"

"If you insist on going back to Dazau," Dennis said, "I can't stop you."

Stop me? He hadn't even hinted at a mild preference for any other course of action.

"But I disapprove on principle of paying ransom to kidnappers," he went on.

"Fine. You aren't paying. I am. Now if that's all, excuse me, I need to arrange the transfers."

"Wait," Dennis said mildly, but I sat back down again. I guess in some part of my pea-sized brain I was still expecting him to express some distress, some interest, some hint of emotional reaction, for Nauzu's sake, about my leaving.

"We can get the kids back without paying ransom," he said. "The first thing you have to do is tell Furo Fykrou that your mathemagics aren't up to par yet."

"Are you crazy?"

"You're going to offer him a bargain," Dennis went on. "Two for the price of one. No Dazauian can resist a deal like that."

I started to feel all warm and soft inside, sort of like you do when the inter-reality transfer kicks in, only with an added flavor of hot fudge sundae. "You're coming with me? You'd do that? Dennis, I can't let you leave your whole life here, you—"

"I have no intention," Dennis interrupted me, "of letting either of us become enslaved or apprenticed to Furo Fykrou."

"Oh! But then what—"

"Go away," Dennis said. He'd opened my Al-Jibber notebook again and was scribbling mathemagical symbols on the blank pages at the back (to be honest, most of the pages were blank. I really hadn't been concentrating on my studies.) "Make the offer. Stall him—say it'll take a while for us both to wind up our affairs in this reality."

"How long?"

"As long as you can."

"The kids will be scared."

"The kids will survive. I need time to work this out."

"Work what out?"

"I think it's got to be some kind of a Fourier transform," Dennis said.

"What does?"

"The mathemagical formula that transfers people and things between realities. See, you can think of a Fourier transform as taking something from the time domain to the frequency domain. It's not exactly clear that the frequency domain has to exist in our reality; it's just an analytical way of looking at these things. And the inversion, of course, is a Laplace transform."

"Oh. Perfectly clear. Except that you can't use a what-you-said transform to get Salla and Jason and Becky back, because there's no mathemagical power in this world."

"I'm not going to use it here," Dennis said. "We'll let Furo Fykrou transport us to Dazau. That's what he wants, isn't it?"

"And then what?"

"You don't want to hear the math," Dennis said. "Go away. Sharpen your sword or something. I think I'd better have all this written out before we get there; I don't want to drop a term in the stress of the moment."

Chapter $\sum_{k=1}^{3} k^2$

Dennis was surrounded by stacks of his old college math textbooks, scribbling equations on a yellow legal pad, when the phone at his elbow rang. I set down the leather strap I'd been oiling and looked at the phone as if it were a wizard about to strike.

"It's the regular phone," Dennis said, flexing his cramped fingers, "not that Trans-Forwarding beeper."

Ring.

"Yeah," I agreed. "So it can't be Furo Fykrou. Can it?"

Ring.

"Whoever it is," Dennis said, "and whatever they want, we don't have time for it."

Ring. Click. Whirr.

"This is a machine." said a childish voice, slightly distorted by the tape noise. "This is not a person. The people here aren't talking and you can't make them, so just leave a message. Nyaah, nyaah, nyaah."

"Salla's been fooling with the answering machine again."

"Yeah. I'll kill her. If I get a chance."

A beep signaled the end of the taped message, and

we heard Norah Tibbs's voice next. "Riva, will you please tell Jason to get back over here? I gotta go to the Meet the Authors party at SalamanderCon in half an hour."

"Nauzu klevulkedimmu! I thought the party didn't start until eight." I looked out the window. "It *is* almost eight. I didn't realize it was that late. Aren't you ready, Dennis?"

Dennis ripped off the top three sheets from the yellow pad and handed them to me. "Memorize these."

I stared in dismay at the pages of K'al-Kul. "You've got to be kidding."

"Okay, just read them aloud so I can make sure you're at least reading them right."

"Why me? I thought you were going to do the mathemagics. I'm just the muscle."

"I want backup," Dennis said. "If he stops me somehow, you've got to complete the transform."

I touched the gleaming sword on my lap. "He won't get near you."

"Read it anyway."

"Riva, dammit, pick up the phone! I know Jason went over there after school. If he doesn't get back and put on some decent clothes he can't come to the—"

Click. Whirr.

"We need a longer answering machine tape," Dennis said thoughtfully.

The phone rang again.

And again.

"I don't think she's going to give up," I said. "I'd better think of some excuse." I picked up the phone. "Norah? I'm sorry, Jason isn't here right now."

"Well, where did he go?"

"Think of something," Dennis hissed.

I covered the mouthpiece. "Like what?"

"Riva? Are you still there? Let me talk to Salla. She'll know where the little brat headed."

"Uh, uh, Salla's not here, either."

"Field trip," Dennis whispered.

"What?"

"Weekend field trip. Both of them."

My brain clicked into gear. "Oh, gosh, Norah, you mean he didn't have your permission? He swore it was all right with you. He and Salla went off on the, umm, the school field trip to . . ." I glanced up at the Texas Hill Country map on the wall for inspiration. "To, umm, Pedernales Falls." I pronounced it the way it was spelled: Ped-ur-nails. "They were over here packing all afternoon," I embellished the story. "It's an overnight trip, you know, and they wanted to borrow some of Dennis's camping gear."

"Oh, really? How come I didn't hear about the trip?"

"You've been real busy finishing a book, haven't you? It's so easy to miss these notes, the school is always sending so many stupid notices home and most of them aren't worth looking at," I babbled. "I didn't read it myself, I didn't even know about this trip until Salla's teacher called up and told me about it today."

I could hear Norah's sigh. "Riva, one of the things I like about you is that you're such a lousy liar. Look. In the first place, this is the opening night of Sala-manderCon and Jason would definitely not miss it for a school field trip to a place we've been to dozens of times on our own. In the second place, the teachers wouldn't have taken him if they didn't have my signed permission slip; they may be ditzy, but they don't want to get sued. And in the third place, if anybody from the school had called to tell you about this field trip, you would know that it's pronounced Perd-na-lees, not Ped-ur-nails. So where is Jason and why don't you want to tell me?"

I gulped and rolled my eyes at Dennis. He threw up his hands.

"Riva." Norah's voice was sharper now. "Do you know where my kid is?"

"Oh, yes. I know exactly where he is."

"So?"

"He's—"

Dennis made an emphatic chopping gesture with one hand.

"I can't tell you."

There was a long, ominous silence on the other end of the line. When Norah spoke again, I jumped.

"Riva. Does this by any chance have anything to do with all the other things you've been carefully not telling me for the last three years?"

"Like what?" I parried.

"Like where you come from. Like what really happened on that fourth-grade field trip where Vera Boatright was sure you'd taken the kids to Six Flags or some theme park, only there isn't one close enough so I know that wasn't it. Like why you freaked out the other day when I mentioned wizards—" Norah stopped. "No. This doesn't make any sense. Never mind. I'm going crazy, believing the stuff I write. Riva, tell me I'm crazy."

I swallowed. "You're . . . not crazy."

"And you know where my kid is."

"Yes. He's with Salla," I added. "And Becky Boatright."

Norah exhaled. "Then I feel deeply sorry for that world, wherever it is. Listen, Riva. If you say it's a field trip, then it's a field trip. At least until tomorrow morning. But get him back."

"I will," I said. "I will." I hung up the handset and stared defiantly at Dennis. "I didn't tell her anything. She figured it out."

"She wasted a lot of your time," Dennis said. "Will you please read over those equations? It's taken me three hours to get them right, and we won't have time for a second try. This has got to work the first time. I wish I had a laptop," he said, looking wistfully at the mass of the clunky, outdated 386 computer with cables trailing to the printer and my beeper. "If I could program the new transform equations and invoke them automatically as soon as we get there, it would be a whole lot easier.

"And I hate the squoogy feeling the transport formula gives you," he said after a few minutes of fiddling with the program. "It's like going down too fast in one of those hotel elevators with all glass walls."

"You get used to it," I said. "Try not to throw up, okay? Ready?

"Ready. Want to sit on my lap?"

"I think I'd better be standing up when we come across."

"Right." Dennis took my hand, leaned over the computer and pressed Enter.

The book-lined walls of the back bedroom shimmered around us. Salla's poster of the lead guitarist for Three Blind Mikes faded slightly. The local distortions of the transfer made the green-haired guitarist seem to be undulating on the walls; his features blurred, then sharpened into the frowning face of a middle-aged man. Dark hair sleeked under a velvet cap framed this face; a robe with sleeves wide enough to brush the ground replaced the guitarist's black T-shirt and metal-studded jeans. Furo Fykrou wavered for a moment like an image borne on the shifting winds between the worlds, then solidified. His sanctum took shape around us: shelves lined with books and scrolls and skulls and bundles of herbs, a long table set before a window that overlooked the rolling barren hills of the north country, a shadowed loft piled high with other books.

"You're late," he said.

"$\int f$ . . ." Dennis began.

Furo Fykrou pointed his long carved staff at Dennis.

"$Log(e^x = x - \frac{1}{x} + \frac{1}{2}(x - \frac{1}{x})^2 + \; . \; . \; .$"

Dennis gasped for breath.

"$\frac{1}{3}(x - \frac{1}{x})^3$ . . ." Furo Fykrou went on.

By now Dennis seemed to be turning blue. Oh, Nauzu! What had Furo Fykrou done? Some kind of infinite series; as it converged, Dennis's ability to breathe was being squeezed out of him. Logarithms. We'd done logarithms. What was the inverse function?

Dennis lifted one finger and sketched a wavy circle in the air, like an ineffective sword parry. What could he mean? Oh, sure. Kill the wizard. Much simpler than fooling around with mathemagics.

Furo Fykrou broke off his incantation, leaving Dennis a bare thread of air—I hoped. He swung his staff at me and began, "$Log(e^x)$ . . ."

Sasulau, singing in my hand, made a single, beautiful arc through the air where the wizard had been standing, ending with a forward lunge that should have perforated his intestines. But he cried out some other mathemagical formula and reappeared in the loft before I could touch him.

The force of my forward lunge carried me on into

the shelves. Small skulls rattled to the floor; a bunch of herbs disintegrated into a powdery dust that filled the air for a moment and brushed Dennis on the face. He sneezed and gasped. That was a relief. At least he was breathing again.

"Piddling herb-magics," sneered Furo Fykrou from the loft. "I can choke him with mathemagics while you're fooling around there. Want to drop the sword and be reasonable?"

I grabbed a handful of the remaining herbs and threw them in Dennis's face. A series of explosive sneezes assaulted him, but so what? At least he was getting enough air to keep sneezing. At the moment, nothing else mattered.

"Naah," I said after making sure I had a good supply of sneezeweed from the stuff on the floor. I leaned on one of the posts supporting the loft. It creaked. "I don't feel real reasonable right now."

"$D/_{dx}$ cot — Watch it, you stupid cow! Those supports were hand-carved with magical formulae. You want to let demons loose?"

If Furo Fykrou didn't like it, it was probably worth doing. I pushed harder. The post gave way with a screech of protest. The loft floor tilted slowly; Furo Fykrou slid to the edge, grabbed a plank with both hands, and dangled slowly in the air.

"Now," I said cheerfully, "do you want to tell me where the kids are and send us all back, or shall I practice fybilka on you? Starting with the feet, since they're within reach."

I drew the tip of my sword across the bottoms of Furo Fykrou's soft slippers. He wailed and drew up his knees. "I'm going to fall!"

"Good."

The series of sneezes that had convulsed Dennis was ending as the cloud of dried herb particles settled towards the floor. Unfortunately, so was his ability to breathe.

"Riva," he whispered at me, "Antilog!" He drew the wavy sign with his finger again.

Oh, that was what he meant. Mathemagics, not swordplay. Okay. I backed towards Dennis, still keeping my sword pointed at the wizard, and took the sheets of yellow paper from his back pocket.

This did not look good. The equations Dennis had scribbled on the yellow pad were advanced K'al-K'ul, far beyond anything I'd studied. And they probably weren't the right ones to neutralize Furo Fykrou's mathemagical attack anyway. They sure didn't look like logarithmic forms.

"Fix Dennis," I suggested instead, poking Sasulau upwards towards the wizard's calves. "Then we talk."

"No more funny tricks?"

"If he dies," I said meditatively, "I can think of some real funny things to do with you. Think you can concentrate enough to stop me with mathemagics while I'm peeling the skin off your thighs?"

Furo Fykrou sighed. "e^x."

Dennis took a deep gasping breath. "Where's Sa—"

Furo Fykrou gabbled a second formula and Dennis's lips closed of their own accord, cutting off the question.

The wizard got a grip on one of the side railings of the loft and hauled himself up out of reach of my sword. Sitting astride what had been the banister at the head of the loft stairs, he looked almost comfortable and a great deal more confident than he had been a moment previously. "You see, Riva," he said, "I can silence your tame mathemagician one way or another. I wasn't really going to let him suffocate, anyway."

"Sure you weren't," I said, keeping Sasulau pointed at him. I could probably reach the knife in my boot and throw it at him while he watched the big sword, but that might not be such a good idea. It's awfully hard to kill somebody with a knife throw, and even if I did succeed, that would leave Dennis with his lips sealed.

"No, really. I wouldn't waste him that way. As soon as you've both taken the bond-oath to me, I'll let him speak again. And I'll send the children back, if you really wish it . . . given that you're going to be staying here. I won't even," said Furo Fykrou with an air of great magnanimity, "charge for the damage you've done to my sanctum."

"Big of you," I said. Maybe it was time to try Dennis's mathemagical formulas. It would have helped a lot if he'd told me what they were for, though. I didn't know whether they would turn Furo Fykrou into a frog or simply render him obedient to our slightest whim. The second would work out better in the long run.

And I needed to keep him distracted, or he'd shut my mouth, too. I leaned on another of the supporting posts. As it creaked and Furo Fykrou scrabbled for another handhold, I began reading the scribbled equations under my breath, substituting Furo Fykrou's name wherever the variable sign occurred.

"$\int \ldots$" What was that funny sign like a figure 8 on its side? Oh, well, maybe it wasn't important. I skipped it and went on. " $\ldots e^{-\pi} \ldots$ " I didn't have a staff to point at Furo Fykrou, but I had Sasulau. She was full of some kind of magical power; she was singing with it while I read the mathemagics.

Furo Fykrou held on to a tilting bannister and tried to kick me in the head. He started an equation, probably the same one that had sealed Dennis's lips. I knocked the staff out of his hand and poked Sasulau at his foot. While he squealed, I finished quickly, "$\int f(t)dt$!"

My hand was empty. Slowly I looked up to the wreckage of the loft. That, too, was empty—at least of wizards.

"Dennis!" I cried. "We did it! It worked! You're a genius!" I sheathed Sasulau and threw my arms around Dennis.

"Mmmmnnp," he said when I let go. "Mpmpng. Mmn!"

"Oh. I forgot. How do I reverse that last spell? Do I integrate or what?"

Dennis snatched the sheets of yellow paper from me. "Mmp mbm!" he mmm'd emphatically, making a scribbling gesture with his index finger.

"Something to write with," I guessed. I prowled around the mess in the study until I found an ink pot and a quill pen. Dennis perched on a stool at the cluttered table and laboriously, with many blots, scrawled the formula that would reverse Furo Fykrou's last spell. I squinted at the paper.

"Is that an alpha or a drop of ink? I don't want to get it wrong."

"Mmmmbp!" Dennis took the paper back and scratched through the misleading blot several times. "Bmbm, mm?"

I pointed Sasulau at Dennis and read the formula extremely carefully, stopping after each word or sign for Dennis's nod. As soon as I finished, his mouth opened and he gasped in a long, sweet breath of air.

"Nauzu save us," I said, "I thought you were breathing okay."

Dennis took in a few more gulps of delicious, herb-scented oxygen and sneezed a couple of times. "I would have been," he said, "except that herbal dust started my allergies. You did great, Riva."

"Now all we have to do," I said, looking around the wreckage of Furo Fykrou's sanctum, "is find the children."

"Listen for the sound of bickering," Dennis suggested.

What we actually heard, when we listened carefully, was a rhythmic thumping from the wall behind the loft. I climbed one of the last remaining supports and ran my fingers along the wall. "Aha!"

"Secret door?"

"Nope. Just bolted." I pulled back the bolt and Salla tumbled into my arms, followed by Jason.

"I heard everything," Salla announced. "Brilliant! What took you so long?"

"Working out the equations," Dennis said. "I wanted to be sure we transported Furo Fykrou to our world before he had a chance to do anything to us."

Salla blinked. "But—"

She looked at Jason, who shrugged. "Don't look at me. I wasn't studying mathemagics, remember? I was downstairs getting dishpan hands."

"Well," said Salla cheerfully, "you did want an equal opportunity quest, didn't you? And you got one."

"You're getting more than you planned on," I said. "I'm going to take you two apart limb from limb and hang you up for the buzzards as soon as we get home. Your mother will probably want to help, Jason. Now let's get Becky and get out of here."

Salla and Jason looked at each other.

"Becky . . . " Salla began.

"It's like this . . . " said Jason.

"Like what?"

"He sold her," the children said in unison.

"Where?"

"Who to?"

"I don't know," said Jason.

"The Bronze Bra Guild," said Salla.

I relaxed. "Okay, that's easy, all we have to do is go to Duke's Zolvorra and I'll buy her back."

Salla swallowed. "Uh . . . this group weren't going to Duke's Zolvorra."

"Well, where was he sending them?"

"I don't think," Salla said carefully, "he was sending them anywhere. From what I heard, the duke was called out of town suddenly to deal with some magical manifestations in the river valley farms. Sika and a couple of lieutenants were leading a group of trainees up to Weariefauld to take care of some dragons. They didn't seem to be quite sure whether they were real dragons or manifestations, though. And Furo Fykrou told them the dragons weren't at Weariefauld anymore."

I sighed. "So where—were—they—going?"

Salla swallowed. "I didn't hear that part," she confessed. "He went outside with them. And Becky. See, he wasn't going to tell them until Sika paid him his twenty zolkys, and she didn't carry the gold on her, it was under guard outside . . ."

"Which way did they march?"

"I don't know that either," Salla confessed. "I tried to get to the window and look out, but Furo Fykrou had put a mist-wraith to guard all the entrances to this room. Even the window."

I looked at Dennis. "Well, there's one simple way

to solve this. You'll have to reverse that last equation and bring Furo Fykrou back here. I feel sure," I said, stroking the hilt of my sword, "that he can be persuaded to tell us where Becky went."

"I think," Salla said, "there might be a slight problem with that."

"Dennis can do anything with mathemagics," I said cheerfully.

"Yeah, but, Mom . . . " Salla looked as if she were going to cry.

"Well?"

"What you were saying, just there at the end: it didn't sound right."

"It got rid of Furo Fykrou, didn't it?"

"Yes, but . . . it didn't *sound* right."

"You know what it should have been?"

"No, but . . . "

Salla and Dennis and Jason tried to explain to me that mathematical equations had a form and rhythm of their own. Sometimes a person with an ear for mathematics could tell when an equation was wrong, just as somebody with an ear for music could tell when somebody played a wrong note in a baroque concerto he'd never heard before.

"And I think Salla's right," Dennis said unhappily. "It sounded to me like you maybe left out a term or something. But I wasn't exactly listening all that carefully. I was trying to breathe through clogged sinuses. And when he vanished, I figured you'd gotten it right after all."

"Oh. Yeah. I couldn't read this little doohicky," I said. "Can you reverse it without that?"

"Gosh," Salla said, peering over my shoulder, "what happens to an integral if you leave out one of the limiting terms?"

"Maybe," Dennis said grimly, "we'd better just reverse it and hope for the best. Let's see, if F is a Fourier transform which sends objects from here into our reality, L(F) ought to reverse the process. The Laplace transformation," he explained.

"Oh, I've heard of those!" I exclaimed, feeling better. "Furo Fykrou said something about building L'Place transforms into my beeper for the return transformulation. I figured it was something that changed Place."

"Er—sort of," Dennis said, looking unhappy. "We haven't studied those yet. $F(s) = L\{F(t)\}$?" he said tentatively.

Nothing happened.

Dennis tried a slight variation on the formula.

More nothing happened.

Jason said in a small voice, "When I was taking the Mathemagical Eptitude Test, he told me that one of the errors I'd made would have transformed me to Outer Yark instead of bringing a monster from there. So maybe you sent him to Outer Yark."

"If that's what happened," I said, "there's not much point in trying to bring him back. He's probably dead by now. And if he isn't dead, he's going to be in a really, really bad mood. Besides, if we start messing around with transforms from Outer Yark, no telling what kind of monsters we could bring in. I vote we forget about mathemagics and do things the straightforward way. One, find Sika's contingent of the Bronze Bra Guild. Two, buy Becky back. Three, get us all home before Mikh destroys any more books with his Leibniz."

"His what?" Dennis exclaimed. "How the—"

"I'll explain on the way," I said. "Jason, Salla, go

down to the kitchens and collect any food you can find. We may have a long march ahead."

"How come Quests involve so much time in the kitchen?" Jason grumbled.

Chapter $\int_{0}^{1}\left(u^2 - 2u + 3\right)du$

"The dragons were headed south," Salla said, "but Furo Fykrou kind of hinted they might have turned off the Great North Road."

"Let's hope they did," I said. "Then we can take the Great North Road straight to Duke's Zolvorra, probably catch up with Sikarouvvana's troop on the way, get Becky back and go home to retrieve the Leibniz."

"The what?" Dennis said.

"I'll explain as we go," I said, slinging a bag of supplies over one shoulder. "Or Salla will. It's really her story."

"No, it's Jason's," Salla said. "He's the one who watched closely enough to figure out what was going on."

Dennis shoved the yellow pages of mathemagical calculations into his hip pocket and picked up the other sack of provisions. "I'll strip my shirt and fly it at the masthead if someone doesn't pick me up soon. What is going on?"

"Will you really?" I said. One of the things I'd discovered in the last three years was that for such a skinny-looking guy, Dennis had great shoulders. It probably had something to do with his habit of standing upside down in yoga poses while he read. He did read a great deal.

"No. I was quoting a character in *The Lady's Not For Burning* who was feeling very nearly as confused as I am. Is this something to do with Sleazeball?"

"You mean Mikhalleviko?"

"You say tomayto, I say tomahto," said Dennis.

Salla snickered, so I decided Dennis wasn't really going crazy; he was just being an inscrutable Paper-Pusher type. "The road," I said, pointing at the dun stretch between scraggy hills, "is that way. I'll watch for bandits. Jason will explain."

So as we started south at the Guild quickstep, Jason and Salla alternately told Dennis about the scene in their classroom, how Bob Boatright had prayed to make the folklore and mythology readings disappear—

"But he didn't do it," Jason said firmly. "It was that new guy, the one that looks kind of like a guilty seal. See, I noticed the Reverend Bob made sure to step out of the way between him and the books, and that looked kind of funny, because you'd think the Rev would want to have his hands right on the things he was praying over. But nothing happened until he moved out of the way. Then the other guy pointed his Leibniz at the books. He tried to keep it mostly inside his sleeve, but he had to have a finger on the function keys."

"How do you know it was a Leibniz?"

"It's not really," I said at the same time that Jason said, "I recognized the logo, of course. The green lightning bolt on the side."

"Ah. So it wasn't a Newton or a— What does IBM call that new palmtop they're pushing?"

"Who cares?" said Jason scornfully. "It's DOS-based. Who's going to fool with that in this day and age?"

"I heard Windows 95.17 is still buggy," Dennis said.

"It's not a Leibniz," I said, loudly enough that they stopped discussing the finer points of computers for a moment and stared at me. "It's his staff. Look. Mikh's a wizard. When he transported himself into our reality, he brought along his staff and his book of spells."

"He told you this, I assume?" Dennis said, raising his eyebrows.

"No."

"Oh. Of course. You must have had so much else to talk about . . . remembering old times and all that."

What was he trying to do, convince me that I wanted Mikhalleviko back? And had I really been feeling depressed about the prospect of leaving this jerk? I told myself that clearly I'd be better off staying some place where I spoke the language—really spoke it, instead of relying on Furo Fykrou's transport spell to manage the details. Salla and I could stay here and send these aliens back to their own reality.

Under my hand, Sasulau hummed in agreement: I was finally thinking the right way.

So why did it feel so lonely?

"I figured. It. Out," I said when I had my voice under partial control. "I know Mikh."

"I'm only too well aware of that," Dennis purred.

I would definitely not be returning with Dennis. But it probably wouldn't be a good idea to take his head off at the neck right now. For one thing, it would upset Salla.

"He can't memorize spells," I explained after a few

minutes of breathing through clenched teeth, "and his
magical eptitude quotient is so low that he can't
summon up the power to do much without holding
his staff, which is full of stored magical power. If he's
working mathemagics in your universe, then he's got
his staff and book of spells somewhere. If he's pointing
something at books to make them disappear, then that
something is his wizard's staff. No matter what it looks
like."

"So we take that away from him," Jason said chirpily,
"and he can't disappear books anymore, and he's no
more problem, right?"

"Ummm. . . ." I said, thinking of his threat to sue
for custody of Salla. But if Salla and I stayed on
Dazau, he wouldn't be able to get at us via Paper-
Pushers' law. And I was still in good enough shape
to get my old job with the Bronze Bra Guild back.
Wasn't I? Especially after the last few weeks of
working out?

"Well . . ." said Dennis at the same time. I wondered
what he was thinking of. But it didn't really matter,
did it? I wouldn't be seeing any more of him once
we'd found Becky and sent them all home.

"Yeah," I said finally. "You'll have to get the Leibniz
away from him. It won't be easy; wizards are never
careless with their tools of power. It would help if you
could get his book of spells, too. If you can figure
out what it looks like."

"Probably the manual for the Leibniz," Jason suggested. "That would be logical."

"You sound as if you don't plan to be there when
we confront Mikhalleviko," Dennis said.

"Well . . ." There wasn't really any point in going
back, was there? I was sure Dennis and Jason could

figure out a way to take care of Mikhalleviko without my help. Well, almost sure.

"I guess it wouldn't be too good for your future relationship with him if you helped us take away his tools of power," Dennis surmised gloomily.

"Look," I started to say, "I don't have any relationship . . . Get down!"

Salla and Jason ducked behind the low-growing motherthorn that bordered the road. Dennis remained upright, squinting through his black-rimmed glasses at the figure that wandered aimlessly this way and that along the horizon.

"He doesn't look dangerous to me, Riva," he said.

"Do you know who he is?"

"Of course not. I don't know anybody on Dazau. Except you, of course. Who is he, then?"

"I don't know either," I explained.

"So you automatically assume he's dangerous?" Dennis grinned. "What is it, does everybody on Dazau have as short a fuse as you?"

"Nauzu klevulkkedimmu! I do not have a short fuse! I'm just trying to keep you idiot Paper-Pushers alive!" The stranger was closer now, though, and I could see that he was not armed. He was acting very odd, though; wandering on and off the road, looking surprised when he stepped on a branch of motherthorn, watching the clouds and the trees as much as he watched us. He was either crazy or very, very subtle. In either case, I did not feel that it was time to relax just yet.

As he ambled towards us, I studied his face. He was pale-skinned like Sikarouvanna's tribe, or like most of the Paper-Pushers; but he was a head taller than any of the Rouvannika, and his face didn't have that look of perpetual tense worry that I associated with adult male Paper-Pushers. He looked oddly young and innocent—all but the eyes, which were as old as a vofur-wizard's.

"I'll be damned," Dennis said softly.

"Do you know him?"

"No, but—" He stopped and bit his lip. "I feel as if I do, somehow. Everything about him seems oddly familiar—the way he carries himself, those old eyes in a young face—and yet I could almost swear I've never seen him before."

"He reminds you of somebody?"

Dennis frowned. "He reminds me of a book. But that doesn't make any sense."

While we were conferring, the stranger had strolled up to within a few feet of us. His hands were open and relaxed. So was his face. I kept one hand on Sasulau, but she did not sing to me of danger.

"Greetings," he said. "May you never thirst."

Dennis jumped as though he had been stabbed in the ribs. "By God, it's not possible!" he muttered.

"I offend you?" The stranger looked very sad. "I do not grok the customs of this place. Please do not discorporate."

"Riva," Dennis said, "give me the water flask."

"You're both crazy," I said.

Jason's eyes had grown as wide as Dennis's. Without speaking, he fished around in the sack Dennis had been carrying and pulled out one of the leather bottles we'd taken from Furo Fykrou's kitchens. He removed the stopper and offered the open flask to the stranger. "May we share water?"

The stranger took the flask in both hands and raised it briefly to his lips. "I thank you for water. May you always drink deep."

"Water brother," said Dennis, "how did you come here?"

The stranger's brows drew together. "I do not grok the manner of my being in this place. Or, indeed, the manner of my being," he added.

"Where did you come from?"

"That, also, I do not grok."

"A stranger in a strange land," Jason murmured. It sounded like a prayer.

"I think so," Dennis said to him, and to the stranger, "Do you want to go home?"

"I do not grok 'home,'" said the stranger. "Is 'home' where I should be?"

"Yes," Dennis said, "and I think I can send you there. But it may take a few minutes to work out. Will you trust me?"

"We have shared water," the stranger said tranquilly.

"My nest is your nest." He sat down in the roadway and appeared to be contemplating the horizon, quite happily.

"It's impossible," Jason said to Dennis.

"All those books that disappeared from Bookstop," Dennis said.

"Yeah, but he's not a book. He's real!"

"That," said Dennis, "is a philosophical question which has exercised many writers. But don't you think he would be happier back in his book?"

Jason nodded. "I sure would like to talk to him first, though."

"Good. Go ahead and talk. Keep him amused while I work out the math. But be sure not to upset him. We don't want him to discorporate."

Jason nodded as though Dennis made perfect sense. He squatted down beside the stranger and began chatting in a low voice.

"Gimme a pen," Dennis demanded.

Salla found a stub of pencil in her backpack. Dennis pulled the yellow paper out of his hip pocket, commandeered my shield for a writing surface, sat down a few feet from Jason and the stranger and began scribbling and erasing mathemagical formulae. I sat down beside him.

"And you were complaining about being confused?" I said. "Would you mind telling me what's going on here?"

Dennis pushed a lock of hair out of his eyes and looked at me. "I would never have figured it out," he said, "if you hadn't told me about Sleazeball's wizard's staff transmuting into a Leibniz Personal Assistant. Things like that don't normally happen when Furo Fykrou transports you between Dazau and our reality, do they? I mean, if you want your sword here, you have your sword in your hand when the transfer starts. You don't start off holding a pen and show up here with a sword."

"No," I agreed. I was beginning to see what he was getting at.

"So maybe your Mikh isn't using a generic Fourier transform. What would happen if he inserted a constant in place of the variable?"

"Huh?"

Dennis looked more disgusted than I felt was really necessary.

"I'm only on Al-Jibber," I reminded him. "Furry R Transforms are K'al-kul."

"Yes, but you understand about constants and variables in equations, don't you?"

"Understand" might have been putting it a bit too strongly. "Mmmm," I said noncommittally.

"So if he inserted the true name of a person or thing into the transform, what would happen?"

"I don't know. Why don't you ask a wizard?"

"Would it mathemagically change the person or thing into a form appropriate to the destination world?"

"Oh!" exclaimed Salla.

"I get it," Jason said.

I kind of hated to spoil the circle of enlightenment, so I said nothing.

"Now I see," said Salla enthusiastically. "You think Mikh just used a form of Fourier transform to get rid of the books? So instead of really making them disappear into thin air, he transferred them to Dazau?"

"There's probably some metamagical law of conservation of mass and energy," Dennis said. "I bet nothing ever really vanishes or is created. It just gets pulled in and out of various realities. And changes form. Yes, I think that's what happened. When he transferred himself to our reality, he inserted his own name into the transformulation so that he and his possessions would be modified to a form consonant with our world. Ha!" Dennis grinned. "Outfoxed himself. He turned his wizard's staff into a notepad computer and his book of spells into a manual for it. No wonder he can't do much mathemagics now!"

"Why not?" I asked.

"Nobody can understand the instructions in the manual," Jason, Salla and Dennis said in chorus.

"Anyway. The changed formula is hardwired into the Leibniz now." Dennis paused. "Or do I mean microcoded?"

"Both out of date," Jason said helpfully. "Nowadays they burn it into ROM."

"Whatever." Dennis dismissed this side issue with a wave of his hand. "In any case, he can't use the generic Fourier transform anymore, because he has to call on the power in his staff. And his staff automatically calls up the modified routine. So when he transfers something from our reality to this one, it gets modified in a way the magic considers appropriate."

"Why is he only transforming books?" I asked.

Jason shrugged. "Maybe he hasn't tried anything else . . . yet."

"That's what Boatright is paying him to do," Dennis pointed out. "Make books vanish."

"It's probably a bug in the program," Salla said. "I bet he can't do anything else, or he would have by now."

I liked that theory.

"The point is," Dennis said, "apparently books turn into their main character."

"What about all those textbooks that vanished at the hearing? Textbooks don't have any characters."

"Maybe they show up as their main idea."

"Not my social studies textbook," Salla said. "It doesn't have any ideas. It would have to transform into a blob of glup."

"Well, we're not dealing with your social studies textbook!" Dennis snapped. "We're dealing with Valentine Michael Smith—at least I hope we are. If my theory is correct, inserting the book title into the equation should send him back to our reality—as a book. $\int^{\infty} e^{-s(STRANGER...)}$ " he began. As he finished the formula, there wasn't a pop, or a puff of dust, or anything. The stranger was just gone.

"Hey," said Jason aggrievedly, "I wasn't through asking him . . ."

"Read the book," Dennis said.

"Ha, ha. Very funny."

I pointed out, quietly and tactfully, that interesting though all this business of transforming books into characters and vice versa might be, we had been sitting around by the roadside now for quite some time when we really needed to be catching up with the Bronze Bra Guild and redeeming Becky.

We made quite good time for the rest of the afternoon, although I did hear some muttering about drill sergeants and basic training from Dennis, and comments about sadistic P.E. coaches from Salla and Jason. I don't know what they were so upset about. They wanted to find Becky, too, didn't they?

Twice we ran into bemused young men with innocent faces. "I wonder how many copies of that book were on the shelves?" Dennis muttered.

"The important question," I said, "is, can you just repeat the Furry R Transform, or do we have to stop and grok and share water and play my-nest-is-your-nest every time?"

Fortunately, Dennis was getting quicker off the mark. By the time we encountered the third Stranger, he started rattling off the transform before anybody was able to say anything social about water. I thought this one looked grateful just before he disappeared, but I wasn't really paying close attention; there were more important things to look at now.

"Why do you want to stop now?" Dennis demanded, gasping slightly, when I nudged him and pointed off to the west of the road.

"Not stop," I said, "turn."

"Why?"

"Nauzu klevulkkedimmu! Are you blind? Look at the scorched motherthorn."

Dennis turned to inspect the bushes I'd noticed, picked up one foot hastily and swore.

"And those are dragon fewmets you just stepped in," I said. "I think . . . They're the wrong color, though." I'd never seen a beast that left white dung before. "We'd better move a little more slowly from now on."

"Okay by me," Dennis said.

"I never thought I'd be glad Coach made us run the track every day," Jason said.

"And be quiet! Do you want them to hear us coming?" I looked at the kids and Dennis. All three looked sweaty, dirty, and utterly exhausted from the afternoon's quick march. I probably looked as bad myself. I certainly felt tired enough to lie down and go to sleep among the motherthorn. But I also knew that if it were really necessary, I'd find the energy to draw Sasulau and fight whatever needed fighting.

Dennis and the kids probably had those reserves of energy, too, but they wouldn't know about them. They'd lived in a nice quiet enclave of Paper-Pushers all their lives. Even Salla didn't know what she could do when she really had to.

"Maybe you three had better stay here," I suggested. "I'll just climb that hill and see if I can follow the dragons' trail."

As I pointed, the crest of the hill flickered with a fiery halo that shot tongues of flame into the sky for a moment. Somebody screamed. It was . . . not a pleasant sound.

"Stay!" I yelled at Salla, who had started moving towards the hill.

Sasulau was in my hand and I was halfway up the hill before I realized that not all the panting I heard came from my own lungs.

"I thought—I told you to stay—where you were," I gasped.

"You— might need—backup." The flames shooting over the crest of the hill danced in Dennis' glasses, making him look like a fiery-eyed monster from Outer Yark.

We could hear the chunky sound of metal going into meat now, and somebody was yelling a rhythmic war chant. I felt a moment's pride in my ex-colleagues. The dragons weren't getting it all their own way.

As we came over the hill, I took in the battle scene in one quick glance. The dragons were bigger than anything native to Dazau; they'd have taken our people in a few quick mouthfuls if they had any notion of strategy or tactics. But Sika was an excellent battle commander. Archers in the trees harassed the dragons from the rear while a line of lancers on foot drove them back into a bog of mud and marsh grass. The dragons were slowly sinking under their own weight while the lancers kept them from escaping the bog.

One of the trees was blackened and bare. That explained the flare of dragonfire that had shown over the hill—and the screams. I made a mental vow to pour a sacrifice to Gredu, Lady of Wrath, for the archers who had been in that tree.

"Lances, retreat, on the double!" Sika called in a high carrying voice. "Archers!" Her right arm rose and fell; the remaining trees erupted in a swarm of buzzing arrows. Most of the arrows fell harmlessly off the dragons' scales; a few struck eyes and open mouths and did a little damage.

The high-pitched chanting went on, one piping little voice set against the rumbling roars of the dragons. I recognized the words now. A cold sweat broke out down my spine. For the first time I felt truly terrified.

"Push 'em back, push 'em back, fight, fight, fight! Cushman Middle School has the might, might, might!" The shortest person on the field of battle leapt onto a tuft of grass in the bog and skewered a dragon's throat with her sword.

"Becky, get out of there!" I screamed.

"Apprentice Bekka, retreat now!" Sika shouted at the same time.

The dragon gave a bellow of agony and fell sideways, feet kicking. Its white flank gleamed eerily against the sucking mud of the bog. Beside it, a smaller dragon reared up and breathed in deeply.

"Nauzu's tears!" I was running forward, but too slowly, the boggy morass where Becky danced among the dragons was too far away, I'd never reach her before the dragon's flame roared out. Time slowed around me; I felt as though I were trying to run through the slough of stinking mud, every step a million years in the taking. Before me, Becky leapt from tuft to tuft of grass, chanting the Cushman Middle School football cheers and sticking her short sword into any soft dragon-parts she could find. And the rearing dragon's mouth flickered with the beginnings of flame.

"ARCHERS!" Sika shouted, and almost at once, "HOLD! You might hit Riva!" The arrows that could have saved Becky remained in the trees. I reminded myself to throttle Sika after we got out of this.

If we got out of this.

"Let $t = DRAGONLANCE$; $\int e^{-st} F(t)dt$!" Dennis yelled from somewhere behind me.

The dragon took a deep breath and blasted a hump of bog moss into cinders.

"Damn," Dennis said quietly. "Guessed wrong. Let $t = \ldots$" he started again.

His shouting was disturbing the dragon. It raised its head and looked straight at him. I knocked him down with one shoulder and plunged forward, under most of the next cloud of fire. Running through the edge of the blast still felt like going from the waterfall of Nauzu's Blood into the Great Fyrkovou Desert at high noon. I grabbed Becky by the back of her leather corselet and yanked her out of range, pivoting on one foot to push her towards Sika's lancers.

She stumbled out of the bog. I didn't. The foot that had been bearing my weight for that last desperate thrust sank down into the mud. I could feel the bog sucking at my knees. I fell forward, clawing for grassy tufts. A hand closed over my arm and hauled me towards the relative solidity of the edge. I tasted mud, spat, rolled over and gasped. The air shimmered with heat around me.

"Let t = DRAGONCLEAVER," Dennis said, and the last heat waves disappeared.

There were feet all around me. "Mmmphky?" I spat out some mud and tried again. "Becky? All right?"

"I'm here," said the voice I'd last heard piping Cushman Middle School football cheers. Two muddy gym shoes came into my field of view. "Riva, what happened to your eyebrows?"

I pushed myself up to a sitting position. Becky's knees were skinned, and her face and arms looked as if she'd been sitting on the beach too long, but she did seem to be all in one piece. Mostly.

"Same thing that happened to yours, I guess," I said.

Becky put one hand to her forehead with a look of dismay.

"I told you we needed mathemagical backup," said Kloreem from behind Sika. She was wearing a lieutenant's insignia stamped on both leather shoulder straps; must have been promoted since I left.

"Becky, guess who we met!" Jason said.

"Riva, when did you come back to work?" demanded Sika. "And don't you ever pull a fool stunt like that again, or I'll personally stake you out for the dragons to roast."

I grinned. My face felt hot, and I probably looked as bad as Becky, but for the moment I didn't care. "Funny coincidence. That's just what I was gonna tell the kid here."

For a few minutes everybody was talking at once. Salla and Jason wanted to tell Becky about the stranger, Sika wanted to tell me about her new apprentice, the woman who'd been complaining about lack of mathemagical backup wanted Sika to offer Dennis a contract, and Dennis wanted to tell the world about how he'd figured out the theory of mathemagical transformulation just in time to dispel the dragons. "Actually," he said, "I worked out the theory earlier. The hard part was figuring out what to insert in the title variable. You have to know the name of the book or series that was transformed in order to reverse the action," Dennis said.

"Couldn't you just have sent them back as dragons?" I asked.

"I was going to," Dennis said. "If necessary. But it wouldn't have been very nice for the people at Bookstop. Or wherever the dragons showed up—if I left too many variables undefined, no telling where they'd go. The responsible thing was to transformulate them back into book form." He swallowed. "I was going to give up being responsible if that last trans-formula didn't work."

"I'm surprised you didn't know the name of the book right off," I said.

Dennis looked pained. "Riva, did you look at those dragons?"

"Yes?"

"White? With bar codes on their flanks?"

"Yeah. Like the cheap cereal and cookies and like that in the generics aisle of the supermarket . . . Oh." I finally caught on.

"Right," Dennis said. "They were generic dragons. They could have come out of any of a dozen series or movie tie-ins or sharecropper packages. I just had to keep trying until I got the right one."

I grinned at him. "I'm glad you got the right one."

"So am I," he said. "I wish I knew how to keep her."

"That's not what I meant."

"I know," Dennis said sadly.

If he really felt that way, why did he keep practically pushing me into Mikh's arms? Not that it was going to work. But— I shook my head, confused. This probably wasn't a good time to demand an explanation.

"Okay, then, how about a one-quarter trial contract, pay to be based on a share of our commissions?" Kloreem asked Dennis.

"I do the negotiating around here," Sika said. "How about a one-quarter trial contract, pay to be based on a share of our commissions?"

"Mom, I need to talk to you," Salla said urgently.

It was definitely not the time to explore Dennis's finer feelings, assuming he had any. I let Salla draw me away from Sika and her lieutenants.

I'd heard some childish voices raised a few moments earlier, but hadn't paid any attention. Now I looked at Jason, standing halfway up the hill and glowering at the women of the Bronze Bra Guild; at Becky, standing beside Sika and staring at the ground; and at Salla, tugging on my arm.

"Whatever it is," I said, "I don't want to know about it, and you kids need to work it out for yourselves."

"Mom," Salla said patiently, "it's important."

"Did you and Jason figure out something new about the Leibniz?"

"Not about the Leibniz. About Becky."

"We've rescued Becky," I pointed out. "And I'm sure her eyebrows—and mine—will grow back in time."

"No, we haven't. She's still an apprentice with the Bronze Bra Guild."

I sighed. "Sika's an old friend. She'll let me buy Becky out." Exactly what I was going to buy the kid out with was another matter, but that was the least of my problems right now. I was tired, dragon-burned, encrusted with stinking marsh mud, and the only man I really wanted seemed to be trying to send me back to Mikhalleviko the Sleazeball. I needed a bath, food, and a long talk with Dennis. Alone. I did not need to contemplate my precarious financial situation.

"Mom," Salla said in the exaggeratedly patient tones of one talking to someone who never gets the point, "Becky doesn't want to be bought out of the Guild. She says she's staying here."

"Well, tough!" I snapped. "She can't stay, and that's that. Vera Boatright would have kittens."

"She's happy here, Mom. She's like a different person."

I glanced over at the sullen kid standing beside Sika.

Her shoulders were slumped and the leather corselet, which must have been borrowed from one of the smaller Guild trainees, gapped open over her growing breasts. She was still staring at the ground. "Looks like the usual Becky to me."

"That's because she thinks you're gonna make her come back with us."

"Darn right," I snapped before I remembered that Salla and I might not be returning to Paper-Pushers. "Look, Salla. You know I can't take Becky away from her parents. That's kidnapping in her universe and stealing here. Either place, it's trouble."

"I know," Salla said, "but we're sorta not in either reality, right? I mean, her parents are there, and she's here, and . . ."

"And you think we ought to have an interuniversal incident over her?"

"She told me," Salla said, staring at the ground like Becky, "that she wanted to stay at least until she learned to fight with a sword. Like you. So . . ."

"Well, that's very flattering, but—"

"So that nobody would ever touch her again if she didn't want them to," Salla said on one long rush of breath.

"Oh."

Salla couldn't know it, but her words sent me back more than a decade—before she was born. For a moment I was in Mikhalleviko's room, hearing him laugh softly as he told me that I had even less magical eptitude than he had but that he'd be willing to keep me and my baby as bond-property. That it would be worth feeding the brat to know that I wouldn't ever be tired or out of sorts or not in the mood again . . . not if my owner wanted me.

I'd been a scared, ignorant girl from the mountains then, and the Guild had been my way out of the mess I'd gotten myself into. If Becky was looking to the Guild for the same reason I had, I wasn't about to stop her. Vera Boatright would have kittens twice if she found out that I'd left her twelve-year-old darling apprenticed to a fighting guild in a strange universe. But I was back in Dazau's reality now, and the longer we stayed, the more I was thinking in Dazau terms. Twelve was the age of apprenticeship on Dazau; by Dazau law, Becky's mother and stepfather had no power to break her contract.

All those years of commuting from Paper-Pushers to give Salla a chance at a better education and a better life now seemed like a dreary waste. What had been the point, anyway? Here I was back in Dazau's reality, with a chance to get my old job back, and nothing and nobody on Paper-Pushers to go back to. My attempt to learn higher mathemagics had been a dead failure—look at the mess I'd made when I tried to neutralize Furo Fykrou. And to tell the truth, I didn't much mind. All the picky little details of Al-Jibber and K'al-Kul were boring. I didn't want to devote my life to reciting long abstract formulas.

I didn't much want to rejoin the Guild as an aging, slowing swordswoman, either, but at least it was honest work. And the years on Paper-Pushers hadn't been a total waste, I told myself. At least Salla had gotten enough grounding in Jomtrie and Al-Jibber to earn herself a decent apprenticeship contract with a wizard here. If I rejoined the Guild, I'd be able to watch over both Salla and Becky as they worked through the years of their apprenticeships.

And if I got really lucky, maybe Dennis would take that contract Sika and Kloreem had mentioned. It was true that the Guild really needed their own wizard, and they could hardly get a better one than Dennis. This mess with the dragons was a perfect example of what happened when you depended on your employer's house wizard: half the time the duke wanted him for something else, and there you were out in the field with no mathemagical backup.

I had just about worked everything out in my own head when reality, as is its nasty habit, confronted me with the unsolved problems.

Jason and Becky had resumed bickering while I thought.

"I don't care if you don't want to be rescued," Jason shouted, loudly enough to break my train of thought, "I've rescued you, and now I want to go home. I don't like this place!"

Okay, we send Jason home, I thought. Dennis could probably manage that on his own; it had to be an easier transformulation than disposing of hordes of generic dragons. Of course, we didn't want to accidentally turn Jason into a book. Might be better to let the Duke's house wizard handle it—if we could find him.

"Sure, I know where Lavvu Lherkode is," Sika said when I asked her. "Just before we got the message about the dragons, he went off with the duke to work on another manifestation. The farmers down along the Vofurron said there were about forty square varengs of sand covering the west side of the river valley. With some kind of sand-crawling snakes in it. The duke told them it was just an illusory manifestation, but they said it was playing hell with the harvest and did he want a nice wizardly illusion of corn in the granaries

this winter, or did he want to do something about it?
So," she finished with a shrug, "he went off to do
something. And if that sand is as real as the dragons
were, I hope Lavvu Lherkode is a fast man with a
trans-reality formula."

I tried to visualize the great relief map in the Duke's
hall. "Isn't the Vofurron the east boundary with old
Lord Gonykivvauno's lands?"

"Not anymore," Sika told me. "Two winters ago he
died without naming an heir. While all his bastards
by all six of his women were quarreling, Rodograunnizo
marched in and took over."

"Seems funny the way all the trouble is happening
near Rodo the Revolting's lands," I said.

"Riva, we know who's causing the manifestations,
and it isn't Rodograunnizo," Dennis reminded me.

"Mikh used to work for Rodo." I was beginning to
wonder if there was some kind of trans-universal plot
going on. Probably not; neither Mikh nor Rodo had
a long enough attention span to stage a public quarrel
and wait two years to start the next stage of their plot.

"Anyway," Sika said, "it's not all happening on the
borders. You should see some of the stuff we've had
in Duke's Zolvorra! And I hear there's something weird
just across the river, in Rodo's territory. A singing metal
tower or something."

Dennis' eyes lit up. "Do we go that way?"

"We?" Sika repeated.

"The duke's house wizard won't have solved this
problem," Dennis said. "You have to put the name
of the book into the transformulation. I just tested
that out with the dragons."

Sika shrugged. "Some of the manifestations just
dissolve after a while. The first one did."

"I bet it never was very solid," Dennis said.

"Well . . . okay, you tell us the transformula and we'll tell Lavvu Lherkode."

Dennis shook his head. "Nothing's free on Dazau. I'll come along and help your wizard dispose of the sandworms, and then the duke will owe me a favor. It'll be in his interest to help, too," he said, "if he doesn't want more manifestations showing up."

"The sand, too," Sika said.

"Huh?"

"You get rid of the sand as well as the snakes, or it's no deal."

"Oh. Right. Don't worry, it will all go away as soon as I say the appropriate inverse transformulation. Can we go down the river to get there?"

"Shorter route than going back to Duke's Zolvorra," Sika said, "if you don't mind a bit of rough traveling."

"I'd like to check out this singing tower," Dennis said mildly. He glanced at me. "And I rather think Riva needs a bath."

Sika looked at me, too, then pinched her nose ostentatiously. "Right. We'd better go by way of the river, or we'll be smelling marsh gas all the way from here to Duke's Zolvorra. But we won't have time for you to detour into Rodo's lands, wizard."

"No detour, no deal."

Sika sighed. "Okay, okay. Tell you what. We can camp in the river bend just above the sand manifestations tonight. Tomorrow morning you can check out the singing tower and then we'll head straight for the duke. I guess one more night of sand-manifestations won't kill any crops that aren't already dead. And Riva needs a chance for a proper bath before she meets the duke again."

Great. Maybe the duke's crops could stand another night, but what about Norah? Would she go to the Paper-Pushers police if I didn't get Jason back to her tonight? Probably not, she was bright enough to see it wouldn't do her much good, but she was not going to be happy. Every minute of waiting must feel to her like twenty years.

And Sika's last comment had just rubbed in another minor problem facing me after we took care of the sand-manifestations. Oh, not Mikh and the Leibniz. I didn't really care, personally, if he transformed every book on Paper-Pushers. Especially if he included *Make Friends With Mr. Euclid* on his hit list.

It was Dennis. I'd been wondering how he felt about Sika's offer of a one-quarter trial contract here; whether he'd be willing to stay in a universe where I could find work and where Mikh couldn't try to get custody of Salla. But a man whose only comment on me was that I stank to high Nauzu wasn't likely to give up his job and take a contract with the Guild for my sake, was he?

So much for that bit of fantasy. It didn't really change anything, I told myself. Salla and I had made it without Dennis before and we'd do fine now. I might miss him like hell, but I'd get over it.

If he stuck around long enough to make a few more of those cracks about how bad I smelled and how I was probably plotting to get back together with Mikhalleviko, it should be real easy to get over him.

Yeah. Should be.

Chapter 2⁴

It was maybe a one-day march from where we were to the lower river valley. If you started early in the morning and your troop was in good shape. Starting in midafternoon, with all of us already tired from traveling and fighting dragons, there was no way we were going to reach the duke and his sand-manifestations that day. But nobody wanted to camp beside a bog, so we pushed ourselves and made it as far as the river before dark. We'd have a little traveling downstream to do the next day, but nothing too bad. At least, I didn't think then that it would be very difficult. I was making certain assumptions, of course, such as that we'd all be marching together and that nothing would be chasing us. You have to watch out for those assumptions.

I had expected to mind watching Sika organize the evening camp, giving the orders I would have been giving a few years ago, reminding me that I was an outsider now. But it wasn't bad at all. In fact, I was perfectly happy to have no more to worry about than washing the bog mud off and pulling sweetgrass to make beds for Dennis and me and the kids, while Sika trotted about setting perimeter guards and assigning cooking details and latrine diggers and telling the trainees to shut up, there was a lot more digging than flashy swordsmanship in the fighting life.

I don't think they'd quite grasped that little fact before this march; most of them had been recruited in Duke's Zolvorra and had only drilled in the Guildhouse camp right outside the walls. Now, when I joined the Guild, I'd had one year of living soft with Mikhalleviko, but before that I'd been raised in a mountain village where everyday life made a Guild march and setting up camp seem like a paid holiday. Maybe Sika was right about bringing in more young apprentices who could get used to the life early and wouldn't grumble like this batch of trainees.

Maybe she was right about Becky. From our camping place, a little apart from the officers' beds but still well within the camp perimeter, I watched Becky cheerfully carrying water, pulling sweetgrass, peeling naupods for soup, and doing any other little task anybody assigned her to. As an untrained apprentice she was getting more than her share of the dirty work, a lot more than any preteen I'd met on Paper-Pushers' would have done without complaining. And she looked happy. Her shoulders were straight and her eyes danced with the light from the cooking fires and she herself almost danced as she carried her loads from one place to another. She looked six inches taller than she did on Paper-Pushers'.

I wasn't feeling any too comfortable around Dennis, especially since he'd arranged the sweetgrass I brought back in four separate and distinct piles—one each for him, me, Jason and Salla. Becky had already informed us that she was sleeping in the trainees' rows.

But regardless of our personal differences, we did

have to settle the matter of what to do with Becky. And he wasn't talking, so I guessed I would have to start.

"Look at Becky," I said.

"Mmmm."

All right, so my conversational skills aren't quite as sharp as my swordplay. I tried again.

"What are we going to do about her?"

"You said you were going to bring all the kids back."

"Yeah, but . . . Things have changed."

"I know your feelings have changed. It's all right. You can stay here. I don't mind."

After a warm and inviting opening like that, I could hardly whack him upside the head with the flat of my sword and yell that I didn't want to stay in this universe while he went back to Paper-Pushers', could I now?

"What I mean," I said, "is about Becky. Salla told me some kind of disturbing things." When I added them to Norah's worry about Becky, and factored in the way Becky looked now as an apprentice, a universe away from her family, what I came up with was a very ugly sum. "I think her stepfather is . . ."

"Yeah," Dennis agreed. He leaned back on one elbow and pushed his black-rimmed glasses up on his nose, studying Becky. "I think so, too. That woman they have for a counselor at Cushman is an idiot of the first order, but even she noticed there was something strange about Becky. Only she thought I was the one who was molesting her."

"You! Dennis, why didn't you tell me?" From her scabbard, Sasulau hummed a thirsty note to match my anger. "Of all the moronic, baseless accusations!"

"I didn't have time to tell you," Dennis said. "It just came up at a meeting this afternoon. Then when

I got home, there were Bob Boatright and his gang of Hitler Youth, and then we had to transport here to rescue the kids, and . . . well, it's been a busy day."

"It has that," I agreed. I was aching in places that would never have bothered me five years ago. Working out in the backyard was all very well, but it was no substitute for my old regimen of full-armor training, weighted marches and teaching sessions with the Guild's armsmistresses. Various muscle groups were now informing me that they thought they were retired, for Nauzu's sake, and what did I think I was doing, calling on them to perform after all this time?

Returning to the Guild was not going to be easy. But that was the only kind of job I'd ever had here, the only one I could imagine myself doing. Two years of studying math with Dennis had convinced me that I would never make a wizard. Furo Fykrou might have been telling me the truth when he said that my Magical Eptitude Quotient was astonishingly high, but what good was that when I couldn't match it with the mathemagical transformulations? A wizard could use me, but he wouldn't make me a partner. The only way I could make a living out of mathemagics would be to team up with somebody who combined mathe-magical ability with total integrity.

And the only guy I knew of who met those criteria wasn't interested in staying with me, let alone staying here.

I sighed and returned to the problem of Becky. "I don't know the laws of your people all that well. If we bring her back, will you be able to see that she is not abused again?"

"I doubt it," Dennis said. "Even aside from the fact

that they're accusing me of doing it. She hasn't said anything directly to you or even Salla, has she? I thought not. Even here, she's not willing to implicate him. Between the hints she's dropped, the way she acts, and the fact that she ran away from home, we can pretty well figure out who it is. But I don't see our social services doing anything for a kid who hasn't got any marks on her and who won't name anybody directly."

"What if we persuaded her to tell someone?"

Dennis looked tired and drawn in the flickering light. I had an urge to reach over and cradle his head against my breast and run my fingers through his hair. I repressed it. "Riva, even if she made a complaint, he'd deny it. The mother strikes me as being totally under his thumb; she'd back him up. He's a preacher. Respectable man. And there's a strong bias to keep families together. Say we make her go back and talk her into accusing him; chances are that after an almighty fuss, she'll be sent right back into the same situation. Only this time," he said quietly, "he'll be angry with her. And she'll have learned that she can't count on us for refuge."

He was saying "us" and "we" as if we were still together. Well, in this matter, tonight, we were. We were both trying to find a solution for Becky.

"Growing up in the Guild isn't exactly safe," I mused, "but at least your enemies come at you openly, and you can defend yourself. And it seems to agree with Becky. But . . . I don't know. If you've been accused of molesting Becky, and she disappears from our house, you're going to be in a lot of trouble. And then there's Vera."

"Never mind me," Dennis said, "I haven't done

anything to her, and they can't prove anything, and
if Jason is idiot enough to tell them where Becky
went—which I don't think he is—they will laugh kindly
and tell him to stop reading so much science fiction,
sonny. As for Vera, she's let it go on all this time. I
don't much care about Vera."

"I don't like her," I said, "but to have your kid
disappear, and never know what happened to her . . .
Dennis, we can't do that. Imagine if it were Salla."

Dennis closed his eyes for a minute. He looked ten
years older. I had to suppress that urge to cuddle him
again.

A fight broke out on the other side of the campfire,
a welcome distraction from the problem of Becky.

"I don't do mending!" one of the trainees was
screeching.

"You tore it, you mend it!" another one yelled. "Or
I'll rub your face in it!" She swung a leather corselet
at the first girl, who punched back. A third joined in,
shouting something about bitterweed in the soup, and
for just a moment the free-for-all threatened to spill
over and engulf the entire camp. Sika and Kloreem
waded in, whacking girls with their scabbarded swords
and handing out demerits at the tops of their voices.
When it was over, Sika came around the campfire and
sat down between Dennis and me.

"I wish you hadn't seen that, Riva."

"Morale," I said cautiously, "seems to have dete-
riorated since my time in the Guild."

"Not morale," Sika said, "manners. Since Savi-
murrina died we haven't had any Guild member
who's ready to retire from active duty to be a
Guildmother. There's nobody to keep the Guildhouse
up to standard and teach the new ones some

manners; they live in a barracks and they act like it, what do you expect?"

I massaged my right calf muscle, which had been protesting ever since I took that dive into the bog. "Way I'm feeling tonight, I might apply for the position. I'm getting too old for this, Sika."

"Nonsense," Sika said, "you've been living soft, that's all. Are you thinking of coming back to the Guild, Riva? We've missed you."

"I've missed you," I admitted. But I wasn't so sure about the life. It was true, what Sika said. I wasn't too old to take up my sword again. But I would be, in—what? Five years? Ten years? A lot of Guild swordswomen kept on past their fighting prime, choosing a quick death at some enemy's hands rather than a slow decline into old age and pottering around the Guildhouse to do housework for the fighting members. Neither future appealed to me.

Dennis snorted. "Well, the two of you should be happy enough now. I'll leave you to your plans; I need a wash." And he stalked off to the river.

The next morning I woke late—well, later than the rest of the camp—to find Dennis arguing with Sika about how many members of the Bronze Bra Guild would escort him across the river to look at this singing tower thing.

"I'll be less conspicuous alone," Dennis said.

"You'll be less alive alone, if they catch you. And then the duke will kill me for letting you get killed. We're giving you a full escort."

"Besides, I have the impression Baron Rodograunizo might take the presence of some of the Duke's men as an incitement to war." With the exception of one word, I thought Dennis had caught on to Dazau customs and attitudes very quickly.

Sika, of course, noticed that word as well. "Women," she said with an edged grin, "and just let him start a war. Duke Zolkir can take that two-time bully—"

"Duke Zolkir can't afford a war if the entire lower Vofurron valley has just been covered with sand," I said, grabbing my armor. "I'll go with him while you guys march on and tell Zolkir that help is on the way. Then none of the duke's people will be involved."

"We'll go too," Jason and Salla chorused.

"Oh, no, you won't. You'll march with Sika's troop and you'll do what you're told. Understand?"

In the end, I left most of the armor with Sika. There wasn't a decent ford within an hour's march of these parts, and I couldn't swim the Vofurron in full body-armor. As it was, I had enough to do, keeping my leather corselet and sword belt and Sasulau dry while I stroked with one arm. Dennis had it easier; his weapons were all in his head.

Once we got across the river and hit on a cart track, we had no trouble finding the manifestation. Big, sloppily painted pictures and arrows guided us and a dozen others to "the wonderful new work of Baron Rodograunnizo's wizards, the tower that sings! (Two copper kauven admission.)"

I don't know what anybody would pay the two kauven for; we could hear the tower well before we came in sight of it. By this time there was quite a crowd traveling with us. Apparently Baron Rodo's musical tower was drawing visitors from all over. Just as well. In the baron's territory, I preferred to be inconspicuous.

I guess you could call it music, the noise the tower was making. Dennis seemed to think so, anyway.

"Wagner," said Dennis. "It's got to be . . ."

The music changed to a jigging, dancing tune that made my toes tap in the dust of the road.

"Wagner followed by Airdrie Lasses," Dennis said happily, and as we crested the hill, "It is her! I knew it! Those idiots can't tell a spaceship from a tower."

It was, I had to admit, a remarkably pointy tower. And I could see no defensive or structural use for the shining metal buttresses that thrust out from its lower end.

"Let t = THE SHIP . . ." Dennis began.

I grabbed his arm and pulled him to the side of the road. "Wait a minute."

"Why?"

"All these people have come a long way to hear the musical tower. And some of them are paying good money to get up close enough to touch it."

"So?"

"So whoever makes it disappear is not going to be real popular," I pointed out. "How about we crawl into these bushes and you do the transformulation very, very quietly so nobody notices?"

Dennis cooperated. But I guess it was overly optimistic of me to hope that nobody would notice. The disappearance of a tower as tall as three dragons and as noisy as a dozen competing jongleurs was not the sort of thing one could pull off inconspicuously.

The only thing that saved us was that finding a good bush to hide in took some time. By the time Dennis finally fired off his transformulation, the other travelers of the morning were down in the valley where the tower had manifested.

"Let $t = THESHIPWHOSANG; \int_0^\infty e^{-st} F(t)dt$!" Dennis called out, pointing at the tower.

The song broke off in midnote; the tower shivered like heat rising from the desert, then vanished.

The people who'd paid to get down in the valley mostly milled around and cursed and demanded their money back. But one or two began to cry wizardry, and then somebody pointed at the bush Dennis and I were hiding in. And I don't know what happened after that, because I grabbed Dennis by the hand and we both ran for it.

We were heading downhill and they had to struggle up out of the valley. It wasn't much of an advantage, but it was all we had. So I kept heading downhill, parallel to the river, until I saw a goat track leading off to the left that should take us to the Vofurron.

Unfortunately, what it took us to was a cliff that goats might be able to climb down, but that wasn't exactly designed for people. Here, what saved us was the narrow track. If we had to go single file, so did our pursuers.

"You'd think—they'd give up—eventually," Dennis panted as we sidled along a rocky ledge and over a boulder that stuck out over the river. "It's only—two cents worth—"

On the other side of the boulder, thank Nauzu, the path slanted downward. If we could stay ahead of the crowd for a little longer, and if they didn't throw too many stones when we were swimming, we might actually make it to the river and across. "It's the most fun they've had since Vordo challenged me to a duel as Rodo's champion," I gasped. And all those two-kauven fees added up to a nice little regular income that the baron would not be happy to lose. I reckoned we were lucky it was just the peasants chasing us and not Rodo's guards.

A spear poked out of the underbrush directly ahead of me. "Stand in the name of the Baron Rodo!" the underbrush demanded.

So much for luck. I looked at Dennis. He shrugged and nodded towards the river. I knew it wouldn't be deep enough for us to dive safely from this height, but Nauzu take it! Our present position wasn't exactly safe either. I shut my eyes and grabbed Dennis's hand. "I never did like this scene in the movie—" he started to say as we jumped for it.

We hit the water and kept on going. My legs, curled up tightly in anticipation of hitting the river bottom, slowly relaxed. The river was deep here, almost like a lake; we touched bottom as gently as feathers falling from a torn mattress, drifted up again. My lungs were bursting. So was my brain. We shouldn't be alive; what had happened?

I tried to breathe and look and swim all at the same time as we broke the surface, with the predictable result that I inhaled a lot of water. But I did see that there was some kind of mountain lying across the river, damming it to create a nice deep backwater just where we needed one. Dennis was swimming for the mountain, dragging me along with him. Sasulau was wet and unhappy about it and making a thin screeching noise, but there wasn't much I could do about that.

The mountain was made of sand. It met the water at such a gentle angle that we were wading long before we came to the dry land.

"Nauzu must love one of us," I said when I was through coughing up river water. "There isn't a lake here. I mean, there never was before."

"It's the manifestation," Dennis said. He shaded his

hand and looked over the undulating sand dunes before us. "We're very lucky, Riva."

"I said that."

"I always said the landscape was the main character in this book," Dennis said.

"What book?" I wrung out my tunic and tried to clean Sasulau with it. The results, as she let me know with an irritable whine, were less than satisfactory.

Two riders came thundering along the northern border of the sand dunes. As they drew closer, I recognized Duke Zolkir's colors. "Up and away!" one of them shouted. "The giant snakes!"

I glanced over my shoulder. One of the dunes was moving towards us. I don't like horses, but I made it up to the saddle of that one in record time. The other rider took up Dennis behind him. They wheeled and galloped back along the solid line. The moving sand dune stopped where the sand did. It opened a mouth and showed us a cavern of sharp teeth.

"They're called worms, actually," Dennis said as we rode towards the duke's camp. "Sandworms."

The horses wheeled to a graceful stop at the base of a rocky ridge that rose several feet above the sea of sand. Higher up, where the rocks leveled out, Duke Zolkir's green-and-gold tent glowed in the morning sunshine. The duke himself stood in front of the tent, watching our arrival with arms folded.

I slid off the back of my horse. My clothes squelched.

"Kneel to the duke," I hissed at Dennis.

He managed a wobbly bow. "Your Grace. I'm here to save your lands."

"Much obliged, I'm sure," said Duke Zolkir. "And very kind of you to bring Rivakonneva with you. We have missed her services. Riva, what happened to your eyebrows?"

"Manifestations," I said. "Dragons. I was in the direct path of their flame, but this powerful wizard from an alternate reality caused the dragons to disappear in the twinkling of an eyelash." Might as well build up Dennis's stock while I could.

Duke Zolkir's house wizard, a portly bald man with three chins and great dignity, frowned at me. "There's no need to bring in extraneous wizards," he informed me. "I have this manifestation well under control."

I looked at the mountains of sand stretching out of sight. I would have raised an eyebrow, if I had one. Instead, I casually mentioned that the Vofurron seemed to be dammed up to a remarkable height by this particular manifestation, and maybe it would be a good idea to remove it before the farmers upstream got flooded out entirely.

Lavvu Lherkode turned his scowl my way and repeated that he had the matter well in hand.

"Er—as one professional mathematician to another," Dennis said, "might I ask how the transformulation has proceeded so far?"

"Transformulation? Don't be ridiculous, boy. It's a simple iteration. Every time I invoke a Trigo Name some more of the manifestation diminishes. Like that!" Lavvu Lherkode pointed at the six inches of bare ground revealed where the borders of the sand had been just a moment earlier.

"It's going to take you a long time at that rate," Sika remarked.

Duke Zolkir looked as if that idea had already occurred to him.

"Sometimes it does much better than that," Lavvu

Lherkode said defensively. "The first time I implemented the equation, nearly three yards of sand disappeared."

"That's true," said Duke Zolkir, "but—"

"And what happened the second time?" Dennis interrupted.

I put my hand on Sasulau, just in case the duke took offense at being interrupted. "No manners, these foreign wizards," he growled, but I thought there was a twinkle in his eye. "You have the right of it, Mage—"

"Dennis Dithrovvu," I said, hastily translating Dennis's name into the standard Dazau form for fully Guild-certified wizards. It would never do to have the duke thinking Dennis was merely a one-name flash in the pan like Mikhalleviko.

"Whatever." The duke waved his hand irritably. I swallowed, reflecting that two interruptions in a row was rather a lot for Zolkir to put up with. "On his second attempt, only a yard of sand disappeared. And each time since then, Lavvu Lherkode has removed proportionately less—"

"$Tan(x) = \frac{\sin(x)}{\cot(x)}$!" Lavvu Lherkode thundered over the duke's words, thumping his staff upon the ground. An impressive aurora of blue and purple flames blazed up where the staff struck. The sand dunes retreated perhaps three grudging inches.

"Don't interrupt me!" Duke Zolkir snarled, grabbing the mage by the jeweled collar of his robe and twisting it.

Dennis cleared his throat. "I think I see what the problem is."

"Yes?" Zolkir growled.

Lavvu Lherkode's eyebrows waggled. His face was turning blue; I supposed that with the duke holding his collar so tightly, he couldn't utter his mathemagical formulae.

Dennis nodded. "I'm afraid you're reaching your limit."

"I reached it some time ago," the duke grumbled. "Yes?"

"I've had some experience with other manifestations by now," Dennis explained. "They're being transferred from my home reality—"

"Then just send them back!" the duke snapped. "Even Lavvu Lherkode should be able to handle a simple Furry R transform!"

"I'm afraid it's not quite that simple," Dennis said. "You see, we need the appropriate value for this variable—" He knelt to scratch his equations in the sand, then looked up over his shoulder. "Let him go, please, Your Grace. I can't consult with a colleague while he's dangling in midair."

Still grumbling, the duke dropped Lavvu Lherkode. Dennis nodded and started writing in the sand. "To get the stuff to go back in its proper form, you have to give this variable the right value."

That wasn't exactly true. As I'd understood Dennis, a generic Furry R transform would send the sand back into Paper-Pushers' reality, all right. But it would manifest as tons of sand, not as a paperback book. However, I didn't see any virtue in explaining this to Duke Zolkir. After all the trouble the manifestations had caused here, he might not be entirely averse to sending a little trouble the other way.

"It has to remain undefined," Lavvu Lherkode protested. "Nobody knows the true name of this manifestation."

"I do," said Dennis. He wiped his hand over the

middle of the equation and substituted a sequence of four letters. "Try this."

"You try it," said Lavvu Lherkode.

"Okay. Let t = DUNE," Dennis said, and finished the equation calmly.

The sand dunes shivered and grew transparent. The giant sand snakes were slower to disappear; for a moment I could see them through the transparent sand, shimmering like ghosts or flames. Then the mountains of sand were gone, and the lake that had been created by the dammed-up river crashed through the valley, washing away topsoil and frothing right up to the rocky crest where we stood. I backed up involuntarily; Duke Zolkir just looked down at the water splashing his boots and nodded with satisfaction. I suppose he assumed that a wizard would have better sense than to drown a duke. Me, I wasn't quite that certain of Dennis's control.

"Very nice," Duke Zolkir shouted over the roar of the released waters. "You'll stay with me, of course. Full house wizard status, coequal with Lherkode, and the usual terms?"

To a sopping wet stranger from nowhere, it was a princely offer. I knew that was how Zolkir meant it, and I was braced for another explosion of wrath when Dennis turned him down. Instead, Dennis said, "That's very generous, Your Grace. Might I beg the favor of some time to discuss it in private?"

"Very well, very well," the duke said. "Come along to my tent."

"Er—I meant, to discuss it with Riva. Your Grace," Dennis added hurriedly.

A broad grin slowly spread over the duke's face. "I see! I see! I suppose when your lady love is a swordswoman, you don't just tell the wench where you're going and throw her over your saddle, eh? Very well, Mage Ditthrovu. I've no doubt the lady will be agreeable."

As he turned away, a group of local farmers bustled up and requested an audience. "All right, all right," I heard him saying, "but I got rid of your sand-manifestation, didn't I? What more do you pestilential peasants want?"

"It's okay, Dennis," I said as soon as Duke Zolkir and his entourage were out of earshot. "I'll get you out of this. I know you don't want to stay here."

"You don't even want me in the same reality with you, do you?"

"Huh?"

"Well, you're planning to go back to the Bronze Bra Guild, aren't you?"

I swallowed. "I . . . sort of thought . . . that was what you wanted. For me to go away. I mean."

"Nauzu's tears!" Dennis said. "Where did you get an idea like that, you idiot?"

"Well, if you weren't desperate to get rid of me, why did you keep shoving me into Mikhalleviko's arms?"

"I never!"

"You did so! Practically all I've heard from you lately has been oblique little cuts about how I must have enjoyed my loooong conversations with Mikh! What am I supposed to think when you go on like that?"

"You might," Dennis said very softly, "think that I'm desperately jealous and wish you would tell me the truth about you and Mikhalleviko."

I stared. "Dennis. I have never lied to you."

"No," he said, "but there's been a lot unsaid between

lies and truth, hasn't there? You never have told me about those nice long friendly chats the two of you were having."

"I didn't tell you everything about Mikh because I didn't want to worry you. As for the 'long friendly chats,' that's something you or he must have invented, choose one. He's been chasing me around Austin talking about suing for custody of Salla. He says that under your law he could claim her. That was the only reason I even thought for a minute about coming back to Dazau."

"You're not homesick?"

"No!"

"You don't miss your old job?"

"No!"

"You're not trying to get away from me?"

"Nauzu klevulkkedimmu! No! How many times do I have to tell you?"

Dennis stared into my eyes. Then he took off his glasses and stared some more.

"Do I pass the exam?" I growled.

His face creased into a weary smile. "Riva. Will you share my bed and board and universe?"

"Yes," I said, "and I want to come back to Paper-Pushers' with you. I don't belong here anymore. But I won't be property. I'll get some kind of a job."

"You'll probably have to support me," Dennis said. "They found out about my teaching credentials. I didn't want to worry you about that."

So that was why he'd been so gloomy! "Perhaps," I said, "in the future we should just go ahead and worry each other about things."

"Perhaps we should," Dennis agreed. "Let's discuss that as soon as we can . . . let's see, we need to get clear of your formidable Duke Zolkir, return all the manifestations to their books, take Mikh's Leibniz away and send him back to this reality, and do something about Becky. Gosh."

"Don't worry about it," I said.

Duke Zolkir was swearing up and down at the farmers when Dennis and I rejoined him. It seemed they had switched from complaining about the sand-manifestation to complaining that Zolkir's wizards might have left a few wagonloads of sand there to improve the naturally marshy ground of the Vofurron valley.

"Never satisfied, peasants," Zolkir summed it up. "And you swordswomen and wizards are just as bad. I suppose you've come to squeeze a few more zolkys out of me before you seal the contract, eh, mage?"

Dennis managed to explain without stammering that he really did not feel able to accept the duke's offer, as he had previous commitments in the reality from which he had come. Furthermore . . .

"I knew it!" Zolkir exploded when Dennis had finished. "Impudence! Never satisfied! You turn down a perfectly good house-wizard contract and now you want me to send my swordswomen of the Bronze Bra Guild into your reality to do you a favor? You're as bad as those pestiferous peasants!"

"With respect, Your Grace," Dennis said firmly, "stopping Mikhalleviko would be doing you as much a favor as it would us."

"I don't see that," grumbled Zolkir. "If you'd stick around, you could just throw back everything he throws at us."

"Not necessarily, Your Grace. My forte is science fiction, and it just happens that Mikhalleviko started his career by transforming the science fiction section of Bookstop. There are many other kinds of books. I might not be able to recognize and transformulate all the manifestations he sends in future."

"There can't be many more," Zolkir said, "there aren't that many books in the world."

"There are in my world, your Grace," Dennis said. "And furthermore, there are many copies of some books."

"What, a dozen or so?"

"Several hundred thousand," Dennis said, "more if it's a really successful book. We learned on the way here, Your Grace, that each copy of a book generates its own manifestation in your reality. If Mikh gets into Ingram's warehouses," he said, "Your Grace will be up to your ducal ass in manifestations."

At that moment, as if to prove his point, a dozen scantily clad beauties appeared in the middle of the camp.

"By the power of Capricorn's Caresses, save me!" cried one.

"My Leo Hero!" cried another, draping herself over Zolkir's knees.

"A fiery, feisty Scorpio is no man's slave!" A redhead stamped her feisty little foot.

"I have to save the world from a giant comet!" proclaimed a busty blonde in a partially unbuttoned lab coat.

Zolkir rolled his eyes and peeled the paper-thin heroine off his legs. "Send 'em back," he pleaded with Dennis.

"I can't," Dennis said. "I told you he would get into other genres."

Zolkir turned to his house wizard. "Lavvu! Can you get a fix on Mikhalleviko's location in the other reality from this latest batch of manifestations?"

Lavvu Lherkode muttered to himself in Al-Jibber, drew glowing lines in the air with his forefinger, and inscribed a diagram of Jomtrie. "Yes, Your Grace. I see him . . . He is in a place of painted monsters . . . There are many people around him . . ."

"Never mind the details," Zolkir growled. "Transform Riva and this squadron of the Bronze Bra Guild down there, now."

"And the children," I prompted Zolkir.

"And the children."

"And Dennis."

"All right, all right! You first, Riva, so you can show your colleagues how to behave in that reality. Sika, you form up your ladies behind Riva, ready for transform."

"And the children, and Dennis," I insisted, "or we'll just let Mikh transform every book in Paper-Pushers'."

Dennis winced but didn't argue with me. I had the feeling he had figured out exactly how far to trust Duke Zolkir.

Chapter $\sqrt{289}$

The coffee shop of Austin's Crimson Griffon Hotel had not actually been decorated in honor of SalamanderCon; it just looked that way. It was a happy coincidence that the murals on its walls were enthusiastic if rather imaginative renderings of the Barton Springs Salamander engaged in typical Austin activities: diving into Barton Springs, leaping out of Barton Springs covered with blue gooseflesh, strolling down Sixth Street in Halloween costume, running red lights, bicycling down the median of I-35, and lugging a sack of paperbacks into Half Price Books. Those murals were the reason SalamanderCon kept returning to the Crimson Griffin for the annual gathering of science fiction fans and authors, despite the high prices, poor service and inadequate lighting. After all, the con committee reasoned, you could find cardboard pastries and $10.95 tuna sandwiches anywhere in Austin, but where else could you consume them under the benevolent gaze of the convention's eponymous totem reptile?

To a normal, red-blooded, decent American male,

however, the bluish-green murals under the flickering lights seemed like a satanic backdrop for the pasty, depraved faces of the fans who drifted in during the late hours of the morning. The picture of the Salamandress sunbathing topless at Barton Springs was especially—

Bob Boatright averted his eyes from the mural with a shudder, met the eyes of the waitress, and under her accusing stare weakly ordered another cup of coffee.

"You're going to float out of here if you don't stop drinking that stuff," said Mikhalleviko.

"We need some excuse to stay here," Boatright muttered, glancing nervously to left and right. On one side a slender, androgynous figure with crewcut hair and five nose studs glanced through a brochure decorated with neon salamanders. On the other side were three ladies who looked almost like normal people except for the iridescent paper dragons nesting in their hair and the tenor of their conversation.

"It's all very well to say that SalamanderCon brings in loads of Significant Writers," one of the dragon-adorned ladies said, "but it doesn't do much for me. I'm a writer. All my friends are writers. I can talk about writing science fiction any time I want to get together with you two. What I like in a convention is some good parties, some serious costuming, and Baen chocolates."

"Decadent," Boatright said. His voice rang out more loudly than he had intended. The writers lowered their menus and looked at him with interest; the Person in Black leaned over and tapped him on the shoulder. Boatright managed not to flinch.

"D'you say you were going to the Decline of

Decadence panel? It's not until three," the Person in Black said helpfully, pointing to a line in the brochure.

"Is that a program of events? Do you mind if we borrow it for just a moment? Thank you so much," Mikhalleviko said, whisking the brochure from the Person in Black before any protest could be voiced.

"Well, I'll be darned," the woman with the green dragon in her hair remarked to her companions, "I could have sworn those two were here for the chiropodists' convention."

"Far out costuming," said one of her friends. "You'd never guess they were fen."

"Maybe they're editors," suggested the third writer, a tall woman wearing jeans and a bright pink T-shirt under a red fanny pack. The purple dragons perched on her knot of silvery hair clashed cheerfully with the rest of the outfit.

"Naah, Susan. They don't have that evil glint in their eyes. I say it's a Businessman Costume, and very well done, too."

"No glitz, though," the woman with the green dragon said regretfully.

"Businessmen aren't supposed to be glitzy, Norah!"

"That," said Norah firmly, "is where the costumer's creativity can show. Now at last year's GalaxyFair opening ceremonies, the emcee was wearing a burgundy satin business suit with flashing lights outlining his tie. I don't care what they say about being ingenious and putting your costume together from stuff at Goodwill, which is what I bet the short guy did. I'll take a little creative glitz every time."

Boatright bristled. "Did you hear that, Mike?" he whispered across the booth to Mikhalleviko.

"Mmm. You bought that suit ready-made, didn't you?"

"It was the most expensive one in Montgomery Ward's Portly Gentlemen department," Boatright said proudly.

"Ummm. Well, there's no substitute for really good tailoring. . . . After we finish this job, I could give you a note to my man in San Francisco. Better take care of this first, though," Mikh said. "According to the schedule, the program starts at noon. People should be showing up any minute." He read from the brochure. "Twelve o'clock. Wivern Room, panel: Do Editors Eat Their Young? Cockatrice Room, panel: Chicks in Chainmail: Credible?"

"That should be a good one," the Person in Black told them. "Quentin Upshaw and Susan Crescent are both on it." He lowered his voice, nodding towards the table on Boatright's other side. "That's her—the one with the purple dragons. She's bound to get into a fight with Upshaw on this panel."

"Why?" Mikhalleviko asked.

"Susan made her first big money with a fantasy trilogy about a woman warrior. Upshaw's a technonerd, despises female fantasy writers."

"Oh," Mikhalleviko said blankly. He scanned the brochure, looking for something more comprehensible. "Here we are, Bob. Ballroom A: Dealers' Room."

"Dear Lord Christ Jesus," Boatright said, mopping his face, "Cannibalism, cross-dressing, and now drug dealing. Is there no end to the depravity of these people?"

"I think," Mikhalleviko said, having glanced through the advertisments decorating the brochure, "the dealers' room is where they sell books."

"Oh!" Boatright felt better. His stomach might be sour from all the hotel coffee he'd consumed since eight o'clock, his youth squad might have deserted him, but here was a definite sign that the Lord was indeed guiding him aright. If there was ever a place in need of purification, this convention had to be it. And there was going to be a whole room full of books for his prayers to waft away. This time somebody had to notice.

He told himself that the Lord tried a man only to lead him to triumph at the end. Twice now he'd worked his miracles for an unbelieving audience; twice the Philistines (Riva) had routed the Army of the Lord (Ronald, Mo, and Thunderhead). This would be the third trial, the one that was destined to succeed. There were supposed to be hundreds of people registered for this decadent, godless gathering. They would all be witnesses to the power of prayer. Some of them might well be converted on the spot. Even the scoffers and unbelievers would carry the word of his doings to the far cities from whence they had come. Waco and Wichita Falls, Salado and San Antonio would hear of the Reverend Bob Boatright's powerful prayers. First Texas, then America, then the world would be watching him.

Boatright felt a momentary quiver of uneasiness at the thought of just what the world might see; then he told himself not to worry, Becky's escapade was just another of the Lord's trials for him. All he had to do was stand firm in his faith and she'd be back, maybe with some of the pride knocked out of her. A twelve-year-old kid wasn't going to run very far. She'd probably be grateful to him for covering up for her, telling Vera that she'd had his permission to spend the night with Salla Konneva. Vera had been surprised by that, she knew how he felt about Dennis and Riva and their sinful household, but she knew better than to question him. And Becky would back him up, because she wouldn't want to tell her mother where she'd really spent the night . . . wherever that was.

Yessirree, she'd be grateful to ol' Daddy Bob for giving her a cover story. Probably never give him any trouble again. Bob Boatright leaned back against the smooth green plastic chair and surreptitiously unbuttoned the top button of his trousers under the table. That coffee was giving him ulcers. "You order some more coffee this time, Mike," he said. "That waitress is looking at us again."

Mikhalleviko glanced up. "No, she isn't. She's looking past you. They're setting up some sort of display in the lobby."

"Books?" Boatright asked hopefully.

"I can't see from here."

The sales rep for Ariel Romances would have been severely disappointed by Mikh's lack of reaction. He had promised his boss that a big display at SalamanderCon would be just the thing to kick off the new Zodiac line of futuristic romances in high style, bringing in all those science fiction fans (weird people, but they bought lots of books) as well as the romance readers. And he had great hopes for the display he was now laboriously setting up. When the foil-covered pieces of cardboard were assembled, the twelve initial Zodiac titles would be displayed in the center of a six-foot silver heart bordered with curls of iridescent pink ribbon. The heart and ribbon curls were the Ariel logo; the promotional bookmarks stacked beside the display bore silver hearts on one side and signs of the Zodiac in pink and silver on the other side.

And leaning casually on the display, dwarfing the heart with his six feet six of lean, tawny-blond, muscular magnificence . . . Vordo himself!

At least that had been the way it was supposed to work out.

"Ah, Vordo, maybe you could lean a little more gently?" the sales rep suggested after the heart swayed and tottered for the third time.

"Nobuddy tell Vordokaunneviko the Great whattado!"

The sales rep sighed. If he didn't know for a fact that the model could respond to photographers' requests for a change in pose, he'd think that one line constituted the whole of Vordo's English. Where had the jerk come from, anyway—a strong man act in a Russian freak show?

"Maybe you could talk to some of these lovely ladies," he suggested, pointing out the three women leaving the coffee shop.

"Vordokaunneviko the Great act, not talk!" Vordo seized Norah Tibbs in the general region of the midsection and bent her backwards for a passionate kiss. "You well-nourished beauty, rich family," he said happily when he came up for air. "I kill your enemies, then I carry you to my tent."

"My turn! Norah, take my camera, I want a picture with Vordo!" The girl with the golden dragons elbowed her friend aside and leaned back against Vordo's arm, lips pursed in anticipation of a kiss.

"Go on, big boy," she urged him, "you don't even have to kill my enemies. I don't have any enemies, do I, Norah?"

Norah Tibbs looked down and fiddled with the camera.

"No enemies? Then I kill your father," Vordo proposed.

Norah snapped a picture. "Here you are, Claudia," she said, dropping the camera strap over Claudia's head. "I want to look at these books. I heard the new Zodiacs were out, but when I went to Bookstop they didn't have any copies and they couldn't explain what happened to the ones that were supposed to be there," she said over her shoulder while reaching at random for a book. "In fact, the whole romance section was empty. So was Science Fiction. They probably stacked the books in the back to reorganize and didn't want to admit it. They're always doing something like that the month I have a book out; last Christmas my book was behind a stand of artificial poinsettias. What are these things like, anyway?" She flipped through the pages of *Capricorn Caress* and burst into laughter.

"Oh, honestly," she burst out, "couldn't you people do any better than this?" She waved *Capricorn Caress* at the sales rep. "You ought to be ashamed, showing this sort of tripe at a science fiction convention!"

"Why, Norah," said the girl with the golden dragons, straightening her skirts after Vordo's embrace, "what a way to talk, when you write romances yourself! And some of them are quite good, dear, or so I hear, though of course I never read that sort of thing myself."

"If you did read them, Claudia, you'd know that at least I get the facts right in my books. They may be potboilers, but they're honest potboilers; I get the history right. And if I wrote futuristic romances, I'd get the science right, too. Listen to this! 'You my woman now,' growled the barbarian warrior. 'You come with Rollo, board his spaceship, fly to distant stars. Rollo come from stars for you, Earth woman.'"

Her companions snickered. "Don't they always talk that way in romances?" Claudia demanded.

"Not in mine," Norah said. "And since this is supposed to be science fiction, and we've already established in the first chapter that this Rollo comes from an advanced civilization, and that he and the girl are conversing via an extremely sophisticated AI translator, how come the sophisticated AI translator makes him sound like Thud on a bad day while she speaks perfect English?"

Susan Crescent dropped her briefcase to applaud the question, then picked up one of the other books from the display. "Oh, I like this story line. Supposedly life on Earth is threatened by the approach of a giant comet, so—get this—our heroine, Laurinda, figures out a way to change the Earth's orbit by speeding it up and slowing it down!"

"What's wrong with that plot line?" demanded the harassed sales rep. "You people are always kvetching about how romances are sexist. So when we give you one with a strong heroine, a scientist heroine, you don't like that either?"

"Come on, Susan," Norah said, taking the tall woman's arm, "don't take anybody's head off at the neck before lunch, it's not polite."

"And nev-er set the cat on fire," sang Claudia under her breath.

"It's a filksong," Norah explained to the befuddled sales rep.

"Don't you mean folk song?"

"Naah. We don't folk. We filk."

"Sci-fi fans are weird."

"The plural," Norah advised him kindly, "is fen, not fans. Never mind. You'll catch on soon enough."

"I will?"

She gave the sales rep a wicked grin. "If you want

to sell any books here, you will. What's your schedule look like, Susan?"

The tall woman pulled a brochure printed with neon salamanders out of her red fanny pack. "I've got that panel on Chicks in Chainmail at noon, and then I'm off until a reading at four. What about you?"

"Doing a signing in the dealers' room at noon," Norah said, "Then at one o'clock I've got the panel on Egg Beater or Torture Implement: Archaeology of the Future."

"Darn," Susan said, "I was hoping you'd join me on the chainmail panel. Alexis called and said she'd be late getting up from Houston, so it's going to be just me and Esther against that neurotic brat Upshaw."

"Uh, Susan, about Esther, I heard—"

"I'd ditch the whole thing and read the new books I just bought," Susan said, "but Upshaw would claim I chickened out of facing him after that little disagreement we had last year."

"Little disagreement," Norah said appreciatively, "I like that. I was moderating that panel, remember? I had to blow a police whistle to get you guys to stop going for each other's throats."

"It was a much-needed public service," Susan said.

Claudia, who had wandered off to read the notices on the bulletin board, suddenly shrieked, "Esther's not coming? I'm desolated! She's such a darling!"

"I didn't realize Claudia was that close to Esther," Norah said.

"She met her last year," Susan said. "For ten minutes."

"She makes it sound as if they were lifelong friends."

"Stick around," Susan said. "Given half an opening, she'll talk about 'Marion' and 'Connie' and 'Ursula' and 'Annie' the same way."

"She's already mentioned her deep, meaningful conversation with Anne McCaffrey." Norah nodded.

"Three minutes," Susan said crisply. "In the autographing line at DragonCon. I was there too. Oh, no." The color drained from her face.

"What's the matter?"

"I just realized what she's saying. Esther's a no-show!"

"Yep. I tried to tell you that a minute ago. I heard she's stuck at home with a sick hamster, or something."

"So that means it's me and Quentin Upshaw, one on one, to discuss the credibility of women warriors in fantasy fiction." Susan clutched at Norah's sleeve. "You have got to ditch the signing and moderate this panel, Norah! No. What am I saying? Of course you mustn't miss your own signing. There's got to be some way out of this."

"Don't panic. You've got fifteen minutes before the panel starts. We'll find somebody who's not scheduled."

"*All* the writers are going to be scheduled for that hour," Susan said in hollow tones. "I can see it coming."

"Then we'll find somebody who isn't a writer." Norah stood on tiptoes and tried to scan the crowd around the Zodiac display. "I wonder if the author of *Capricorn Caress* is going to show? Whatever she is, she's definitely not a writer!"

"My whole life is flashing before my eyes," Susan said despairingly, "and my best friend is making lousy jokes. I give up. I shall await my fate peacefully. At least I can read for a few minutes before the carnage begins." She found a bench by the wall and drew a copy of *Good Women, Expensive Horses* from her briefcase.

She had barely begun reading when a sonorous voice rolled over the buzz of fennish conversations and greetings.

"Almighty and Everlasting Lord! Grant that these Your children may be redeemed from the abyss of filth and decadence into which the minions of the Evil One are leading them."

"Hey, buddy! Wait for the masquerade before you start your act, okay? Some of us are trying to have a conversation here."

"Dear Lord Christ Jesus, remove the scales of error from their eyes as You remove these prurient books from their hands . . . Move over, will you!" the man in the shiny blue suit ended on a most untheological note. "I'm trying to get to that book stand!"

"Keep yer pants on, Bub," the fan who'd been standing in his way advised. "You wanta read the romances? Fine. I don't wanta read 'em." He moved aside and gave Boatright a clear path to the display of Zodiac Futuristic Romances.

"Dear Lord," Boatright began again, "Now by Your grace through me let these pornographic books disappear from off the face of the earth! Now," he repeated, and then, somewhat more loudly, "Now!"

The right-hand half of the display was suddenly no longer there, only a gaping hole in the six-foot silver heart. Susan closed *Good Women, Expensive Horses* over one finger to mark her place and watched appreciatively.

"Like wow," said a reverent voice from somewhere in the back of the lobby. "Way cool special effects!"

"Probably some publicity stunt from Zodiac," suggested another voice.

Boatright turned to confront the speakers. "It is not

a publicity stunt! You are seeing the power of the Lord Jesus, and if you've got any sense you'll fall to your knees and worship!"

"Hey," Norah said from beside Susan, "I know that guy."

"Which one?"

"The short one in the cheap-looking suit."

"The other one's a fox," said Claudia. "Introduce me?"

"Why, Claudia! You're married!"

"I'm married, but I'm not dead."

"I'da thought Jesus could get rid of all the books," said the fan who'd suggested the whole thing was a stunt put on by the Zodiac sales rep.

"He will," Boatright said. "Move aside! O heavenly Father, let it please You to show these unbelievers . . ."

Half the fen in the lobby moved away to give Boatright room to work. Unfortunately, the other half took their places to get a front-row view of the "special effects." They jostled Boatright and his companion. It looked as if a laser gun set on "wide disperse" had swept through the display. The books in the bottom corner of the display vanished. So did the stack of Zodiac promotional bookmarks, seventeen SalamanderCon programs held by various fen, and the book Susan had been reading.

"Hey!" Susan said indignantly. "I want that back!"

Seventeen fen said the same thing with varying degrees of urgency.

"The Lord moves in mysterious ways," said Boatright, "his wonders to perform. Repent and be saved!"

He stalked off towards the dealers' room.

"Seventeen ninety-five that book cost me," Susan grumbled. "Oh, well, I got some others at the same time." She took a copy of *Women Who Love Horses Too Much* out of her briefcase.

"You don't have time to read that," Norah said. "It's two minutes of twelve. You've got a panel, and I've got a signing. . . . " Her voice trailed off as she stared into the crowd. A tall, dusky woman in battered bronze armor and sweaty leather harness stood amid the surging fen.

"Riva!" Norah exclaimed. "Where did you come from? And what happened to you?"

Riva pushed her way through the crowd of fen, pricking a few of them with the point of her short sword when they didn't move quickly enough to suit her. "You know."

"I don't know what happened to your eyebrows."

"Look, I don't want to discuss it here. I need to find—"

"And where's Jason?"

"He should be along any minute."

"He'd better be," Norah said. "Listen, it's a good thing you showed up just now. We really need your help."

"I know," Riva said, "that's why I'm here." She glanced around the room. "I wonder where the rest of them are? They should be here by now."

"How did you know Esther and Alexis weren't coming?"

"Who?"

"Oh, never mind. We don't have time, anyway. Susan," Norah said, "I want you to meet Riva Konneva. She's the perfect fill-in for your panel about Chicks in Chaimail."

Susan looked up. "I don't think Quentin will be very polite to a costumer."

"This isn't a costume," Riva said. "It's my work outfit."

"Riva," Norah said, "is an expert on women warriors." She looked at Riva. "Yes, I know I'm not supposed to know about that, but give me a break. I've been putting things together since last night. 'Security guard'—hah!"

"I have," Riva said mildly, "worked security. On occasion." She sheathed her sword. "Oh, well. I'm supposed to be waiting for backup, anyway. What is a panel?"

"You'll enjoy it," Norah told her.

Chapter $\sum_{i=5}^{7} i$

I couldn't figure out why Norah wanted me to be part of a wall. But as she pointed out, I owed her one for trusting me and keeping her mouth shut about Jason's disappearance.

"Who's that?" exclaimed somebody behind us.

I turned and saw Sikarouvvana.

"What took you so long?"

"Sorry about the delay," Sika said. "I had to show the duke's men how to stack heroines. The others should be along any minute now."

"Uh, people, you better move out of the way," I said. The transform function was supposed to check boundary conditions so that you never transformed into anything solid, but it just might get overloaded handling this many people. "Sika, can you clear a space?"

She didn't even have to draw her sword to do that; just turned around and glared at the people pressing close to her. They backed off, treading on each other's toes, just as Kloreem and Linnizyvv showed up. By the time the troop of trainees started appearing, most of the Paper-Pushers' people were backed up against the wall or edging through a door leading to some kind of big room. I heard murmurs of admiration. "Far out costuming!"

"What is it, some kind of show for the Chicks in Chainmail panel?"

"Well, I say it's tacky," some dweeb in a white shirt and rimless glasses complained. "We don't come to SalamanderCon for costuming and magic tricks. This con is supposed to be for serious intellectual discussion."

"I'd like to have a serious intellectual discussion with the one on the far right," said his friend.

"Jason!" Norah cried. "Are you all right?"

"Aw, Mom. Don't embarrass me in front of all these people!" Jason ineffectually fended off Norah's hugs.

Dennis appeared behind the trainees, holding Salla by one hand and Becky by the other. "Lemme go!" Becky yelled. "I belong with the Guild now!" She yanked her hand free of Dennis's and darted into the midst of the trainees.

"Where's Mikh?" Dennis asked.

"I don't know. I just got here myself, and Norah keeps trying to get me to be part of a wall."

"Huh?"

"A panel," Norah corrected. "We've had two no-shows for this panel, and I can't cover it because I'm supposed to be doing a signing—" she looked at her watch "—three minutes ago, actually."

"Go ahead, Riva," Dennis said. "With all these ladies as backup, I can handle the sleazeball."

"You owe me," Norah said. "You said, if ever you could do something for me? Well, now's your chance." She took my arm and steered me away from the crowd, down a short hall to a door with a white sign

on it. The sign read, "CHICKS IN CHAIMAIL: CREDIBLE?
FRIESNER, CRESCENT, UPSHAW, LATNER. 12:00."

"Go up front and sit next to Susan," Norah told me.
"She'll explain everything. I gotta go."

Norah's friend Susan Crescent was sitting behind
a long table at the far end of the room. A dark-haired
man with a sulky pout on his face was slumped at
the other end of the table. In the center was a pitcher
of water and a stack of glasses.

I made my way past rows of chairs filled with
chattering people and took a chair between Susan and
the sulky-looking guy, right by the water pitcher.
Poured myself a glass of icy water and swallowed it
in one gulp. That was good. A shower would be even
better, but you can't have everything.

"Okay, I'm here, what am I supposed to do?" I asked
Susan.

"You're sitting in the middle, so you're the moderator," she told me.

"How do I moderate?"

"Oh, introduce the panelists—that's not much, seeing
there are only two of us—say something about the
topic, keep the discussion going."

"So what's the topic?"

"Whether it's credible to have women warriors in
fantasy novels."

I shrugged. The whole thing made no sense to me,
but I might as well oblige Dennis and Norah while
the Bronze Bra Guild was taking care of Mikh and
his transformulated wizard's staff. I felt sure Sika could
handle the sleazeball with one hand tied behind her
back; Dennis was right, they didn't really need me.

I hated to miss out on all the fun, though.

With a sigh of regret for missing my last chance to

beat the living daylights out of Mikh, I reached for the microphone and cleared my throat. "Okay, people. I still don't quite get it, but I'll try to do the job anyway. Um, I'm supposed to introduce these folks. On my right is Susan Crescent, author of the fantasy trilogy *Starsword* as well as . . . many other books." Whose titles I couldn't quite remember at the moment. Why wasn't Dennis doing this? He knew science fiction. But, of course, he also knew mathemagics, and Sika might need him for backup against Mikh. Oh well. "I don't know this guy on my left, so I can't introduce him."

The crowd broke into laughter. I gathered that Sulky-Face was somebody so famous they couldn't imagine I didn't know who he was, so I must be making a joke. "And the topic of the panel is, are women warriors in fantasy fiction credible? Now personally I don't get it. Unless there are some rules about fantasy novels that I haven't heard about, why not have fighting women in them, just like in the real world?"

The audience cracked up again, and while they were giggling the guy on my left seized the microphone.

"For those of you who didn't find that dazzling introduction sufficient," he said with a sneer towards me, "I'm Quentin Upshaw, author of *The Technoghetto, Isobars, The Variance Device*, and, of course, my new book due out next month, *Nanoknights*."

He held up a book in a shiny new cover and flashed it around so the audience could see and clap. "With all appreciation of our lovely moderator's ingenious costuming," Upshaw continued, "I have to say that I prefer books like *Nanoknights*, which give a true impression of the dirty street warfare of the near future—"

"How can you give a true impression of something that hasn't happened yet?" I asked.

"—to these charming fantasies of scantily dressed bimbos playing at swordfighting," Upshaw went on. "In my opinion, this trend towards fantasy novels featuring female warriors is just one more example of the commodification which is corrupting our entire life. Instead of accepting and enjoying their natural roles as wives, mothers, and support systems, some women want to take over roles for which they're naturally unfitted and even to be paid for these jobs they can't do. Look at the mess caused by letting women get into combat in the Gulf War!"

"Just a minute!" Susan said. "I want to speak to that. Gimme the mike." She reached for it, but Upshaw ignored her and went on, microphone firmly clenched in one hand. "Of course those people who've made money off such fantasies," he sneered, "want us to believe that it's really possible for a woman to pull her own weight in battle. Maybe women can handle a computerized support center well behind the lines—"

"Quentin. Give me the mike!"

"—but in real combat, one-on-one combat, we all know they just can't hack it."

I tapped Upshaw's wrist with the edge of my sheathed shortsword, not hard, just enough to sting and make him want to relax his muscles and drop the mike. "Ow!" he yelped. "That hurt!"

"No, it didn't," I said, passing the microphone to Susan. "Now be a good boy and let somebody else speak, or I'll demonstrate what 'hurt' really means."

"I deplore violence," Upshaw said. He edged his chair so far away from me that he was in danger of falling off the dais.

"Especially when it's directed at you?" Susan said sweetly. "Don't be so frightened, Quentin. Remember, women can't fight men on equal terms."

Upshaw reached across me and grabbed the mike back. "I would never hit a woman," he said. "I'm a gentleman. But if I did take a good punch at you or this costume-horse here, you'd be in deep trouble. It's a simple scientific fact that men have far more upper-body strength, plus we have the fighting instinct which women naturally lack. You can't go against millennia of evolution, Susan." He smirked and his fans in the audience clapped.

"Oh, please," I said. "Please try it."

"I told you," Upshaw said, "I don't approve of violence."

"Look. I'll take off my sword-belt. I'll take off my armor." I laid Sasulau on the table and unhooked my bronze corselet and shoulder-guards. The leather corselet underneath only covered my torso; my arms and shoulders were bare.

"I bet she strips better than you do, Upshaw," yelled a girl in the audience. "Whyn'cha take off your shirt and let us see those manly muscles?"

The soft flesh bulging under Upshaw's T-shirt quivered. "I protest this!" he shouted. "This is supposed to be an intellectual discussion, not a sideshow! What kind of moderator are you, anyway?"

"A draftee," I said mildly. "But as a soldier, I was a volunteer. Where did you get your combat experience?"

"I don't approve of war," Upshaw muttered.

"He sat out Vietnam in Canada," yelled the girl who'd suggested he should take off his T-shirt. "While Susan was in the Marines."

I sighed and turned to Susan. "No wonder your

people can't believe in women fighters. As far as I can tell nobody in this reality will stand up and fight."

"This trend of commodification and costuming is corrupting SalamanderCon," Quentin Upshaw whined. "We're not like other science fiction cons. We're serious. We're here to discuss literature."

"Oh, come on, Quentin," Susan said, "most of us aren't writing great literature. We're writing entertainment—and darned good entertainment, too. Why don't you lighten up a little?"

"You may not be writing anything of literary merit," Quentin smirked, "but *Nanoknights* is getting reviewed in the *New York Times*. Some of us are doing serious work that's worth taking seriously, literature that will last for the ages."

The door opened and a Guild trainee I didn't recognize poked her head in. "Uh, Riva? Sorry to interrupt, but there's kind of a mess in the dealers' room."

"I knew this panel was a mistake," I sighed. "I hereby declare the panel over. I gotta go."

"You can't do that!" Upshaw protested. "Even if you run off, the rest of us can stay and talk."

I was getting very tired of this bozo's whiny voice. "Okay," I said, "keep the mike if you want it so much." I wrapped the cord of the microphone around his neck and shoved it into his mouth.

"UNGH UNGH UNGH!" he roared over the sound system.

"Here, Quentin," Susan said sweetly as I shouldered my way through the crowd to the door, "let me help you."

"What's happening?" I asked the trainee.

"We heard a lot of yellin' from this big room in the front of the palace," she started.

"It's a hotel, not a palace—oh, never mind. I suppose that sleazeball Mikh was making the noise?"

"No, ma'am. It was a bunch of Paper-Pushers waving their arms and shouting about how all their books had disappeared."

"Correction," I sighed, "Mikh was causing the noise. Okay, didn't Sika tell you that your mission was to take out his wizard's staff?"

"Yes'm, but we didn't see nobody in no wizard's robes, nor no staff, neither."

That's what happens when you send the troops out without adequate briefing. I hadn't thought to mention to them that Mikh was dressed like a Paper-Pusher and that his wizard's staff had transformulated into a small black box with push-buttons. Nauzu klevul-kedimmu! I knew it was a mistake to let Norah distract me from the main job.

"Then the new apprentice hauled off and hit some fat guy in the stomach," the trainee continued, "and yelled that she wasn't ever going to let him touch her again, and your girl Salla said she could see the wizard and ran off to where the new apprentice was, and we were just going to follow here when all these manifestations started showing up. Monsters with silver skin and monsters with big eyes and I don't know what all. So Sika says, get Riva, she'll know what's happening here, and I went and got you."

"Sika vastly overestimates me," I muttered as we reached the milling crowd in the big room. "Why are we getting manifestations now?"

✧   ✧   ✧

The Zodiac heroines were only a minor nuisance in the duke's camp. Sika asked Lavvu Lherkode to wait a moment before translating her to Paper-Pushers' reality, showed the duke how to fold and stack the paper-thin characters, and suggested putting a nice large rock on top of them to keep them from fluttering around and getting in the way. And there were, after all, only twelve of them.

But only minutes after Sika and the others had been transported, new manifestations came out of nowhere. The first ones were not so bad; crude sketches of many-armed monsters with bulging eyes and steely-jawed men waving slide rules. If Dennis had still been there, he would have realized that Mikh was working his way through the Golden Age Collectables booth at SalamanderCon. The duke simply had the new manifestations folded and stacked on top of the Heroines. Some of the Scientist-Engineers protested that they would get cooties from being so close to girls, but all they could do about it was flap in the wind and complain.

Unfortunately, the next manifestations were a little more substantial.

At first the duke's personal guards formed a tight ring around the tent and fought off acid-spitting spiders, glowing green rings of light, and men in strange silvery armor and transparent, bubble-like helmets. It wasn't all that hard; most of the manifestations were only cardboard-thick, and all of them were seriously confused about what had happened. But there were so many of them, and more appeared every minute.

A man on flames flickered in and out of the protected circle of the duke's tent. A man in a sweeping black cloak appeared and advanced on Zolkir, mouth half-open to show the overly long incisors. The duke cut that manifestation down where it stood, but a moment later, three identical beings appeared in the same place. Two soldiers of the guard broke ranks to deal with this threat from within. While they were removing the vampires, a flock of white dragons with black stripes on their flanks appeared in the marshy ground near the river. A silver-haired man in a long-sleeved gown flickered into existence behind Zolkir.

"The dragons aren't really a threat, you know," he said. "Lucky they manifested in the marsh. They'll sink too far to move."

"Avaunt, dread manifestation!" cried a guard, thrusting a lance into the silver-haired man's face.

"$n = \frac{ld^2V_1}{kds^2}$!"

The point of the lance drooped like a wilted lily. "Don't you know me, Sauklourrizo?" Furo Fykrou asked reproachfully. "I can't have been gone that long; you and the duke don't look a day older."

"Mage!" Sauklourrizo dropped his lance.

"Are you sure you're not a manifestation?" the duke asked. "Last time I saw you, you had black hair."

"Much have I suffered," Furo Fykrou declaimed, "and much wisdom have I gained since last we met. That idiot Riva got her mathemagics wrong and transported me to Outer Yark. I had Nauzu's own trouble of a time working out the reverse equations to get myself back. Nothing to write on. I had to do it all in my head."

"Outer Yark? Where the monsters come from?" Sauklo asked. "How did you survive? What's it like there?"

Furo Fykrou closed his eyes and shuddered slightly.

"Trust me, Sauklo, you don't want to know. Let's just say it opens up some . . . intriguing possibilities for exile of troublemakers. And like I said," he went on briskly, regaining his dignified tone as he spoke, "much wisdom have I gained and many magics have I worked during my time of exile and horrible trials."

"Enough to get rid of the manifestations?" Duke Zolkir asked.

"Pshaw! Nothing to it. The merest elementary transformation."

"It's not that easy," Lavvu Lherkode said. "The foreign wizard explained it. You have to know the things' true names."

Duke Zolkir nodded slowly. "That's right. This Dennis Dithrovvu claimed that it was necessary to know their true names in his reality in order to return them to their true forms in that reality."

Furo Fykrou shrugged. "Why go to all that trouble? We can transport them in their present forms. Let the people of Paper-Pushers' reality deal with the monsters they would thrust upon us!"

He raised his staff and began reciting the transform, turning slowly in a circle as he spoke. The spiders and the creatures in bubble-armor disappeared; the dragons vanished. The burning man appeared and disappeared like a flash of light.

Before Furo Fykrou had completed the circle, though, new manifestations sprang up: man-shaped things of gleaming metal, jellyfish-like beasts with many squirming tentacles, a man in a monk's hood plodding across a desert landscape that coexisted with the actual marsh beneath him.

"This," Furo Fykrou said, "is getting tiring. $\int e^{-st} F(t)dt$. Really, one might as well be back in Outer Yark.

$\int_0^\infty e^{-st} F(t) dt$. Why don't you dispatch somebody to stop the mage who's sending these things, Your Grace?"

"Riva," Duke Zolkir said. "Her mage-friend Dennis Ditthrovu. A whole troop of the Bronze Bra Guild, commanded by Sika. I don't know why they haven't stopped the wizard yet; I shall require a full trip report when Sika returns."

The dealers' room was almost empty of books, though it was so crowded that I didn't notice the bare shelves right away. In the exact center of the room, Bob Boatright was making his usual loud noises about Lord God Christ Jesus while Mikh smirked and thumbed the buttons of his Leibniz. Around them there milled a confused crowd of fans, costumers and manifestations: a man in a black cape with long gleaming fangs, a skinny boy in jeans and a Grateful Dead T-shirt, two women in low-cut velvet dresses, something with bulging eyes and many tentacles, several nerdy guys in white shirts, a three-foot spider, a slim girl with a dragon in her hair, some square-jawed men in white coats, a dozen robots, and a whole slew of people in various designs of space suits. You could tell the real people from the manifestations by their actions. The manifestations were wandering aimlessly; the real people were either fighting to get into the room or fighting to get out of it, depending on how they felt about seeing their fictional dreams come true. Besides that, most of the manifestations gave themselves away when they turned sidewise; they varied in thickness from tissue-paper to corrugated cardboard. But a few were as solid as any "real" person or thing.

Dennis was standing on a table to one side. "$F(s) = L\{F(t)\}!$," he shouted.

When nothing happened, he tried snappping out a series of integrals.

None of the manifestations disappeared, but a dozen feisty heroines fluttered down from empty air and draped themselves over people's heads.

I pushed my way to the table and grabbed Dennis by the ankle. "It won't work," I shouted over the babble of the crowd. "Mathemagics doesn't work here . . . unless you can draw power from Dazau. We need to get Mikh's staff—I mean, his Leibniz. He might have enough mathemagical power stored there to undo all this."

"Right!" Dennis hopped off the table and bounced into a gleaming bronze figure. The robot turned and shoved him in the chest. Dennis went down and three people stepped on him in their eagerness to get out the door. I kicked the next one and bought us a moment for Dennis to get to his feet.

The moment cost us the Leibniz.

Vordokaunneviko the Slow On the Uptake had finally noticed that something interesting was going on in Ballroom A. When he did lumber into the room, his height gave him a good view over the crowd of people and manifestations. When he saw Mikh, he gave an inarticulate roar and shoved people out of the way to get at him. And Mikh had nowhere to go; he was surrounded by spiders and fans and robots and costumers and spacemen.

"Feelthy foukobu cheat!" Vordo roared, reaching for Mikh's neck. "You transporting me into middle of former Union of Soviet Socialist Republics while you take self straight to land of peace and plenty! Trying to losing me in civil war and chaos, forcing me to walk thousands of varengs to rich land! And then I having to hurt head learning foukobu Anglish language with many irregular verbs which you give self directly by transform function! Nobuddy treat Vordokaunneviko the Great thattaway!" His big hands closed around Mikh's neck and lifted him bodily off the floor.

"Do something!" he cried to Boatright. But Bob Boatright was sidling away as quickly as a portly man could move in the press of fans and aliens. He might have made it out if he hadn't mistaken a costumed man for a manifestation and tried to walk over him. The man in the spacesuit costume punched Boatright in the face. He wobbled dizzily into the thick of the crowd.

"Wait a minute," Sika called, "that man is Duke Zolkir's prisoner!"

Vordo grinned over his shoulder. "Duke Zolkir welcome to what I leaving of him," he said, punctuating the statement with a series of brisk shakes.

On the third shake the Leibniz flew out of Mikh's hand. It arched over the heads of the crowd and fell into somebody's outstretched hands. "Gimme that!" Kloreem yelled, diving into the crowd.

I got two or three glimpses of bodies hurtling this way and that. The green flash of the Leibniz logo appeared and disappeared like a glowfish in the murky waters of the Vofurron. Where was it now? If I could just figure out who had it, I could bash him politely over the head until he gave it up. I plunged into the crowd, tracking the spot where I'd last seen the Leibniz.

Unfortunately, Kloreem and Linnizyvv and the brighter two-thirds of the trainees all had the same idea. We met in the center of the room, breathing hard and ignoring a chorus of complaints, wheezes and admiration for our "costuming" from the people we'd pushed past.

"It's gotta be here somewhere," Kloreem said. "Linni, put a guard on the doors. Nobody else gets out of this room until we get the Leibniz, okay? We'll search these people one by one if we have to."

Linnizyvv snapped orders at a couple of trainees who were standing near the door. Just as they reached it, a plump little woman in a cotton housedress charged in.

"Becky Boatright, you get over here right this minute, you hear?" she shrilled. "Goodness knows what your daddy would say if he found you in this God-less. . . ."

Her voice trailed off and she stared at Bob Boat-right. His suit was ripped at the shoulder and he had the beginnings of a beautiful black eye. "Bob?"

"He's not my daddy," a shrill voice proclaimed. Becky Boatright, still outfitted in brass and leather as befitted a Guild apprentice, pushed past a giant spider and pointed her short sword at Boatright. "He's not my daddy, and if he ever touches me again I'll put this into his guts, and I'm not staying here no matter what you say, and . . . Mommmmmy," she wailed, finally sounding like a twelve-year-old kid instead of a Junior Guild Apprentice.

The room seemed less crowded than it had just a moment ago. I glanced over my shoulder. No, nobody could have left; Linni and the trainees were standing shoulder to shoulder at the closed doors, swords out and ready for action.

Becky buried her head against her mother's shoulder and murmured something. I saw Vera Boatright's face change. She looked like someone who had heard her worst nightmare confirmed. It hurt to look at her. I stared past her, at Sika and Kloreem holding out their shields against an acid-spitting spider, at . . .

There wasn't any spider.

I rubbed my eyes and looked again. The spider was definitely gone. As I watched, the golden robot behind it vanished also.

And there were books all over the floor.

"I know it's true, Becky," Vera interrupted her daughter. "You don't have to prove anything to me. It all makes sense now. All the nights when he made me go out to the church meetings and he said he had to stay home and work."

Becky nodded violently. "I'm not going back," she said.

"No. We aren't." Vera took Becky's hand and rose to her feet. "Although where we'll go," she said under her breath, "I don't know . . ."

"I do," Becky said. "We'll go back to the Guildhouse. I'm only an apprentice now, but in four years I'll be earning, Mommy. And you can be a Guildmother—they don't have one just now, Sika said so."

"Sikarouvvana to you, Apprentice Bekka," Sika said, but her eyes were smiling. "And it would be most irregular . . . but we do need someone to teach the trainees decent manners."

Vera looked uncertainly at Sika, then at her daughter. "I dunno," she said doubtfully. "But we cain't stay with Boatright . . ."

It seemed time to give Vera the benefit of my experience. I cleared my throat and stepped forward.

"It's only a matter of living where your kid can go to the right school," I told her. "I moved here so Salla could get an education."

"And what kind of education will Becky get in this Guild of yours?"

"She won't be doing a lot of book reports or Al-Jibber . . . I mean, algebra," I admitted, "but she'll be learning a trade she's good at and work she loves."

"Please, Mommy," Becky urged.

"Can you keep up your schoolwork and do this Guild training both?"

"They don't have our kind of schools there!"

Vera nodded. "Plenty of good Christian women home-school their children, and I reckon I can do the same. All right. We'll give it a try, if these ladies—" she nodded at Sika and her lieutenants "—will have me. But the first time you fall behind in your schooling, young lady, you leave this Guild. Understand?"

Becky nodded.

"As I said," Sika murmured, "we do need somebody to teach manners to the young ones."

"Vera Boatright and Dazau," Dennis murmured. "An explosive combination."

I smiled at him. "Any worse than Rivakonneva and the Planet of the Paper-Pushers?"

"Probably not," he allowed.

I'd been so intent on Vera and Becky that I had hardly noticed the room emptying out. Now I looked around and saw that all the manifestations—or nearly all—had vanished. The floor was covered with books. Book dealers knelt amid the piles, sorting out their scrambled stocks. A few fans were gathered in one corner, excitedly comparing notes on what had just happened. Some of them seemed to think it was a rehearsal for the masquerade; others claimed it was a publicity stunt from Zodiac, citing as evidence the neat pile of twelve Zodiac Romances in the center of the room.

Nobody seemed inclined to give Bob Boatright and the Lord Jesus Christ any credit at all.

"Linni," I said. "Where is Boatright?"

She jerked her head towards the hotel lobby. "Been letting people out, one by one," she said. "After searching 'em to make sure they didn't have the you-know-what." She gave me a long look. "Don't remember passing the wizard through, but looks like he's gone, too."

"And good riddance!" I said loudly.

But where could Mikh's staff have gone? There was nobody left but dealers, fans, the Bronze Bra Guild, and the children. Jason and Salla were seated cross-legged on the floor in a corner stacked high with books. Jason's head was bent over an old Doc Savage novel, and Salla . . .

Was holding something behind her open book. I knew the comic-book-behind-the-textbook stance well enough. Whatever she had there, she was concentrating very hard. The tip of her tongue protruded between her lips, curling in rhythm with her tapping fingers. I edged around the room, trying to come up behind her without being noticed.

She tapped a sequence of keys and pressed the green button. A neat stack of papers appeared on the floor in front of her. They looked like university course transcripts.

"Okay," Salla murmured, "now let's try this." She pressed two function keys, entered a number, and pressed the green button again. The lighted panel of the Leibniz flickered. Whirling dust motes in the air slowly coalesced, becoming flat and white; letters appeared on the paper as it formed itself.

"Good!" Salla patted the Leibniz. "Now let's take care of this."

This time she had to tap a long sequence of number and function keys. Before she even touched the green button, the display dimmed until it was almost unreadable. Salla held the keypad close to her cheek, tapping and coaxing. "Come on now," she murmured, "you can do it." She entered another long sequence—or maybe it was the same one, I wouldn't know—and pressed the green button while the display flickered.

Red letters flashed on the display. "POWER OUT," they read. "BATTERY BACKUP . . . POWER OUT . . . BATTERY BACKUP . . . POWER OUT . . ." Then the display went completely blank.

"Salla, dear," I said.

She glanced up, elaborately casual. "Oh, hi, Mom," she said in a bright and very innocent tone. "Look, somebody dropped this calculator."

I took the Leibniz from her. "Looks like you've completely drained the magical power from it," I commented. "I hope it was worth it."

"Oh, I think so," Salla said. She grabbed the papers she'd created and folded them over before I could read them. "But I wasn't quite finished. I'm sorry. I found the Undo function, and it put almost all the manifestations back, but I couldn't get that one to turn into its book again." She pointed at a slender person in black with five nose studs and a flowing tail of peacock feathers.

"That, Salla my love, is a costumer," I told her.

"Oh. A real person?" She stared shamelessly.

"They're all real," Jason said. "In the books or out of them."

Epilogue

Two days after SalamanderCon, a freshly plucked leegryz and a leather flask of caumopi sauce appeared beside my computer, with a scroll inscribed, "Compliments of Zolkir, Duke of Zolvarra and the Outlying Provinces." A neon-pink Post-it note attached to the back of the scroll turned out to be a request from Vera to forward a few basic supplies to Dazau.

"I gather that a few of the Guild trainees have joined Becky's home schooling," Dennis said, looking over the request for extra copies of the sixth grade math textbooks. "But what on earth does she want with two dozen manicure sets and cuticle sticks?"

"She's probably teaching the Guild members never to go into battle with chipped nail polish," I surmised. Looked like I had gotten out of Dazau just in time. Personally I'd never felt any need to trim my cuticles. "Anyway, I don't care what she does with the manicure sets; the question is, who should we have over to share the leegryz in caumopi sauce?"

"And what wine goes with leegryz?"

"Beer," I said firmly. "Dos Equis."

Norah agreed with me. So did Salla and Jason. I tried

to tell them they were too young for beer, but Salla argued that if she was old enough to save the planet, she was old enough for half a glass of Dos Equis.

"Er—I'd been meaning to ask you about that, Salla," said Dennis. "What exactly did you do to Sleazeball's Leibniz?"

Since that day at SalamanderCon, the Leibniz had shown no hint of magical power. With a recharged battery it functioned reasonably well as a wallet-sized personal computer, or so Salla said; I thought the keyboard was too small. But whatever use she had made of it seemed to have drained the last of Mikh's store of power.

Salla squirmed, took a cautious bite of the leegryz, and followed it with a gulp of Dos Equis. "Ick," she said, "this stuff tastes like, like—"

"Like beer?" Dennis suggested.

"Yeah."

"Have a Big Red."

Having successfully defended her right to share in adult celebrations, Salla switched over to soda pop with no visible regrets.

"About the Leibniz?" I prompted when she had swallowed half the contents of the bottle. "And the manifestations turning back into books? And—"

"Easy," said Salla. "There's an Undo function on the Leibniz. I told you that, Mom."

"You weren't just pushing buttons when I found you," I said. "You were uttering mathemagical equations."

"Just playing around?" Salla suggested.

"And draining power," I reminded her. "Come on. What did you use it for?"

"Um. Well," Salla said, "I was going to tell you anyway. First I got Dennis a teaching certificate."

"You what?"

Salla pushed back her chair, dashed into her bedroom and rummaged in her top desk drawer. "I know I put it somewhere in here. . . . No, that's the Social Studies report. . . . Oh, of course! I filed it with the SalamanderCon program." She came out clutching a handful of grimy, crumpled papers. "Here you are. College transcripts. Teaching certificate. A letter of apology and reinstatement from the superintendent of schools."

Dennis looked over the top of his glasses at her. "And where exactly did you learn to use mathemagics to create a paper trail?"

"I was Furo Fykrou's apprentice," Salla said sweetly. "Remember?"

"For half a day!"

"He gave me the run of his study." She paused. "Actually, it was real interesting. Actually, I wouldn't mind going—"

"*No,*" Dennis and I said together, just as Jason said, "Not me, thank you!"

Salla stuck her tongue out at him. "Who asked you?"

"Calm down, both of you," I said. "What else did you do, Salla?"

"Hardly anything," she said. "I, um, fixed it so if Mr. Boatright ever touches any little girls he'll get a real bad case of Montezuma's Revenge. And I sort of transformulated Mikhalleviko to Outer Yark."

"Was that when the Leibniz ran out of power?"

"Um. No. I thought I was being kind of selfish," Salla said, "so I decided to do good. I think it was trying to end world hunger that wore it out."

I would like to think she was making that up, but the newspapers have been full of stories about mysterious food shipments showing up in places like Ethiopia and India.

Maybe we should let the kid go back to Dazau for more mathemagical training.

While I was thinking that over, Norah changed the subject. "So now that Dennis has his job back, Riva, are you going to look for work or keep studying math?"

"Neither," I told her. "I've figured out how to earn lots of money in a glamorous career that I can pursue at home in my spare time."

"Oh, really? Want to share the secret?"

"It was your idea, really," I told her. "I'm going to write down all this stuff that happened and publish it. As science fiction. Then I'll be rich and famous, right?"

Norah choked on her Dos Equis and never got around to answering that question.

Appendix: Proofs

Chapter 1: e^0

$e^0 = 1$

Chapter 2: $(\sqrt{2})^2$

$(\sqrt{2})^2 = \sqrt{2} * \sqrt{2} = 2$

Chapter 3: $[\pi]$

The greatest integer less than or equal to π is 3

Chapter 4: $4(\lim\limits_{x \to 2^+} \frac{x-[x]}{x-2})$

Let $f(x) = \frac{x-[x]}{x-2}$.

([x] denotes the greatest integer less than or equal to x).

Since f(x) cannot be evaluated at 2, $\lim\limits_{x \to 2} f(x)$ does not exist.

However, observe that f(x) = 1 for every x in the open interval (2,3).

Hence the right-hand limit $\lim\limits_{x \to 2^+} \frac{x-[x]}{x-2}$ exists and is equal to 1.

Therefore $4(\lim\limits_{x \to 2^+} \frac{x-[x]}{x-2}) = 4*1 = 4$.

Chapter 5: $f(-1) | f(x) = x^2 - 3x + 1$

$f(-1) = (-1)^2 - 3(-1) + 1 = 1 + 3 + 1 = 5$

Chapter 6: (3!)

$3! = 3*2*1 = 6$

Chapter 7: 111_2

$2^2 + 2^1 + 1 = 4 + 2 + 1 = 7$

Chapter 8: $\int_{-2}^{0} 3x^2 dx$

If $f(x) = 3x^2$ then the antiderivative $g(x) = x^3$.

$\int_{-2}^{0} f(x) = g(0) - g(-2) = 0 - (-8) = 8$.

Chapter 9: $3\left(\lim_{t \to 1} \frac{t^3 - 1}{t - 1}\right)$

Let $F(t) = \frac{t^3 - 1}{t - 1}$.

Note that $t^3 - 1 = (t-1)(t^2 + t + 1)$.

Thus $F(t) = \frac{t^3 - 1}{t - 1} = \frac{(t-1)(t^2 + t + 1)}{(t-1)} = t^2 + t + 1$.

This form of $F(t)$ can be evaluated at t=1.

As t approaches 1, $F(t)$ approaches 3.

Thus $3\left(\lim_{t \to 1} \frac{t^3 - 1}{t - 1}\right) = 3*3 = 9$.

Chapter 10: $3^2 + 1$

$3^2 + 1 = 3*3 + 1 = 10$.

Chapter 11: $\sqrt{121}$

$11*11 = 121$, therefore $\sqrt{121} = 11$.

Chapter 12: 20_6

Without a subscript, a number is understood to be written in base 10 notation; thus

$20 = 2*10 + 0*1 = 20_{10}$.

The subscript $_6$ indicates base 6 notation; thus

$20_6 = 2*6 + 0*1 = 12_{10}$.

Chapter 13: $\left|\lim_{x \to 3}(x^3 - 5x^2 + 2x - 1)\right|$

Let $f(x) = x^3 - 5x^2 + 2x - 1$.

This function is continuous and can be evaluated at 3.

As x approaches 3, f(x) approaches f(3).

Therefore $\lim_{x \to 3} f(x) = f(3) = 3^3 - 5*3^2 + 2*3 - 1$

$= 27 - 45 + 6 - 1 = -13$.

$|-13| = 13$.

Chapter 14: $\sum_{k=1}^{3} k^2$

$\sum_{k=1}^{3} k^2 = 1^2 + 2^2 + 3^2 = 1 + 4 + 9 = 14$.

Chapter 15: $\int (u^2 - 2u + 3) du$

If $f(u) = u^2 - 2u + 3$ then the antiderivative $g(u) = \frac{u^3}{3} - u^2 + 3u$.

$\int_{1}^{4} f(u) = g(4) - g(1) = \frac{4^3}{3} - 4^2 + 3*4 - \frac{1^3}{3} + 1^2 - 3*1 = 21\frac{1}{3} - 16 + 12 - \frac{1}{3} + 1 - 3 = 15$

Chapter 16: 2^4

$2^4 = 2*2*2*2 = 16$.

Chapter 17: $\sqrt{289}$

$17*17 = 289$, therefore $\sqrt{289} = 17$.

Chapter 18: $\sum_{i=5}^{7} i = 18$

$\sum_{i=5}^{7} i = 5 + 6 + 7 = 18$.

THE SHIP WHO SANG IS NOT ALONE!

Anne McCaffrey, with Margaret Ball, Mercedes Lackey, S.M. Stirling, and Jody Lynn Nye, explores the universe she created with her ground-breaking novel, The Ship Who Sang.

PARTNERSHIP
by Anne McCaffrey & Margaret Ball

"[*PartnerShip*] captures the spirit of *The Ship Who Sang*...a single, solid plot full of creative nastiness and the sort of egocentric villains you love to hate."
—Carolyn Cushman, **Locus**

THE SHIP WHO SEARCHED
by Anne McCaffrey & Mercedes Lackey

Tia, a bright and spunky seven-year-old accompanying her exo-archaeologist parents on a dig, is afflicted by a paralyzing alien virus. Tia won't be satisfied to glide through life like a ghost in a machine. Like her predecessor Helva, *The Ship Who Sang*, she would rather strap on a spaceship!

THE CITY WHO FOUGHT
by Anne McCaffrey & S.M. Stirling

Simeon was the "brain" running a peaceful space station—but when the invaders arrived, his only hope of protecting his crew and himself was to become *The City Who Fought*.

THE SHIP WHO WON
by Anne McCaffrey & Jody Lynn Nye

"*Oodles of fun.*" —*Locus*
"*Fast, furious and fun.*" —*Chicago Sun-Times*

HARRY TURTLEDOVE:
A MIND FOR ALL SEASONS

EPIC FANTASY

Werenight (72209-3 ♦ $4.99) ☐
Prince of the North (87606-6 ♦ $5.99) ☐
In the Northlands rules Gerin the Fox. Quaintly, he intends to rule for the welfare and betterment of his people—but first he must defeat the gathering forces of chaos, which conspire to tumble his work into a very dark age indeed....

ALTERNATE FANTASY

The Case of the Toxic Spell Dump (72196-8 ♦ $5.99) ☐
Inspector Fisher's world is just a *little* bit different from ours...Stopping an ancient deity from reinstating human sacrifice in L.A. and destroying Western Civilization is all in a day's work for David Fisher of the Environmental *Perfection* Agency.

ALTERNATE HISTORY

Agent of Byzantium (87593-0 ♦ $4.99) ☐
In an alternate universe where the Byzantine Empire never fell, Basil Agyros, the 007 of his spacetime, has his hands full thwarting un-Byzantine plots and making the world safe for Byzantium. "Engrossing, entertaining and very cleverly rendered...I recommend it without reservation." —**Roger Zelazny**

A Different Flesh (87622-8 ♦ $4.99) ☐
An extraordinary novel of an alternate America. "When Columbus came to the New World, he found, not Indians, but primitive ape-men.... Unable to learn human speech...[the ape-men] could still be trained to do reliable work. Could still, in other words, be made slaves.... After 50 years of science fiction, Harry Turtledove proves you can come up with something fresh and original." —**Orson Scott Card**

To Read About Great Characters Having Incredible Adventures You Should Try 🖝 🖝 🖝

BAEN

IF YOU LIKE . . .	YOU SHOULD TRY . . .
Arthurian Legend...	*The Winter Prince* by Elizabeth E. Wein
Computers...	Rick Cook's *Wizard's Bane* series
Cats...	Larry Niven's *Man-Kzin Wars* series
	Cats in Space ed. by Bill Fawcett
Horses...	*Hunting Party* and *Sporting Chance* by Elizabeth Moon
	Dun Lady's Jess by Doranna Durgin
Fantasy Role Playing Games...	*The Bard's Tale* ™ Novels by Mercedes Lackey et al.
	The Rose Sea by S.M. Stirling & Holly Lisle
	Harry Turtledove's *Werenight* and *Prince of the North*
Computer Games...	*The Bard's Tale* ™ Novels by Mercedes Lackey et al.
	The *Wing Commander* ™ Novels by Mercedes Lackey, William R. Forstchen, et al.

IF YOU LIKE... YOU SHOULD TRY...

Norse Mythology... *The Mask of Loki* by Roger Zelazny & Thomas T. Thomas

The Iron Thane by Jason Henderson

Sleipnir by Linda Evans

Puns... *Mall Purchase Night* by Rick Cook

The Case of the Toxic Spell Dump by Harry Turtledove

Quests... *Pigs Don't Fly* and *The Unlikely Ones* by Mary Brown

The Deed of Paksenarrion by Elizabeth Moon

Through the Ice by Piers Anthony & Robert Kornwise

Vampires... *Tomorrow Sucks* by Greg Cox & T.K.F. Weisskopf